LILA

Robert M. Pirsig

LILA

An Inquiry into Morals

BANTAM BOOKS

New York   *Toronto*   *London*   *Sydney*   *Auckland*

Grateful acknowledgment is made for permission to reprint the following:

Excerpt from *Patterns of Culture* by Ruth Benedict. Copyright 1934 by Ruth Benedict. Copyright © renewed 1961 by Ruth Valentine. Reprinted by permission of Houghton Mifflin Company.

Excerpt from *The Message in the Bottle* by Walker Percy. Copyright © 1975 by Walker Percy. Reprinted by permission of Farrar, Straus and Giroux, Inc.

Excerpt from *The Crack-Up* by F. Scott Fitzgerald. Copyright 1945 by New Directions Publishing Corporation. Reprinted by permission of New Directions Publishing Corporation.

Excerpt from "In Search of the April Fool" by Cathie Slater Spence. Courtesy of the author.

Lyrics from "Get Down Tonight" by Harry Wayne Casey and Richard Finch. Copyright 1975 by Longitude Music Company. All rights reserved. Reprinted by permission of Longitude Music Company.

LILA

A Bantam Book / November 1991

The author wishes to give special thanks to the Guggenheim Foundation for the grant under which this book was written.

Library of Congress Cataloging-in-Publication Data

Pirsig, Robert M.
  Lila / Robert Pirsig.
    p.   cm.
  ISBN 0-553-07737-6
  ISBN 0-553-07873-9 (Limited Edition)
  I. Title.
PS3566.I66L54   1991
813'.54—dc20   91-16417
                                                   CIP

Published simultaneously in the United States and Canada

PRINTED IN THE UNITED STATES OF AMERICA

BVG   0 9 8 7 6 5 4 3 2 1

TO WENDY AND NELL

Part One

1.

Lila didn't know he was here. She was sound asleep, apparently in some fearful dream. In the darkness he heard a grating sound of her teeth and felt her body suddenly turn as she struggled against some menace only she could see.

The light from the open hatch above was so dim it concealed whatever lines of cosmetics and age were there and now she looked softly cherubic, like a small girl with blond hair, wide cheekbones, a small turned-up nose, and a common child's face that seemed so familiar it attracted a certain natural affection. He got the feeling that when morning came she should pop open her sky-blue eyes and they should sparkle with excitement at the prospect of a new day of sunlight and parents smiling and maybe bacon cooking on the stove and happiness everywhere.

But that wasn't how it would be. When Lila's eyes opened in a hung-over daze she'd look into the features of a gray-haired man she wouldn't even remember—someone she met in a bar the previous night. Her nausea and headache might produce some remorse and self-contempt but not much, he thought—she'd been through this many times—and she'd slowly try to figure out how to return to whatever life she'd been leading before she met this one.

Her voice murmured something like "Look out!" Then she said something unintelligible and turned away, then pulled the blanket up around her head, perhaps against the cold breeze that came down through the open hatch. The berth of the sailboat was so narrow that this turn of her body brought her up against him again and he felt the whole length of her and then her warmth. An earlier lust came back and his arm went over her so that his hand held her breast—full there but too soft, like something over-ripe that would soon go bad.

He wanted to wake her and take her again but as he thought about this a sad feeling rose up and forbade it. The more he hesitated the more the sadness grew. He would like to know her better. He'd had a feeling all night that he had seen her before somewhere, a long time ago.

That thought seemed to bring it all down. Now the sadness came on in full and blended with the darkness of the cabin and with the dim indigo light through the hatch above. Up there were stars, framed by the hatch opening so that they seemed to move when the boat rocked. Part of Orion momentarily disappeared, then appeared again. Soon all the winter constellations would be back.

Cars rolling over a bridge in the distance sounded clearly through the cold night air. They were on their way to Kingston, somewhere on the bluffs above, over the Hudson River. The boat was berthed here in this tiny creek for a night's rest on the way south.

There was not much time. There was almost no green left in the trees along the river. Many of the turned leaves had already fallen. During these last few days, gusts of cold wind had swept down the river valley from the north, swirling the leaves up off their branches into the air in sudden spiraling flights of red and maroon and gold and brown across the water of the river into the path of the boat as it moved down the buoyed channel. There had been hardly any other boats in the channel. A few boats at docks along the riverbank seemed abandoned and forlorn now that summer had ended and their owners had turned to other pursuits. Overhead the V's of ducks and geese had been everywhere, flying down on the north wind from the Canadian arctic. Many of them must have been just ducklings and goslings when he first began this voyage from the inland ocean of Lake Superior, a thousand miles behind him now and what seemed like a thousand years ago.

There was not much time. Yesterday when he first went up on deck his foot slipped and he caught himself and then he saw the entire boat was covered with ice.

Phædrus wondered where he had seen Lila before, but he didn't know. It seemed as though he had seen her, though. It was autumn then too, he thought, November, and it was very cold. He remembered the streetcar was almost empty except for him and the motorman and the conductor and Lila and her girlfriend sitting back three seats behind him. The seats were yellow woven rattan, hard and tough, designed for years of wear, and then a few years later the busses replaced them and the tracks and overhead cables and the streetcars were all gone.

He remembered he had seen three movies in a row and smoked too many cigarettes and had a bad headache and it was still about half an hour of pounding along the tracks before the streetcar would let him off and then he would have a block and a half through the dark to get home where there would be some aspirin and it would be about an hour and a half after that before the headache would go away. Then he heard these two girls giggle very loudly and he turned to see what it was. They stopped very suddenly and they looked at him in such a way that there could have been only one thing they were giggling at. It was him. He had a big nose and poor posture and wasn't anything to look at, and tended to relate poorly to other people. The one on the left who looked like she had been giggling the loudest was Lila. The same face, exactly—gold hair and smooth complexion and blue eyes—with a smothered smile she probably thought covered up what she was laughing at. They got off a couple of blocks later, still talking and laughing.

A few months later he saw her again in a downtown rush-hour crowd. It happened in a moment and then it was over. She turned her head and he saw in her face that she recognized him and she seemed to pause, waiting for him to do something, say something. But he didn't act. He didn't have that skill of relating quickly to people, and then it was too late, somehow, and they each went on and he wondered for a long time that afternoon, and for days after that, who she was and what it would have been like if he had gone over and said something. The next summer he thought he saw her at a bathing beach in the south part of the city. She was lying in the sand so that when he walked past her he saw her face upside down and he was suddenly very excited. This time he wouldn't just stand there. This time he would act, and he worked up his courage and went back and stood in the sand at her feet and then saw that the right-side-up face wasn't Lila. It was someone else. He remembered how sad that was. He didn't have anybody in those days.

But that was so long ago—years and years ago. She would have changed. There was no chance that this was the same person. And he didn't know her anyway. What difference did it make? Why should he remember such an insignificant incident like that all these years?

These half-forgotten images are strange, he thought, like dreams. This sleeping Lila whom he had just met tonight was someone else too. Or not someone else exactly, but someone less specific, less individual. There is Lila, this single private person who slept beside him now, who was born and now lived and tossed in her dreams and will soon enough die and then there is someone else—call her *lila*—who is immortal, who inhabits Lila for a while and then moves on. The sleeping Lila he had just met tonight. But the waking Lila, who never sleeps, had been watching him and he had been watching her for a long time.

It was so strange. All the time he had been coming down the canal through lock after lock she had been making the same journey but he didn't know she was there. Maybe he had seen her in the locks at Troy, looked right at her in the dark but had not seen her. His chart had shown a series of locks close together but they didn't show altitude and they didn't show how confusing things could get when distances have been miscalculated and you are running late and are exhausted. It wasn't until he was actually in the locks that danger was apparent as he tried to sort out green lights and red lights and white lights and lights of locktenders' houses and lights of other boats coming the other way and lights of bridges and abutments and God knows what else was out there in that black that he didn't want to hit in the middle of the darkness or go aground either. He'd never seen them before and it was a tense experience, and it was amidst all this tension that he seemed to remember seeing her on another boat.

They were descending out of the sky. Not just thirty or forty or fifty feet but hundreds of feet. Their boats were coming down, down through the night out of the sky where they had been all this time without their knowing it. When the last gate opened up from the last lock they looked on a dark oily river. The river flowed by a huge construction of girders toward a loom of light in the distance. That was Troy and his boat moved toward it until the swirl of the confluence of the rivers caught it and the boat yawed quickly. Then with the engine at full throttle he angled against the current across the river to a floating dock on the far side.

"We have four-foot tides here," the dock attendant said.

Tides! he had thought. That meant sea-level. It meant that all the inland man-made locks were gone. Now only the passage of the moon over the ocean controlled the rise and fall of the boat. All the way to Kingston this feeling of being connected without barriers to the ocean gave him a huge new feeling of space.

The space was really what this sailing was all about and this evening at a bar next to the dock he had tried to talk about it to Rigel and Capella. Rigel seemed tired and preoccupied and uninterested, but Bill Capella, who was his crewman, was full of enthusiasm and seemed to know.

"Like at Oswego," Capella said, "all that time we were waiting for the locks to open, crying about how terrible it was we couldn't get going, we were having the time of our lives."

Phædrus had met Rigel and Capella when rain from a September hurricane caused floods to break through canal walls and submerge buoys and jam locks with debris so that the entire canal had to be closed for two weeks. Boats heading south from the Great Lakes were tied up and their crewmen had nothing to do. Suddenly a space was created in everyone's lives. An unexpected gap of time had opened up. The reaction of everyone at first was frustration. To sit around and do nothing, that was just terrible. The yachtsmen had been busy about their own private cruises not really wanting very much to speak to any one else, but now they had nothing better to do than sit around on their boats and talk to each other day after day after day. Not trivially. In depth. Soon everyone was visiting somebody on somebody else's boat. Parties broke out everywhere, simultaneously, all night long. Townspeople took an interest in the jam-up of boats, and some of them became acquainted with the sailors. Not trivially. In depth. And more parties broke out.

And so this catastrophe, this disaster that everyone originally bewailed, turned out to be exactly as Capella described it. Everyone was actually having the time of their lives. The thing that was making them so happy was the space.

Except for Rigel and Capella and Phædrus the tavern had been almost empty. It was just a small place with a few pool tables at the far room, a bar in the center opposite the door and a lot of dingy tables at their own end. It omitted all appearances of style. And yet the feelings were good. It didn't intrude on your space. That's what did it. It was just a bar being a bar without any big ideas.

"I think it's the space that does it," he'd said to Rigel.

"What do you mean?" Rigel asked.

"About the space?"

Rigel was squinting at him. Despite Rigel's jaunty striped shirt and knit sailor's cap he seemed unhappy about something he wasn't talking about. Maybe it was that his whole purpose for this trip was to sell his boat down in Connecticut.

So as not to get into an argument Phædrus had told Rigel carefully, "I think what we're buying with these boats is space, nothingness, emptiness . . . huge sweeps of open water . . . and sweeps of time with nothing to do. . . . That's worth a lot of money. You can't hardly find that stuff any more."

"Shut yourself up in a room and lock the door," Rigel had said.

"That doesn't work," he had answered. "The phone rings."

"Don't answer."

"UPS knocks at the front door."

"How often? You don't have to answer."

Rigel was just looking for something to argue about. Capella joined in for the fun of it. "The neighbors will take it," Capella said.

"Then the kids will come home and turn up the TV."

"Tell them to turn it down," Capella said.

"Then you're out of the room."

"Okay, then just ignore them," Capella said.

"Okay, all right, fine. Now. What happens to someone who sits in a locked room and doesn't answer the phone, and refuses to come out when someone is knocking at the front door, even when the kids are home and have turned up the TV?"

They thought about it and finally smiled a little.

The bartender's face, when they had come in, had been completely bored. He had hardly any business. But since they had arrived four or five more customers had come in. He was talking to two of them, old customers it looked like, relaxed and used to the place. Two others were holding pool cues, apparently from some tables in an adjoining room.

"There isn't any space," Rigel said. He still wanted to quarrel. "If you were from here you'd know that."

"What do you mean?"

"There's no space here," Rigel repeated. "It's all crowded with history. It's all dead now but if you knew this region you'd see there's no space. It's full of old secrets. Everyone covers up around here."

He asked Rigel, "What secrets?"

"Nothing's the way it seems," Rigel said. "This little creek we're on here, do you know where it leads? You wouldn't think it goes back more than a few hundred yards after it completes that turn back there, would you? How far would you guess you could go, on this little tiny creek here, before it stops?"

Phædrus guessed twenty miles.

Rigel smiled. "In the old days, you'd go forever," he said. "It goes all the way to the Atlantic Ocean. People don't know that any more. It goes *behind* the whole state of New Jersey. It used to connect to a canal that went over the mountains and down into the Delaware. They used to run coal through here on barges all the way from Pennsylvania. My great-grandfather was in that business. He had money invested in all sorts of enterprises around here. Did well at it, too."

"So your family comes from around here," Phædrus said.

"Since just after the Revolution," Rigel said. "They didn't move from here until about thirty years ago."

Phædrus waited for Rigel to go on but he didn't say any more.

A cold draft hit as the door opened and a large crowd came in. One of them waved at Rigel. Rigel nodded back.

"Do you know him?" Phædrus asked.

"He's from Toronto," Rigel said.

"Who is he?"

"I've raced against him," Rigel said. "They're all Canadians. They come down at this time of year."

One Canadian wore a red sweater, a second had a blue Navy

watchcap cocked back on his head and a third wore a bright green jacket. They all moved together in a way that indicated they knew each other very well but did not know this place at all. They had an outdoorsy exuberance, like some visiting hockey team.

Now he remembered he had seen them before, in Oswego, on a large boat called the *Karma*, and they had seemed a little clannish.

"They act like they don't think much of this place," Capella said.

"They just want to get south," Rigel said.

"There's something about them though," Capella said, "like they don't *approve* of what they see."

"Well I approve of *that*," Rigel said.

"What do you mean?" Capella asked.

"They're moral people," Rigel said. "We could use a little of that."

One of the Canadians who had been studying jukebox selections had pushed some buttons and lights now radiated from it and rotated around the room.

A blast of noise hit them. The speaker was set way too loud. Phædrus tried to say something to Capella. Capella cupped his hand to his ear and laughed. Phædrus threw up his hands and they both sat back and listened and drank their ale.

More people had come in and now the place was really getting crowded; a lot of local people it seemed like, but they seemed to mix with the sailors just fine, as though they were used to each other. With all the ale and noise and friendliness of strangers this was beginning to be sort of a great little joint. He drank and listened and watched little patches of light from some sort of disco machine attached to the jukebox circle around on the ceiling.

His thoughts began to drift. He thought of what Rigel had said. The East *was* a different country. The difference was hard to identify —you felt it more than you saw it.

Some of the Hudson valley architecture had a "Currier-and-Ives" feeling of the early 1800s, a feeling of slow, decent orderly life that preceded the industrial revolution. Minnesota, where Phædrus came from, never shared that. It was mostly forests and Indians and log cabins back then.

Traveling across America by water was like going back in time and seeing how it must have been long ago. He was following old trade routes that were used before railways became dominant. It was amazing how parts of this river still looked the same as the old Hudson River school of painting showed it, with beautiful forests, and mountains in the distance.

As the boat moved south he'd seen a growing aura of social structure, particularly in the mansions that had become more numerous. Their styles were getting more and more removed from the frontier. They were getting closer and closer to Europe.

Two of the Canadians at the bar were a man and a woman up against each other so close you couldn't have slipped a letter-opener between them. When the music stopped Phædrus motioned to Rigel and Capella to notice them. The man had his hand on the woman's thigh and the woman was smiling and drinking as though nothing was happening.

Phædrus asked Rigel, "Are these some of your moral Canadians?" Capella laughed.

Rigel glanced over for a second and glanced back with a frown. "There are two kinds," he said. "The one kind disapproves of this country for all the junk they find here, and the other kind *loves* this country for all the junk they find here."

He motioned with his head to the two and was going to say something but then the music and the lights started up again and he threw up his hands and Capella laughed and they sat back again.

After a while, it began to feel cold. The door was open. A woman stood there, her eyes combing the room as though she was looking for someone.

Someone shouted, "CLOSE THE DOOR!"

The woman and Rigel looked at each other for a long time. It looked as though he was the one she was looking for but then she kept on looking.

"CLOSE THE DOOR!" someone else shouted.

"They're talking to *you*, Lila," Rigel said.

Apparently she saw what she was looking for because suddenly her entire expression turned furious. She slammed the door with all her might.

"That SUIT you?" she shouted.

Rigel looked at her without expression and then turned back to the table.

The music stopped. Phædrus asked with a wink, "Is that one of the ones who love us?"

"No, she's not even a Canadian," Rigel said.

Phædrus asked, "Who is she?"

Rigel didn't say anything.

"Where's she from?"

"Don't have anything to do with her," Rigel said.

Suddenly they were hit again by another blast of noise.

"TAKE A BREAK! . . ." it blared out.

The colored lights flashed around the room again.

"LET'S GET TOGETHER! . . ."

"ME AND YOU! . . ."

Capella held up an ale can questioningly to see if anyone wanted more. Phædrus nodded yes and Capella went off.

"AND DO THE THING . . ."

"AND DO THE THING . . ."

"THAT WE LIKE . . ."

"TO DO! . . ."

Rigel said something, but Phædrus couldn't hear him. The tall Canadian with the roving hand and his girlfriend were on the dance floor. He watched them for a while, and as you might know, they were good.

"DO A LITTLE DANCE . . ."

"MAKE A LITTLE LOVE . . ."

"GET DOWN TONIGHT . . ."

"GET DOWN TONIGHT . . ."

Sensual. Short driving bursts of sound. A black sermon, up from the ghetto.

He watched Lila, who was now sitting by herself at the bar. Something about her really held his attention. Sex, he guessed.

She had the usual junk cosmetics; blond tinted hair, red nails, nothing original, except that it all came out X-rated. You just sort of felt instantly right away without having to think twice about it what it was she did best. But there was something in her expression that looked almost explosive.

When the music stopped the sexy Canadian and his girl came off from the dance floor. They saw her and almost stopped, then went forward slowly to the bar. Then Phædrus saw her say something to them and three people around them suddenly stiffened. The man turned around and actually looked scared. He took his arm off the girlfriend and turned to Lila. He must have been the one Lila was looking for. He said something to her and she said something back to him and then he nodded and nodded again, then he and the woman looked at each other and turned to the bar and said nothing to Lila at all. The others around them gradually turned back to talking again.

This ale was getting to Phædrus. Still his head seemed strangely clear.

He studied Lila some more: Her legs were crossed and her skirt was above her knees. Wide hips. Shiny satin blouse, V-necked and tucked tight into a belt. Under it was a bustline that was hard to look away from. It was a defiant kind of vulgarity, a kind of "Mae West" thing. She looked a little like Mae West. "C'mon and *do* something, if you've got the nerve," she seemed to say.

Some X-rated thoughts passed through his mind. Whatever it is that's aroused by these cues isn't put off by any lack of originality. They were doing all kinds of things to his endocrine system. He'd been alone on the water a long time.

"DO A LITTLE DANCE . . ."

"MAKE A LITTLE LOVE . . ."

"GET DOWN TONIGHT . . ."

"GET DOWN TONIGHT . . ."

"Do you know her?" he shouted at Rigel.

Rigel shook his head. "Don't have anything to do with her!"

"Where's she from?"

"The *sewer*!" Rigel said.

Rigel gave him a narrow-eyed glance. Rigel sure was giving a lot of advice tonight.

The door opened and more people came in. Capella returned with an armload of cans.

"DO A LITTLE DANCE . . ."

"MAKE A LITTLE LOVE . . ."

Capella shouted in Phædrus' ear, "NICE, QUIET, REFINED PLACE WE PICKED!!!"

Phædrus nodded up and down and smiled.

He could see Lila start to talk to one of the other men at the bar and the man seemed to answer familiarly. But the others kept a distance and held their faces stiff as though they were on guard against something.

"DO A LITTLE DANCE . . ."

"MAKE A LITTLE LOVE . . ."

"GET DOWN TONIGHT . . ."

"GET DOWN TONIGHT . . ."

"GET DOWN TONIGHT!"

"GET DOWN TONIGHT!"

He wondered if he had the nerve to go up and talk to her.

"BABY!!"

He sure as hell had the desire.

He took his time and finished his ale. The relaxation from the alcohol and tension from what was coming just exactly balanced each other in an equilibrium that resembled stone sobriety but was not. He watched her for a long time and she knew that he was watching her and he knew that she knew he was watching her, and he knew that she knew that he knew; in a kind of regression of images that you get when two mirrors face each other and the images go on and on and on in some kind of infinity.

Then he picked up his can and headed toward the spot next to her at the bar.

At the bar-rail the smell of her perfume penetrated through the tobacco and liquor smells.

After a while she turned and stared into him. The face was mask-like from the cosmetics, but a faint smile showed pleasure, as though she had been waiting for this a long time.

She said, "Where have I seen you before?"

A cliché, he thought, but there was a protocol to this sort of thing. Yeah, "Where have I seen you before?" He tried to think of the protocol. He was rusty. The protocol was you're supposed to talk about the places you might have seen her in and who you know there, and this is supposed to lead to further subjects in a progression of intimacy, and he was trying to think of some places to talk about when he looked at her, and my God, it was *her*, the one on the streetcar and she's asking, "Where have I seen you before?" and that was what started the illumination.

It was stronger toward the center of her face but it didn't come *from* her face. It was as though her face were on the center of a screen and the light came from behind the screen.

My God it was really *her*, after all these years.

"Are you on a boat?" she said.

He said he was.

"Are you with Richard Rigel?"

"You know him?" he asked.

"I know a lot of people," she said.

The bartender brought the ales he ordered, and he paid for them.

"Are you crewing for Richard?"

"No. My boat's rafted against his. Everything's crowded with all these boats coming down at the same time."

Where have you been all this time? he wanted to say, but she wouldn't know what he was talking about. *Why did you go away in the crowd that time? Were you laughing at me then too?* Something about boats. He was supposed to say something about boats.

"We came down the canals together from Oswego," he said.

"Then why didn't I see you there?" Lila said.

You did see me there before, he thought, but now the illumination had disappeared and her voice wasn't the way he had always thought it would be and so now this was just another stranger like all the others.

She said, "I saw Richard in Rome and Amsterdam but I didn't see you."

"I didn't go into town with him. I stayed on my boat."

"Are you all alone?"

"Yes."

She looked at him with a kind of question in her eye and then said, "Invite me to your table."

Then she said loudly enough so that the others could hear, "I can't *stand* the *trash* at this *bar*!" But the two she intended it for just looked at each other knowingly and didn't look over at her at all.

Rigel was gone from the table when they got there but Capella gave Lila a big hello and she flashed a big smile on him.

"How are you, Bill?" she said.

Capella said okay.

"Where's Richard?" she asked.

"He went to play pool," Capella said.
She looked at Phædrus and said, "Richard's an old friend."
There was a pause when he didn't answer this.
Then she asked how far he was going.
Phædrus said he wasn't sure yet.
Lila said she was going south for the winter.
She asked him where he was from and Phædrus told her the Midwest. She didn't have much interest in that.

He told her about seeing someone like her before in the Midwest but she said she'd never been there. "Lots of people look like me," she said.

After a while Capella left for the bar. Phædrus was alone with her, facing up to a kind of emptiness. Something needed to be said but he didn't know what to say. He could see it was beginning to bother her too. He wasn't her "type," she was beginning to see that, but the ale was helping. It obliterated the differences. Enough ale and everything got reduced to pure biology, where it belonged.

After a while Lila asked him to dance. He said he didn't and so they just sat there. But then the tall Canadian and his girlfriend got on the floor and started to dance again. They were good. They really moved together, but when Phædrus looked over at Lila he saw the same look she had when she first came in.

Her face had that explosive look again. "That son-of-a-bitch!" she said. "He *came* with me. He *invited* me on this trip! And now he's with *her*. God, that just *kills* me."

Then the music started again and the disco lights rotated and Lila looked at him in a curious way. It was just a glance, and the disco light moved on but in just that moment he noticed what a beautiful pale blue her eyes were. They didn't seem to match the way she talked or the way the rest of her looked either. Strange. Out of memory. They were like the eyes of some child.

The ale cans were empty and he offered to get some more but she said, "C'mon, let's dance."

"I'm no good," he said.

"That doesn't matter," she said. "Just do anything you feel like," she said, "I'll go along."

He did, and she *did* go along and he was surprised. They got into a sort of a whirl thing. Going round and round with the disco lights and they began to get into it more and more.

"You're better than you think," she said, and it was true: he *was*.

"GET DOWN TONIGHT . . ."

"GET DOWN TONIGHT . . ."

He was aware that people were watching them, but all he could see was Lila and the lights whirling around and around.

Around and around. And around and around—red and blue and pink and orange and gold. They were all over the room and they moved across the ceiling and sometimes they shined on her face and sometimes they shined in his eyes—red and pink and gold.

Do a little dance . . .

Make a little love . . .

Get down tonight . . .

Get down tonight . . .

The hesitation was gone and the ale and the music and the perfume from Lila took over and her pale blue eyes were watching him with that strange look of *are you the one?* and his mind kept saying to her *yes, I am the one* and this answer extended slowly into his arms and hands where he held her and then into her body and she could feel it and she began to quiet down from her anger and he began to quiet down from his awkwardness.

Do a little dance . . .

Make a little love . . .

Get down tonight . . .

Get down tonight . . .

Once the Canadian dancer came over and wanted to cut in. Lila told him to "get lost" and he could tell from a change in her body how good she felt about that. After that they both knew that something had been settled, for tonight, at least, and beyond that was too far to think about.

He could hardly remember how he got back to his boat with her. What came through in memory was the beat of the music and that pale, blue-eyed questioning look, and then here on the bunk the way she embraced him, clinging with all her might, like a drowning person holding on for dear life.

Do a little dance . . .

Make a little love . . .
Get down tonight . . .
Get down tonight . . .
He began to feel sleepy.

It's so strange, he thought. All the tricks and games and lines and promises to get them into bed with you and you work so hard at it and nothing happens. And then someone like *this* comes along and you don't try much of anything at all and then *she's* the one you wake up next to.

It doesn't make any sense at all, he thought sleepily . . . no sense at all. And the tune kept playing on and on in his mind—over and over again and again until he fell asleep.

Do a little dance . . .
Make a little love . . .
Get down tonight . . .
Get down tonight . . .

2.

When Phædrus awoke he saw through the hatch that the sky had become less black. Dawn was coming.

Then he realized he wasn't alone. In fact he was blocked physically from getting out of the bunk by a body between him and the boat's passageway. This was Lila, he remembered.

He saw that with some careful maneuvering he could slink up through the open hatch and come around on deck and re-enter the cabin from the cockpit.

He lifted himself up carefully and then got through the hatch without disturbing her.

Nice work.

The cold deck on his bare feet really woke him up. He couldn't feel any ice, but the fiberglass coachroof was the next thing to it. It helped to shake off all the alcohol fumes in his head. Nothing like walking around bare-naked on top of a freezing boat to wake you up for the day.

Everything was so quiet now. The dawn was still so early the turn of the creek in the distance was barely visible. Hard to believe what Rigel said; that around that turn a coal-barge could go all the way to the ocean.

He went over and checked the lines going over to Rigel's boat. They were a little loose and he took up on one of the spring lines and then tightened all of them. He should have done that before he went to bed. He'd been too drunk to take care of details like that.

He looked around and, despite the cold, a dawn mystery took

hold of him. Some other boats had come in since he had, and were rafted ahead and behind him. Possibly one of them was the boat Lila had come on. The harbor looked scuzzy and old in places but showed some signs of gentrification in others. Pseudo-Victorian, it looked like, but not bad. Off in the distance was a crane and other masts. The Hudson River was completely out of sight.

It felt good not to be related to this harbor in any way. He didn't know what was above the banks of the river or behind the harbor buildings or where the roads led to or who the houses belonged to or what people would appear here today or what people they would meet. It was like a picture-book and he was a child, watching it, waiting for a page to be turned.

Shivering broke the spell. His skin was covered with goose-bumps. He went back to the stern of the boat, hung off the boom gallows with one arm and relieved into the creek. Then he stepped down to the cockpit, pushed the heavy teak hatch cover back and let himself down with the grace that came from a familiar motion. It was a "grace" he'd acquired the hard way. When he first got the boat he walked around like it was a house, slipped on some diesel oil, plunged head-first down the companionway ladder, and broke a collarbone. Now he'd learned to move like a spider monkey, particularly in storms when the whole boat rose and pitched and rolled like a flying trapeze.

In the cabin he felt his way to an overhead light and flicked it on. The darkness was filled instantly with familiar teak and mahogany.

He went forward into the deck forecabin and found his clothes in the bunk opposite Lila. She had evidently rolled over since he left. Her shadowy shape looked about the same from this side as it had from the other a few minutes ago.

He closed the forecabin door and went into the main cabin where he pulled open a wood bin-cover, took out his old heavy brown sweater and drew it over his head. When he pushed the cover shut, the snap of its catch disturbed the silence. He went back to the companionway ladder, put the hatch's drop-boards in place, and slid the heavy hatch-cover shut.

This place needed some heat.

Next to the ladder, by the chart table, he found matches and alcohol. He carefully brought a little cupful of the alcohol to a small coal stove mounted on a bulkhead at the other end of the cabin and poured the alcohol over some charcoal briquets inside. On the picture-book shore out there everything was done by magic. They got their heat and electricity without even thinking about it. But in this little floating world, whatever you needed you had to get for yourself.

He lit a match, tossed it in and watched the alcohol go "Pouf!" and fill the stove with a pale, blue-purple flame. He was glad he'd loaded the stove yesterday. He wouldn't want to have to do it now. . . . Was that just yesterday? It seemed like a week. . . .

He closed the stove door, watched it for a moment until out of the corner of his eye he saw an enormous suitcase that he had never seen before.

Where did that come from, he wondered.

It wasn't his.

Lila must have brought it with her.

He thought about it as he struck another match at a gimballed brass kerosene lamp. He adjusted the wick until the flame seemed right. Then he turned off the overhead electric light and sat down on the berth under the lamp, his back against a rolled sleeping bag.

As far as he could figure he must have made some sort of deal with her to come on the boat or she wouldn't have brought this suitcase.

Now the kerosene light glowed over all the wood and bronze and brass and fabric shapes of the cabin and another invisible glow of warmth came from the black coal stove that now made cricking heating noises. Soon it would heat everything enough to make it all comfortable.

Except for that suitcase. What was coming back to mind wasn't making him comfortable at all. He remembered she'd dropped the suitcase on Rigel's deck. Really hard. When they walked across to come aboard he'd turned and told her to keep it quiet. He remembered she shouted, "Don't you tell *me* to keep it quiet!" in a voice you could hear all over the harbor.

It was all coming back: going over to her boat, waiting for her to pack, listening to her talk about that "dirty double-crosser George" and his "*whore*, Debbie."

Oh-oh.

He guessed it couldn't be so bad, though. Just a couple of days into Manhattan and then she would be gone. No harm done.

He saw that her suitcase had shoved all his trays of slips over to one side of the pilot berth. They were for a book he was working on and one of the four long card-catalog-type trays was by an edge where it could fall off. That's all he needed, he thought, about three thousand four-by-six slips of notepad paper all over the floor.

He got up and adjusted the sliding rest inside each tray so that it was tight against the slips and they couldn't fall out. Then he carefully pushed the trays back into a safer place in the rear of the berth. Then he went back and sat down again.

It would actually be easier to lose the boat than it would be to lose those slips. There were about eleven thousand of them. They'd grown out of almost four years of organizing and reorganizing and reorganizing so many times he'd become dizzy trying to fit them all together. He'd just about given up.

Their overall subject he called a "Metaphysics of Quality," or sometimes a "Metaphysics of Value," or sometimes just "MOQ" to save time.

The buildings out there on shore were in one world and these slips were in another. This "slip-world" was quite a world and he'd almost lost it once because he hadn't written any of it down and incidents came along that had destroyed his memory of it. Now he had reconstructed what seemed like most of it on these slips and he didn't want to lose it again.

But maybe it was a good thing that he had lost it because now, in the reconstruction of it, all sorts of new material was flooding in—so much that his main task was to get it processed before it log-jammed his head into some kind of a block that he couldn't get out of. Now the main purpose of the slips was not to help him remember anything. It was to help him to forget it. That sounded contradictory but the purpose was to keep his head empty, to put all his ideas of the past four years on that pilot berth where he didn't have to think of them. That was what he wanted.

There's an old analogy to a cup of tea. If you want to drink new tea you have to get rid of the old tea that's in your cup, otherwise your cup just overflows and you get a wet mess. Your head is like that cup. It has a limited capacity and if you want to learn something about the world you should keep your head empty in order to learn it. It's very easy to spend your whole life swishing old tea around in your cup thinking it's great stuff because you've never really tried anything new, because you could never get it in, because the old stuff prevented its entry because you were so sure the old stuff was so good, because you never really tried anything new . . . on and on in an endless circular pattern.

The reason Phædrus used slips rather than full-sized sheets of paper is that a card-catalog tray full of slips provides a more random access. When information is organized in small chunks that can be accessed and sequenced at random it becomes much more valuable than when you have to take it in serial form. It's better, for example, to run a post office where the patrons have numbered boxes and can come in to access these boxes any time they please. It's worse to have them all come in at a certain time, stand in a queue and get their mail from Joe, who has to sort through everything alphabetically each time and who has rheumatism, is going to retire in a few years, and who doesn't care whether they like waiting or not. When any distribution is locked into a rigid sequential format it develops Joes that dictate what new changes will be allowed and what will not, and that rigidity is deadly.

Some of the slips were actually about this topic: random access and Quality. The two are closely related. Random access is at the essence of organic growth, in which cells, like post-office boxes, are relatively independent. Cities are based on random access. Democracies are founded on it. The free market system, free speech, and the growth of science are all based on it. A library is one of civilization's most powerful tools precisely *because* of its card-catalog trays. Without the Dewey Decimal System allowing the number of cards in the main catalog to grow or shrink at any point the whole library would soon grow stale and useless and die.

And so while those trays certainly didn't have much glamour they nevertheless had the hidden strength of a card catalog. They ensured that by keeping his head empty and keeping sequential formatting to a minimum, no fresh new unexplored idea would be forgotten or shut out. There were no ideological Joes to kill an idea because it didn't fit into what he was already thinking.

Because he didn't pre-judge the fittingness of new ideas or try to put them in order but just let them flow in, these ideas sometimes came in so fast he couldn't write them down quickly enough. The subject matter, a whole metaphysics, was so enormous the flow had turned into an avalanche. The slips kept expanding in every direction so that the more he saw the more he saw there *was* to see. It was like a Venturi effect which pulled ideas into it endlessly, on and on. He saw there were a million things to read, a million leads to follow. . . too much . . . too much . . . and not enough time in one life to get it all together. Snowed under.

There'd been times when an urge surfaced to take the slips, pile by pile, and file them into the door of the coal stove on top of the glowing charcoal briquets and then close the door and listen to the cricking of the metal as they turned into smoke. Then it would all be gone and he would be really free again.

Except that he *wouldn't* be free. It would still be there in his mind to do.

So he spent most of his time submerged in chaos, knowing that the longer he put off setting into a fixed organization the more difficult it would become. But he felt sure that sooner or later some sort of a format would have to emerge and it would be a better one for his having waited.

Eventually this belief was justified. Periods started to appear when he just sat there for hours and no slips came in—and this, he saw, was at last the time for organizing. He was pleased to discover that the slips themselves made this organizing much easier. Instead of asking "Where does this metaphysics of the universe begin?"—which was a virtually impossible question—all he had to do was just hold up two slips and ask, "Which comes first?" This was easy and he always seemed to get an answer. Then he would take a third slip, compare it with the first one, and ask again, "Which comes first?" If the new slip came after the first one he compared it with the second. Then he had a three-slip organization. He kept repeating the process with slip after slip.

Before long he noticed certain categories emerging. The earlier slips began to merge about a common topic and later slips about a different topic. When enough slips merged about a single topic so that he got a feeling it would be permanent he took an index card of the same size as the slips, attached a transparent plastic index tab to it, wrote the name of the topic on a little cardboard insert that came with the tab, put it in the tab, and put the index card together with its related topic slips. The trays on the pilot berth now had about four or five hundred of these tabbed index cards.

At various times he'd tried all kinds of different things: colored plastic tabs to indicate subtopics and sub-subtopics; stars to indicate relative importance; slips split with a line to indicate both emotive and rational aspects of their subject; but all of these had increased rather than decreased confusion and he'd found it clearer to include their information elsewhere.

It was fascinating to watch this thing grow. No one that he knew had ever written a whole metaphysics before and there were no rules for doing it and no way of predicting how it would progress.

In addition to the topic categories, five other categories had emerged. Phædrus felt these were of great importance:

The first was UNASSIMILATED. This contained new ideas that interrupted what he was doing. They came in on the spur of the moment while he was organizing the other slips or sailing or working on the boat or doing something else that didn't want to be disturbed. Normally your mind says to these ideas, "Go away, I'm busy," but that attitude is deadly to Quality. The UNASSIMILATED pile helped solve the problem. He just stuck the slips there on hold until he had the time and desire to get to them.

The next non-topical category was called PROGRAM. PRO-GRAM slips were instructions for what to do with the rest of the slips. They kept track of the forest while he was busy thinking about in-dividual trees. With more than ten thousand trees that kept wanting to expand to one hundred thousand, the PROGRAM slips were ab-solutely necessary to keep from getting lost.

What made them so powerful was that *they too* were on slips, one slip for each instruction. This meant the PROGRAM slips were ran-dom access too and could be changed and resequenced as the need arose without any difficulty. He remembered reading that John Von Neumann, an inventor of the computer, had said the single thing that makes a computer so powerful is that the program *is* data and can be treated like any other data. That seemed a little obscure when Phædrus had read it but now it was making sense.

The next slips were the CRIT slips. These were for days when he woke up in a foul mood and could find nothing but fault everywhere. He knew from experience that if he threw stuff away on these days he would regret it later, so instead he satisfied his anger by just describing all the stuff he wanted to destroy and the reasons for destroying it. The CRIT slips would then wait for days or sometimes months for a calmer period when he could make a more dispassionate judgment.

The next to the last group was the TOUGH category. This contained slips that seemed to say something of importance but didn't fit into any topic he could think of. It prevented getting stuck on some slip whose place might become obvious later on.

The final category was JUNK. These were slips that seemed of high value when he wrote them down but which now seemed awful. Sometimes it included duplicates of slips he had forgotten he'd written. These duplicates were thrown away but nothing else was discarded. He'd found over and over again that the junk pile is a working category. Most slips died there but some reincarnated, and some of these reincarnated slips were the most important ones he had.

Actually, these last two piles, JUNK and TOUGH, were the piles that gave him the most concern. The whole thrust of the organizing effort was to have as few of these as possible. When they appeared he had to fight the tendency to slight them, shove them under the carpet, throw them out the window, belittle them, and forget them. These were the underdogs, the outsiders, the pariahs, the sinners of his system. But the reason he was so concerned about them was that he felt the quality and strength of his entire system of organization depended on how he treated them. If he treated the pariahs well he would have a good system. If he treated them badly he would have a weak one. They could not be allowed to destroy all efforts at organization but he couldn't allow himself to forget them either. They just stood there, accusing, and he had to listen.

The hundreds of topics had organized themselves into larger sections, the sections into chapters, and chapters into parts; so that what the slips had organized themselves into finally was the contents of a book; but it was a book whose organization was from the bottom up rather than from the top down. He hadn't started with a master idea and then selected in Joe-fashion only those slips that would fit. In this case, "Joe," the organizing principle, had been democratically elected by the slips themselves. The JUNK and TOUGH slips didn't participate in this election, and that created an underlying dissatisfaction. But he felt that you can't expect a perfect system of organization of anything. He'd kept the junk pile as small as possible without deliberately suppressing it and that was the most anyone could ask.

A description of this system makes it all sound a lot easier than it actually was. Often he got into a situation where incoming TOUGH slips and the JUNK slips would indicate his whole system of making topics was wrong. Some slips would fit in two or three categories and other slips would fit into no categories at all and he began to see that he would have to tear the whole system of organization apart and begin to reorganize it differently, because if he didn't, the JUNK pile and the TOUGH pile and the CRIT pile would start howling at him louder and louder until he had to do it.

Those were bad days, but sometimes the new reorganization would leave the JUNK piles and the TOUGH piles *bigger* than they were when he started. Slips that had fit the old organization now didn't fit the new one, and he began to see that what he had to do now was go back and redo it all over again the old way. Those were the *really* bad days.

Sometimes he would start to make a PROGRAM procedure that would allow him to go back where he started, but in the process of making it he saw that the PROGRAM procedure needed modification so he started to modify that, but in the process of modification he saw that the modification needed modification, so he started to modify *that*, but then he saw that *even that* was no good, and then just about at this time the phone would ring and it would be someone wanting to sell him something or congratulate him on the previous book he had written or invite him to some conference or get him to lecture somewhere. They were usually well-intentioned callers, but when he was done with them he would just sit there, blocked.

He began to think that if he just got away from people on this boat and had enough time it would come to him, but it hadn't worked out as well as he'd hoped. You just get other kinds of interruptions. A storm comes up and you worry about the anchor. Or another yacht pulls up and they come over and want to socialize. Or there's a drunken party down on the dock . . . on and on. . . .

He got up, went over to the pilot berth, got some more charcoal briquets and put them in the coal stove. It was getting nice and warm now.

He picked up one of the trays and looked at it. The front of it showed rust through the paint. You couldn't keep anything of steel from rusting on a boat, even stainless, and these boxes were ordinary mild-steel sheet metal. He would have to make some new ones out of marine plywood and glue when he had the time. Maybe when he got South.

This tray was the oldest one. It had slips he hadn't looked at for more than a year now.

He brought it over to the table with him.

The first topic, at the very front of the tray, was DUSENBERRY. He looked at it nostalgically. At one time he had thought DUSEN-BERRY was going to be at the center of the whole book.

After a while he took a blank pad from the back of the tray and wrote on the top slip, "PROGRAM," and then under it, "Hang up everything until Lila gone." Then he tore the slip off the notepad and put the slip in the front of the PROGRAM pile and put the notepad in the back of the tray. It was important, he'd found, to write a PROGRAM slip for what you are currently doing. It seems unnecessary at the time you are writing it but later when interruptions have interrupted interruptions which have interrupted interruptions you're glad you did it.

The CRIT slips had been saying for months that DUSENBERRY had to go but he never seemed to be able to get rid of it. It just stayed there for what seemed to be sentimental reasons. Now it had been shoved into lesser and lesser importance by incoming slips and was just hanging on, teetering on the edge of the JUNK pile.

He took the whole DUSENBERRY topic section out. The slips were getting brown around the edges and the ink was turning brown too, on the first slip.

It said: "Verne Dusenberry, Assoc. Prof., English Dept., Montana State College. Died, brain tumor, 1966, Calgary, Alberta."

He'd made the slip, probably, so he'd remember the year.

3.

Nineteen-sixty-six. My God, how the years had sped up.

He wondered what Dusenberry'd be like now if he'd lived. Not much, maybe. There were signs before he died that he was going downhill, that he'd been at the peak of his powers at about the time Phædrus knew him in Bozeman, Montana, where they both were members of the English department.

Dusenberry was born in Bozeman and had graduated from the college there, but after twenty-three years on the faculty his assignment was just three sections of freshman composition; no literature courses, no advanced composition courses of any kind. Academically he had long before been placed on the TOUGH pile of scholars whom the department would just as soon have gotten rid of. Tenure was all that saved him from the JUNK pile. He had little to do with the rest of the department socially. Other members seemed to be in various degrees of alienation from him.

This seemed odd to Phædrus because in his own conversations with him Dusenberry was not at all unsociable. He sometimes looked unsociable with his arched eyebrows and downturned mouth, but when Phædrus had gotten to know him, Dusenberry was actually gabby in a high-spirited, gleeful, maiden-auntish sort of way. It was a slightly "gay" style; tart, and somewhat backbiting; and at first Phædrus thought this was why they were so down on him. Montanans in those days were supposed to look and act like Marlboro ads, but in time Phædrus saw that wasn't what caused the alienation. It was just Dusenberry's general overall eccentricity. Over the years small eccentric differences in a small college department can grow into big differences, and Dusenberry's differences were not so small. The biggest difference was revealed in a line Phædrus heard a number of times, a disdainful: "Oh, yes, Dusenberry . . . Dusenberry and his Indians."

When Dusenberry spoke of other faculty it was with equal disdain: "Oh yes, the *English* department." But he seldom spoke of them at all. The only subject he spoke about with any sincere enthusiasm was Indians, and particularly the Rocky Boy Indians, the Chippewa-Cree on the Canadian border about whom he was writing his Ph.D. thesis in anthropology. He let it be known that except for the Indians he had befriended for twenty-one of his twenty-three years as a teacher he regarded all these years as a waste of his life.

He was the advisor for all the Indian students at the college and had held this post for as long as anyone could remember. The students were a connecting link. He'd made a point to know their families and visit them and use this as an entry point into their lives. He spent all the weekend and vacation time he could on the reservations, participating in their ceremonies, running errands for them, driving their kids to the hospital when they were sick, speaking to state officials when they got in trouble, and beyond that, completely losing himself into the ways and personalities and secrets and mysteries of these people he loved a hundred times better than his own.

Within a few years when his degree was completed he would be leaving English teaching forever and teaching anthropology instead. One would guess that this would be a happy solution for him, but from what Phædrus heard it was already apparent that it would not be. He was not only an eccentric in the field of English, he was an eccentric in anthropology as well.

The main part of his eccentricity seemed to be his refusal to accept "objectivity" as an anthropological criterion. He didn't think objectivity had any place in the proper conduct of anthropological study.

This is like saying the Pope has no place in the Catholic Church. In American anthropology that is the worst possible apostasy and Dusenberry was quickly informed of it. Of all the American universities he had applied to for Ph.D. study, every one had turned him down. But rather than change his beliefs he had gone *around* the whole American university system to Prof. Åke Hultkranz in Uppsala, Sweden's oldest university, and was about to receive his Ph.D. there. Whenever Dusenberry talked about this, a cat-who-ate-the-canary smile would come over his face. An American taking a Ph.D. in Sweden on the Anthropology of American Indians? It was ludicrous!

"The trouble with the objective approach," Dusenberry said, "is that you don't *learn* much that way. . . . The only way to find out about Indians is to care for them and win their love and respect . . . then they'll do almost anything for you. . . . But if you don't do that . . ." He would shake his head and his thoughts would go trailing off.

"I've seen these 'objective' workers come on the reservations," he said, "and get absolutely nowhere . . .

"There's this pseudo-science myth that when you're 'objective' you just disappear from the face of the earth and see everything undistorted, as it really is, like God from heaven. But that's rubbish. When a person's objective his attitude is remote. He gets a sort of stony, distant look on his face.

"The Indians see that. They see it better than we do. And when they see it they don't like it. They don't know where in hell these 'objective' anthros are at and it makes them suspicious, so they clam up and don't say anything. . . .

"Or they'll just tell them nonsense . . . which of course a lot of the anthros believe at first because they got it 'objectively' . . . and the Indians sometimes laugh at them behind their backs.

"Some of these anthropologists make big names for themselves in their departments," Dusenberry said, "because they know all *that* jargon. But they really don't know as much as they think they do. And they especially don't like people who tell them so . . . which I do. . . ." He laughed.

"So that's why I'm not objective about Indians," he said. "I *believe* in them and they believe in me and that makes all the difference. They've told me things they've said they never told any other white man because they know I'll never use it against them. It's a whole different way of relating to them. Indians first, anthropology second. . . .

"That limits me in a lot of ways. There's so much I can't say. But it's better to know a lot and say little, I think, than know little and say a lot. . . . Don't you agree?"

Because Phædrus was new to the English department Dusenberry took a curious interest in him. Dusenberry was curious about everything, and as he got to know Phædrus better the curiosity grew. Here to Dusenberry's surprise was someone who seemed even more alienated than he was, someone who had done graduate work in Hindu philosophy at Benares, India, for God's sake, and knew something about cultural differences. Most important, Phædrus seemed to have a very analytic mind.

"That's what *I* don't have," Dusenberry had said. "I know volumes about these people but I can't structure it. I just don't have that kind of mind."

So every chance he got he poured hours and hours of information about American Indians into Phædrus' ears, hoping to get back from him some overall structure, some picture of what it all meant in larger terms. Phædrus listened but he never had any answers.

Dusenberry was particularly concerned about Indian religion. He was sure it explained why the Indians were so slow in integrating into the surrounding white culture. He'd noticed that tribes with the strongest religious practices were the most "backward" by white standards and he wanted Phædrus to provide some theoretical support for this. Phædrus thought Dusenberry was probably right but couldn't think of any theoretical support and thought the whole thesis was somewhat dull and academic. For more than a year Dusenberry never tried to correct this impression. He just kept on feeding information about Indians to Phædrus and getting back Phædrus' lack of ideas. But then, a few months before Phædrus was to leave Bozeman for another teaching job, Dusenberry said to him, "There's something I think I have to show you."

"Where?" Phædrus asked.

"On the Northern Cheyenne reservation, down in Busby. Have you been there?"

"No," Phædrus said.

"Well, it's a wretched place but I've promised to take some students down and you should come along too. I want you to see a meeting of the Native American Church. The students won't be going to it, but you should."

"You're going to convert me?" Phædrus said facetiously.

"Maybe," Dusenberry said.

Dusenberry explained that they would be sitting in a teepee all night long until sunup. After midnight Phædrus could leave if he wanted, but before that no one was permitted to leave.

"What do we do all night?" Phædrus asked.

"In the center of the teepee there will be a fire, and there will be ceremonies connected to it, and a lot of singing and drumming. Not much talking. After the meeting is over in the morning there'll be a ceremonial meal."

Phædrus thought about it and then agreed and asked what the meal was like.

Dusenberry smiled with a kind of arch smile. He said, "One time they were supposed to have the food, you know, from before the white men came. Blueberries and venison and all that and so what did they do? They broke out three cans of Del Monte corn and started opening all the cans with a can opener. I stood it as long as I could. Finally I told them 'No! No! No! Not *canned* corn,' and they laughed at me. They said, 'Just like a white man. Has to have everything just right.'

"Then after that, all night long they did everything the way I said and they thought that was an even bigger joke because now they weren't only using white man's corn, they were having a white man *run* the ceremony. And they were all laughing at me. They're always doing stuff like that. We just *love* each other. I just have the *best* time when I'm down there."

"What's the purpose of staying up all night?" Phædrus asked.

Dusenberry looked at him meaningfully, "Visions," he said.

"From the fire?"

"There's a sacramental food that you take that induces them. It's called 'peyote.' "

That was the first time Phædrus had ever heard the name. This was just before Leary and Alpert's notoriety and the great age of hippies, trippers, and flower children that peyote and its synthetic equivalent, LSD, helped to produce. Peyote back then was all but unknown to almost everyone except anthropologists and other specialists in Indian affairs.

In the tray of slips, just back of the ones on Dusenberry, was a section of slips on how the Indians had quietly brought peyote up from Mexico in the late nineteenth century, eating it to induce an altered mental state that they considered a form of religious communion. Dusenberry had indicated that Indians who used it regarded it as a quicker and surer way of arriving at the condition reached in the traditional "vision quest" where an Indian goes out into isolation and fasts and prays and meditates for days in the darkness of a sealed lodge until the Great Spirit reveals itself to him and takes over his life.

On one of his slips Phædrus had copied a reference that showed the similarity of the peyote experience to the old vision quest descriptions. According to the description it produces "light-headedness, a state of well-being, and increased attention to all perceptions, sensations, and inner mental events."

> *Perceptual modifications follow, initially manifested by vivid and spontaneous visual imagery, which evolves to illusions and finally to visual hallucinations. Emotions are intensified, vary widely in content, and may include euphoria, apathy, serenity, or anxiety. The intellect is drawn to the analysis of complex realities or transcendental questions. Consciousness expands to include all these responses simultaneously. In later stages, following a large dose of a hallucinogen, a person may experience a feeling of union with nature associated with a dissolution of personal identity, engendering a state of beatitude or even ecstasy. A dissociative reaction, in which the subject loses contact with immediate reality, may also occur. A subject may experience abandonment of the body, may see elaborate visions, or feel the imminence of death, which could lead to terror and panic. The experience is determined by the person's mental state, the structure of his or her personality, the physical setting, and cultural influences.*

The source Phædrus had taken this material from concluded that "current research and discussion are clouded by political and social issues," which since the 1960s has certainly been true. One slip noted

that Dusenberry had been asked to testify before the Montana leg-
islature on the matter. The president of the college had told him not
to say anything, presumably to avoid political repercussions. Dusenberry complied, and told Phædrus later how guilty he felt about this.

After the sixties the whole issue of peyote became one of those
no-win political contests between individual freedom on the one hand
and democracy on the other. Clearly LSD was injuring some innocent
people with hallucinations that led to their death, and clearly the
majority of Americans wanted drugs such as LSD made illegal. But
the majority of Americans were not Indians and certainly they were
not members of the Native American Church. There was a persecution of a religious minority going on here, something that's not
supposed to happen in America.

The majority opposition to peyote reflected a cultural bias, the
belief, unsupported by scientific or historical evidence, that "hallucinatory" experience is automatically bad. Since hallucinations are a
form of insanity, the term, "hallucinogen," is clearly pejorative. Like
early descriptions of Buddhism as a "heathen" religion and Islam as
"barbaric," it begs some metaphysical questions. The Indians who
use it as part of their ceremony might with equal accuracy call it a
"de-hallucinogen," since it's their claim that it removes the hallucinations of contemporary life and reveals the reality buried beneath
them.

There is actually some scientific support for this Indian point of
view. Experiments have shown that spiders fed LSD do not wander
around doing purposeless things as one might expect a "hallucination"
would cause them to do, but instead spin an abnormally perfect,
symmetrical web. That would support the "de-hallucinogen" thesis.
But politics seldom depends on facts for its decisions.

Behind the index card for the "PEYOTE" slips was another card
called "RESERVATION." There were more than a hundred "RES-
ERVATION" slips describing that ceremony Dusenberry and
Phædrus attended—way too many. Most would have to be junked.
He'd made them because at one time it looked as though the whole
book would center around this long night's meeting of the Native
American Church. The ceremony would be a kind of spine to hold
it all together. From it he would branch out and show in tangent after

tangent the analysis of complex realities and transcendental questions that first emerged in his mind there.

The place can be seen from U.S. 212, about two hundred yards from the highway, but all you see from the road is tar-papered shacks and grungy dogs and maybe a poorly dressed Indian walking on an earth footpath past some junked cars. As if to make a point of the shabbiness, a clean white steeple of a missionary church stands in the middle of all this.

Away from the steeple, off by itself (and probably gone by now) was a large teepee that looked like it might have been put up as a tourist attraction except that there was no way you could drive to it from the road and there were no billboards or signs around advertising anything for sale.

The physical distance to that teepee from the highway was about two hundred yards, but culturally the distance bridged with Dusenberry that night was more like thousands of years. Phædrus couldn't have gone that distance without the peyote. He would have just sat there "observing" all this "objectively" like a well-trained anthropology student. But the peyote prevented that. He didn't *observe*, he participated, exactly as Dusenberry had intended he should do.

From twilight, when the peyote buttons were passed around, until midnight he sat staring across the flames of the ceremonial fire. The ring of Indian faces around the edge of the teepee had seemed ominous at first in the alternating light and shadow from the fire. The faces seemed misshapen, with sinister expressions like the storybook Indians of old; then that illusion passed and they seemed merely inscrutable.

After that there was a scaling down of thoughts that occurs whenever you adjust to a new physical situation. "What am I doing here?" he wondered. "I wonder how things are doing now back home? . . . How am I going to get those English papers corrected by Monday?" . . . and so on. But the thoughts gradually became less and less demanding and he settled down more and more into where he was and what he was watching.

Sometime after midnight, after he had listened to the singing and beating on the drum for hours and hours, something began to change. The exotic aspects began to fade. Instead of being an onlooker, feeling greater and greater distance from all this, his perceptions began to go in the opposite direction. He began to feel a warmth toward the songs. He murmured to John Wooden Leg, the Indian sitting next to him, "John, that's a great song!" and he meant it. John looked at him with surprise.

Some huge unexpected change was taking place in his attitude toward this music and toward the people who were singing it. Something in the way they spoke and handled things and related to each other struck a resonance too, way deep inside him, at levels that had seldom resonated favorably to anything.

He couldn't figure out what it was. Was the peyote just making him sentimental? He didn't think so. It ran deeper than sentimentality. Sentimentality is a narrowing of experience to the emotionally familiar. But this was something new opening up. There was a contradiction here. It was something new opening up that gave the sentimental feeling one might get from his childhood home when he sees a tree he once climbed or a swing he used to play on. A feeling of coming home. Coming home to some place one had never been before.

Why should he feel at home? This was the last place on earth where he should feel that.

He really didn't. Only a part of him felt at home. The other part still felt estranged and analytic and watchful. It seemed as though he was splitting into two people, one of whom wanted to stay there forever, and the other wanted to leave immediately. The latter one he understood, but who was this first person? This first person was a mystery.

This first person seemed like it must be some secret side of his personality, a dark side, that seldom spoke and didn't show itself to other people. He guessed he knew about it. He just didn't like to think about it. It was the side with the sullen, scowling, outlook; a side that didn't like authority, had "never amounted to anything," and never would, and knew that, and was sad about it, but couldn't help it. It could never be happy anywhere but always wanted to move on.

This wild side was saying for the first time, "stop wandering," and "these are your real people," and that was what he began to see there, listening to the songs and drums and staring into the fire. Something about these people seemed to say to this "bad" side of himself, "We know *exactly* how you feel. We feel this way ourselves."

The other side, the "good" analytic side, just watched, and before long it slowly began to spin an enormous symmetrical intellectual web, larger and more perfect than any it had ever spun before.

The nucleus of this intellectual web was the observation that when the Indians entered the teepee, or went out, or added logs, or passed the ceremonial peyote, or pipe, or food, they just *did* these things. They didn't go *about* doing them. They just *did* them. There was no waste motion. When they moved a branch into the fire to build it up they just *moved* it. There was no sense of ceremony. They were *engaged* in a ceremony but the way they did it there *wasn't* any ceremony.

Normally he wouldn't have attached much importance to this, but now, with the peyote opening up his mind and with his attention having nowhere else to go, he bored in on it with intensity.

This directness and simplicity was in the way they spoke, too. They spoke the way they moved, without any ceremony. It seemed to always come from deep within them. They just said what they wanted to say. Then they stopped. It wasn't just the way they pronounced the words. It was their attitude—plain-spoken, he thought. . . .

Plains spoken. They were speaking in the language of the Plains. This was the pure Plains American dialect he was listening to. It wasn't just Indian. It was white too. It was a kind of Midwestern and Western accent you hear in Woody Guthrie songs and cowboy movies. When Henry Fonda appears in *The Grapes of Wrath* or Gary Cooper or John Wayne or Gene Autry or Roy Rogers or William S. Boyd appear in any of a hundred different Westerns this is how they talk, not like some fancy college professor, but *Plains* spoken; laconic, understated, very little tonal change, no change of expression. Yet there was a warmth beneath the surface that you couldn't point to the source of.

Films have made the whole world know the dialect so well it's almost a cliché, but the way these Indians were speaking it wasn't any cliché. They were speaking the American Western dialect just as authentically as any cowboy he had ever heard. *More* authentically. It wasn't something they were putting on. It was *them*.

The web expanded when Phædrus began to consider the fact that English wasn't even the native language of these people. They didn't speak English in their homes. How was it that these linguistic "foreigners" spoke the Plains dialect of American English not only as *well* as their white neighbors but actually *better*? How could they possibly imitate it so perfectly when it was obvious from their lack of ceremony that they weren't trying to imitate anything at all?

The web grew wider and wider. They were *not* imitating. If there's one thing these people didn't do it was imitate. Everything was coming straight from the heart. That seemed to be the whole idea—to get things down to a point where everything's coming straight on, direct, no imitation. But if they weren't imitating, why did they talk this way? Why were they imitating?

Then the huge peyote illumination came:

They're the *originators*!

It expanded until he felt as though he had walked through the screen of a movie and for the first time watched the people who were projecting it from the other side.

Most of the rest of the whole tray of slips, many more than a thousand of them before him here, was a direct growth from this one original insight.

Tucked in among them was a copy of a speech made at the Medicine Lodge council of 1867 by Ten Bears, a Comanche chief. Phædrus had copied it from a book on Indian oratory to use as an example of Plains speech by someone who could not possibly have learned it from the whites. Now he read it again.

Ten Bears spoke to the assembled tribes and specifically to the representatives of Washington, saying:

There are things which you have said to me which I do not like. They were not sweet like sugar, but bitter like gourds. You said that you wanted to put us upon a reservation, to build us houses and to make us Medicine lodges. I do not want them.

I was born on the prairie, where the wind blew free, and there was nothing to break the light of the sun. I was born where there were no enclosures, and where everything drew a free breath. I want to die there, and not within walls. I know every stream and every wood between the Rio Grande and the Arkansas. I have hunted and lived over in that country. I lived like my fathers before me, and like them I lived happily.

When I was at Washington, the Great Father told me that all the Comanche land was ours, and that no one should hinder us in living upon it. So why do you ask us to leave the rivers, and the sun, and the wind, and live in houses? Do not ask us to give up the buffalo for the sheep. The young men have heard talk of this and it has made them sad and angry. Do not speak of it any more. I love to carry out the talk I get from the Great Father. When I get goods and presents, I and my people feel glad since it shows that he holds us in his eye. If the Texans had kept out of my country, there might have been peace. But that which you now say we must live on is too small.

The Texans have taken away the places where the grass grew the thickest and the timber was the best. Had we kept that, we might have done this thing you ask. But it is too late. The white man has the country which we loved and we only wish to wander on the prairie until we die. Any good thing you say to me shall not be forgotten. I shall carry it as near to my heart as my children and it shall be as often on my tongue as the name of the Great Spirit. I want no blood upon my land to stain the grass. I want it all clear and pure, and I wish it so, that all who go through among my people may find peace when they come in, and leave it when they go out.

As Phædrus read it again this time he saw that it wasn't quite as close to cowboy speech as he'd remembered—it was a damn sight *better* than cowboy speech—but it was still closer to the white Plains dialect than is the language of the European. Here were the straight, head-on, declarative sentences without stylistic ornamentation of any kind, but with a poetic force that must have put the sophisticated bureaucratic speech of Ten Bears' antagonists to shame. This was no imitation of the involuted Victorian elocution of 1867!

From that original perception of the Indians as the originators of the American style of speech had come an expansion: The Indians were the originators of the American style of *life*. The American personality is a mixture of European and Indian values. When you see this you begin to see a lot of things that have never been explained before.

Phædrus' problem now was to organize all this into a persuasive book. It was so radically different from the usual explanations of America, people would never believe it. They'd think he was just babbling. If he just talked in generalities he knew he would lose it. People would just say, "Oh yes, well that's just another one of those interesting ideas people are always coming up with," or "You can't generalize about Indians because they're all different," or some other cliché like that and walk away from it.

He'd thought for a while he might come at it obliquely, starting with something very concrete and specific such as a cowboy film that people already know about, for example, *Butch Cassidy and the Sundance Kid*.

There is an opening scene in that film where everything is shown in brown monochrome probably to give a historic, legendary feeling to it. The Sundance Kid is playing poker, and the scene is slowed a little to give it a dramatic tension. The Kid's face is all you see. Only a fragment of one of the other players is sometimes seen, and an occasional wisp of smoke passing before the Sundance Kid's countenance. The Kid is without expression but is alert and self-controlled.

The voice of an unseen gambler says, "Well it looks like you cleaned everybody out, fella. You haven't lost a hand since you got the deal."

There is no change in the Kid's expression.

"What's the secret of your success?" the gambler's voice continues. It is threatening. Ominous.

Sundance looks down for a while as if thinking about it, then looks up unemotionally. "Prayer," he says.

He doesn't mean it but he doesn't say it sarcastically either. It's a statement poised on a knife edge of ambiguity.

"Let's just you and me play," the gambler says.

A showdown is about to occur. It is *the* cliché of the Wild West. It has been repeated in hundreds of films shown in thousands of theatres and millions of TV sets again and again. The tension grows but the Sundance Kid's expression doesn't change. His eye movements, his pauses, are in a kind of relaxed harmony between himself and his surroundings even though we see that he is in a growingly dangerous situation, which soon explodes into violence.

What Phædrus wanted to do now was use just that one scene as an opening illustration. To it he would add just one explanation which no one ever notices, but which he was sure was true. "What you have just seen," he would explain, "is a rendition of the cultural style of an American Indian."

Then would be seen, identified for what they were, the famous old traits of the American Indian: silence, a modesty of manner, and a dangerous willingness to sudden, enormous violence.

It would be a dramatic way of making the point, he thought. Before you are alerted to it you don't see it, but once you become aware, it's obvious. The source of values that Robert Redford tapped and that the American public overwhelmingly responded to is the cultural value pattern of the American Indian. Even the color of Redford's face in the sepia monochrome was changed to that of an Indian.

Certainly it wasn't the intention of the film to personify an Indian. It came "naturally" as a way of showing the Wild West. But the point of Phædrus' thesis was that the *reason* it came "naturally" and that audiences responded to it "naturally" was that the film reached into a root source of American feelings for what is good. It is this source of what is good, this historic cultural system of American values, which is Indian.

If you take a list of all the things European observers have stated to be the characteristics of white Americans, you'll find that there is a correlation with the characteristics white American observers have customarily assigned to the Indians. And if, furthermore, you take another list of all the characteristics that Americans use to describe Europeans you'll get a pretty good correlation with Indian opinions of white Americans.

To prove this point Phædrus intended to reverse the situation: instead of showing how a cowboy resembles an Indian, he would show how an Indian resembles a cowboy. For this he'd found a description by the anthropologist, E. A. Hoebel, of a Cheyenne Indian male:

> Reserved and dignified, . . . [the Cheyenne male] . . . moves with a quiet sense of self-assurance. He speaks fluently, but never carelessly. He is careful of the sensibilities of others and is kindly and generous. He is slow to anger and strives to suppress his feelings, if aggravated. Vigorous on the hunt, in war he prizes the active life. Towards enemies he feels no merciful compunctions, and the more aggressive he is the better. He is well versed in ritual knowledge. He is neither flighty nor dour. Usually quiet, he has a lightly displayed sense of humor. He is sexually repressed and masochistic but that masochism is expressed in culturally approved rites. He does not show much creative imagination in artistic expression but he has a firm grip on reality. He deals with the problems of life in set ways while at the same time showing a notable capacity to readjust to new circumstances. His thinking is rationalistic to a high degree and yet colored with mysticism. His ego is strong and not easily threatened. His superego, as manifest in the strong social conscience and mastery of his basic impulses, is powerful and dominating. He is "mature," serene and composed, secure in his social position, capable of warm social relations. He has powerful anxieties but these are channelized into institutionalized modes of collective expression with satisfactory results. He exhibits few neurotic tendencies.

Now if that isn't a description of William S. Boyd playing *Hopalong Cassidy* in twenty-three or fifty or however-many films, there never was one. With the single exception of the Indian "mysticism" the characterization is perfect.

Whether the American cowboy ever really was like William S. Boyd is not really relevant. What is relevant is that in the 1930s, during the darkest days of the Great Depression, Americans shoveled out millions of dollars to look at his movies. They didn't have to. Nobody forced them to. But they went anyway, just as they later went to see *Butch Cassidy and the Sundance Kid*.

They did so because those movies were a confirmation of the values they believed in. Those movies were rituals, almost religious rituals, for transmitting the cultural values of America to the young and reconfirming them in the old. It wasn't a deliberate, conscious process; people were just doing what they liked. It is only when one analyzes what they liked that one sees the assimilation of Indian values.

Others of the thousands of slips in Phædrus' trays continued this analysis: Many Europeans think of white Americans as a sloppy, untidy people, but they're not nearly as untidy as the Indians on the reservations. Europeans often think of white Americans as being too direct and plain-spoken, bad-mannered and sort of insolent the way they do things, but Indians are even more that way. In World War II Europeans noted that American troops drank too much, and when they got drunk they made a lot of trouble. The comparison with Indians is obvious. But on the other hand, European military commanders rated the stability of American troops under fire as high, and that is also an Indian characteristic.

That steady "When you say that, smile!" look the cowboy movies love to portray (and Europeans tend to abhor) is pure Indian, except that when the Indian looks that way it doesn't necessarily mean he is threatening. What causes that steady look comes from something much deeper.

Indians don't talk to fill time. When they don't have anything to say, they don't say it. When they don't say it, they leave the impression of being a little ominous. In the presence of this Indian silence, whites sometimes get nervous and feel forced as a matter of politeness or kindness to fill the vacuum with a kind of small-talk which often says one thing and means another. But these well-mannered circumlocutions of aristocratic European speech are "forked-tongue" talk to the Indian and are infuriating. They violate his morality. He wants you to either speak from the heart or keep quiet. This has been a source of Indian-white conflict for centuries and although the modern white American personality is a compromise of that conflict, the conflict still exists.

To this day Americans are mistakenly characterized by Europeans as "like children," naïve, immature, and tending toward violence because they don't know how to control themselves. That mistake is also made about Indians. To this day white Americans are also mistakenly characterized by Indians as a bunch of snobs who think you are so stupid you can never see how phony they are. That mistake is also made about Europeans.

This anti-snobbery of all Americans, particularly Western Americans, is derived from this Indian attitude. The Cheyenne name for white man is *wihio*, meaning "spider." Arapaho use *niatha* to mean the same thing. To the Indian, whites *seemed* like spiders when they talked. They sat there and smiled and said things they didn't mean, and all the time their mind was spinning a web around the Indian. They got so lost in their own web-spinning thoughts they didn't even see that the Indian was watching them too and could see what they were doing.

The American politics of isolationism, in its refusal to become "entangled in the meshes of European politics" comes from this root, Phædrus thought. Most of American isolationism has come from regions that are closest to the American Indian.

The slips went on and on detailing European and Indian cultural differences and their effects, and as the slips had grown in number a secondary, corollary thesis had emerged: that this process of diffusion and assimilation of Indian values is not over. It's still with us, and accounts for much of the restlessness and dissatisfaction found in America today. Within each American these conflicting sets of values still clash.

This clash, Phædrus thought, explained why others hadn't seen long before what he had seen at the peyote meeting. When you borrow traits and attitudes from a hostile culture you don't give them credit for it. If you tell a white from Alabama that his Southern accent is derived from Negro speech he is likely to deny and resent it, although the geographical congruity of the Southern accent with areas of huge black population makes this pretty obvious. Similarly if you tell a Montana white living near a reservation that he resembles an Indian he may take it as an insult. And if you'd said it a hundred years ago you might have had a real fight on your hands. Then Indians were fiends from hell! The only good one was a dead one.

But even though Indians were never given proper credit for their contribution to the American frontier personality values, it's certain that these values couldn't have come from anyone else. One often hears "frontier values" spoken of as though they came from the rocks, the rivers, or the trees of the frontier, but trees, rocks, and rivers do not by themselves confer social values. They've got trees, rocks, and rivers in Europe.

It was the people living among those trees, rocks, and rivers who are the source of the values of the frontier. The early frontiersmen such as the "Mountain Men" deliberately and enthusiastically imitated Indians. They were delighted to be told that they were indistinguishable from Indians. Settlers who came later copied the Mountain Men's frontier style but didn't see its source, or if they did, denied it and credited it to their own hard work and isolation.

But the clash between European and Indian values still exists, and Phædrus felt he himself was one of those in whom the battle was taking place. That was why he had the feeling of "coming home" at that peyote meeting. The division he'd felt within himself and thought was something wrong with himself was not within himself at all. What he was seeing was a source of "himself" that had never been formally acknowledged. It was a division within the entire American culture that he had projected upon himself. It was in many others too.

In one of his long contemplations of this subject the name of Mark Twain appeared. Twain was from Hannibal, Missouri, along the Mississippi, the great dividing line between the American East and West, and one of his most fearsome villains was "Injun Joe," who personified the Indian the settlers feared at that time. But Twain's biographers had also noted a deep division in his own personality that shaped his choice of heros. On the one side was an orderly, intelligent, obedient, clean, and relatively responsible young lad whom he fictionalized as Tom Sawyer; and on the other, a wild, freedom-loving, uneducated, lying, irresponsible, low-status American he called Huckleberry Finn.

Phædrus noticed that the division of Twain's personality fitted the cultural split he'd been talking about. Tom was an Eastern person with the manners of a New Englander, much closer to Europe than to the American West, but Huck was a Western person, closer to the Indians, forever restless, unattached, unbelieving in the pompousness of society, wanting more than anything else just to be free.

Freedom. That was the topic that would drive home this whole understanding of Indians. Of all the topics his slips on Indians covered freedom was the most important. Of all the contributions America has made to the history of the world, the idea of freedom from a social hierarchy has been the greatest. It was fought for in the American Revolution and confirmed in the Civil War. To this day it's still the most powerful, compelling ideal holding the whole nation together.

And yet, although Jefferson called this doctrine of social equality "self-evident," it is not at all self-evident. Scientific evidence and the social evidence of history indicate the opposite is self-evident. There is no "self-evidence" in European history that all men are created equal. There's no nation in Europe that doesn't trace its history to a time when it was "self-evident" that all men are created *un*equal. Jean Jacques Rousseau, who is sometimes given credit for this doctrine, certainly didn't get it from the history of Europe or Asia or Africa. He got it from the impact of the New World upon Europe and from contemplation of one particular kind of individual who lived in the New World, the person he called the "Noble Savage."

The idea that "all men are created equal" is a gift to the world from the American Indian. Europeans who settled here only trans-mitted it as a doctrine that they sometimes followed and sometimes did not. The real source was someone for whom social equality was no mere doctrine, who had equality built into his bones. To him it was inconceivable that the world could be any other way. For him there was no other way of life. That's what Ten Bears was trying to tell them.

Phædrus thought the Indians haven't yet lost this one. They haven't yet won it either, he realized; the fight isn't over. It's still the central internal conflict in America today. It's a fault line, a dis-continuity that runs through the center of the American cultural per-sonality. It's dominated American history from the beginning and continues to be a source of both national strength and weakness today. And as Phædrus' studies got deeper and deeper he saw that it was to this conflict between European and Indian values, between freedom and order, that his study should be directed.

4.

After Phædrus left Bozeman he saw Dusenberry just twice: once when Dusenberry came for a visit and had to rest because he "felt strange"; a second time in Calgary, Alberta, after he had learned that the "strangeness" was brain cancer and he had only a few months to live. Then he was withdrawn and sad, preoccupied with internal preparations for his own end.

Some of his sadness was caused by the feeling he'd failed the Indians. He'd wanted to do so much for them. He spent so many years accepting their hospitality and now there was nothing he would ever do in return. Phædrus felt he'd failed Dusenberry's plea to help analyze all his data, but Phædrus was involved in enormous problems of his own and there was nothing he could do about it, and now it was too late.

But six years later, after publication of a successful book, most of these problems had disappeared. When the question arose of what would be the subject of a second book there was no question about what it would be. Phædrus loaded his old Ford pickup truck with a camper and headed back into Montana again, to the eastern plains where the reservations were.

At this time there was no such thing as a Metaphysics of Quality and no plans for one. His book had covered the subject of Quality. Any further discussion would be like a lawyer who, after swinging the jury in his favor, keeps on talking and talking until he finally swings them back the other way again. Phædrus just wanted to talk about Indians now. There was plenty to say.

On the reservations he talked to Indians he had met when he was with Dusenberry, hoping to pick up the threads Dusenberry had left. When he told them he was Dusenberry's friend they would always say, "Oh yes, Dusenberry—he was a *good* man." They would talk for a while, but before long the conversation would become difficult and die down.

He couldn't think of anything to say. Or when he did, he would say it so awkwardly and self-consciously that it disturbed the flow of the conversation. He didn't have the knack for casual conversation that Dusenberry had. He wasn't the person for the job. Dusenberry could sit there all weekend and gab on and on with them about their families and their friends and anything they thought was important, and he just loved that. That's what he was really in anthropology for. That was his idea of a wonderful weekend. But Phædrus had never learned how to make small-talk like that and as soon as he got into it his mind always drifted off into his own private world of abstractions and the conversation died.

He thought that maybe if he did some reading in the field of anthropology he might know better what to ask the Indians. So he said goodbye for a while and drove from the hot plains up into the Rocky Mountains near Bozeman. At the college there, now a university, he took out the best books he could find on anthropology, then drove up to an old remote campground near the timberline and settled down to do some reading. He hoped to stay there until he had some kind of plan for a book sketched out.

It felt good to be back in the stunted pines and wild flowers and chilly nights and hot days again. He enjoyed the ritual of getting up in the morning in the freezing camper, turning on the heat, and then going for a jog up a mountain trail. When he came back for tea and breakfast the camper would be all warm and he could settle down to a morning of reading and note-taking.

It could have been a great way to do a book but unfortunately it didn't turn out that way. What he read in the anthropology texts slowed him down more and more until it stopped him.

Phædrus saw with disbelief at first and then with growing anger that the whole field of anthropology was rigged and stacked in such a way that everything he had to say about Indians would be unacceptable. There was no question about it. Page after page kept making it clearer and clearer that there was no way he could continue. He could write a totally honest, true and valuable book on the subject, but if he dared call it anthropology it would be either ignored or attacked by the professionals and discarded.

He remembered Dusenberry's hostility and bitterness toward what he called "objective anthropology," but he always thought Dusenberry was just being iconoclastic. Not so.

The professionals' refutation of his book would go something like this:

A thesis of this sort is colorful and interesting but it cannot be considered useful to anthropology without empirical support. Anthropology tries to be a science of man, not a collection of gossip and intuitions about man. It is not anthropology when someone with no training or experience spends one night on a reservation in a teepee full of Indians taking a hallucinogenic drug. To pretend he has discovered something that hundreds of carefully trained methodical workers who have spent a lifetime in the field have missed, exhibits a certain "overconfidence" that the discipline of anthropology tries to restrain.

It should be mentioned that such theses are not at all unusual in anthropology. In fact, during the early history of anthropology, they dominated the field. It was not until the beginning of this century, when Franz Boas and his co-workers started to ask seriously, "Which of this material is science and which is not?" that speculative intuitive rubbish unsupported by any real facts was methodically weeded out of the field.

Every anthropologist at one time or another arrives at speculative theses about the cultures he studies. It is part of the fascination that keeps him interested in the field. But every anthropologist is trained to keep these theses to himself until he is sure, from a study of actual facts and proofs, that he knows what he is talking about.

Very formidable. First you say things our way and then we'll listen to you. Phædrus had heard it before.

What it always means is that you have hit an invisible wall of prejudice. Nobody on the inside of that wall is ever going to listen to you; not because what you say isn't true, but solely because you have been identified as outside that wall. Later, as his Metaphysics of Quality matured, he developed a name for the wall to give it a more structured, integrated meaning. He called it a "cultural immune system." But all he saw now was that he wasn't going to get anywhere with his talk about Indians until that wall had been breached. There was no way he was going to make any contribution to anthropology with his non-credentials and crazy ideas. The best he could do was mount a careful attack upon that wall.

In the camper he did less and less reading and more and more thinking about the problem. The books that surrounded him on the seat and floor and shelves were of no use to him. Many of the anthropologists seemed to be bright, interested, humane people but they were all operating within the wall of the anthropological cultural immune system. He could see that some of the anthropologists were struggling to get outside that wall, but within the wall there were no intellectual tools that would let them out.

As he reflected further on that wall he thought about how all paths within it seemed to lead to Franz Boas, who in 1899 had become Columbia University's first professor of anthropology, and had so completely dominated his field that most of the anthropology in America today still seems to lie in his shadow. Students working within his intellectual domain became famous: Margaret Mead, Ruth Benedict, Robert Lowie, Edward Sapir, Alfred Kroeber, Paul Radin and others. They produced a flowering of anthropological literature so great and so rich that their work is sometimes mistaken for all of cultural anthropology. The key to getting through the wall lay in re-examining the philosophical attitudes of Boas himself.

Boas' training was in mathematics and physics in nineteenth century Germany. His influence lay not in the establishment of a single particular theory of anthropology but in the establishment of a method of anthropological investigation. This method followed the principles of the "hard" science he had been trained in.

Margaret Mead said, "He feared premature generalization like the plague, and continually warned us against it." Generalization should be based on the facts and only on the facts.

"It is indubitable that science was his religion," Kroeber said. "He called his early convictions materialistic. Science could tolerate nothing 'subjective'; value judgments—and by infection even values considered as phenomena—must be absolutely excluded."

On one slip, headed "Goldschmidt," Phædrus copied down the statement that, "This empiricism, this concern with fact, with detail, with preserving the record, Boas transmitted to his students and to anthropology. It is so major an element in anthropological thinking that the term 'armchair anthropologist' is one of opprobrium, and two generations later we still insist on field work as a requisite to any claim for anthropological competence."

By the time Phædrus finished reading about Boas he was confident he'd identified the source of the immune system he was up against, the same immune system that had so rejected Dusenberry's views. It was classical nineteenth-century science and its insistence that science is only a method for determining what is true and not a body of beliefs in itself. There have been many schools of anthropological theory other than Boas' but Phædrus could find none that opposed him on the matter of scientific objectivity.

As he read on, Phædrus could see more and more of what the negative effects of this application of Victorian science to cultural anthropology had been. What had happened was that Boas, by superimposing the criteria of the physical sciences upon cultural anthropology, had shown that not only were the theories of the armchair anthropologists unsupported by science but that any anthropological theory was unsupported by science, since it could not be proved by the rigorous methods of Boas' own field of physics. Boas seemed to think that someday such a theory would emerge out of the facts but it's been nearly a century since Boas had those expectations and it hasn't emerged yet. Phædrus was convinced it never would. Patterns of culture do not operate in accordance with the laws of physics. How are you going to prove in terms of the laws of physics that a certain attitude exists within a culture? What is an attitude in terms of the laws of molecular interaction? What is a cultural value? How are you going to show *scientifically* that a certain culture has certain values?

You can't.

Science has no values. Not officially. The whole field of anthropology was rigged and stacked so that nobody could prove anything of a general nature about anybody. No matter what you said, it could be shot down any time by any damn fool on the basis that it wasn't scientific.

What theory existed was marked by bitter quarrels over differences that were not anthropological at all. They were almost never quarrels about accuracy of observation. They were quarrels about abstract meanings. It seemed almost as though the moment anyone said anything theoretical it was a signal for the commencement of an enormous dog fight over differences that could not be resolved with any amount of anthropological information.

The whole field seemed like a highway filled with angry drivers cursing each other and telling each other they didn't know how to drive when the real trouble was the highway itself. The highway had been laid down as the scientific objective study of man in a manner that paralleled the physical sciences. The trouble was that man isn't suited to this kind of scientific objective study. Objects of scientific study are supposed to hold still. They're supposed to follow the laws of cause and effect in such a way that a given cause will always have a given effect, over and over again. Man doesn't do this. Not even savages.

The result has been theoretical chaos.

Phædrus liked a description he read in a book called *Theory in Anthropology* by Robert Manners and David Kaplan of Brandeis University. "Scattered throughout the anthropological literature," they wrote, "are a number of hunches, insights, hypotheses, and generalizations. They tend to remain scattered, inchoate, and unrelated to one another, so that they often get lost or are forgotten. The tendency has been for each generation of anthropologists to start afresh.

"Theory building in cultural anthropology comes to resemble slash-and-burn agriculture," they said, "where the natives return sporadically to old fields grown over by bush and slash and burn and plant for a few years."

Phædrus could see the slash and burn everywhere he looked. Some anthropologists were saying a culture is the essence of anthropology. Some were saying there isn't any such thing as a culture. Some were saying it's all history, some said it's all structure. Some said it's all function. Some said it was all values. Some, following Boas' scientific purity said there were no values at all.

That idea that anthropology has no values Phædrus marked down in his mind as the "spot." That was the place where the wall could best be breached. No values, huh? No Quality? This was the point of focus where he could begin an attack.

What many were trying to do, evidently, was get out of all these metaphysical quarrels by condemning all theory, by agreeing not to even *talk* about such theoretical reductionist things as what savages do in general. They restricted themselves to what *their* particular savage happened to do on Wednesday. That was scientifically safe all right—and scientifically useless.

The anthropologist Marshall Sahlins wrote, "The very term 'universal' has a negative connotation in this field because it suggests the search for broad generalization that has virtually been declared unscientific by twentieth-century academic, particularistic American anthropology."

Phædrus guessed anthropologists thought they had kept the field "scientifically pure" by this method, but the purity was so constrictive it had all but strangled the field. If you can't generalize from data there's nothing else you can do with it either.

A science without generalization is no science at all. Imagine someone telling Einstein, "You can't say '$E = mc^2$.' It's too general, too reductionist. We just want the facts of physics, not all this high-flown theory." Cuckoo. Yet, that's what they were saying in anthropology.

Data without generalization is just gossip. And as Phædrus continued on and on that seemed to be the status of what he was reading. It filled shelf after shelf with volume after dusty volume about this savage and that savage, but as far as he could see, anthropology, the "science of man," had had almost no guiding effect on man's activities in this scientific century.

Whacko science. They were trying to lift themselves by their bootstraps. You can't have Box "A" contain within itself Box "B," which in turn contains Box "A." That's whacko. Yet here's a "science" which contains "man" which contains "science" which contains "man" which contains "science"—on and on.

He left the mountains near Bozeman with boxes full of slips and many notebooks full of quotations and the feeling that there was nothing within anthropology he could do.

· · ·

Back down in the plains, in a country motel one night with nothing to read, Phædrus had found a small dog-eared *Yankee* magazine, thumbed through it, and stopped on a brief account by Cathie Slater Spence entitled, "In Search of the April Fool."

It was about a child prodigy who had possibly the highest intelligence ever observed, and who in his later life went nowhere. "Born on April 1, 1898," it said, "William James Sidis could speak five languages and read Plato in the original Greek by the age of five. At eight he passed the entrance for Harvard but had to wait three years to be admitted. Even so he became Harvard's youngest scholar and graduated *cum laude* in 1914 at the age of 16. Frequently featured in 'Ripley's Believe It or Not,' Sidis made the front page of the *New York Times* 19 times."

But after graduating from Harvard, the "Boy Wonder" pursued his own obscure and seemingly meaningless interests. The press that had lionized him turned on him. The most scathing example came in the New Yorker *in 1937. Entitled "April Fool," the magazine article ridiculed everything from Sidis's hobbies to his physical characteristics. Sidis sued for libel and invasion of privacy. Though he won a small out-of-court settlement for libel, the invasion of privacy charge was dismissed by the U.S. Supreme Court in a landmark decision. "The article is merciless in its dissection of intimate details of its subject's personal life," the court conceded, but Sidis was "a public figure" and thus could not claim protection from the interest of the press, which continued to hound him until his death in 1944. Obituaries called him "a prodigious failure" and "a burnt-out genius" who had never achieved anything of significance despite his talents.*

Dan Mahony of Ipswich, Massachusetts, read about Sidis in 1976 and was puzzled. "What was he really doing and thinking all that time?" Mahony wondered. "It's true he held low-paying jobs, but Einstein came up with the theory of relativity while working in a patent office. I had a feeling Sidis was up to more than most people thought."

Mahony has spent the last ten years looking into Sidis's work. In one dusty attic, he found a bulky manuscript called The Tribes and the States *in which Sidis argues persuasively that the New England political system was profoundly influenced by the democratic federation of the Penacook Indians.*

At this sentence, a kind of shock passed through Phædrus, but the article went on.

When Mahony sent Sidis's book The Animate and Inanimate *to another eccentric genius, Buckminster Fuller, Fuller found it "a fine cosmological piece" that astoundingly predicted the existence of black holes—in 1925!*

Mahony has unearthed a science fiction novel, economic, and political writings, and 89 weekly newspaper columns about Boston that Sidis wrote under a pen name. "The amazing thing is that we may only have tapped the surface of what Sidis produced," says Mahony. "For instance, we've found just one page of a manuscript called The Peace Paths, *and people who knew Sidis have said they saw many more manuscripts. I think Sidis may still have a few surprises in store for us."*

Phædrus set down the magazine and felt as though someone had thrown a rock through the motel window. Then he read the article over and over again in a sort of daze, as the impact of what he was reading sank deeper and deeper. That night he could hardly sleep.

It looked as though way back in the thirties Sidis had been on exactly the same thesis about Indians. He was trying to tell people some of the most important things that could be said about their country and they were rewarding him by publicly calling him a "fool" and failing to publish what he had written. There didn't even seem to be any way to find out what Sidis had said.

Phædrus tried to contact the Mahony mentioned in the article but couldn't find him, partly, he supposed, because his effort was only half-hearted. He knew that even if he did get a look at Sidis' material there wasn't much he could do about it. The problem wasn't that it wasn't true. The problem was that nobody was interested.

5.

It felt cold again and Phædrus got up and reloaded the coal stove with more charcoal briquets.

After that depressing experience in the mountains he had wanted to give the whole thing up and move on to something more profitable, but as it turned out, the depression he was feeling was just a temporary setback. It was a prelude to a much larger and more important explanation of the Indians. This time it would not be just Indians versus whites, treated within a white anthropological format. It would be whites and white anthropology versus Indians and "Indian anthropology" treated within a format no one had ever heard of yet. He would get out of the impasse by expanding the format.

The key was values, he thought. That was the weakest spot in the whole wall of cultural immunity to new ideas the anthropologists had built around themselves. Value was a term they had to use, but under Boas' science value does not really exist.

And Phædrus knew something about values. Before he had gone up into the mountains he had written a whole book on values. Quality. Quality was value. They were the same thing. Not only were values the weakest spot in that wall, he might just be the strongest person to attack that spot.

He found surprising support for this attack from one of Boas' students, Alfred Kroeber, who with Harvard anthropology professor Clyde Kluckhohn had led a drive for the reinsertion of values into anthropology. Elsewhere Kluckhohn had said, "Values provide the only basis for fully intelligible comprehension of culture because the actual organization of all cultures is primarily in terms of their values.

This becomes apparent as soon as one attempts to present the picture of a culture without reference to its values. The account becomes a meaningless assemblage of items having relationship to one another only through coexistence in locality and moment—an assemblage that might as profitably be arranged alphabetically as in any other order; a mere laundry list."

Kluckhohn conceded that, "The degree to which even lip-service to values has been avoided until recently, especially by anthropologists, is striking. The hesitation of anthropologists can perhaps be laid to the natural history tradition which persists in our science for better or worse." But in *Culture: a Critical Review of Concepts and Definitions* they said that, "culture must include the explicit and systematic study of values and value-systems viewed as observable, describable, and comparable phenomena of nature."

They explained that negativism toward the use of values resulted from attitudes of objectivity. It was the same objectivity, Phædrus noted, that Dusenberry had so much trouble with. "It is this subjective side of values that led to their being long tabooed as improper for consideration by natural science," Kroeber and Kluckhohn said. "Instead (values) were relegated to a special set of intellectual activities called 'the humanities' included in the 'spiritual science' of the Germans. Values were believed to be eternal because they were God-given, or divinely inspired or at least discovered by that soul part of man which partakes somewhat of divinity, as his body and other bodies and tangibles of the world do not. A new and struggling science, as little advanced beyond physics, astronomy, anatomy and the rudiments of physiology as Western science was only two centuries ago, might cheerfully concede this reservation of the remote and unexpected territory of values to the philosophers and theologians and limit itself to what it could treat mechanistically."

Kluckhohn conceded that values are ill-defined and subject to a multiplicity of competing definitions, but asserted that verbal definitions of values are not necessary to field work. He said that whether they were well-defined or not everyone agreed with what they were in actual practice. He tried to solve the problem by allowing everyone in his *Values Project* to define values any way they wanted to, but in formal social science that's unacceptable.

In his *Values Project* Kluckhohn described five neighboring Southwest American cultures in terms of their evaluations of their neighbors, and provided a good description of these cultures by this method. But as Phædrus continued reading elsewhere, he discovered that values, like every other general term in anthropology, were subject to the usual bilious attack. Sociologists Judith Blake and Kingsley Davis had the following to say about values:

> *As long as the cultural configurations, basic value attitudes, prevailing mores or whatnot are taken as the starting point and principal determinant, they have the status of unanalyzed assumptions. The very questions that would enable us to understand the norms tend not to be asked, and certain facts about society become difficult if not impossible to comprehend.*

Mores, determinants, norms . . . these were the jargon terms of sociology into which they converted things they wanted to attack. That's how you know when you're within a walled city, Phædrus thought. The jargon. They've cut themselves off from the rest of the world and are speaking a jargon only they can really understand.

"Worse yet," they went on,

> *the deceptive ease of explanation in terms of norms or value attitudes encourages an inattentiveness to methodological problems. By virtue of their subjective emotion and ethical character, norms and especially values are among the world's most difficult objects to identify with certainty. They are bones of contention and matters of disagreement. . . . An investigator . . . tends to be explaining the known by the unknown, the specific by the unspecific. His identification of the normative principles may be so vague as to be universally useful, i.e. anything and everything becomes explicable. Thus, if Americans spend a great deal of money on alcoholic beverages, theater and movie tickets, tobacco, cosmetics, and jewelry, the explanation is simple: They have a good-time ideology. If, on the other hand, there is a lack of social intimacy between Negro and white, it is because of a "racism" value. The cynical critic might advise that, for convenience in causal interpretation, the values of a "culture" should always be described in pairs of opposites.*

"Explicit definitions when given, demonstrate the nebulous character of 'value,' " Blake and Davis said. "Here, for example, is the definition of 'value-orientation' in a 437-page book on value orientations:

> *Value orientations are complex but definitely patterned (rank-ordered) principles resulting from the transactional interplay of three analytically distinguishable elements of the evaluative process—the cognitive, the affective, and the directive elements—which give order and direction to the ever-flowing stream of human acts and thoughts as these relate to the solution of 'common human' problems."*

Poor Kluckhohn, Phædrus thought. That was *his* definition. With that lead balloon for a vehicle there was no way he could succeed.

The attack made Phædrus want to get in there and start arguing. The statement that values are vague and therefore shouldn't be used for primary classification is not true. There's nothing vague about a value judgment. When a voter goes to the polling booth he's making a value judgment. What's so vague about that? Isn't an election a cultural activity? What's so vague about the New York stock exchanges? Aren't values what they're dealing in? How about the U.S. Treasury? Who in this world is more specific than the Internal Revenue Service? As Kluckhohn kept saying, values are not the least vague when you're dealing with them in terms of actual experience. It's only when you bring back statements about them and try to integrate them into the overall jargon of anthropology that they become vague.

This attack on Kroeber and Kluckhohn's "values" was a good example of what had stopped Phædrus' own entry into the field. You can't get anywhere because you are forced to resolve arguments every step of the way about the basic terms you are using. It's hard enough to talk about Indians alone without having to resolve a metaphysical dispute at the end of each sentence. This should have been done *before* anthropology was set up, not afterward.

That was the problem. The whole field of cultural anthropology is a house built on intellectual quicksand. As soon as you try to build the data into anything of theoretical weight it sinks and collapses. The field that one might have expected to be one of the most useful and productive of the sciences had gone under, not because the people in it were no good, or the subject was unimportant, but because the structure of scientific principles that it tries to rest on is inadequate to support it.

What was clear was that if he was going to do anything with anthropology the place to do it was not in anthropology itself but in the general body of assumptions upon which it rests. The solution to the anthropological blockage was not to try to construct some new anthropological theoretic structure but to first find some solid ground upon which such a structure can be constructed. It was this conclusion that placed him right in the middle of the field of philosophy known as metaphysics. Metaphysics would be the expanded format in which whites and white anthropology could be contrasted to Indians and "Indian anthropology" without corrupting everything into a white anthropological walled-in jargonized way of looking at things.

Whew! What a job! He wondered if he was biting off ten times as much as he could possibly chew. This could fill a whole shelf full of books. A whole corridor of shelves! But the more he thought about it the more he saw that the only alternative was to quit entirely.

There was a sense of relief though. Metaphysics was an area of study that had interested him more than any other as an undergraduate philosophy student in the United States and later as a graduate student in India. There was a sense of opening up after the endless tangles and nettles of unfamiliar anthropology. He had finally landed in his own briar patch.

Metaphysics is what Aristotle called the First Philosophy. It's a collection of the most general statements of a hierarchical structure of thought. On one of his slips he had copied a definition of it as "that part of philosophy which deals with the nature and structure of reality." It asks such questions as, "Are the objects we perceive real or illusory? Does the external world exist apart from our consciousness of it? Is reality ultimately reducible to a single underlying substance? If so, is it essentially spiritual or material? Is the universe intelligible and orderly or incomprehensible and chaotic?"

You might think from this primary status of metaphysics that everyone would take its existence and value for granted, but this is definitely not so. Even though it has been a central part of philosophy since Ancient Greek times it is not a universally approved field of knowledge.

It has two kinds of opponents. The first are the philosophers of science, most particularly the group known as *logical positivists*, who say that only the natural sciences can legitimately investigate the nature of reality, and that metaphysics is simply a collection of unprovable assertions that are unnecessary to the scientific observation of reality. For a true understanding of reality, metaphysics is too "mystical." This is clearly the group with which Franz Boas, and because of him modern American anthropology, belongs.

The second group of opponents are the mystics. The term mystic is sometimes confused with "occult" or "supernatural" and with magic and witchcraft but in philosophy it has a different meaning. Some of the most honored philosophers in history have been mystics: Plotinus, Swedenborg, Loyola, Shankaracharya and many others. They share a common belief that the fundamental nature of reality is outside language; that language splits things up into parts while the true nature of reality is undivided. Zen, which is a mystic religion, argues that the illusion of dividedness can be overcome by meditation. The Native American church argues that peyote can force-feed a mystic understanding upon those who were normally resistant to it, an understanding that Indians had been deriving through Vision Quests in the past. This mysticism, Dusenberry thought, is the absolute center of traditional Indian life, and as Boas had made clear, it is absolutely outside the domain of positivistic science and any anthropology that adheres to it.

Historically mystics have claimed that for a true understanding of reality metaphysics is too "scientific." Metaphysics is not reality. Metaphysics is *names* about reality. Metaphysics is a restaurant where they give you a thirty-thousand page menu and no food.

Phædrus thought it portended very well for his Metaphysics of Quality that *both* mysticism and science reject metaphysics for completely opposite reasons. It suggested that if there *is* a bridge between the two, between the understanding of the Indians and the understanding of the anthropologists, metaphysics is where that bridge is located.

Of the two kinds of hostility to metaphysics he considered the mystics' hostility the more formidable. Mystics will tell you that once you've opened the door to metaphysics you can say good-bye to any genuine understanding of reality. Thought is not a path to reality. It sets obstacles in that path because when you try to use thought to approach something that is prior to thought your thinking does not carry you toward that something. It carries you *away* from it. To define something is to subordinate it to a tangle of intellectual relationships. And when you do that you destroy real understanding.

The central reality of mysticism, the reality that Phædrus had called "Quality" in his first book, is not a metaphysical chess piece. Quality doesn't have to be defined. You understand it without definition, ahead of definition. Quality is a direct experience independent of and prior to intellectual abstractions.

Quality is indivisible, undefinable and unknowable in the sense that there is a knower and a known, but a metaphysics can be none of these things. A metaphysics must be divisible, definable, and knowable, or there isn't any metaphysics. Since a metaphysics is essentially a kind of dialectical definition and since Quality is essentially outside definition, this means that a "Metaphysics of Quality" is essentially a contradiction in terms, a logical absurdity.

It would be almost like a mathematical definition of randomness. The more you try to say what randomness is the less random it becomes. Or "zero," or "space" for that matter. Today these terms have almost nothing to do with "nothing." "Zero" and "space" are complex relationships of "somethingness." If he said anything about the scientific nature of mystic understanding, science might benefit but the actual mystic understanding would, if anything, be injured. If he really wanted to do Quality a favor he should just leave it alone.

What made all this so formidable to Phædrus was that he himself had insisted in his book that Quality cannot be defined. Yet here he was about to define it. Was this some kind of a sell-out? His mind went over this many times.

A part of it said, "Don't do it. You'll get into nothing but trouble. You're just going to start up a thousand dumb arguments about something that was perfectly clear until you came along. You're going to make ten thousand opponents and zero friends because the moment you open your mouth to say one thing about the nature of reality you automatically have a whole set of enemies who've already said reality is something else."

The trouble was, this was only one part of himself talking. There was another part that kept saying, "Ahh, do it anyway. It's interesting." This was the intellectual part that didn't like undefined things, and telling it not to define Quality was like telling a fat man to stay out of the refrigerator, or an alcoholic to stay out of bars. To the intellect the process of defining Quality has a compulsive quality of its own. It produces a certain excitement even though it leaves a hangover afterward, like too many cigarettes, or a party that has lasted too long. Or Lila last night. It isn't anything of lasting beauty; no joy forever. What would you call it? Degeneracy, he guessed. Writing a metaphysics is, in the strictest mystic sense, a degenerate activity.

But the answer to all this, he thought, was that a ruthless, doctrinaire avoidance of degeneracy is a degeneracy of another sort. That's the degeneracy fanatics are made of. Purity, identified, ceases to be purity. Objections to pollution are a *form* of pollution. The only person who doesn't pollute the mystic reality of the world with fixed metaphysical meanings is a person who hasn't yet been born—and to whose birth no thought has been given. The rest of us have to settle for being something less pure. Getting drunk and picking up bar-ladies and writing metaphysics is a part of life.

That was all he had to say to the mystic objections to a Metaphysics of Quality. He next turned to those of logical positivism.

Positivism is a philosophy that emphasizes science as the only source of knowledge. It sharply distinguishes between fact and value, and is hostile to religion and traditional metaphysics. It is an outgrowth of empiricism, the idea that all knowledge must come from experience, and is suspicious of any thought, even a scientific statement, that is incapable of being reduced to direct observation. Philosophy, as far as positivism is concerned, is limited to the analysis of scientific language.

Phædrus had taken a course in symbolic logic from a member of logical positivism's famed Vienna circle, Herbert Feigl, and he remembered being fascinated by the possibility of a logic that could extend mathematical precision to solve problems of philosophy and other areas. But even then the assertion that metaphysics is meaningless sounded false to him. As long as you're inside a logical, coherent universe of thought you can't escape metaphysics. Logical positivism's criteria for "meaningfulness" were pure metaphysics, he thought.

But it didn't matter. The Metaphysics of Quality not only *passes* the logical positivists' tests for meaningfulness, it passes them with the highest marks. The Metaphysics of Quality *restates* the empirical basis of logical positivism with more precision, more inclusiveness, more explanatory power than it has previously had. It says that values are not outside of the experience that logical positivism limits itself to. They are the *essence* of this experience. Values are *more* empirical, in fact, than subjects or objects.

Any person of any philosophic persuasion who sits on a hot stove will verify without any intellectual argument whatsoever that he is in an undeniably low-quality situation: that the *value* of his predicament is negative. This low quality is not just a vague, woolly-headed, crypto-religious, metaphysical abstraction. It is an *experience*. It is not a judgment about an experience. It is not a description of experience. The value itself is an experience. As such it is completely predictable. It is verifiable by anyone who cares to do so. It is reproducible. Of all experience it is the least ambiguous, least mistakable there is. Later the person may generate some oaths to describe this low value, but the value will always come first, the oaths second. Without the primary low valuation, the secondary oaths will not follow.

The reason for hammering on this so hard is that we have a culturally inherited blind spot here. Our culture teaches us to think it is the hot stove that directly causes the oaths. It teaches that the low values are a property of the person uttering the oaths.

Not so. The value is *between* the stove and the oaths. *Between* the subject and the object lies the value. This value is more immediate, more directly sensed than any "self" or any "object" to which it might be later assigned. It is more *real* than the stove. Whether the stove is the cause of the low quality or whether possibly something else is the cause is not yet absolutely certain. But that the quality is low is absolutely certain. It is the primary empirical reality from which such things as stoves and heat and oaths and self are later intellectually constructed.

Once this primary relationship is cleared up an awful lot of mysteries get solved. The reason values seem so woolly-headed to empiricists is that empiricists keep trying to assign them to subjects or objects. You can't do it. You get all mixed up because values don't belong to either group. They are a separate category all their own.

What the Metaphysics of Quality would do is take this separate category, Quality, and show how it contains within itself both subjects and objects. The Metaphysics of Quality would show how things become enormously more coherent—*fabulously* more coherent— when you start with an assumption that Quality is the primary empirical reality of the world. . . .

. . . but showing that, of course, was a very big job. . . .

. . . He noticed a strange noise, unlike any boat sound he was used to. He listened for a while and then realized that it was coming from the forecabin. It was Lila. She was snoring. He heard her mutter something. Then she was quiet again. . . .

After a while he heard the putt-putting of a small boat approaching. An early fisherman, probably, heading down the creek. Soon the entire cabin rocked gently and the lamp swung a little from the boat's wake. After a while the sound passed and it became quiet again. . . .

. . . He wondered if he was going to get any more sleep himself. He remembered when he used to be a "night person," going to bed at three or four in the morning and waking up at around noon. It seemed then that nothing of any importance could ever happen during the hours between dawn and late afternoon, and he avoided them as much as possible. Now it was the opposite. He had to be up with the sun or something was missing. It didn't matter that there was nothing to do.

He picked up the slips on Dusenberry, put them back into the tray where they had been removed and then got up and tucked the tray into the pilot berth where it had come from. Above the pilot berth the portholes of the cabin showed light outside. He saw that the sky was somewhat overcast. It might clear up. The buildings across the harbor were gray. Some trees on the bank still had their leaves but they were brown and ready to fall. October colors.

He pushed the hatch back and stuck his head out.

It was cold out, but not as cold as before. A mild breeze rippled the water toward the stern of the boat, and he felt it on his face.

6.

Richard Rigel awoke and looked at his watch. It was 7:45 already. He felt tired and cross. He had not had much sleep since that fool author and Lila Blewitt stumbled across his deck.

All night long, in and out, in and out, the wakes from passing boats caused that author's barge next to him to push his own boat in and out against the dock like a railroad Pullman car. And there was nothing he could do about it.

He could have gotten up and adjusted the author's lines himself. But that wasn't *his* job.

What was really angering was that he hadn't even granted the author *permission* to raft. The author had been told in Oswego he could raft because of the emergency there and evidently had taken it as a lifetime privilege.

Now no more sleep was possible. He would have to make the best of it. Bill would have to get up too. There was much to be done today.

Richard Rigel went to the forecabin of the boat, found Capella with a pillow over his head and pulled it off. "Get up, Bill," he said.

Capella opened his eyes, looked startled and then sat up quickly.

"Much to do today," Rigel repeated.

Capella yawned and looked at his watch. "They said they'd take us at nine to get the mast up."

Rigel replied, "We should be ready for an earlier opening."

He went back to his aft cabin, removed his pajamas, carefully folded them and put them in the drawer. Only a week left before going back. He could get Simonsen to take over his court appearances, but if he were lucky and there were no more delays he might still get back in time. . . . What a completely rotten vacation.

Capella's voice said, "What about next door?"

"You mean the 'Great Author'?" Rigel replied. "I don't think the 'Great Author' will be up this morning."

"Why not?" Capella asked.

"Didn't you *hear* him last night?"

"No."

"You certainly must have been sleeping soundly . . . Of course! You were forward. He fell on *my* cabin."

"He *fell?*"

"Yes, he and that woman he was dancing with stumbled across the deck and fell evidently. I didn't want to get into it so I didn't go up there. What a commotion!"

In the boat's head Richard Rigel drew a basin of heated water with which to wash his face and shave. He said loudly, "We've got to get free of his boat before we can move. You'll have to go over and wake him up."

"Wake him up?" Capella repeated.

"Yes," Richard Rigel replied. "He was in no condition to set an alarm clock."

He added, more softly, "I wonder what his situation is, to pick up someone like her."

The water was steaming hot but there wasn't much satisfaction in that now. Two years ago it had cost him an arm and a leg to have this hot water system installed. He had to wait a whole summer for it. Now he was selling the boat. Everything changes. Nothing is predictable any more.

Rigel vigorously soaped the warm wash cloth and applied it to his face. He thought the Great Author's respectful readers should have seen him last night dancing with Lila. They probably wouldn't have minded though. Among *his* respectful readers drunkenness and whoring were probably considered some form of "Quality."

It was interesting to get a look at someone like him up close. In Oswego he seemed so reserved. They look so fine from a distance but when you see them up close for what they really are then all the cracks and blemishes appear. He wasn't reserved. He was just boorish.

Last night was typical. After listening to the author talk on and on about some pet idea about "nothingness," Rigel had tried to illustrate the point with a fishing story. The Great Author didn't even listen. Rigel had tried to warn him about sailing alone off shore and he wouldn't listen. And then after he had warned him about Lila he had the nerve to invite her to their table.

Boorish. What made it so hard to stand was that it wasn't deliberate. He just didn't know any better. . . . He seemed so naïve most of the time and yet there was something . . . *clever* about him that infuriated. He shouldn't let him make him so angry like this. He didn't really matter that much. . . . If he wasn't careful he was going to cut himself with this razor.

There were enough people like that, of course, but what made this all so insufferable was that here was a man who was passing himself off as an expert on "Quality," with a capital "Q." And he got *away* with it! It was like watching some ambulance chaser sway a jury. Once he got them emotionally on his side there wasn't much you could do about it.

Richard Rigel emptied the basin, rinsed it neatly, then folded the towel and put it on its rack to dry properly.

Capella said, "If I'm going to wake him up, what am I going to tell him about his boat?"

Rigel thought for a while. "I suppose I should be the one to talk to him," he said.

He would do it tactfully. He'd invite him to breakfast, and then when the author turned the invitation down, he would be up and awake so that he could be told his boat needed moving.

Now clean and shaven Richard Rigel felt a little better. He watched in the mirror as he combed his hair into respectability, then tried on a tie. It didn't look right. With Cary Grant features like his own it would be inappropriate to be overdressed, particularly in a place like this. He removed the tie, unbuttoned the collar and carefully opened it a little. Much better.

He climbed to the deck and looked around at the harbor. There were old rotting timbers and hulks that had to be crossed by a series of precarious gangplanks to get to dry land. One was lucky if he didn't break his neck. Probably it would be a whole day wasted here.

Richard Rigel turned and was surprised to see himself being watched. The Great Author himself was in the next cockpit.

"Hello!" Richard Rigel said loudly.

"Hello."

His neighbor's expression seemed bland. He was wearing the same blue chambray shirt he had worn yesterday, with the same food stain above one pocket.

"I didn't expect to find you up this early," Richard Rigel said.

The author replied, "If you want to take your boat down to the crane dock I can cast off now."

He must be some sort of a mind-reader, Rigel thought. He said, "There may be another boat at the dock."

"No, I checked."

He seemed to be in remarkably good shape after his performance last night. He *would* be, Rigel thought.

"It's still too early," Rigel said. "There may be a boat scheduled ahead of me. Are you interested in breakfast?"

As he said it he realized it was no longer necessary to invite the author to breakfast, but it was too late.

"That sounds good," the author answered. "I'll see if I can get Lila up."

"What?" Richard Rigel was startled. "No, of course not. Let the woman have her sleep. Just you come."

"Why?" the author asked.

There it was again, that boorishness. He knew perfectly well why. "Because this is undoubtedly the last time we will be seeing one another," Rigel smiled, "and I would prefer to chat alone."

Capella appeared on deck and the three crossed the gangplanks to shore in a single file.

Inside the restaurant Capella said, "It's hard to believe this is the same place."

Rigel saw the jukebox silent in one corner. "Be thankful for small favors," he said.

A blackboard in front of the bar mirror contained the breakfast menu. Beside it an old woman talked across the bar to three workmen eating breakfast at the table beside them. Probably the wife of last night's bartender, he thought.

The author was being his indifferent self again. His attention seemed to drift outside the window toward the boat-yard debris and docks where they had come from. Perhaps he was looking for Lila.

Capella said to him, "Where did you learn to dance like that? You really stopped the action."

The author's attention returned. "Why?" he asked, "Were you watching?"

"Everybody was," Richard Rigel said.

"No." The author grinned. "I don't know how to dance." He looked quizzically at both of them.

"You're way too modest." Rigel smiled. "You dazzled us all . . . particularly the lady."

The author looked at them suspiciously. "Ah, you people are teasing."

"Maybe you had so much to drink you don't remember."

Capella laughed, and the author exclaimed, "*I* wasn't so drunk."

"No, *you* weren't so drunk," Rigel said. "That's why you tiptoed so softly across my deck at two."

"Sorry about that," the author said. "She dropped her suitcase."

Rigel and Capella looked at each other. "Suitcase!" Capella said.

"Yes," the author answered. "She's leaving the boat she was on and coming with me to Manhattan to stay with some friends there."

"Wow!" Capella said, winking at Rigel, "One dance with him and they pack up their suitcases." He said to Rigel, "I wish I knew his secret. How do you suppose he does it?"

Richard Rigel frowned and looked around. He didn't like the direction this was going. He wondered when the old woman was going to take their order. He motioned to her to come.

When she arrived he ordered ham and eggs and toast and orange juice. The others ordered too.

While they were waiting Richard Rigel said that the tide would turn at about ten. He told the author his best strategy was to wait until about nine o'clock, which was the last hour of the flood tide, then go as fast as possible with the ebb tide as far as he could before the tide changed again, moor for the night and wait for the next day's ebb into Manhattan. The author thanked him for the information.

They ate most of the breakfast in silence. Rigel felt stymied, pushed into a corner by this person. There was something about him that prevented you from saying anything to him, something that didn't leave you any room to say it. He was in such another world, talking away so glibly about Quality.

When they were finished eating Richard Rigel turned to the author. He didn't like what he had to say to him but he felt an obligation to say it anyway.

"It's none of my business whom you select for company," he said. "You seemed to pay no attention to me at all last night. But I think I have an obligation to advise you one last time to get Lila off your boat."

The author looked surprised. "I thought you said I needed a crew."

"Not *her!*"

"What's wrong with her?"

There it was again. "You're not *that* naïve," Rigel said.

The author mumbled, almost to himself, "Lila may be better than she looks."

Richard Rigel contradicted him. "No, Lila is much *worse* than she looks."

The author looked at Capella, who was smiling, and then at Rigel with narrowing eyes. "What makes you think that?" he said.

Richard Rigel studied the author for a while. The author really *was* innocent. "I've known Lila Blewitt for a long, long time," he said. "Why don't you just take my word for it?"

"Who is she?" the author said.

"She's a very unfortunate person of very low quality," he said.

At the word, "quality," the author looked up as though it was some kind of challenge thrown at him. It was, of course.

The author's eyes shifted. "What does she do for a living?" he asked, evasively.

When Capella glanced at him Richard Rigel couldn't resist a smile. "She meets people like *you*, my friend," he said. "Didn't anyone ever *tell* you about people like her?"

Another challenge. The wheels were turning almost visibly inside the author's head.

Rigel wondered whether to push it any farther. There was no point in doing so, really. But there was something about the author's complacency, particularly after last night, that made him want to do it anyway. But then he decided not to. "If you need a crew," he said, "why don't you wait a few days in Manhattan and then Bill will be available. I think Bill knows enough that the two of you could make it."

Bill nodded with a smile.

They talked more about the sail into Manhattan. It was all straightforward. They should call ahead to the 79th Street Marina since even this late in the year it was hard to get in there without a reservation. An October cruise to the Chesapeake might be something he would enjoy himself, Rigel said. But of course, he wouldn't have the time.

The author said suddenly, "I don't think you know what you're talking about. How do you know that?"

"Know *what?*" Rigel asked.

"About Lila."

"I know it from the experience of a very close friend whose divorce case I handled," Richard Rigel answered.

In his memory a picture returned of Lila, arm in arm with Jim, coming into his office. Poor Jim, he thought. "Your friend Lila completely ruined his life."

"She used to be much more attractive than she is now," Rigel added. "She seems to be going downhill fast."

Capella said, "You never told me about that."

"It's not a public matter," Rigel said. "And I won't mention his name, Bill, or you'd recognize it."

Then he looked at the author seriously. "You've never seen such a sad, forsaken man. He lost his wife, his children, most of his friends—his reputation was gone. He had to quit his job at the bank where he had a promising future—in fact was scheduled for a vice-presidency. Eventually he had to move to get re-established. But knowing the bank's president I'm sure he put it on Jim's record, and that was the end of his career, I'm afraid. No board will ever promote him to any position of real responsibility."

"That's really bad," the author said, and looked down at the table.

"It was completely necessary," Richard Rigel said. "No one wants to trust millions of dollars to a man who hasn't enough self-control to keep his hands off a common bar-whore."

Another challenge. This time the author's eyes hardened. It looked as though he was going to take it.

"Who was to blame?" he said.

"What do you mean?" Richard Rigel asked.

"I mean was it Lila who was to blame for your friend's misfortune or was it his wife and his so-called friends and his superiors at the bank? Who *really* did him in?"

"I don't follow," Richard Rigel said.

"Was it *her* love or was it *their* hatred?"

"I wouldn't call it *love.*"

"Would you call it *hatred* on their part? What exactly did he do to *them* that justified their hatred?"

"Now you're no longer being naïve," Richard Rigel said. "Now you're being deliberately stupid. Are you trying to tell me his wife had no *right* to be angry?"

The author thought for a while. "I don't know," he said, "but there's something wrong there."

"I think there is," Richard Rigel said.

"There's always been something wrong, logically," the author went on. "How can an act of love, that does no injury to anyone, be so evil? . . . Think about it. Who was injured?"

Richard Rigel thought about it. He said, "It wasn't any act of love. Lila Blewitt doesn't know what love means. It was an act of deceit."

He could feel anger growing. "I've heard that word 'love' so many times from the mouths of so many people who don't know what it is." He could still see Jim's wife sitting in his office. She had shielded her eyes with her hand and tried hard to keep her voice steady. *There* was love.

He said, "Let me try another word: 'Honor.' The person we are talking about dishonored his wife and he dishonored his children and he dishonored everyone who put trust in him, as well as himself. People forgave him for his weakness, but they lost respect for him and that was what finished him for any position of responsibility.

"But it wasn't weakness on Lila's part. She knew what she was doing."

The author stared at him. Dumbly it seemed.

"And I don't know what the circumstances of your own personal family are my friend, but I warn you, if you're not careful she'll do it to you."

As an afterthought he added, "If she hasn't already."

Rigel looked at the author to see what the effect was. There was no change of expression. Nothing, apparently, penetrated that thick crust.

"But who did she hurt?" Capella asked.

Rigel looked at Bill with surprise. Him too? He thought Capella was more sensible. It was a sign of the times.

"Well there are some of us left," he said, returning to the author, "who are still holding out against your hedonistic 'Quality' philosophy or whatever it is."

"I was just asking a question," the author said.

"But it's a question that expresses a certain point of view," Richard Rigel answered, "and it's a point of view that *some* people, including myself, find loathsome."

"I'm still not sure why."

God he was insufferable. "All right, I'll tell you why. Will you listen?"

"Of course."

"No, I mean *really* listen?"

The author was silent.

"You made a statement in your book that everyone knows and agrees to what 'Quality' is. Obviously everyone does not! You refused to define 'Quality,' thus preventing any argument on the subject. You tell us that 'dialecticians' who debate these matters are scoundrels. I guess that would include lawyers too. That's pretty good. You carefully tie your critics' hands and feet so that they cannot give you any opposition, tar their reputations for good measure, and then you say, 'Okay, come on out and fight.' Very brave. Very brave."

"May I come out and fight?" the author said. "My exact statement was that people *do* disagree as to what Quality is, but their disagreement is only on the objects in which they think Quality inheres."

"What's the difference?"

"Quality, on which there is complete agreement, is a universal source of things. The objects about which people disagree are merely transitory."

My oh my, what *smart talk*, Richard Rigel thought. "*What* 'universal source of things'? Some of us can do *without* that universal source of things, that no one else seems to be able to talk about but you. Some of us would rather stick with our good old-fashioned transitory objects. By the way, how do you keep in touch with that marvelous 'universal source of things'? Do you have some sort of special radio set? Hmmm? How do you keep in touch?"

The author did not answer.

"I'm waiting to hear," Richard Rigel said. "How do you keep in touch with Quality?"

The author still didn't answer.

Relief poured through Richard Rigel. He suddenly felt better than he had all morning. He finally communicated something to him. "There are answers," the author finally said, "but I don't think I can give them all to you this morning."

He wasn't going to get off that easy.

"Let me ask an easier question then," Richard Rigel said. "You are in contact with this 'universal source of things,' aren't you?"

"Yes," said the author. "You are too, if only you'd understand it."

"Well I'm *trying*," said Richard Rigel, "but you're just going to have to help me a little. This 'universal source of things' moreover tells you what's good and what's not good, doesn't it? Isn't that right?"

"Yes," said the author.

"Well, we've been talking in a rather general way so far, now let me ask a rather specific question: Did the universal source of things, that is responsible for the creation of Heaven and Earth, broadcast on your radio receiver as you stumbled across my boat at two a.m. this morning that the woman you were stumbling with was an Angel of Quality?"

"*What?*" the author asked.

"I'll repeat," he said. "Did God tell you that Miss Lila M. Blewitt of Rochester, New York, with whom you stumbled across my deck at two this morning, has *Quality?*"

"What God?"

"*Forget* God. Do you *personally* think Miss Lila M. Blewitt is a Woman of Quality?"

"Yes."

Richard Rigel stopped. He hadn't expected *this* answer.

Could the Great Author really be so stupid? . . . Maybe he had some trick up his sleeve. . . . Richard Rigel waited but nothing came.

"Well," he said after a long pause, "the Great Source of All Things is really coming up with some surprises these days."

He leaned forward and addressed the Great Author with deep gravity. "Please will you, in future days, consider the possibility that the 'Great Source of All Things,' that speaks only to you and not to me, is, like so many of your ideas, just a figment of your own fertile imagination, a figment that allows you to justify any act of your own immorality as somehow God-given. I consider that undefined 'Quality' to be a very dangerous commodity. It's the stuff fools and fanatics are made of."

He waited for the author to drop his gaze or wince or blanch or get angry or walk out or give some sign of defeat, but he seemed to just settle back into his usual detachment.

He's really out of it, Richard Rigel thought. But no matter. The spine of his whole case for "Quality" was broken.

When the old woman came to take their dishes the author finally asked, "*Do* you get along entirely without Quality?"

He can't defend himself, Richard Rigel thought, and now he wants to cross-examine *me*. He looked at his watch. There was enough time. "No, I don't get along without Quality entirely," he said.

"Then how do you define it?"

Richard Rigel settled back in his chair. "To begin with," he said, "quality that is independent of experience doesn't exist. I've done very well without it all these years and I'm sure I will continue without any difficulty whatsoever."

The author interrupted, "I didn't say Quality was independent of experience."

"Well now you asked me to define quality," Richard Rigel snapped, "and I've started to do that. Why don't you just let me continue?"

"All right."

"I find quality to be always involved with experience of specific things, but if you ask me which things have quality and which don't I'd have a hard time answering without enumerating. But I'd say that in general, and with many qualifications, quality is found in values I've learned in childhood and grown up with and used all my life and have found nothing wrong with. Those are values that are shared by personal friends and family, my law associates and other companions. Because we believe in these common values we're able to act morally toward one another.

"In the practice of law," he said, "we come into contact with a fair-sized number of people who do not share traditional moral values, but feel rather that what is good and what is bad is a matter of their own independent judgment. Does that sound familiar?"

The author nodded. He'd better. He could hardly do anything else.

"Well, we give them a name," Rigel continued. "We call them criminals."

The author looked as if he wanted to interrupt again but Rigel waved him down. "Now you may argue, and many do, that the values of the community and the laws they produce are all wrong. That's permissible. The law of the land guarantees you the right to hold that opinion. And moreover, the laws provide you with political and judicial recourses by which to change the 'bad' laws of the community. But as long as those recourses are there and until those laws are changed neither you or Lila or anyone else can just go acting as you please in disregard of everyone else, deciding what does and what does not have 'Quality.' You *do* have a moral and legal obligation to obey the same rules others do."

Rigel continued, "One of the things that angered me most about your book was its appearance at a time when so many young people all over the country put themselves above the law with criminal acts— draft dodgers, arsonists, political traitors, revolutionists, even *assassins*, all of them justifying themselves with the belief that they alone can see the God-given truth that no one else can see.

"You talked for chapter after chapter about how to preserve the underlying form of a motorcycle, but you didn't say a single word about how to preserve the underlying form of society. And so your book may have been a big seller among some of these radicals and cult groups who are looking for that sort of thing. They're looking for anything that will justify their doing as they please. And you gave them support. You gave them encouragement." He felt his voice becoming angry. "I've no doubt that your intentions were good, but whatever your intentions may have been it was the devil's work you were doing."

He sat back. The author looked stunned. Good. Capella looked sober too. Good. Bill was a good boy. These radical intellectuals can sometimes get hold of people his age and fill them with their damned fads and get them believing them because they aren't old enough yet to see what the world is really like. But Bill Capella he had hopes for.

"It's not the devil's work I'm doing," said the author.

"You're trying to do what has 'quality,' isn't that right?"

"Yes," the author said.

"Well, do you see what happens when you get all involved in fine-sounding words that nobody can define? That's why we *have* laws, to define what quality *is*. These definitions may not be as perfect as you'd like them, but I can promise you they're a whole lot better than having everybody run around doing as he pleases. We've seen the results of that."

The author looked confused. Capella looked amazed. Richard Rigel felt pleased at that. He had made his point at last, and he always enjoyed that, even when he wasn't getting paid for it. That was his skill. Maybe he should write a book about quality and what it *really* was.

"Tell me," he said, "do you really and sincerely believe that Lila Blewitt has quality?"

The author thought for a long time. "Yes," he said.

"Well why don't you just try to explain to us how on earth you can possibly think that Lila has quality. Do you think you can do that?"

"No, I don't think I can."

"Why not?"

"It's too difficult."

It wasn't the answer Richard Rigel had expected. He saw it was time to put an end to this and leave. "Well," he said conciliatingly, "maybe there's something I don't see."

"I think so," the author said.

He sounded sick. He had been sailing alone for a long time now. Richard Rigel looked again at his watch. It was time to go. "Let me say just one last thing," he said, "and I hope you will not take it as a personal insult but rather as something to think about: I've noticed last night and in Oswego that you're one of the most isolated individuals I have ever seen. I think you will always be that way unless by some possibility you find your way to understanding and integrating yourself with the values of the community around you. Other people count. You should understand that."

"I understand that . . ." the author began. But it was clear to Rigel that he didn't.

"We *must* go," he said to Capella, and got up from the table. He went to the bar, paid the check and joined the author at the door.

"I'm surprised that you listened to me just now," Richard Rigel said as they walked toward their boats at the dock. "I didn't really think you were capable of that."

As the boats came into view they saw Lila standing on the deck of his boat. She waved to them. They all waved back.

7.

In Kingston Phædrus' boat had been a tethered home from which the dock and harbor seemed like a local neighborhood. But here, out on the broad river, the "neighborhood" was gone and that below-decks home was just a storage area in which the chief concern was that things did not shift and crash when the boat heeled in the wind. Now, above deck, his attention was given to sail shape and wind direction and river current, and to the chart on the deck beside him folded to correspond to landmarks and day beacons and the progression of red and green buoys showing the way to the ocean. The river was brown with silt and there was a lot of debris in it but nothing he couldn't avoid. There was a nice running-breeze, but it was gusting and shifting a little, probably from deflection by the river valley.

He felt depressed. That Rigel had really gotten to him. Someday, maybe, he would develop a thick enough skin to not get bothered by someone like that, but the day hadn't arrived yet. Somehow he'd gotten the idea that a sailboat provided isolation and peace and tranquillity, in which thoughts could proceed freely and calmly without outside interference. It never happened. A sailboat under way means one hazard after another with little time to think about anything but *its* needs. And a sailboat at the dock is an irresistible magnet for every conversation-making passerby in sight.

He'd gotten resigned to it, and Rigel, when he'd met him, was just one of the hundreds of here-today-gone-tomorrow people that cruising causes you to meet. Lila was in that class too . . . and there was a lot to be said for the kind of wandering life where you never knew who you would be tied up against—or sleeping with—the next night.

What depressed him most was the stupid way he had let himself be set up for Rigel's attack. He had probably been invited to breakfast just to receive that little sermon. Now he'd brood for days and go over everything that was said and recycle every word over and over again and think of perfect answers that he should have said at the time.

A small power boat approached, coming the other way. As they passed, the helmsman waved from inside the cabin, and Phædrus waved back.

The weather was turning out better than he'd thought it would. Yesterday's stiff north wind was dying and warm southwesterlies would probably take over, which meant a few days of good weather. The river was broad here and the current would be with him for most of the day. This would be a nice day if it hadn't been for that scene this morning.

The feeling left was one of enormous confusion and weariness, a kind of back-to-the-drawing-board, back-to-square-one feeling you get where you're thinking you're making great progress and then suddenly some question like this comes along and sets you back to where you started. He didn't even want to think about it.

There are so many kinds of problem people like Rigel around, he thought, but the ones who go posing as moralists are the worst. Cost-free morals. Full of great ways for others to improve without any expense to themselves. There's an ego thing in there, too. They use the morals to make someone else look inferior and that way look better themselves. It doesn't matter what the moral code is—religious morals, political morals, racist morals, capitalist morals, feminist morals, hippie morals—they're all the same. The moral codes change but the meanness and the egotism stay the same.

The trouble was, pure meanness didn't completely explain what happened this morning. Something else was going on. Why should *Rigel* be so concerned about morals at *that* early hour in the morning? It just didn't scan right. . . . Not for some yachtsman-lawyer like that. Not in this century anyway. Maybe back in 1880 some church deacon lawyer might have talked like that but not now. All that stuff Rigel was referring to about sacred duties and home and family went out fifty years ago. That wasn't what Rigel was mad about. It didn't make sense for him to go running around sermonizing people on morals . . . at eight o'clock in the morning . . . on his *vacation*, for God's sake.

It wasn't even Sunday.

It was just bizarre. . . .

He was mad about something else. What he was trying to do was catch Phædrus in the old trap of sexual morality. If Phædrus answered that Lila had Quality then he would be saying sex was Quality which was not right. But if he said Lila had no Quality the next question was, "Why were you sleeping with her?" That had to be the world's oldest guilt trap. If you didn't go for Lila you're some kind of prissy old prude. If you did go for her you were some kind of dirty old man. No matter what you did you were guilty and should be ashamed of yourself. That trap's been around since the Garden of Eden, at least.

A broad lawn rising back from the bluff above the water's edge led to a grove of trees that partly concealed a large Victorian *fin de siècle* mansion. The lawn had the same deserted look he'd seen yesterday—uninhabited. No children or animals played anywhere.

He noticed again, as he had coming down here, how this old Hudson River valley looked like paintings of it made more than a hundred years ago. The banks of the river were steep and heavily forested, giving the river a quiet and tranquil look. Things seemed to have been the same here for a long time. Since he'd entered the Erie Canal system he'd noticed how things seemed older and more tired. Now that feeling was even more dominant.

Hundreds of years ago these old waterways were the only way to travel in this continent. For a while he had wondered why his boat always seemed to stop in the oldest part of each city it came to, and then he realized that small boats stopping right there is what got the city started in the first place.

Now there's a sadness that attaches to these old river and lake ports that were once bustling and important. Before the railroads took over, this Hudson River and Erie Canal system were the main shipping route to the Great Lakes and the West. Now there's almost nothing, just an occasional oil barge. The river is almost abandoned.

A depression always came over him when he came East like this, but the oldness and abandonment weren't the only reasons for it. He was a Midwesterner and he shared the prejudices of many Midwesterners against this region of the country. He didn't like the way everything gets more stratified here. The rich start looking richer and the poor start looking poorer. What was worse, they looked as though they thought this was the way things *ought* to be. They had settled for this. There was no sign it was going to change.

In a state like Minnesota or Wisconsin you can be poor and still feel some sense of dignity if you work hard and live fairly cleanly and you keep your eye on the future. But here in New York it seemed as if when you're poor you're just poor. And that means you're nobody. Really nobody. And if you're rich you're really somebody. And that fact seemed to explain ninety-five percent of everything else that went on in this region.

Maybe he was just noticing it more because he'd been thinking about Indians. Some of these differences are just urban-rural differences, and the East is more urban. But some of these differences reflected European values too. Every time he came this way he could feel the people getting more formal and impersonal and . . . *crafty*. Exploitative. European. And petty too, and ungenerous.

Out West among the Indians it's a standing joke that the chief is the poorest man in the tribe. Every time somebody needs something he's the one they go to, and by the Indian code, "the generosity of the frontier," he has to help them. Phædrus didn't think you'd see much of that along this river. He could just imagine some strange riverboat man pulling up at Astor's mansion and saying, "I just saw a light on and thought I'd stop in and say 'hello.' " He wouldn't get past the butler. They'd be horrified at his impertinence. Yet in the West they'd probably feel obliged to invite him in.

It just got worse and worse around here. The rich got glitzier and glitzier and the poor got scuzzier and scuzzier until you finally got to New York City. Homeless crazies hovering over ventilator grates while billionaires are escorted past them to their limousines. With each somehow accepting this as natural.

Oddly it's this valley that's the worst. If you cross into Vermont or Massachusetts it starts to weaken. He didn't know how to explain that. Something historical maybe.

New England was settled by a completely different pattern of immigration. That was it. In the early days New England was all one big WASP family staying put, but this valley was everybody on the move. Dutch, English, French, German, Irish—and their relations were often hostile. So right from the start there was this aggressive, exploitative atmosphere. Maybe they had just as much class distinction and exploitativeness in New England, maybe even more, but they muted it so as not to upset the family. Here they just flaunted it openly. That's what these "Castles on the Hudson" were: an open flaunting of wealth.

He supposed maybe some of Rigel's "morality" this morning was Eastern too.

. . . No, that wasn't it. It was something else. If he were a true Easterner he would have just kept quiet about it and increased his distance. Why did he want to get involved? He didn't have to. He was angry.

. . . The celebrity thing maybe.

Once you become a celebrity it satisfies some people to try to tear you down, and there's not much you can do about it. Phædrus hadn't seen any of that all summer: where someone suddenly jumps on you for no reason at all just because they think you're a celebrity. Maybe that's what it was. In the past when it occurred it was usually at parties when someone had a few drinks in them. Never at *breakfast.*

Usually you get a warning when they're all over you with praise. Then you know they've got some false image of you they're talking to. Rigel was that way in Oswego, but it had been so far back Phædrus had forgotten about it.

That celebrity business is another whole phenomenon that's related to Indian-European conflict of values. It's a peculiarly American phenomenon, to catapult people suddenly into celebrity, lavish praise and wealth upon them, and then, at the moment they at last become convinced of their worth, try to destroy them. At their feet and then at their throat. He thought the reason was that in America you're supposed to be socially superior like a European and socially equal like an Indian at the same time. It doesn't matter that these goals are contradictory.

So what you get is this tension, this business executives' tension, where you're the most relaxed, smiling, easy-going guy in the world— who is also absolutely killing himself to beat the competition and get ahead. Everybody wants their children to be valedictorians, but no-body is supposed to be better than anybody else. A kid who comes out somewhere near the bottom of his class is guilt ridden, self-destructive, and he thinks, "It's not fair! Everybody's equal!" And then the celebrity, John Lennon, steps out to sign an autograph for him. That's the end of the celebrity, John Lennon.

Spooky. Until you're the celebrity you don't see how spooky it is. They love you for being what they want to be but they hate you for being what they're not. There's always this two-faced relationship with celebrity and you never know which face will appear next. That's how it was with Rigel. First he was smiling because he thought he was talking to some big shot and that satisfied his European patterns, but now he's furious because he thinks the big shot is acting superior or something like that.

The old Indians knew how to handle it. They just got rid of anything anybody wanted. They didn't own property, they dressed in rags, some of them. They kept it down, laid low, and let the aristocrats and egalitarians and sycophants and assassins all look on them as worthless. That way they got a lot accomplished without all the celebrity grief.

This boat was good for that. When you're moving along like this on these old abandoned waterways you can relate to people on a one-to-one basis, without all the celebrity business standing in between. Rigel was just a fluke.

Some noises came from the cabin. Phædrus wondered if something had broken loose. Then he remembered his passenger. She was prob-ably getting dressed or something.

"There's no *food* on this boat," Lila's voice said.

"There's some down there somewhere," he answered.

"No, there isn't."

Her face appeared in the hatchway. She looked belligerent. He'd better not tell her he'd already had breakfast.

She looked different. Worse. Her hair wasn't combed. Her eyes were reddened and lined underneath. She looked a lot older than she did last night.

"You didn't search around enough," he said. "Look in the ice-box."

"Where is that?"

"That huge wooden lid with the ring in it by the post there." Her face disappeared again and soon he heard some more noises of her rummaging.

"There's something near the bottom, it looks like," she said. "There are three boxes of junk food and one jar of peanut butter. The jar is almost empty. . . . That is all. No eggs, no bacon, no nothing. . . ."

"Well, we're under way now," he said. "We have to use this current while it's with us or we lose a whole day. Tonight we'll have a big meal."

"*Tonight?!*"

"Yeah," he said.

He heard her mutter "Peanut butter and junk food. . . . Don't you have anything at all? . . . Oh, wait a minute, she said, "here's a half a bar of chocolate."

Then he heard her say "Ugh!"

"What's the matter?" he asked.

"There's something wrong with it. It tastes stale. . . . How about some coffee? Do you have any coffee?" Her voice sounded pleading.

"Yes," he said. "Come on up and steer and I'll go down to make some."

As she rose from the hatchway he saw that she wore a white T-shirt, skin-tight, with the word "L-O-V-E" printed in large red block letters.

She saw him stare and said, "Summer clothes again. Pretty good weather."

He said, "I'll bet you never expected yesterday it would be like this."

"I never know what's going to happen next," she answered. "I thought I was going to have breakfast next."

She moved to sit across from him. The four letters of "L-O-V-E" shifted around in provocative directions.

"Do you know how to steer one of these boats?" he asked.

"Of course," she said.

"Then keep to the right of that red nun-buoy up there." He pointed to make sure she saw it. Then he stood up, stepped out of the cockpit into the hatchway, and went below.

He started to search through some storage bins for food, but after looking for a while he saw that she was right, there *wasn't* any food on this boat. He hadn't known his supplies were so low. He found a box of cheese crackers that looked about a third full.

"How about some cheese crackers and coffee," he said.

No answer.

He tried again. "With peanut butter . . . sort of a 'Continental breakfast.' "

After a while her voice said, "All right."

He unlocked the gimbals from the stove so that it leveled itself against the boat's heel; then from a shelf he brought out a propane torch to pre-heat the stove's kerosene burner.

This burner was a real problem. It had delicate brass needle valves attached to doorknob-sized handles which meant that one normal turn wrecked the whole mechanism.

"How soon until we get somewhere?" Lila asked.

"We can't stop," he said. "I told you. That would get us out of phase with the current and we'd have to buck it down around West Point." He wasn't sure if she knew this river flowed backward twice a day.

"Rigel says there are moorings at Nyack," he added, "and from there it's an easy sail into Manhattan. I want to keep that last distance short. . . . Leave some margins. . . . There's no telling what's down there."

With a match he lit the propane torch and then directed the flame onto one side of the burner so that it would become hot enough to vaporize the kerosene. These stoves could not burn kerosene liquid—they could only burn kerosene gas.

"Is Richard going to be there?" Lila asked.

"Where?"

"Where we stop."

"I doubt it," Phædrus said. "In fact I'm sure he isn't."

When the burner was red hot from the propane torch he turned its doorknob handle a crack. A hot blue flame took hold. Phædrus shut off the propane torch and put it on a shelf where the hot tip couldn't touch anything. Then he filled a kettle of water from the galley sink and put it on top of the burner.

Lila said, "How long have you known him?"

"Who?"

"Richard."

"Too long," he said.

"Why do you say that?"

"I just like to be by myself," he said.

"You're a loner, eh?" Lila said. "Just like me."

He went up the ladder halfway and looked out to see if she was still on course. It was all right.

"It must be nice to have a boat like this all your own," she said. "Nobody ever tells you what to do. You just move on."

"Yeah," he said. It was the first time he had ever seen her smile. "I'm sorry about breakfast," he said. "That was a working dock we were at. We were right next to the crane. We had to get off so they could use it."

When the coffee was done he brought it up, and sat across from her and took the tiller.

"This is nice," Lila said. "That last boat I was on was too crowded. Everybody was in everybody else's way."

"That's not a problem here," he said.

"Do you always sail alone?" she asked.

"Sometimes alone, sometimes with friends."

"You're married, aren't you?"

"Separated."

"I knew it," Lila said. "And not very long, either."

"How do you know that?"

"Because there isn't any *food* on this boat. Real bachelor men always cook. They don't just have junk food in the ice box."

"We'll have the biggest steak in town when we get to Nyack," he said.

"Where's Nyack?"

"It's just a little way from Manhattan, on the New Jersey side. From there it's just a few miles."

"Good," she said.

"Do you know a lot of people in New York?"

"Yes," she said. "Lots."

"Did you use to live there?"

"Yes."

"What did you do?"

She glanced up at him for a second. "I used to work there."

"Where?"

"Lots of different jobs."

"What did you do?"

"Secretary," she said.

"Oh," he said.

That sort of exhausted that. He didn't want to hear about her typing.

He tried to think of some other topic. He wasn't any good at small talk. Never was. Dusenberry should be here. This was getting like the reservation again.

"Do you like New York?" he asked.

"Yes."

"Why?"

"The people are so friendly."

Was she being sarcastic? No, her expression didn't show it. It was just blank. Like she'd never been to New York.

"Where did you live?" he asked.

"West Forties," she said.

He waited for her continue, but she didn't. That, apparently, was it. Real chatterbox. She was *worse* than the Indians.

What a change from last night. No illumination today. Just this kind of dull face staring ahead not looking at anything in particular.

He watched her for a while.

It certainly wasn't an evil face, though. Not low quality. You could see it as pretty if you wanted to.

Her whole head is wide, he thought. Brachycephalic, a physical anthropologist would call it. A Saxon head, probably, judging from her name. A commoner's head, a medieval yeoman's head, good for cudgeling, with the lower lip ready to curl. But not evil.

The eyes were out of place somehow. Her whole face and body and style of talking and action were all tough and ready for anything, but those eyes when she looked right at you were something else, like some frightened child looking up from the bottom of a well. They didn't fit at all.

This was a beautiful valley, spectacular valley, the day was great, but she wasn't even noticing it. He wondered why she had come sailing in the first place. He supposed all that break-up with those people on the previous boat was depressing her, but he didn't want to get into it.

He asked, "How well do you get along with Richard Rigel?"

She seemed a little startled. "What makes you think I don't get along with him?" she said.

"Last night when you first came in the bar he told you to shut the door, remember? And you slammed it and said, 'Does that suit you?' and I got the impression you knew each other and were both angry."

"I know him," Lila said. "We know some of the same people."

"Well, why was he mad at you?"

"He wasn't mad at me. He just talks that way."

"Why?"

"I don't know," she said.

She finally said, "He's very moody. One moment he's very friendly and the next moment he acts like that. That's just the way he is."

To know that much about him she had to know him *very* well, Phædrus thought. Obviously she wasn't telling everything, but what she said certainly rang true. It explained Rigel's attack this morning in a way that had never occurred to him. Rigel was just cranky and quixotic and attacked people without *any* explanation.

But something in him didn't buy that explanation either. There was a better one. He just hadn't heard it yet. All this didn't explain why Rigel was attacking her and why she seemed to defend him. Usually when one person hates another the feeling is mutual.

"How is Rigel regarded back in Rochester?" he asked.

"How do you mean?" Lila said.

"Do people like him?"

"Yes, he's popular," Lila said.

"Even though he's moody and turns on people who haven't done anything to him?"

Lila frowned.

"Would you say he's a very 'moral' person?" Phædrus continued.

"No, not particularly," Lila said. "Like anyone else." She looked really annoyed. "Why are you asking all these questions? Why don't you ask *him*? He's *your* friend, isn't he?"

Phædrus answered, "He seemed to act awfully stuffy and moral and preachy this morning, and I thought that if you knew him you might be able to tell me why."

"Richard?"

"He seemed to object to my being with you last night."

"When did you talk to him?"

"This morning. We had some conversation before the boat got off."

"It's none of his business what I do," Lila said.

"Well why should he make such a fuss?"

"I told you, that's the way he gets sometimes. He's moody. Also he likes to tell other people what to do."

"But you said he was not especially moral. Why would he pick on morals?"

"I don't know. He gets it from his mother. He gets everything from his mother. That's the way he talks sometimes. But he doesn't really mean it. He's just moody."

"Well, what . . ."

A really angry glare came into Lila's blue eyes. "Why do you want to know about him so much?" she said. "It sounds like you're trying to get something on him. I don't like your questions. I don't want to hear about it. I thought he was your friend."

Her jaw clamped shut and her cheek muscles were tense. She turned away from him and stared down over the boat's bulwark at the passing water.

A railroad train came along the shore, on its way to Albany probably. There was a roar as it went by and then disappeared to the north. He hadn't even known that the track was there.

What else hadn't he noticed? He had a feeling there were a lot of things. "Secrets," Rigel had said. Forbidden things. This was the Atlantic Seaboard starting up now: a whole other culture.

Back from the shore stood another mansion like the one Phædrus had noticed earlier. This one was of gray stone, so bleak and oppressive it looked like a setting for some great historic tragedy. Another old Eastern robber-baron, Phædrus thought. Or his descendants . . . or maybe their creditors.

He studied the mansion for a while. It was set back above a huge lawn. Everything was in its place. All the leaves were raked and the grass was mowed. Even the trees were carefully spaced and carefully trimmed. It looked like the work of some obedient caretaker who had been at it, patiently, all his life.

Lila got up and said she needed to wash. She looked angry but Phædrus didn't know exactly what to do about it. He told her how to pump the water to wash with, and she picked up the empty box of cheese crackers and her cup and stepped into the hatchway.

Halfway down the ladder she turned and said, "Give me your cup, and I'll wash it." No expression. He gave her his cup and then she disappeared.

He kept looking back again at the mansion rising back of the trees, as the boat moved away from it. It was huge and gray and shabby, and somewhat frightening. They sure knew how to dominate the spirit.

He picked up the binoculars for a closer look. Under one small grove of oak trees by the shore were empty white-painted chairs around a white table. From their curlicued shapes he guessed they were made of ornamental cast iron. Something about them seemed to convey the mood of the whole place. Brittle, cold, and uncomfortable. That was the Victorian spirit: a whole attitude toward life. "Quality," they called it. European quality. Full of status and protocol.

It had the same feeling as Rigel's sermon this morning. The social pattern that created that sermon on morality and the one that created these mansions were the same. It wasn't just Eastern; it was Victorian. Phædrus hadn't thought about that factor so much, but these mansions, and lawns and ornamental iron furniture made it unmistakable.

He remembered his graduate school adviser, white-haired Professor Alice Tyler, at the beginning of her first lecture on the Victorians saying, "This is the period of American history I just *hate* to teach." When asked why, she said, "It's so depressing."

Victorians in America, she explained, were *nouveau riche* who had no guidelines for what to do with all their sudden wealth and growth. What was depressing about them was their ugly gracelessness: the gracelessness of someone who has outgrown his own codes of self-regulation.

They didn't know how to relate to money. That was the problem. It was partly the new post-Civil War industrial revolution. Fortunes were being made in steel, lumber, cattle, machinery, railroads, and land. Everywhere one looked new innovations were creating fortunes where there was nothing before. Cheap labor was pouring in from Europe. No income taxes and no social codes really forced a sharing of the wealth.

After scrambling for their lives to get it, they couldn't just give it away. And so the whole thing became involuted.

That's a good word, "involuted." Twisted in upon itself like the curves of their ornamental woodwork and the paisley patterns of their fabrics. Victorian men with beards. Victorian women with long involuted dresses. He could see them walking among the trees. Stiff, somber. It was all a pose.

He remembered elderly Victorians who had been nice to him as a child. It was a niceness that set him on edge. They were trying to improve him. It was expected that he would benefit from their attention. The Victorians always took themselves seriously, and the thing they took most seriously of all was their code of morality, or "virtue," as they liked to call it. The Victorian aristocrats *knew* what quality was and defined it very carefully for persons with a less fortunate upbringing than their own.

He got an image of them standing back of Rigel's shoulder at breakfast this morning endorsing every word Rigel said. They would have, too. That superiority Rigel asserted this morning was exactly the pose they would have affected.

You can duplicate it perfectly by pretending you're a king of some

European country, preferably England or Germany. Your subjects are devoted and demanding of you. You must show respect to your own "station in life." It is not permitted that your inner personal feelings be publicly displayed. Your whole Victorian purpose in life is to capture and maintain that pose.

The tormented children of the Victorians often spoke of their morality as "Puritanism" but this really slanders the Puritans. The Puritans were never the gaudy, fraudulent, ornamental peacocks the Victorians were. Puritan moral codes were as simple and unadorned as their houses and clothes. And they had a certain beauty because, in their early period at least, the Puritans really believed in them.

It wasn't from Puritans but from contemporary Europe that the Victorians got their moral inspiration. They thought they followed the highest English standards of morality, but the English morality they looked up to wasn't anything Shakespeare would have recognized. Like Victoria herself, it was more out of the German Romantic tradition than anything English.

Smug posing was the essence of their style. That's what these mansions were, poses—turrets and gingerbread and ornamental cast iron. They did it to their bodies with bustles and corsets. They did it to their whole social and psychic lives with impossible proprieties of table manners and speech and posture and sexual repression. Their paintings captured it perfectly—expressionless, mindless, cream-skinned ladies sitting around ancient Greek columns, draped in ancient Greek robes, in perfect form and posture, except for one breast hanging out, which no one noticed, presumably, because they were so elevated and so pure.

And they called it "quality."

For them the pose *was* quality. Quality *was* the social corset, the ornamental cast iron. It was a "quality" of manners and egotism and suppression of human decency. When Victorians were being moral, kindness wasn't anywhere in sight. They approved whatever was socially fashionable and suppressed or ignored anything that was not.

The period ended when, after having defined for all time what "Truth" and "Virtue" and "Quality" are, the Victorians and their Edwardian successors sent an entire generation of children into the trenches of World War I on behalf of these ideals. And murdered them. For nothing. That war was the natural consequence of Victorian moral egotism. When it was over the children who survived never got tired of laughing at Charlie Chaplin comedies of those elderly people with the silk hats and too many clothes and noses up in the air. Young people of the twenties read Hemingway, Dos Passos and Fitzgerald, drank bootleg gin, danced tangos into the night, drove fast roadsters, made illicit love, called themselves a "lost generation," and never wanted anything to remind them of Victorian morality again.

Ornamental cast iron. If you hit it with a sledge-hammer it doesn't bend. It just shatters into ugly, coarse fragments. The intellectual social reforms of this century just shattered those Victorians. All that's left of them now is ugly fragments of their ornamental cast-iron way of life turning up at odd places, such as these mansions and in Rigel's talk this morning.

Instead of improving the world forever with their high-flown moral codes they did just the opposite: left the world a moral vacuum we're still living in. Rigel too. When Rigel starts all that breakfast oratory about morals he's just blowing hot air. He doesn't know what he's talking about. He's just trying to imitate a Victorian because he thinks it sounds good.

Phædrus had told Rigel he couldn't answer Rigel's question because it was too difficult, but that didn't mean it couldn't be done. It could be done, but not with direct answers. Clever, hip-shot answers have to come out of the culture you're living in and the culture we're living in doesn't have any quick answer to Rigel. To answer him you have to go all the way back to fundamental meanings of what is meant by morality and in this culture there aren't any fundamental meanings of morality. There are only old traditional social and religious meanings and these don't have any real intellectual base. They're just traditions.

That's why Phædrus got such a weary feeling from all this. All the way back to the beginning. That's where he had to go.

Because Quality *is* morality. Make no mistake about it. They're *identical*. And if Quality is the primary reality of the world then that means morality is also the primary reality of the world. The world is primarily a moral order. But it's a moral order that neither Rigel nor the posing Victorians had ever, in their wildest dreams, thought about or heard about.

8.

The idea that the world is composed of nothing but moral value sounds impossible at first. Only objects are supposed to be real. "Quality" is supposed to be just a vague fringe word that tells what we think about objects. The whole idea that Quality can create objects seems very wrong. But we see subjects and objects as reality for the same reason we see the world right-side up although the lenses of our eyes actually present it to our brains upside down. We get so used to certain patterns of interpretation we forget the patterns are there.

Phædrus remembered reading about an experiment with special glasses that made users see everything upside down and backward. Soon their minds adjusted and they began to see the world "normally" again. After a few weeks, when the glasses were removed, the subjects again saw everything upside down and had to relearn the vision they had taken for granted before.

The same is true of subjects and objects. The culture in which we live hands us a set of intellectual glasses to interpret experience with, and the concept of the primacy of subjects and objects is built right into these glasses. If someone sees things through a somewhat different set of glasses or, God help him, takes his glasses off, the natural tendency of those who still have their glasses on is to regard his statements as somewhat weird, if not actually crazy.

But he isn't. The idea that values create objects gets less and less weird as you get used to it. Modern physics on the other hand gets more and more weird as you get into it and indications are that this weirdness will increase. In either case, however, weirdness isn't the test of truth. As Einstein said, common sense—non-weirdness—is just a bundle of prejudices acquired before the age of eighteen. The tests of truth are logical consistency, agreement with experience, and economy of explanation. The Metaphysics of Quality satisfies these.

The Metaphysics of Quality subscribes to what is called empiricism. It claims that all legitimate human knowledge arises from the senses or by thinking about what the senses provide. Most empiricists deny the validity of any knowledge gained through imagination, authority, tradition, or purely theoretical reasoning. They regard fields such as art, morality, religion, and metaphysics as unverifiable. The Metaphysics of Quality varies from this by saying that the values of art and morality and even religious mysticism are verifiable, and that in the past they have been excluded for metaphysical reasons, not empirical reasons. They have been excluded because of the metaphysical assumption that all the universe is composed of subjects and objects and anything that can't be classified as a subject or an object isn't real. There is no empirical evidence for this assumption at all. It is just an assumption.

It is an assumption that flies outrageously in the face of common experience. The low value that can be derived from sitting on a hot stove is obviously an experience even though it is not an object and even though it is not subjective. The low value comes first, then the subjective thoughts that include such things as stove and heat and pain come second. The value is the reality that brings the thoughts to mind.

There's a principle in physics that if a thing can't be distinguished from anything else it doesn't exist. To this the Metaphysics of Quality adds a second principle: if a thing has no value it isn't distinguished from anything else. Then, putting the two together, *a thing that has no value does not exist.* The thing has not created the value. The value has created the thing. When it is seen that value is the front edge of experience, there is no problem for empiricists here. It simply restates the empiricists' belief that experience is the starting point of all reality. The only problem is for a subject-object metaphysics that calls itself empiricism.

This may sound as though a purpose of the Metaphysics of Quality is to trash all subject-object thought but that's not true. Unlike subject-object metaphysics the Metaphysics of Quality does not insist on a single exclusive truth. If subjects and objects are held to be the ultimate reality then we're permitted only one construction of things—that which corresponds to the "objective" world—and all other constructions are unreal. But if Quality or excellence is seen as the ultimate reality then it becomes possible for more than one set of truths to exist. Then one doesn't seek the absolute "Truth." One seeks instead the highest quality intellectual explanation of things with the knowledge that if the past is any guide to the future this explanation must be taken provisionally; as useful until something better comes along. One can then examine intellectual realities the same way he examines paintings in an art gallery, not with an effort to find out which one is the "real" painting, but simply to enjoy and keep those that are of value. There are many sets of intellectual reality in existence and we can perceive some to have more quality than others, but that we do so is, in part, the result of our history and current patterns of values.

Or, using another analogy, saying that a Metaphysics of Quality is false and a subject-object metaphysics is true is like saying that rectangular coordinates are true and polar coordinates are false. A map with the North Pole at the center is confusing at first, but it's every bit as correct as a Mercator map. In the Arctic it's the only map to have. Both are simply intellectual patterns for interpreting reality and one can only say that in some circumstances rectangular coordinates provide a better, simpler interpretation.

The Metaphysics of Quality provides a better set of coordinates with which to interpret the world than does subject-object meta-physics because it is more inclusive. It explains more of the world and it explains it better. The Metaphysics of Quality can explain subject-object relationships beautifully but, as Phædrus had seen in anthropology, a subject-object metaphysics can't explain values worth a damn. It has always been a mess of unconvincing psychological gibberish when it tries to explain values.

For years we've read about how values are supposed to emanate from some location in the "lower" centers of the brain. This location has never been clearly identified. The mechanism for holding these values is completely unknown. No one has ever been able to add to a person's values by inserting one at this location, or observed any changes at this location as a result of a change of values. No evidence has been presented that if this portion of the brain is anesthetized or even lobotomized the patient will make a better scientist as a result because all his decisions will then be "value-free." Yet we're told values must reside here, if they exist at all, because where else could they be?

Persons who know the history of science will recognize the sweet smell of phlogiston here and the warm glow of the luminiferous ether, two other scientific entities which were arrived at deductively and which never showed up under the microscope or anywhere else. When deduced entities are around for years and nobody finds them it is a sign that the deductions have been made from false premises; that the body of theory from which the deductions are made is wrong at some fundamental level. This is the real reason values have been avoided by empiricists in the past, not because values aren't experienced, but because when you try to fit them into this absurd brain location you get a sinking feeling that tells you that somewhere back down the line you have gone way off the track and you just want to drop the whole subject and think about something else that has more of a future to it.

This problem of trying to describe value in terms of substance has been the problem of a smaller container trying to contain a larger one. Value is not a subspecies of substance. Substance is a subspecies of value. When you reverse the containment process and define substance in terms of value the mystery disappears: substance is a "stable pattern of inorganic values." The problem then disappears. The world of objects and the world of values is unified.

This inability of conventional subject-object metaphysics to clarify values is an example of what Phædrus called a "platypus." Early zoologists classified as mammals those that suckle their young and as reptiles those that lay eggs. Then a duck-billed platypus was discovered in Australia laying eggs like a perfect reptile and then, when they hatched, suckling the infant platypi like a perfect mammal.

The discovery created quite a sensation. What an enigma! it was exclaimed. What a mystery! What a marvel of nature! When the first stuffed specimens reached England from Australia around the end of the eighteenth century they were thought to be fakes made by sticking together bits of different animals. Even today you still see occasional articles in nature magazines asking, "Why does this paradox of nature exist?"

The answer is: it doesn't. The platypus isn't doing anything paradoxical at all. It isn't having any problems. Platypi have been laying eggs and suckling their young for millions of years before there were any zoologists to come along and declare it illegal. The real mystery, the real enigma, is how mature, objective, trained scientific observers can blame their own goof on a poor innocent platypus.

Zoologists, to cover up their problem, had to invent a patch. They created a new order, monotremata, that includes the platypus, the spiny anteater, and that's it. This is like a nation consisting of two people.

In a subject-object classification of the world, Quality is in the same situation as that platypus. Because they can't classify it the experts have claimed there is something wrong with it. And Quality isn't the only such platypus. Subject-object metaphysics is characterized by herds of huge, dominating, monster platypi. The problems of free will versus determinism, of the relation of mind to matter, of the discontinuity of matter at the sub-atomic level, of the apparent purposelessness of the universe and the life within it are all monster platypi created by the subject-object metaphysics. Where it is centered around the subject-object metaphysics, Western philosophy can almost be *defined* as "platypus anatomy." These creatures that seem like such a permanent part of the philosophical landscape magically disappear when a good Metaphysics of Quality is applied.

The world comes to us in an endless stream of puzzle pieces that we would like to think all fit together somehow, but that in fact never do. There are always some pieces like platypi that don't fit and we can either ignore these pieces or we can give them silly explanations or we can take the whole puzzle apart and try other ways of assembling it that will include more of them. When one takes the whole ill-shaped, misfitting structure of a subject-object explained universe apart and puts it back together in a value-centered metaphysics, all kinds of orphaned puzzle pieces fit beautifully that never fit before.

. . .

Almost as great as this "value" platypus is another one handled by the Metaphysics of Quality: the "scientific reality" platypus. This is a very large monster that has been disturbing a lot of people for a long time. It was identified a century ago by the mathematician and astronomer, Henri Poincaré who asked, "Why is the reality most acceptable to science one that no small child can be expected to understand?"

Should reality be something that only a handful of the world's most advanced physicists understand? One would expect at least a majority of people to understand it. Should reality be expressible only in symbols that require university-level mathematics to manipulate? Should it be something that *changes* from year to year as new scientific theories are formulated? Should it be something about which different schools of physics can *quarrel* for years with no firm resolution on either side? If this is so then how is it fair to imprison a person in a mental hospital for life with no trial and no jury and no parole for "failing to understand reality"? By this criterion shouldn't all but a handful of the world's most advanced physicists be locked up for life? Who is crazy here and who is sane?

In a value-centered Metaphysics of Quality this "scientific reality" platypus vanishes. Reality, which is value, is understood by every infant. It is a universal starting place of experience that everyone is confronted with all the time. Within a Metaphysics of Quality, science is a set of static intellectual patterns describing this reality, but the patterns are *not* the reality they describe.

A third major platypus handled by the Metaphysics of Quality is the "causation" platypus. It has been said for centuries that, empirically speaking, there is no such thing as causation. You never see it, touch it, hear it or feel it. You never experience it in any way. This has not been a minor philosophic or scientific platypus. This has been a real show-stopper. The amount of paper consumed in dissertations on this one metaphysical problem must equal whole forests of pulpwood.

In the Metaphysics of Quality "causation" is a metaphysical term that can be replaced by "value." To say that "A *causes* B" or to say that "B *values* precondition A" is to say the same thing. The difference is one of words only. Instead of saying "A magnet *causes* iron filings to move toward it," you can say "Iron filings *value* movement toward a magnet." Scientifically speaking neither statement is more true than the other. It may sound a little awkward, but that's a matter of linguistic custom, not science. The language used to describe the data is changed but the scientific data itself is unchanged. The same is true in every other scientific observation Phædrus could think of. You can always substitute "B values precondition A" for "A causes B" without changing any facts of science at all. The term "cause" can be struck out completely from a scientific description of the universe without any loss of accuracy or completeness.

The only difference between causation and value is that the word "cause" implies absolute certainty whereas the implied meaning of "value" is one of preference. In classical science it was supposed that the world always works in terms of absolute certainty and that "cause" is the more appropriate word to describe it. But in modern quantum physics all that is changed. Particles "prefer" to do what they do. An individual particle is not absolutely committed to one predictable behavior. What appears to be an absolute cause is just a very consistent pattern of preferences. Therefore when you strike "cause" from the language and substitute "value" you are not only replacing an empirically meaningless term with a meaningful one; you are using a term that is more appropriate to actual observation.

The next platypus to fall is "substance." Like "causation," "substance" is a derived concept, not anything that is directly experienced. No one has ever seen substance and no one ever will. All people ever see is data. It is assumed that what makes the data hang together in consistent patterns is that they inhere in this "substance." But as John Locke pointed out in the seventeenth century, if we ask what this substance is, devoid of any properties, we find ourselves thinking of nothing whatsoever. The data of quantum physics indicate that what are called "subatomic particles" cannot possibly fill the definition of a substance. The properties exist, then disappear, then exist, and then disappear again in little bundles called "quanta." These bundles are not continuous in time, yet an essential, defined characteristic of "substance" is that it *is* continuous in time. Since the quantum bundles are not substance and since it is a usual scientific assumption that these subatomic particles compose everything there is, then it follows that there is no substance anywhere in the world nor has there ever been. The whole concept is a grand metaphysical illusion. In his first book, Phædrus had railed against the conjuror, Aristotle, who invented the term and started it all.

But if there is no substance, it must be asked, then why isn't everything chaotic? Why do our experiences *act* as if they inhere in something? If you pick up a glass of water why don't the properties of that glass go flying off in different directions? What is it that keeps these properties uniform if it is not something called substance? That is the question that created the concept of substance in the first place.

The answer provided by the Metaphysics of Quality is similar to that given for the "causation" platypus. Strike out the word "substance" wherever it appears and substitute the expression "stable inorganic pattern of value." Again the difference is linguistic. It doesn't make a whit of difference in the laboratory which term is used. No dials change their readings. The observed laboratory data are exactly the same.

The greatest benefit of this substitution of "value" for "causation" and "substance" is that it allows an integration of physical science with other areas of experience that have been traditionally considered outside the scope of scientific thought. Phædrus saw that the "value" which directed subatomic particles is not identical with the "value" a human being gives to a painting. But he saw that the two are cousins, and that the exact relationship between them can be defined with great precision. Once this definition is complete a huge integration of the humanities and sciences appears in which platypi fall by the hundreds. Thousands.

One of the first to fall, he was happy to note, was the one that got all this started in the first place—the "Theory of Anthropology" platypus. If science is a study of substances and their relationships, then the field of cultural anthropology is a scientific absurdity. In terms of substance there is no such thing as a culture. It has no mass, no energy. No scientific laboratory instrument has ever been devised that can distinguish a culture from a non-culture.

But if science is a study of stable patterns of value, then cultural anthropology becomes a supremely scientific field. A culture can be defined as a network of social patterns of value. As the Values Project anthropologist Kluckhohn had said, patterns of value are the essence of what an anthropologist studies.

Kluckhohn's enormous mistake was his attempt to define values. He assumed that a subject-object view of the world would allow such a definition. What was destroying his case was not the accuracy of his observations. What was destroying his case were these substance-oriented metaphysical assumptions of anthropology that he failed to detach from his observations. Once this detachment is made anthropology is out of the metaphysical quicksand and onto hard ground at last.

Phædrus found again and again that a Quality-centered map of the universe provides overwhelming clarity of explanation where all has been fog before. In the arts, which are primarily concerned with value, this was expected. A surprise, however, came in fields that were supposed to have little to do with value. Mathematics, physics, biology, history, law—all of these had value foundations built into them that now came under scrutiny and all sorts of surprising things were revealed.

Once a thief is caught a whole string of crimes is often solved.

9.

In any hierarchy of metaphysical classification the most important division is the first one, for this division dominates everything beneath it. If this first division is bad there is no way you can ever build a really good system of classification around it.

In his book Phædrus had tried to save Quality from metaphysics by refusing to define it, by placing it outside the dialectical chess board. Anything that is undefined is outside metaphysics, since metaphysics can only function with defined terms. If you can't define it you can't argue about it. He had demonstrated that even though you can't define Quality you still must agree that it exists, since a world from which value is subtracted becomes unrecognizable.

But he realized that sooner or later he was going to have to stop carping about how bad subject-object metaphysics was and say something positive for a change. Sooner or later he was going to have to come up with a way of dividing Quality that was better than subjects and objects. He would have to do that or get out of metaphysics entirely. It's all right to condemn somebody else's bad metaphysics but you can't replace it with a metaphysics that consists of just one word.

By even using the term "Quality" he had already violated the nothingness of mystic reality. The use of the term "Quality" sets up a pile of questions of its own that have nothing to do with mystic reality and walks away leaving them unanswered. Even the name, "Quality," was a kind of definition since it tended to associate mystic reality with certain fixed and limited understandings. Already he was

in trouble. Was the mystic reality of the universe really more im-
manent in the higher-priced cuts of meat in the butcher shop? These
were "Quality" meats weren't they? Was the butcher using the term
incorrectly? Phædrus had no answers.

. . . That was the problem this morning too, with Rigel. Phædrus
had no answers. If you're going to talk about Quality at all you have
to be ready to answer someone like Rigel. You have to have a ready-
made Metaphysics of Quality that you can snap at him like some
catechism. Phædrus didn't have a Catechism of Quality and that's
why he got hit.

Actually the issue before him was not whether there should be a
metaphysics of Quality or not. There already *is* a metaphysics of
Quality. A subject-object metaphysics is in fact a metaphysics in which
the first division of Quality—the first slice of undivided experience—
is into subjects and objects. Once you have made that slice, all of
human experience is supposed to fit into one of these two boxes. The
trouble is, it doesn't. What he had seen is that there is a metaphysical
box that sits above these two boxes, Quality itself. And once he'd
seen this he also saw a huge number of ways in which Quality can
be divided. Subjects and objects are just one of the ways.

The question was, which way was best?

Different metaphysical ways of dividing up reality have, over the
centuries, tended to fan out into a structure that resembles a book
on chess openings. If you say that the world is "one," then somebody
can ask, "Then why does it look like more than one?" And if you
answer that it is due to faulty perception, he can ask, "How do you
know which perception is faulty and which is real?" Then you have
to answer *that*, and so on.

Trying to create a perfect metaphysics is like trying to create a
perfect chess strategy, one that will win every time. You can't do it.
It's out of the range of human capability. No matter what position
you take on a metaphysical question someone will always start asking
questions that will lead to more positions that lead to more questions
in this endless intellectual chess game. The game is supposed to stop
when it is agreed that a particular line of reasoning is illogical. This
is supposed to be similar to a checkmate. But conflicting positions go
on for centuries without any such checkmate being agreed upon.

Phædrus had spent an enormous amount of time following what turned out to be lousy openings. A particularly large amount of this time had been spent trying to lay down a first line of division between the *classic* and *romantic* aspects of the universe he'd emphasized in his first book. In that book his purpose had been to show how Quality could unite the two. But the fact that Quality was the best way of uniting the two was no guarantee that the reverse was true—that the classic-romantic split was the best way of dividing Quality. It wasn't. For example, American Indian mysticism is the same platypus in a world divided primarily into classic and romantic patterns as under a subject-object division. When an American Indian goes into isolation and fasts in order to achieve a vision, the vision he seeks is not a romantic understanding of the surface beauty of the world. Neither is it a vision of the world's classic intellectual form. It is something else. Since this whole metaphysics had started with an attempt to explain Indian mysticism Phædrus finally abandoned this classic-romantic split as a choice for a primary division of the Metaphysics of Quality. The division he finally settled on was one he didn't really choose in any deliberative way. It was more as if *it* chose *him*. He'd been reading Ruth Benedict's *Patterns of Culture* without any particular search in mind, when a relatively minor anecdote stopped him. It stayed with him for weeks. He couldn't get it out of his mind.

The anecdote was a case-history in which there was a conflict of morality. It concerned a Pueblo Indian who lived in Zuñi, New Mexico, in the nineteenth century. Like a Zen *koan* (which also originally meant "case history") the anecdote didn't have any single right answer but rather a number of possible meanings that kept drawing Phædrus deeper and deeper into the moral situation that was involved.

Benedict wrote: "Most ethnologists have had . . . experiences in recognizing that persons who are put outside the pale of society with contempt are not those who would be placed there by another culture. . . .

"The dilemma of such an individual is often most successfully solved by doing violence to his strongest natural impulses and accepting the role the culture honours. In case he is a person to whom social recognition is necessary it is ordinarily his only possible course."

She said the person concerned was one of the most striking individuals in Zuñi.

*In a society that thoroughly distrusts authority of any sort, he had
native personal magnetism that singled him out in any group. In a
society that exalts moderation and the easiest way, he was turbulent
and could act violently upon occasion. In a society that praises a
pliant personality that "talks lots"—that is, that chatters in a friendly
fashion—he was scornful and aloof. Zuñi's only reaction to such
personalities is to brand them as witches. He was said to have been
peering through a window from outside, and this is a sure mark of
a witch. At any rate he got drunk one day and boasted that they could
not kill him. He was taken before the war priests who hung him by
his thumbs from the rafters till he should confess to his witchcraft.
This is the usual procedure in a charge of witchcraft. However he
dispatched a messenger to the government troops. When they came his
shoulders were already crippled for life, and the officer of the law
was left with no recourse but to imprison the war priests who had
been responsible for the enormity. One of these war priests was probably the most respected and important in recent Zuñi history and
when he returned after imprisonment in the state penitentiary he never
resumed his priestly offices. He regarded his power as broken. It was
a revenge that is probably unique in Zuñi history. It involved, of
course, a challenge to the priesthoods, against whom the witch by his
act openly aligned himself.*

*The course of his life in the forty years that followed this defiance
was not, however, what we might easily predict. A witch is not barred
from his membership in cult groups because he has been condemned,
and the way to recognition lay through such activity. He possessed a
remarkable verbal memory and a sweet singing voice. He learned
unbelievable stores of mythology, of esoteric ritual, of cult songs. Many
hundreds of pages of stories and ritual poetry were taken down from
his dictation before he died, and he regarded his songs as much more
extensive. He became indispensable in ceremonial life and before he
died was the governor of Zuñi. The congenital bent of his personality
threw him into irreconcilable conflict with his society, and he solved
his dilemma by turning an incidental talent to account. As we might*

well expect, he was not a happy man. As governor of Zuñi and high in his cult groups, a marked man in his community, he was obsessed by death. He was a cheated man in the midst of a mildly happy populace.

It is easy to imagine the life he might have lived among the Plains Indians where every institution favoured the traits that were native to him. The personal authority, the turbulence, the scorn, would all have been honoured in the career he could have made his own. The unhappiness that was inseparable from his temperament as a successful priest and governor of Zuñi would have had no place as a war chief of the Cheyenne; it was not a function of the traits of his native endowment but of the standards of the culture in which he found no outlet for his native responses.

When Phædrus first read this passage he felt a kind of eerie feeling—a feeling he might have had if he had passed in front of a strange mirror and suddenly seen a reflection of someone he'd never expected to see. It was the same feeling he got at the peyote meeting. This Zuñi Indian was not exactly someone else.

This was not just an isolated tribal incident going on here. This was something of universal importance happening. This was *everyman.* There is not a person alive who is not in some way or other in the kind of situation this "witch" was in. It was just that his circumstances were so exotic and so extreme one could now see it, by itself, out in the open.

The story was of a struggle between good and evil, but the koan it raised was, "Which was which?" Was this person really good or was he perhaps also evil?

At first reading he might seem a model of goodness, a lone, virtuous man surrounded by wicked persecutors, but this was too facile. Circumstances of the story argued against it. One of his tormentors was "probably the most important and respected person in Zuñi history." If his tormentor was so evil why was he so respected? Was the whole Zuñi culture evil? That was ridiculous. There was a lot more to it than that.

Phædrus saw that the question was thrown off by a connotation of "witch." This word alone loaded the case against the priests since

anyone who calls someone else a witch is obviously a bigoted per-
secutor. But did they really call him a witch? A witch is a Druid
priestess reduced by legend to an old crone who wears a pointed black
hat and rides a broomstick in front of the moon on Halloween. Was
that what they were calling him?

In his koan-like recycling of the event in his mind Phædrus came
to think that Benedict had given the event an interpretation that didn't
do it justice. She was finding stories to support her thesis that different
cultures create different personality traits, which is important, and
undoubtedly true. But this man was more than just a "misfit." There
was something deeper than that going on.

"Misfit" is one of those words that seem to explain things but
does not. "Misfit" says only that something is *not* explained. If he
was a misfit why didn't he leave? What persuaded him to stay? It
certainly wasn't timidity. And why did the citizens of Zuñi change
their minds and make this former "witch" their governor? There's no
indication that he changed or they changed. She said he turned "an
incidental talent to account" in order to satisfy his need for social
recognition. Probably so, but Zuñi or no Zuñi, it takes stronger social
forces than a good singing voice and a need for social recognition to
turn a misfit and torture victim into a governor.

How did he do it? What were his "powers"? Was there something
special in the way Pueblo Indians think that after ten thousand years
of continuous culture they would let a drunkard and a window-peeper
get away with this?

Phædrus did not think so. He thought a better name for him might
have been *sorcerer*, or *shaman*, or *brujo*, a Spanish term used extensively
in that region that denotes a quite different kind of person. A *brujo*
is not a semi-mythical, semi-comic figure that rides a broomstick but
a real person who claims religious powers; who acts outside of and
sometimes against the local church authorities.

This was not a case of priests persecuting an innocent person.
This was a much deeper conflict between a priesthood and a shaman.
A passage from the anthropologist, E. A. Hoebel, confirmed Phædrus'
idea:

Although in many primitive cultures there is a recognized division
of function between priests and shamans, in the more highly developed

cultures in which cults have become strongly organized churches, the priesthood fights an unrelenting war against shamans. . . . Priests work in a rigorously structured hierarchy fixed in a firm set of traditions. Their power comes from and is vested in the organization itself. They constitute a religious bureaucracy.

Shamans, on the other hand, are arrant individualists. Each is on his own, undisciplined by bureaucratic control; hence a shaman is always a threat to the order of the organized church. In the view of the priests they are presumptive pretenders. Joan of Arc was a shaman for she communed directly with the angels of God. She steadfastly refused to recant and admit delusion and her martyrdom was ordained by the functionaries of the Church. The struggle between shaman and priest may well be a death struggle.

For weeks Phædrus returned to these questions before he saw that the key lay in the war priest's statement that his "powers had been broken." Something very grave had occurred. The priest refused to return to a priestly office after return from the penitentiary. What had occurred had been enormous.

Phædrus concluded that a huge battle had taken place for the entire mind and soul of Zuñi. The priests had proclaimed themselves good and the *brujo* evil. The *brujo* had proclaimed himself good and the priests evil. A showdown had occurred and the *brujo had won*!

Phædrus began to suspect that Benedict missed all this because she was trained in the "objectivity" of science by Boas. She tried to show only those aspects of Zuñi culture that were independent of the white observer.

This explains why the *brujo* is analyzed only in terms of relations within his own culture, although by her own accounting he was very much in contact with the whites. It was the white man to whom he sent for help and who saved him. It was the white anthropologists, presumably, who took dictation of all his songs and stories and made him well known in books of which his tribesmen could not have been ignorant.

Phædrus concluded that the real reason the people of Zuñi made the *brujo* governor had to be because of this. The *brujo* had shown he could deal successfully with the one tribe that could easily wipe them out any time it wanted to. It wasn't just a sweet singing voice that made him governor of Zuñi. He had real political clout.

Sometimes you can see your own society's issues more clearly when they are put in an exotic context like that of the *brujo* in Zuñi. That is a huge reward from the study of anthropology. As Phædrus thought about this context again and again it became apparent there were two *kinds* of good and evil involved.

The tribal frame of values that condemned the *brujo* and led to his punishment was one kind of good, for which Phædrus coined the term "static good." Each culture has its own pattern of static good derived from fixed laws and the traditions and values that underlie them. This pattern of static good is the essential structure of the culture itself and defines it. In the static sense the *brujo* was very clearly evil to oppose the appointed authorities of his tribe. Suppose everyone did that? The whole Zuñi culture, after thousands of years of continuous survival, would collapse into chaos.

But in addition there's a *Dynamic* good that is outside of any culture, that cannot be contained by any system of precepts, but has to be continually rediscovered as a culture evolves. Good and evil are not *entirely* a matter of tribal custom. If they were, no tribal change would be possible, since custom cannot change custom. There has to be another source of good and evil outside the tribal customs that produces the tribal change.

If you had asked the *brujo* what ethical principles he was following he probably wouldn't have been able to tell you. He wouldn't have understood what you were talking about. He was just following some vague sense of "betterness" that he couldn't have defined if he had wanted to. Probably the war priests thought he was some kind of egotist trying to build his own image by tearing down tribal authority. But he showed later on that he really wasn't. If he'd been such an egotist he wouldn't have stayed with the tribe and helped keep it together.

The *brujo*'s values were in conflict with the tribe at least partly because he had learned to value some of the ways of the new neighbors and they had not. He was a precursor of deep cultural change. A tribe can change its values only person by person and someone has to be first. Whoever is first obviously is going to be in conflict with everybody else. He didn't have to change his ways to conform to the culture only because the culture was changing its ways to conform to him. And that is what made him seem like such a leader. Probably he wasn't telling anyone to do this or to do that so much as he was just being himself. He may never have seen his struggle as anything but a personal one. But because the culture was in transition many people saw this *brujo*'s ways to be of higher Quality than those of the old priests and tried to become more like him. In this Dynamic sense the *brujo* was good because he saw the new source of good and evil before the other members of his tribe did. Undoubtedly he did much during his life to prevent a clash of cultures that would have been completely destructive to the people of Zuñi.

Whatever the personality traits were that made him such a rebel from the tribe around him, this man was no "misfit." He was an integral *part* of Zuñi culture. The whole tribe was in a state of evolution that had emerged many centuries ago from cliff-dwelling isolation. Now it was entering a state of cooperation with the whites and submission to white laws. He was an active catalytic agent in that tribe's social evolution, and his personal conflicts were a part of that tribe's cultural growth.

Phædrus thought that the story of the old Pueblo Indian, seen in this way, made deep and broad sense, and justified the enormous feeling of drama that it produced. After many months of thinking about it, he was left with a reward of two terms: Dynamic good and static good, which became the basic division of his emerging Metaphysics of Quality.

It certainly felt right. Not subject and object but static and Dynamic is the basic division of reality. When A. N. Whitehead wrote that "mankind is driven forward by dim apprehensions of things too obscure for its existing language," he was writing about Dynamic Quality. Dynamic Quality is the pre-intellectual cutting edge of reality, the source of all things, completely simple and always new. It was the moral force that had motivated the *brujo* in Zuñi. It contains no pattern of fixed rewards and punishments. Its only perceived good is freedom and its only perceived evil is static quality itself—any pattern of one-sided fixed values that tries to contain and kill the ongoing free force of life.

Static quality, the moral force of the priests, emerges in the wake of Dynamic Quality. It is old and complex. It always contains a component of memory. Good is conformity to an established pattern of fixed values and value objects. Justice and law are identical. Static morality is full of heroes and villains, loves and hatreds, carrots and sticks. Its values don't change by themselves. Unless they are altered by Dynamic Quality they say the same thing year after year. Sometimes they say it more loudly, sometimes more softly, but the message is always the same.

During the next few months that Phædrus reflected he began to transpose the static-Dynamic division out of the moral conflict of Zuñi into other seemingly unrelated areas. The negative esthetic quality of the hot stove in the earlier example was now given some added meaning by a static-Dynamic division of Quality. When the person who sits on the stove first discovers his low-Quality situation, the front edge of his experience is Dynamic. He does not think, "This stove is hot," and then make a rational decision to get off. A "dim perception of he knows not what" gets him off Dynamically. Later he generates static patterns of thought to explain the situation.

A subject-object metaphysics presumes that this kind of Dynamic action without thought is rare and ignores it when possible. But mystic learning goes in the opposite direction and tries to hold to the ongoing Dynamic edge of all experience, both positive and negative, even the Dynamic ongoing edge of thought itself. Phædrus thought that of the two kinds of students, those who study only subject-object science and those who study only meditative mysticism, it would be the mystic students who would get off the stove first. The purpose of mystic meditation is not to remove oneself from experience but to bring one's self closer to it by eliminating stale, confusing, static, intellectual attachments of the past.

In a subject-object metaphysics morals and art are worlds apart, morals being concerned with the subject quality and art with object quality. But in the Metaphysics of Quality that division doesn't exist. They're the same. They both become much more intelligible when references to what is subjective and what is objective are completely thrown away and references to what is static and what is Dynamic are taken up instead.

He found an example within the field of music. He said, imagine that you walk down a street past, say, a car where someone has the radio on and it plays a tune you've never heard before but which is so fantastically good it just stops you in your tracks. You listen until it's done. Days later you remember exactly what that street looked like when you heard that music. You remember what was in the store window you stood in front of. You remember what the colors of the cars in the street were, where the clouds were in the sky above the buildings across the street, and it all comes back so *vividly* you wonder what song they were playing, and so you wait until you hear it again. If it's that good you'll hear it again because other people will have heard it too and have had the same feelings and that will make it popular.

One day it comes on the radio again and you get the same feeling again and you catch the name and you rush down the street to the record store and buy it and can hardly wait until you can get it home and play it.

You get home. You play it. It's really good. It doesn't quite transform the whole room into something different but it's really good. You play it again. Really good. You play it another time. Still good, but you're not so sure you want to play it again. But you play it again. It's okay but now you definitely don't want to play it again. You put it away.

The next day you play it again, and it's okay, but something is gone. You still like it and always will, you say. You play it again. Yeah, that's sure a good record. But you file it away and once in a while play it again for a friend and maybe months or years later bring it out as a memory of something you were once crazy about.

Now what has happened? You can say you've gotten tired of the song but what does that mean? Has the song lost its quality? If it has, why do you still say it's a good record? Either it's good or it's not good. If it's good why don't you play it? If it's not good why do you tell your friend it's good?

If you think about this question long enough you will come to see that the same kind of division between Dynamic Quality and static quality that exists in the field of morals also exists in the field of art. The first good, that made you want to buy the record, was Dynamic

Quality. Dynamic Quality comes as a sort of surprise. What the record did was weaken for a moment your existing static patterns in such a way that the Dynamic Quality all around you shone through. It was free, without static forms. The second good, the kind that made you want to recommend it to a friend, even when you had lost your own enthusiasm for it, is static quality. Static quality is what you normally expect.

Soon after that Phædrus ran across another example that concerned neither art nor morality but referred indirectly to mystic reality itself.

It was in an essay by Walker Percy called "The Delta Factor." It asked,

> *Why is a man apt to feel bad in a good environment, say suburban Short Hills, New Jersey, on an ordinary Wednesday afternoon? Why is the same man apt to feel good in a very bad environment, say in an old hotel in Key Largo, in a hurricane. . . . Why is it that a man riding a good commuter train from Larchmont to New York, whose needs and drives are satisfied, who has a good home, loving wife and family, good job, and enjoys unprecedented "cultural and recreational facilities" often feels bad without knowing why?*
>
> *Why is it that if such a man suffers a heart attack and, taken off the train at New Rochelle, regains consciousness and finds himself in a strange place, he then comes to himself for the first time in years, perhaps in his life, and begins to gaze at his own hand with a sense of wonder and delight?*

These are haunting questions, but with Quality divided into Dynamic and static components, a way of approaching them emerges. A home in suburban Short Hills, New Jersey, on an ordinary Wednesday afternoon is filled with static patterns. A hurricane in Key Largo promises a *Dynamic* relief from static patterns. The man who suffers a heart attack and is taken off the train at New Rochelle has had all his *static* patterns shattered, he can't find them, and in that moment only *Dynamic* Quality is available to him. That is why he gazes at his own hand with a sense of wonder and delight.

Phædrus saw that not only a man recovering from a heart attack but also a baby gazes at his hand with mystic wonder and delight. He remembered the child Poincaré referred to who could not understand the reality of objective science at all but was able to understand the reality of value perfectly. When this reality of value is divided into static and Dynamic areas a lot can be explained about that baby's growth that is not well explained otherwise.

One can imagine how an infant in the womb acquires awareness of simple distinctions such as pressure and sound, and then at birth acquires more complex ones of light and warmth and hunger. *We* know these distinctions are pressure and sound and light and warmth and hunger and so on but the baby doesn't. We could call them stimuli but the baby doesn't identify them as that. From the baby's point of view, something, he knows not what, compels attention. This generalized "something," Whitehead's "dim apprehension," is Dynamic Quality. When he is a few months old the baby studies his hand or a rattle, not knowing it is a hand or a rattle, with the same sense of wonder and mystery and excitement created by the music and heart attack in the previous examples.

If the baby ignores this force of Dynamic Quality it can be speculated that he will become mentally retarded, but if he is normally attentive to Dynamic Quality he will soon begin to notice differences and then correlations between the differences and then repetitive patterns of the correlations. But it is not until the baby is several months old that he will begin to really understand enough about that enormously complex correlation of sensations and boundaries and desires called an *object* to be able to reach for one. This object will not be a primary experience. It will be a complex pattern of static values *derived* from primary experience.

Once the baby has made a complex pattern of values called an object and found this pattern to work well he quickly develops a skill and speed at jumping through the chain of deductions that produced it, as though it were a single jump. This is similar to the the way one drives a car. The first time there is a very slow trial-and-error process of seeing what causes what. But in a very short time it becomes so swift one doesn't even think about it. The same is true of objects. One uses these complex patterns the same way one shifts a car, without thinking about them. Only when the shift doesn't work or an "object" turns out to be an illusion is one forced to become aware of the deductive process. That is why we think of subjects and objects as primary. We can't remember that period of our lives when they were anything else.

In this way static patterns of value become the universe of distinguishable things. Elementary static distinctions between such entities as "before" and "after" and between "like" and "unlike" grow into enormously complex patterns of knowledge that are transmitted from generation to generation as the mythos, the culture in which we live.

This, Phædrus thought, was why little children are usually quicker to perceive Dynamic Quality than old people, why beginners are usually quicker than experts, why primitive people are sometimes quicker than those of "advanced" cultures. American Indians are exceptionally skilled at holding to the ever-changing center of things. That is the real reason they speak and act without ornamentation. It violates their mystic unity. This moving and acting and talking in accord with the Great Spirit and almost nothing else has been the ancient center of their lives.

Their term *manito* is often used interchangeably with "God" by whites who usually think all religion is theistic and by Indians themselves who don't make a big deal out of any verbal distinctions. But as David Mandelbaum noted in his book *The Plains Cree*, "The term *manito* primarily referred to the Supreme Being but also had many other usages. It was applied to manifestations of skill, fortune, blessing, luck, to any wonderous occurrence. It connoted any phenomenon that transcended the run of everyday experience."

In other words, "Dynamic Quality."

With the identification of static and Dynamic Quality as the fundamental division of the world, Phædrus felt that some kind of goal had been reached. This first division of the Metaphysics of Quality now covered the spectrum of experience from primitive mysticism to quantum mechanics. What remained for Phædrus to do next was fill in the gaps as carefully and methodically as he could.

In the past Phædrus' own radical bias caused him to think of Dynamic Quality alone and neglect static patterns of quality. Until now he had always felt that these static patterns were dead. They have no love. They offer no promise of anything. To succumb to them is to succumb to death, since that which does not change cannot live. But now he was beginning to see that this radical bias weakened his own case. Life can't exist on Dynamic Quality alone. It has no staying power. To cling to Dynamic Quality alone apart from any static patterns is to cling to chaos. He saw that much can be learned about Dynamic Quality by studying what it is not rather than futilely trying to define what it is.

Static quality patterns are dead when they are exclusive, when they demand blind obedience and suppress Dynamic change. But static patterns, nevertheless, provide a necessary stabilizing force to protect Dynamic progress from degeneration. Although Dynamic Quality, the Quality of freedom, creates this world in which we live, these patterns of static quality, the quality of order, preserve our world. Neither static nor Dynamic Quality can survive without the other.

If one inserts this concept into a case such as that of the *brujo* in Zuñi, one can see the truth of it. Although the Dynamic *brujo* and the static priests who tortured him appeared to be mortal enemies, they were actually necessary to each other. Both types of people had to exist. If most of Zuñi went around drunk and bragging and looking in windows, that ancient way of life could never have lasted. But without wild, disreputable outcasts like the *brujo*, ready to seize on any new outside idea and bring it into the community, Zuñi would have been too inflexible to survive. A tension between these two forces is needed to continue the evolution of life.

The beauty of that old Indian, Phædrus thought, is that he seemed to have understood this. He wasn't interested in just knocking things down and walking off into the sunset with some kind of a moral victory. The old priestly ways would have come back and all his suffering would have been wasted. He didn't do that. He stayed around the rest of his life, became a part of the static pattern of the tribe, and lived to see his reforms become a part of the tribe's ongoing culture.

Slowly at first, and then with increasing awareness that he was going in a right direction, Phædrus' central attention turned away from any further explanation of Dynamic Quality and turned toward the static patterns themselves.

10.

Lila sat on the cabin berth and thought about the bad taste in her mouth from the coffee. There was something wrong with it. It was that rubbery taste in the water. That was bad too. It was in the coffee too.

She didn't feel good. Her head still hurt. From last night. How much had she spent? she wondered. She didn't have much money left. Then she remembered: *he* paid for most of it. . . . Her head really hurt bad.

God she was hungry. At least she'd get him to buy her a big steak tonight . . . with mushrooms . . . and onions. . . . Oh, she could hardly *stand* it!

Everything was all changed again. Yesterday she was going to Florida on the *Karma*. Now she was on *this* boat. Her life was really getting worse and worse. She knew it. She used to at least plan things a little. Now everything happened without any plans at all.

She wondered where the *Karma* was now. And George and Debbie. He was probably still shacked up with her! She hoped they'd *both* drown. She didn't even ask for her money back. She knew they wouldn't give it to her.

She should have asked for it, though. She really needed it. She was getting that old feeling again. It meant trouble. She always got into trouble when she got mad. If she hadn't got mad at George and Debbie she'd be on the *Karma* right now. She could have got George back. That was dumb to get mad at him. That just made things worse.

And now she was mad at this new Captain. She was mad at every-body these days. What was the purpose of that? There wasn't anything really wrong with him. He was just a dumbbell, that was all. All those dumb questions about Richard. She wondered why Richard had any-thing to do with him. Probably just someone he met and she thought they were good friends.

Maybe Richard would be in New York when they got there.

Anyway she was stuck with this Captain now. At least until New York, or wherever they were going to stay tonight. She could stand him that long.

She might need him when they got to New York.

She watched him for a while over the top of the stairway. He looked like a schoolteacher she thought, the kind that never liked her. Like someone who was always getting mad at her for doing something she shouldn't. He looked like he'd been frowning about her for a long time.

She had to get out of these bad feelings. She knew what would happen to her if she didn't. She ought to try going up one more time. She didn't have to look at him. She could just sit there.

She watched the Captain for a while longer then braced herself, put on a smile, climbed the stairs to the deck and sat down again.

There, that wasn't so hard.

She brought her sweater with her and now she stood up to put it on. "It's gotten cool," she said.

"We're lucky it isn't any colder," the Captain said. "At this time of year we can't count on anything any more."

"It's the wind," he added. "Watch out for the boom. The winds are fluky in river valleys like this."

"Where are we?" she asked.

"We're south of Poughkeepsie," he said. "It's getting a little more industrial now. You can see some mountains up ahead."

"I was watching you," she said.

"When?"

"Just now."

"Oh."

"You frown a lot. You were talking to yourself a lot. That's the way Morris was."

"Who's Morris?"

"A friend of mine. He would just sit for hours and not say a word and I'd think he was really mad at me and he wasn't mad at all. Some men are like that. He was just thinking about something else."

"Yes, that's the way I am too."

After a while she saw there was all sorts of stuff floating in the water. She saw some branches and what looked like grass and there was foam all around it.

"What's all that in the water?" she asked.

"It's from the hurricane," he said. "We seem to hit thick patches of it and then it thins out for a while."

"It looks awful," Lila said.

"They were talking about it back in Castleton," he added. "They said everything's been coming down the river. Trees, garbage cans, old picnic benches. A lot of it's half-submerged. . . . One of the reasons I'm using the sails is so we don't hit anything with the propeller."

He pointed up ahead. "When we get to the mountain up there the wind will probably start doing funny things. We'll have to stop sailing and run the engine." Where he pointed, the river seemed to run right into some mountains. "At a turn called World's End," he added.

A few minutes went by and then she saw that far ahead, by a branch or something sticking up out of the water, it looked like some animal was floating with its feet up.

They got closer and she saw it was a dog. It was all swelled up and it was on its side with two of its feet up in the air.

She didn't say anything.

The Captain didn't say anything either.

Later, after they got by it, she could smell it and she knew he could smell it too.

"These rivers are like sewers," the Captain said. "They take all the debris and poisons from the land and carry them out to sea."

"What poisons?"

"Salts and chemicals. If you irrigate land without drainage it loads up with poisons and becomes dead. Nothing grows. The rivers keep the land clean and fresh. All of this debris is on the same journey we are."

"Where? What do you mean?"

"To the ocean."

"Oh. . . . Well, we're just going to New York," she said.

The Captain didn't say anything.

"How soon will we be there?" Lila asked.

"Tomorrow, unless something goes wrong," the Captain answered. "Are you in a hurry?"

"No," Lila said. She really didn't have to get there at all. She really didn't know anybody to stay with except Jamie and some of the others but that was so long ago they were probably all gone by now.

She asked, "Is your buyer going to be there?"

"What buyer?"

"For your boat."

"Not me. I'm going to Florida."

Florida? Lila wondered. She said, "I thought you said you were going to sell your boat in New York."

"Not me."

"You said so last night."

"Not me," the Captain said. "It was Rigel. I'm going to Florida. You must have heard me wrong."

"Ohhhh," Lila said, "I thought *Richard* was going to Florida."

"No. . . . I want to get south of Cape Hatteras before the end of the month," the Captain said, "but everything seems to slow me down. The fall storms are in now and these could pin the boat down for days."

Florida, Lila thought. In Florida the light was always golden orange and everything looked different. Even the light on the sand was different in Florida. She remembered the beach at Fort Lauderdale and the palm trees and the warm sand under her towel and the hot sun on her back. That was so good.

"You're going to go all by yourself?" she asked.

"Sure."

"With no food?"

"I'll get food."

In Florida there were all kinds of good food. Good seafood—pompano, shrimp and snapper. She sure could go for some of that now. *Oh*, she shouldn't *think* about it!

"You need a cook," she said. "You don't cook. You need someone to cook."

"I get along," he said.

Once she went shrimp fishing at night under a bridge with lights and afterward they all cooked the shrimp and took it to the beach and drank cold beer and there was more than anyone could eat. *Oh, they were good.* She could remember how soft and warm the wind was and they were all so stuffed and they laid down under the palm trees and they drank rum-and-Coke and they talked and they all made love all night long until the sun came up over the ocean. She wondered where they were now, those guys. She'd probably never see them again.

And the boats, she thought, the boats were everywhere.

"How long will it take you?" she asked.

"A long time," he said. "A month maybe."

"That's a long time. . . . How long have you been sailing like this?"

"Since August eleventh."

"Are you retired?"

"I'm a writer," he said.

"What do you write about?"

"Traveling, mostly, I guess," he said. "I go places and see things and think about what I see and then I write about that. There are lots of writers who do that."

"You mean you would write about what we're seeing right now?"

"Sure."

"Why would anyone want to write about this? Nothing is happening."

"There's always something happening," he said. "When you say 'nothing is happening' you're just saying nothing is happening that fits your cliché of what something is."

"What?"

"It's hard to explain," he said. "Something is happening right now and you think it's unimportant because you've never seen a movie of it. But if you saw three movies in a row of people sailing down the Hudson River and maybe a TV documentary about Washington Irving and the history of the Hudson River and *then* you got on this trip you'd say, 'Boy, this is sure something,' because what you were seeing fit some mental picture you already had planted in your mind."

Lila didn't know what that was all about. He said it like he thought it was pretty smart.

She looked at him for a long time and wondered whether to say something, but changed her mind. She watched the water pass under her elbow.

After a while she asked, "You want to have a really good dinner tonight?"

"Sure," he said.

"I'll make it," Lila said.

"You will?"

"We'll bring the steaks and you just watch how I cook them. Is it a deal?"

"You don't have to," he said.

"No, that's all right," she said, "I can cook. I just *love* to cook. Cooking is one of my favorite things to do."

She looked at the shirt he was wearing. There was a big food spot over the front pocket. She wondered how long he'd worn that shirt. He hadn't changed shirts for days.

"I'm going to put that shirt in the laundry in New York," she said. He smiled a little.

She thought some more about Florida.

After a while she turned to him again and asked, "Do you want to see something really beautiful?"

"What?" the Captain asked.

"I'll show you," she said.

She went below, got out her suitcase, spread it on the berth and opened it. Inside one corner pocket was a bundle of papers with a red ribbon around it. She untied the ribbon and removed a colored pamphlet with "JUNGLE QUEEN" printed in big red letters across the top. Beneath it was a picture of the most beautiful boat in the world. Lila spread the picture out and carefully turned back one corner that had got folded over.

She brought it up to the deck and sat down next to the Captain and showed it to him. She hung on to it hard so it wouldn't blow away.

"That's a boat I was on in Fort Lauderdale, Florida, three years ago," she said. "With my girlfriend. See where that 'X' is? That's where we used to sit."

The boat looked like a great big beautiful wedding cake with two layers and covered with curlicued frosting. On the front was the state flag of Florida. She knew everything about that boat. Because she had been *on* it. Many times. The sky was sort of pink and blue with big cottony clouds blowing by in the wind. The boat left just before sunset and that's how the sky looked. All the flags on the boat were fluttering in the breeze. That was the trade wind. And all around were dark green coconut palm trees waving in the trade wind and the water was pink and blue all around the boat from the sunset with ripples from the breeze. That's the way it really was. The picture looked so real you wanted to stick your finger in it and feel how warm the water was.

The Captain took the pamphlet in one hand while he steered with the other. He looked at it for a while and then she could see he was reading the part at the bottom. She knew it by heart:

A *MUST* in Fort Lauderdale.

WORLD FAMOUS ORIGINAL JUNGLE QUEEN

"Acclaimed Florida's Finest Evening"

Come aboard our new 550 passenger boat. Bar-B-Q and Shrimp Dinner Cruise—7 p.m. Alcoholic Beverages Available Make reservations at your Hotel or Motel or Phone.

His expression didn't change. He squinted at it like a doctor examining somebody. Then he frowned and said, "Do you know the owners, or something?"

"No," Lila said, "It's just a boat we rode on a few years ago."

"That's a *head-boat*," he said.

"What's a head-boat?"

"Where they charge by the head to go cruising."

"Of course," Lila said. She didn't understand why he was frowning. "But they don't charge very much. Open it up."

The Captain opened up the pamphlet to a big picture of the Jungle Queen. He asked, "Why is this so important to you?"

"I don't know," Lila said. She looked up at him to see if he was really listening. "I can remember so many worlds," she said. "I'm not sure what I mean by that . . . but there are so many worlds and I just touch them and I'm in them for a moment and then I'm out of them again. . . . Things like my grandfather's house where I used to play. And my dog that I used to have . . . things like that. They don't really mean anything to anybody else except once in a while you can share them with someone."

The Captain looked down and read, "A Lauderdale tradition for over thirty years. . . . The 'all you wish to eat' dinner, the vaudeville show and the sing-a-long have made it a 'must' in Fort Lauderdale. There is nothing else like it. . . ."

The Captain looked up. "What's a sing-a-long?" he asked.

"She was my favorite," Lila said.

"Who?"

"The woman who led the sing-a-long. She could have been my sister. I wish she *was* my sister. At first everyone was so stuffed with food no one wanted to sing very much, but she got them all going.

"She's not like me at all," Lila said. "She had dark hair, really beautiful dark hair and a beautiful figure and she had what you call a 'magnetic personality.' You know what I mean? She really liked everybody who was there and they all liked her too. She didn't act like she thought she was any better than anybody else. . . . There was this old man sitting in front of us and he wouldn't say anything . . . he was just like you. . . ." Lila watched the Captain. "So she sat next to him and put her arms around him and started to sing 'Put Your Arms Around Me Baby' to him and pretty soon he couldn't keep from grinning. She wouldn't let anybody sit there and act like they were all alone.

"You could see she was very smart. I mean how quick she was to catch on to everything. One man tried to grab her and she just smiled as sweet as if he handed her a ten-dollar bill or something. She said, 'You just save that for your wife, honey,' and everybody laughed. And *he* liked it too. She knew how to take care of herself.

"She sang 'Oh, You Great Big Beautiful Doll,' and 'Yes, Sir, That's My Baby,' and 'Nothing Could Be Finer Than to be in Carolina,' and lots of others. I wish I could remember them all. And all the time the boat was floating down the river through the palm trees in the dark and it was so beautiful. And then she sang, 'Shine On Harvest Moon,' and just as the boat came around a corner of the river the palm trees opened up and there it was. A full moon. Everybody went 'Ohhhhhh!' See, she *planned* it that way so that she would be singing that just as they came around the corner."

"Ugh." The Captain looked angry.

"What's the matter?"

"That's too much."

"*What's* too much?" Lila asked.

"That's all static," he said.

"What's *that?*"

"It's just clichés, one after another!"

He pointed to the picture of the Jungle Queen. "Look at those smokestacks coming out the top. Those are for a steamboat. That isn't any steamboat."

"They're just there to look pretty."

"They *don't* look pretty. A pretty boat doesn't have all that fake gingerbread and phony smokestacks."

Lila took the pamphlet back. "It's a very beautiful boat," she said.

The Captain shook his head. "Beauty isn't things trying to look like something else."

He's something else, Lila thought.

"Beauty is things being just what they are," he said. "There probably isn't one thing on that boat that's original."

"Why does it have to be original?"

"It's *play*-acting. It's *make*-believe."

"What difference does *that* make? If it's what people like?"

He didn't have any answer for that.

"Disneyland's all fake too," Lila said. "I suppose you don't like that either?"

"No."

"How about movies? TV? That's all fake too, I guess, huh?"

"It depends on what they do," the Captain said.

"You sure must enjoy yourself a lot," Lila said. She folded up the pamphlet carefully. Arguing with him seemed to make the Captain mad. He didn't want anybody to argue with him.

He said, "I suppose if the boat gave three million rides they must be doing something right. But it's all—he shook his head—prostitution."

"Prostitution?"

"Yeah. It's all taking the customer's money and giving him exactly what he wants and then leaving him poorer than when he started. That's what that singer was doing with those songs. She could have sung something original and left them richer, but she didn't want to do that, because if she sang something they never heard before they might not like that and might ignore her or turn on her and she'd lose her job and she wouldn't get her money any more. And she knew that and that's why she never sang anything that was really her own, did she? She was just imitating some kind of person she was sure they liked and they went along with it. That's why she's a hustler. They were *paying* her to imitate someone making love to them."

Watch out, Lila, she thought. She was really getting mad. She *was* herself! *He* was the phony! How did *he* know what she was like? He wasn't even *there*.

"People should be themselves," he went on. "Not phony singers on a phony boat."

Hang on Lila.

She smiled a little and said, "I'm getting cold." She got up carefully and went back down inside the cabin again.

There she let out her breath.

God, that made her mad!

Oh boy! Oh boy!

A *smokestack*. A big blowhard smokestack, that's what he is. "Yeah! A big phony *smokestack*. That's exactly what he *is*. He thinks he's so smart. It's all over his face. And he's *not* smart. He's *stupid*. He doesn't know *anything*. He doesn't even know what a hustler is. He doesn't even know how stupid he *is*."

Lila opened her suitcase again, carefully folded the brochure, tied it together with her other things with the red ribbon, and then put it in its special compartment and closed the suitcase and locked it.

Hang on, Lila. Never get mad at people like that, she thought. Don't let yourself get angry. That's what they want.

Her hands were shaking.

Oh-oh.

She knew what that meant.

She got her purse from the berth, opened it and took out the pills, got a plastic glass by the sink and pumped some water into it and then swallowed them. She had to do that quick, or they didn't work. She'd been feeling the wave coming all morning. She'd been riding in front of it too long. She should have blown up at him. Then this wouldn't have happened.

Smokestack! He looked at that picture like it was some kind of an ant or something. That's what smokestacks like him do. Just to prove how smart they are. She knew what *they* were like. Just when you start being nice to them they turn on you like that. There's just one thing someone like him loves—to hear himself blow smoke.

Well, that was that, she guessed. Nothing more to do on *this* boat until they got to New York. And then get off.

Suddenly she felt cold. That always happened after her hands started to shake. She hoped the pills would work in time. Sometimes they didn't. She unlocked the suitcase again, took out another sweater and put it on over the one she already had on, then closed the suitcase and locked it again and put it away on the upper berth.

It would be good to get back to living on land again, Lila thought. She was really done with all this boat life. It wasn't the way she thought it was going to be. Nothing ever was. She didn't have to put up with him one more night, but she didn't want to pay for a bus.

On the ledge back of the berth was a radio. Lila opened it and tried to turn it on. It wouldn't work. She turned on all the switches, back and forth, but none of them worked. Then she found a switch and she could hear some static noise. It worked.

There were lots of stations. One of the announcers said something about Manhattan.

She listened for a while. They were close now. Some music from one station was close and dreamy, the kind anyone could dance to.

She just wanted to get to New York now. Would it be four years now? No, *five*! Five whole years. Where did they go so fast?

Jamie would *never* be there. Just to see him again the way he used to look, the way he used to smile at her when he was feeling good. That's all she wanted. And a little money too.

He'd be hard to find. She would have to ask around. Mindy might know. Probably she was gone too. No one ever stayed any place long. She'd find someone who knew.

She wondered what the old place looked like now. Once in a while they would play an old slow one like that and Jamie would go slow with it. The way he held his hands on her. The way he touched and handled her. It all came back with the music. She was a real princess then, but she didn't know it.

"Lila," she could hear him say, "you got something on your mind. I can just *tell*. What is it?" And then after a while she'd just tell him and he'd always listen and he'd never argue with her no matter what she told him. She was crazy to leave. She never should have left.

Even with two sweaters on Lila was still cold. She needed a blanket. She remembered now that she'd had one when she woke up last night but now it wasn't here. She got up, went to the front of the boat, took the blanket off the bed and brought it back to the main cabin.

The shaking of her hands was getting worse. It always happened after she got mad like that and there wasn't anything she could do about it. She should have screamed at the Captain but it was too late for that now. When she could scream or hit somebody or even just swear at them then sometimes the wave would stop.

She turned off the radio.

She listened to the sound of the wind above and the lapping sound of water on the hull. So quiet. So different from the *Karma*.

She wondered what she would do in Manhattan. To get money. Waitressing probably. She wasn't much good for anything else anymore. She'd find somebody. She always did. She wished the Captain was different and they could sail all the way to Florida together. But he was a stupid smokestack. He reminded her of Sidney. Sidney was the kind you always knew was going to be a doctor or lawyer or something like that. He was always supposed to be so nice but you could never talk to him really. He was always looking down on you and he thought you didn't know it.

That's the kind her mother always wanted her to pay attention to.

The Captain had the same expression—like he was always thinking about something. Sidney was a pediatrician now making lots of money and had four kids, she had heard. "See!" her mother'd say.

Oh, God, not *her*. Why was it her mother appeared when her hands started shaking. The men her mother liked were always rich. Like the Captain here. And Sidney. They're the real hustlers. The women who marry for the money. She shouldn't think that about her mother. She shouldn't think about her mother at all.

It was coming. The wave was coming. The pills weren't going to stop it.

The Captain wasn't Sidney though. He was something different. Really strange, like he knew something he wasn't telling.

When she danced with him last night she remembered, it was like at first he was just an ordinary person but then it got more and more like he was somebody else. He got real light, like he didn't weigh anything at all.

He *knew* something. She wished she could remember what he said. He talked about some Indians and he said something about good and evil.

Why should he talk like that?

There was something else. It had something to do with her grandfather's house.

She tried to remember.

Her grandfather always talked about good and evil. He was a preacher.

Something to do with the Captain. The way he looked at that dead dog and didn't say anything. No, he *did* say something! He said they were all going where the dog was going!

On her grandfather's wall, she remembered now, there'd been a great big picture in his living room where a man was standing in a boat going across a river to an island. At the bottom it said something in German. Her grandfather said it meant "Island of the Dead." Then her grandfather was dead and she always thought of him as going to that island. Where Lucky was. Lucky met him when he got there.

He was always talking about good and evil and how she would go to hell for her sins if she wasn't good. The boatman was taking people across the river to hell to the island because they had sinned.

Lucky, her black and white dog. He looked just like that dog today, floating with his two feet up in the air.

Why did she remember it now? That picture burned up in a fire when her grandfather's house burned down. That's why God burned her grandfather's house down. To send him to hell. It was all mixed up.

Nothing makes any sense, Lila thought. Nothing ever did but now it was worse.

Who *was* he? she wondered. Everything seemed so dreamy. Like she didn't really belong here. There was something wrong with her, she knew there was. But nobody would tell her what it was.

She listened to the wind. It was getting louder. The boat was tipping more and more on its side. Why was this river so empty? Why was this river so lonely? Weren't they supposed to be getting near New York? Where were the other boats?

Why was the wind getting louder?

The people along the bank of the river. They never made a sound when the boat went by. It was as if they couldn't even *see* the boat.

A sudden gust of wind hit and the boat rocked way over to one side and Lila hung on and looked up through the hatchway and could see the Captain. He couldn't see she was watching him and his face was sad and serious as though he was at a funeral. As though he was carrying a coffin. Something was wrong.

Something terrible was coming. Something was going to happen. It couldn't go on like this. She could just feel it in her bones. It was coming. Seeing that dog like that in the water.

It looked like *Lucky*. Why should he come back now?

She knew! They were coming to that place in the mountains! What did the Captain say it was? *"End of the World!"* What did he mean by that!?

What did he MEAN!!

Lila sat back on her berth. She pulled the blanket up around her face and listened. All she could hear was the howl of the the wind and the sound of the water against the side of the boat.

Suddenly came a huge RRRRROAR!!! . . .

She screamed!

11.

Phædrus throttled the engine back to a fast rumbling idle. Then he headed the boat up into the howling wind which caught the sail and cracked it like a whip. He dashed forward and freed the halyard. He pulled the sail down as fast as he could, furled it with a single stop and got back to the tiller again before the boat lost its heading.

Crazy wind. Damn gale through here. They didn't tell him about this in Castleton. Whew!

The water was full of whitecaps and spray. He should have seen that before he reached it. He wasn't paying attention.

He uncleated the topping lift and lowered the boom into its gallows notch, then sat down again.

With the sail down and the engine guiding the boat everything now seemed under control. Storm King Mountain loomed over him to the right and Breakneck Ridge to the left. Up ahead was West Point and the dog-leg in the river called "World's End." Apparently this wind was some sort of funnel-effect from the mountains.

After a while he saw that the wind wasn't getting any worse. It just seemed to hold at a mild gale force.

He'd bought this boat with the illusion that when you sailed you just sat and admired the scenery. It seemed like he hadn't sat still for five minutes in all these days without something needing attention.

Now he saw that he'd furled the sail too sloppily and it was blowing loose. He tied the tiller, went forward again, and this time got all the sail tucked in properly and the stops carefully knotted.

He wondered why Lila was still below somewhere and hadn't

reacted to all this. He supposed he could have gotten her up here to take the tiller while he fixed the sail but something told him it would be easier just to tie it off himself. She wasn't the "aye-aye-sir" sort of crewman you needed for jobs like this.

Up ahead were waves caused by the change in the direction of the river. The water looked angry at having been forced to change its path. As he approached he saw it boil up from below and whirl around in strange eddy currents. He headed the boat away from them.

Everything he said turned out wrong with her. No point in aggravating the situation any further. She lived in another world. She really did. And you could never break into this world by superimposing on it patterns of your own.

What he'd told her about that head-boat was valuable if she'd been listening. But she wasn't. She wasn't a listener. She had a set of fixed static patterns of value and if you argued with her she'd get mad at you and maybe spite you in some way and that's about all. He'd seen enough of that. He'd been bucking that stuff all his life.

At the south entrance to the military academy the wind died away to a mild breeze. The boat passed under the high castle-like walls and he thought of calling Lila up to look at it but decided he'd better not. She wouldn't be interested.

After a while the academy was out of sight and the wind started to pick up again into a sailing breeze. He decided not to put up the sail. The day was running on. He felt tired now. The engine could do it from here.

He sure didn't feel like going anywhere tonight. All he wanted to do was sleep.

Does Lila have Quality? There it was again, Rigel's infuriating question. It would come back again and again like that until he had an answer for it. That was the way his mind worked. Why did he ever answer "yes"? She seemed determined to prove Rigel was right. He shouldn't have given any answer at all.

Does a dog have a Buddha-nature? It's the same question. It's exactly the same question.

You could transpose it right into that whole Zen verse by Mumon:

Does Lila have Quality?
That's the most important question of all.
But if you answer "yes" or you answer "no,"
You lose your own Quality.

That's a perfect transposition. That's exactly what happened. He answered "yes." That was his mistake. He let himself get caught in the kind of "picking-and-choosing" situation that Zen avoids, and now he was stuck.

. . . It wasn't that the question wasn't answerable. It was answerable but the answer went on and on and you never got done.

. . . It isn't Lila that has quality; it's Quality that has Lila. Nothing can have Quality. To have something is to possess it, and to possess something is to dominate it. Nothing dominates Quality. If there's domination and possession involved, it's Quality that dominates and possesses Lila. She's created by it. She's a cohesion of changing static patterns of this Quality. There isn't any more to her than that. The words Lila uses, the thoughts she thinks, the values she holds, are the end product of three and a half billion years of the history of the entire world. She's a kind of jungle of evolutionary patterns of value. She doesn't know how they all got there any more than any jungle knows how it came to be.

And yet there in the middle of this "Lila Jungle" are ancient prehistoric ruins of past civilizations. You could dig into those ruins like an archaeologist layer by layer, through regressive centuries of civilization, measuring by the distance down in the soil, the distance back in time.

That was an intriguing idea. You could structure a whole analysis around this one person, interview her, find out what her values were and then show the entire metaphysics in terms of one specific case. . . . This whole metaphysics was crying for something to bring it down to earth. He could ask her questions all the way to Florida.

He thought about it for a while.

It would be an ideal interviewing situation.

What could she tell him, though? Those patterns might be there but she doesn't know what they are. She'd just sit there and tell him about her typing and her head-boat and all the different kinds of food she likes, and complain about the coffee and he wouldn't get anything. Some trip that would be.

Something else sounded wrong too. It was too contrived, too full of objective "observational" stuff. It ignored the whole Dynamic aspect. There is always this open end of Dynamic indeterminacy. It would be impossible to predict anything from what she said.

Also, she didn't think much of him. She probably wouldn't tell him anything. Just like the Indians and the "objective" anthros.

Dusenberry should be here. He could get it out of her. All I'm good for is theory, Phædrus thought.

But the theory was okay. Lila is composed of static patterns of value and these patterns are evolving toward a Dynamic Quality. That's the theory, anyway. She's on her way somewhere, just like everybody else. And you can't say where that somewhere is.

The theory had arrived in his mind several months ago with the statement, "All life is a migration of static patterns of quality toward Dynamic Quality." It had been boiling around in his mind ever since.

In traditional, substance-centered metaphysics, life isn't evolving toward anything. Life's just an extension of the properties of atoms, nothing more. It has to be that because atoms and varying forms of energy are all there is. But in the Metaphysics of Quality, what is evolving isn't patterns of atoms. What's evolving is static patterns of value, and while that doesn't change the data of evolution it completely up-ends the interpretation that can be given to evolution.

Historically this assumption by a subject-object metaphysics that all the world is composed of substance put a strain on the Theory of Evolution right from its beginning. At the time of its origin it wasn't yet understood that at the level of photons and electrons and other small particles the laws of cause and effect no longer apply; that electrons and photons simply appear and disappear without individual predictability and without individual cause. So today we have as a result a theory of evolution in which "man" is ruthlessly controlled by the cause-and-effect laws of the universe while the particles of his body are not. The absurdity of this seems to be neglected. The problem doesn't lie in anyone's department. Physicists can ignore it because they are not concerned with man. Social scientists can ignore it because they are not concerned with subatomic particles.

So although modern physics pulled the rug out from under the deterministic explanation of evolution many decades ago, it has survived by default because no other more plausible explanation has been available. But right from the beginning, substance-caused evolution has always had a puzzling aspect that it has never been able to eliminate. It goes into many volumes about how the fittest survive but never once answers the question of why.

This is the sort of irrelevant-sounding question that seems minor at first, and the mind looks for a quick answer to dismiss it. It sounds like one of those hostile, ignorant questions some fundamentalist preacher might think up. But why do the fittest survive? Why does any life survive? It's illogical. It's self-contradictory that life should survive. If life is strictly a result of the physical and chemical forces of nature then why is life opposed to these same forces in its struggle to survive? Either life is with physical nature or it's against it. If it's with nature there's nothing to survive. If it's against physical nature then there must be something apart from the physical and chemical forces of nature that is motivating it to be against physical nature. The Second Law of Thermodynamics states that all energy systems "run down" like a clock and never rewind themselves. But life not only "runs up," converting low energy sea-water, sunlight and air into high-energy chemicals, it keeps multiplying itself into more and better clocks that keep "running up" faster and faster.

Why, for example, should a group of simple, stable compounds of carbon, hydrogen, oxygen and nitrogen struggle for billions of years to organize themselves into a professor of chemistry? What's the motive? If we leave a chemistry professor out on a rock in the sun long enough the forces of nature will convert him into simple compounds of carbon, oxygen, hydrogen and nitrogen, calcium, phosphorus, and small amounts of other minerals. It's a one-way reaction. No matter what kind of chemistry professor we use and no matter what process we use we can't turn these compounds back into a chemistry professor. Chemistry professors are unstable mixtures of predominantly unstable compounds which, in the exclusive presence of the sun's heat, decay irreversibly into simpler organic and inorganic compounds. That's a scientific fact.

The question is: Then why does nature reverse this process? What on earth causes the inorganic compounds to go the other way? It isn't the sun's energy. We just saw what the sun's energy did. It has to be something else. What is it?

Nowhere on the pages of all that he had read about evolution did Phædrus see any answer. He knew of theological answers, of course, but these aren't supported by scientific observation. Evolutionists, in their reply, simply say that in the scientific observation of the facts of the universe no goal or pattern has ever appeared toward which life is heading.

This last statement so neatly sweeps the whole matter under the carpet one would never guess that it was of much concern to evolutionists at all. But a reading of the early history of the theories of evolution shows this is not true. The first major evolutionist, who was not Darwin but Jean Baptiste Lamarck, maintained that all life was evolving toward perfection, a synonym for Quality. Alfred Wallace, who forced Darwin to publish by independently arriving at an almost identical theory, also maintained that natural selection was not enough to account for the development of man. After Darwin many others continued to deny the goallessness of life.

Phædrus had found a good summary of the entire matter in a *Scientific American* article by Ernst Mayr.

> *Those who rejected natural selection on religious or philosophical grounds or simply because it seemed too random a process to explain evolution continued for many years to put forward alternative schemes with such names as orthogenesis, nomogenesis, aristogenesis or the "Omega Principle" of Teilhard de Chardin, each scheme relying on some built-in tendency or drive toward perfection or progress. All these theories were finalistic; they postulated some form of cosmic teleology or purpose or program.*

> *The proponents of teleological theories, for all their efforts, have been unable to find any mechanism (except supernatural ones) that can account for their postulated finalism. The possibility that any such mechanism can exist has now been virtually ruled out by the findings of molecular biology.*

> *Evolution is recklessly opportunistic: it favors any variation that provides a competitive advantage over other members of an organism's*

own population or over individuals of different species. For billions of years this process has automatically fueled what we call evolutionary progress. No program controlled or directed this progression. It was the result of spur of the moment decisions of natural selection.

Mayr certainly seemed to consider the matter settled and this attitude, no doubt, reflected a consensus among everyone except anti-evolutionists. But after reading it Phædrus wrote on one of his slips, "It seems clear that no mechanistic pattern exists toward which life is heading, but has the question been taken up of whether life is heading away from mechanistic patterns?"

He guessed that the question had not been taken up at all. The concepts necessary for taking it up were not at hand. In a metaphysics in which static universal laws are considered fundamental, the idea that life is evolving away from any law just draws a baffled question mark. It doesn't make any sense. It seems to say that all life is headed toward chaos, since chaos is the only alternative to structural patterns that a law-bound metaphysics can conceive.

But Dynamic Quality is not structured and yet it is not chaotic. It is value that cannot be contained by static patterns. What the substance-centered evolutionists were showing with their absence of final "mechanisms" or "programs" was not an air-tight case for the biological goallessness of life. What they were unintentionally showing was a superb example of how values create reality.

Science values static patterns. Its business is to search for them. When non-conformity appears it is considered an interruption of the normal rather than the presence of the normal. A deviation from a normal static pattern is something to be explained and if possible controlled. The reality science explains is that "reality" which follows mechanisms and programs. That other worthless stuff which doesn't follow mechanisms and programs we don't pay any attention to.

See how this works? A thing doesn't exist because we have never observed it. The reason we have never observed it is because we have never looked for it. And the reason we have never looked for it is that it is unimportant, it has no value and we have other better things to do.

Because of his different metaphysical orientation Phædrus saw instantly that those seemingly trivial, unimportant, "spur of the moment" decisions that Mayr was talking about, the decisions that directed the progress of evolution are, in fact, Dynamic Quality itself. Dynamic Quality, the source of all things, the pre-intellectual cutting edge of reality, always appears as "spur of the moment." Where else could it appear?

When this prejudice against "spur of the moment" Dynamic Quality is removed new worlds of reality open up. Naturally there is no mechanism toward which life is heading. Mechanisms are the enemy of life. The more static and unyielding the mechanisms are, the more life works to evade them or overcome them.

The law of gravity, for example, is perhaps the most ruthlessly static pattern of order in the universe. So, correspondingly, there is no single living thing that does not thumb its nose at that law day in and day out. One could almost define life as the organized disobedience of the law of gravity. One could show that the degree to which an organism disobeys this law is a measure of its degree of evolution. Thus, while the simple protozoa just barely get around on their cilia, earthworms manage to control their distance and direction, birds fly into the sky, and man goes all the way to the moon.

A similar analysis could be made with other physical laws such as the Second Law of Thermodynamics, and it seemed to Phædrus that if one gathered together enough of these deliberate violations of the laws of the universe and formed a generalization from them, a quite different theory of evolution could be inferred. If life is to be explained on the basis of physical laws, then the overwhelming evidence that life deliberately works around these laws cannot be ignored. The reason atoms become chemistry professors has got to be that something in nature does not like laws of chemical equilibrium or the law of gravity or the laws of thermodynamics or any other law that restricts the molecules' freedom. They only go along with laws of any kind because they have to, preferring an existence that does not follow any laws whatsoever.

This would explain why patterns of life do not change solely in accord with causative "mechanisms" or "programs" or blind operations of physical laws. They do not just change valuelessly. They change in ways that evade, override and circumvent these laws. The patterns of life are constantly evolving in response to something "better" than that which these laws have to offer.

This would at first seem to contradict the one thing that evolutionists insist upon most: that life is not responding to anything but the "survival of the fittest" process of natural selection. But "survival-of-the-fittest" is one of those catch-phrases like "mutants" or "misfits" that sounds best when you don't ask precisely what it means. Fittest for what? Fittest for survival? That reduces to "survival of the survivors," which doesn't say anything. "Survival of the fittest" is meaningful only when "fittest" is equated with "best," which is to say, "Quality." And the Darwinians don't mean just any old quality, they mean undefined Quality! As Mayr's article makes clear, they are absolutely certain there is no way to define what that "fittest" is.

Good! The "undefined fittest" they are defending is identical to Dynamic Quality. Natural selection is Dynamic Quality at work. There is no quarrel whatsoever between the Metaphysics of Quality and the Darwinian Theory of Evolution. Neither is there a quarrel between the Metaphysics of Quality and the "teleological" theories which insist that life has some purpose. What the Metaphysics of Quality has done is unite these opposed doctrines within a larger metaphysical structure that accommodates both of them without contradiction.

The river was opening up now into a broad lake that the chart beside Phædrus identified as the Tappan Zee. Like the Zuider Zee, he supposed. Nice that they'd kept the old Dutch name. He turned and looked behind him and there was the mountain range that he'd passed through. The last range. The American continent was coming to an end. Soon this strong heavy boat would be out in the Atlantic for the first time, where it really belonged. That felt exciting after all these weeks. The boat was built to cross oceans and circumnavigate continents, not just "run the buoys" down placid inland waterways.

It was still early afternoon. The boat was making ferocious speed. He supposed that contraction of the river by the mountains must have made it speed up. Now, according to his calculations, the tide would begin to reverse and it would be slower going.

· · ·

Anyway, that "migration of static patterns toward Dynamic Quality" he'd been thinking so much about seemed to hold up so far. In the past when ideas like it had been defeated they were always knocked down by the assumptions of a conventional metaphysics of substance, but with the Metaphysics of Quality behind it, it stood up. He'd tried dozens of times to think of how it could be knocked down with one argument or another but he'd never found anything that worked. And so in the months since it had emerged he had tried to work out various refinements.

The explanation of life as a "migration of static patterns toward Dynamic Quality" not only fitted the known facts of evolution, it allowed new ways of interpreting them.

Biological evolution can be seen as a process by which weak Dynamic forces at a subatomic level discover stratagems for overcoming huge static inorganic forces at a superatomic level. They do this by selecting superatomic mechanisms in which a number of options are so evenly balanced that a weak Dynamic force can tip the balance one way or another.

The particular atom that the weak Dynamic subatomic forces have seized as their primary vehicle is carbon. All life contains carbon yet a study of properties of carbon atom shows that except for the extreme hardness of one of its crystalline forms there is not much unusual about it. In terms of other physical constants of melting point, conductivity, ionization, and so on it does just about what its position on the periodic table of the elements suggests it might do. Certainly there's no hint of any miraculous powers waiting to spring chemistry professors upon a lifeless planet.

One physical characteristic that makes carbon unique is that it is the lightest and most active of the group IV of atoms whose chemical bonding characteristics are ambiguous. Usually the positively valanced metals in groups I through III combine chemically with negatively valanced non-metals in groups V through VII and not with other members of their own group. But the group containing carbon is halfway between the metals and non-metals, so that sometimes carbon combines with metals and sometimes with non-metals, and sometimes it just sits there and doesn't combine with anything, and sometimes it combines with itself in long chains and branched trees and rings.

Phædrus thought this ambiguity of carbon's bonding preferences was the situation the weak Dynamic subatomic forces needed. Carbon bonding was a balanced mechanism they could take over. It was a vehicle they could steer to all sorts of freedom by selecting first one bonding preference and then another in an almost unlimited variety of ways.

And what a variety has been chosen. Today there are more than two million known compounds of carbon, roughly twenty times as many as all the other known chemical compounds in the world. The chemistry of life is the chemistry of carbon. What distinguishes all the species of plants and animals is, in the final analysis, differences in the way carbon atoms choose to bond.

But the invention of Dynamic carbon bonding represents only one kind of evolutionary stratagem. The other kind is preservation of what has been invented. A Dynamic advance is meaningless unless it can find some static pattern with which to protect itself from degeneration back to the conditions that existed before the advance was made. Evolution can't be a continuous forward movement. It must be a process of ratchet-like steps in which there is a Dynamic movement forward up some new incline and then, if the result looks successful, a static latching-on of the gain that has been made; then another Dynamic advance, then another static latch.

What the Dynamic force had to invent in order to move up the molecular level and stay there was a carbon molecule that would preserve its limited Dynamic freedom from inorganic laws and at the same time resist deterioration back to simple compounds of carbon again. A study of nature shows the Dynamic force was not able to do this but got around the problem by inventing two molecules: a static molecule able to resist abrasion, heat, chemical attack and the like; and a Dynamic one, able to preserve the subatomic indeterminacy at a molecular level and "try everything" in the ways of chemical combination.

The static molecule, an enormous, chemically "dead," plastic-like molecule called protein, surrounds the Dynamic one and prevents attack by forces of light, heat and other chemicals that would prey on its sensitivity and destroy it. The Dynamic one, called DNA, reciprocates by telling the static one what to do, replacing the static one when it wears out, replacing itself even when it hasn't worn out, and changing its own nature to overcome adverse conditions. These two kinds of molecules, working together, are all there is in some viruses, which are the simplest forms of life.

This division of all biological evolutionary patterns into a Dynamic function and a static function continues on up through higher levels of evolution. The formation of semi-permeable cell walls to let food in and keep poisons out is a static latch. So are bones, shells, hide, fur, burrows, clothes, houses, villages, castles, rituals, symbols, laws and libraries. All of these prevent evolutionary degeneration.

On the other hand, the shift in cell reproduction from mitosis to meiosis to permit sexual choice and allow huge DNA diversification is a Dynamic advance. So is the collective organization of cells into metazoan societies called plants and animals. So are sexual choice, symbiosis, death and regeneration, communality, communication, speculative thought, curiosity and art. Most of these, when viewed in a substance-centered evolutionary way, are thought of as mere incidental properties of the molecular machine. But in a value-centered explanation of evolution they are close to the Dynamic process itself, pulling the pattern of life forward to greater levels of versatility and freedom.

Sometimes a Dynamic increment goes forward but can find no latching mechanism and so fails and slips back to a previous latched position. Whole species and cultures get lost this way. Sometimes a static pattern becomes so powerful it prohibits any Dynamic moves forward. In both cases the evolutionary process is halted for a while. But when it's not halted the result has been an increase in power to control hostile forces or an increase in versatility or both. The increase in versatility is directed toward Dynamic Quality. The increase in power to control hostile forces is directed toward static quality. Without Dynamic Quality the organism cannot grow. Without static quality the organism cannot last. Both are needed.

Now when we come to the chemistry professor, and see him studying his empirically gathered data, trying to figure out what it means, this person makes more sense. He's not just some impartial visitor from outer space looking in on all this with no purpose other than to observe. Neither is he some static, molecular, objective, biological machine, doing all this for absolutely no purpose whatsoever. We see that he's conducting his experiments for exactly the same purpose as the subatomic forces had when they had first began to create him billions of years ago. He's looking for information that will expand the static patterns of evolution itself and give both greater versatility and greater stability against hostile static forces of nature. He may have personal motives such as "pure fun," that is, the Dynamic Quality of his work. But when he applies for funds he will normally and properly tie his request to some branch of humanity's overall evolutionary purpose.

12.

Phædrus had once called metaphysics "the high country of the mind"—an analogy to the "high country" of mountain climbing. It takes a lot of effort to get there and more effort when you arrive, but unless you can make the journey you are confined to one valley of thought all your life. This high country passage through the Metaphysics of Quality allowed entry to another valley of thought in which the facts of life get a much richer interpretation. The valley spreads out into a huge fertile plain of understanding.

In this plain of understanding static patterns of value are divided into four systems: inorganic patterns, biological patterns, social patterns and intellectual patterns. They are exhaustive. That's all there are. If you construct an encyclopedia of four topics—Inorganic, Biological, Social and Intellectual—nothing is left out. No "thing," that is. Only Dynamic Quality, which cannot be described in any encyclopedia, is absent.

But although the four systems are exhaustive they are not exclusive. They all operate at the same time and in ways that are almost independent of each other.

This classification of patterns is not very original, but the Metaphysics of Quality allows an assertion about them that is unusual. It says they are not continuous. They are discrete. They have very little to do with one another. Although each higher level is built on a lower one it is not an extension of that lower level. Quite the contrary. The higher level can often be seen to be in opposition to the lower level, dominating it, controlling it where possible for its own purposes.

This observation is impossible in a substance-dominated metaphysics where everything has to be an extension of matter. But now atoms and molecules are just one of four levels of static patterns of quality and there is no intellectual requirement that any level dominate the other three.

An excellent analogy to the independence of the levels, Phædrus thought, is the relation of hardware to software in a computer. He had learned something about this relationship when for several years he wrote technical manuals describing complex military computers. He had learned how to troubleshoot computers electronically. He had even wired up some of his own digital circuits which, in those days before integrated circuit chips, were composed of independent transistors, diodes, resistors and capacitors all held together with wire and solder. But after four years in which he had acquired all this knowledge he had only the vaguest idea of what a program was. None of the electrical engineers he worked with had anything to do with programs. Programmers were off in another building somewhere.

Later, when he got into work with programmers, he discovered to his surprise that even advanced programmers seldom knew how a flip-flop worked. That was amazing. A flip-flop is a circuit that stores a "1" or a "0." If you don't know how a flip-flop works, what do you know about computers?

The answer was that it isn't necessary for a programmer to learn circuit design. Neither is it necessary for a hardware technician to learn programming. The two sets of patterns are independent. Except for a memory map and a tiny isthmus of information called the "Machine Language Instruction Repertoire"—a list so small you could write it on a single page—the electronic circuits and the programs existing in the same computer at the same time have nothing whatsoever to do with each other.

The Machine Language Instruction Repertoire fascinated Phædrus because he had seen it from such different perspectives. He had written hardware descriptions of many hundreds of blueprints showing how voltage levels were transferred from one bank of flipflops to another to create a single machine language instruction. These Machine Language instructions were the final achievement toward which all the circuits aimed. They were the end performance of a whole symphony of switching operations.

Then when he got into programming he found that this symphony of electronic circuits was considered to be a mere single note in a whole other symphony that had no resemblance to the first one. The gating circuits, the rise and decay times, the margins for voltage levels, were gone. Even his banks of flip-flops had become "registers." Everything was seen from a pure and symbolic world of logical relationships that had no resemblance at all to the "real" world he had worked in. The Machine Language Instruction Repertoire, which had been the entire design goal, was now the lowest element of the lowest level programming language. Most programmers never used these instructions directly or even knew what they meant.

Although both the circuit designer and the programmer knew the meaning of the instruction, "Load Accumulator," the meaning that each knew was entirely different from the other's. Their only relationship was that of analogy. A register is analogous to a bank of flip-flops. A change in voltage level is analogous to a change in number. But they are not the same. Even in this narrow isthmus between these two sets of static patterns called "hardware" and "software" there was still no direct interchange of meaning. The same machine language instruction was a completely different entity within two different sets of patterns.

On top of this low-level programming language was a high-level programming language, FORTRAN or COBOL in those days, which had the same kind of independence from the low-level language that the low-level language had from electronic circuits. And on top of the high-level language was still another level of patterns, the application, a novel perhaps in a word-processing program. And what amazed him most of all was how one could spend all of eternity probing the electrical patterns of that computer with an oscilloscope and never find that novel.

What makes all this significant to the Metaphysics of Quality is its striking parallelism to the interrelationship of different levels of static patterns of quality.

Certainly the novel cannot exist in the computer without a parallel pattern of voltages to support it. But that does not mean that the novel is an expression or property of those voltages. It doesn't have to exist in any electronic circuits at all. It can also reside in magnetic domains on a disk or a drum or a tape, but again it is not composed of magnetic domains nor is it possessed by them. It can reside in a notebook but it is not composed of or possessed by the ink and paper. It can reside in the brain of a programmer, but even here it is neither composed of this brain nor possessed by it. The same program can be made to run on an infinite variety of computers. A program can change itself into a different program while it is running. It can turn on another computer, transfer itself into this second computer and shut off the first computer that it came from, destroying every last trace of its origins—a process with similarities to biological reproduction.

Trying to explain social moral patterns in terms of inorganic chemistry patterns is like trying to explain the plot of a word-processor novel in terms of the computer's electronics. You can't do it. You can see how the circuits make the novel possible, but they do not provide a plot for the novel. The novel is its own set of patterns. Similarly the biological patterns of life and the molecular patterns of organic chemistry have a "machine language" interface called DNA but that does not mean that the carbon or hydrogen or oxygen atoms possess or guide life. A primary occupation of every level of evolution seems to be offering freedom to lower levels of evolution. But as the higher level gets more sophisticated it goes off on purposes of its own.

Once this independent nature of the levels of static patterns of value is understood a lot of puzzles get solved. The first one is the usual puzzle of value itself. In a subject-object metaphysics value has always been the most vague and ambiguous of terms. What is it? When you say the world is composed of nothing but value, what are you talking about?

Phædrus thought this was why no one before had ever seemed to have come up with the idea that the world is primarily value. The word is too vague. The "value" that holds a glass of water together and the "value" that holds a nation together are obviously not the same thing. Therefore to say that the world is nothing but value is just confusing, not clarifying.

Now this vagueness is removed by sorting out values according to levels of evolution. The value that holds a glass of water together is an inorganic pattern of value. The value that holds a nation together is a social pattern of value. They are completely different from each other because they are at different evolutionary levels. And they are completely different from the biological pattern that can cause the most skeptical of intellectuals to leap from a hot stove. These patterns have nothing in common except the historic evolutionary process that created all of them. But that process is a process of value evolution. Therefore the name "static pattern of values" applies to all.

That's one puzzle cleared up. Another huge one is the mind-matter puzzle.

If the world consists only of patterns of mind and patterns of matter, what is the relationship between the two? If you read the hundreds of volumes of philosophy available on this matter you may conclude that nobody knows—or at least knows well enough to convince everybody else. There is the materialist school that says reality is all matter, which creates mind. There is the idealist school that says it is all mind, which creates matter. There is the positivist school which says this argument could go on forever; drop the subject.

That would be nice if you could, but unfortunately it is one of the most tormenting problems of the physics to which positivism looks for guidance. The torment occurs not because of anything discovered in the laboratory. Data are data. It is the intellectual framework with which one deals with the data that is at fault. The fault is within subject-object metaphysics itself.

A conventional subject-object metaphysics uses the same four static patterns as the Metaphysics of Quality, dividing them into two groups of two: inorganic-biological patterns called "matter," and social-intellectual patterns called "mind." But this division is the source of the problem. When a subject-object metaphysics regards matter and mind as eternally separate and eternally unlike, it creates a platypus bigger than the solar system.

It has to make this fatal division because it gives top position in its structure to subjects and objects. Everything has got to be object or subject, substance or non-substance, because that's the primary division of the universe. Inorganic-biological patterns are composed of "substance," and are therefore "objective." Social-intellectual patterns are not composed of "substance" and are therefore called "subjective." Then, having made this arbitrary division based on "substance," conventional metaphysics then asks, "What is the relationship between mind and matter, between subject and object?"

One answer is to fudge both mind and matter and the whole question that goes with them into another platypus called "man." "Man" has a body (and therefore is not himself a body) and he also has a mind (and therefore is not himself a mind). But if one asks what is this "man" (which is not a body and not a mind) one doesn't come up with anything. There isn't any "man" independent of the patterns. Man is the patterns.

This fictitious "man" has many synonyms: "mankind," "people," "the public," and even such pronouns as "I," "he," and "they." Our language is so organized around them and they are so convenient to use it is impossible to get rid of them. There is really no need to. Like "substance" they can be used as long as it is remembered that they're terms for collections of patterns and not some independent primary reality of their own.

In a value-centered Metaphysics of Quality the four sets of static patterns are not isolated into separate compartments of mind and matter. Matter is just a name for certain inorganic value patterns. Biological patterns, social patterns, and intellectual patterns are supported by this pattern of matter but are independent of it. They have rules and laws of their own that are not derivable from the rules or laws of substance. This is not the customary way of thinking, but, when you stop to think about it you wonder how you ever got conned into thinking otherwise. What, after all, is the likelihood that an atom possesses within its own structure enough information to build the city of New York? Biological and social and intellectual patterns are not the possession of substance. The laws that create and destroy these patterns are not the laws of electrons and protons and other elementary particles. The forces that create and destroy these patterns are the forces of value.

So what the Metaphysics of Quality concludes is that all schools are right on the mind-matter question. Mind is contained in static inorganic patterns. Matter is contained in static intellectual patterns. Both mind and matter are completely separate evolutionary levels of static patterns of value, and as such are capable of each containing the other without contradiction.

The mind-matter paradoxes seem to exist because the connecting links between these two levels of value patterns have been disregarded. Two terms are missing: biology and society. Mental patterns do not originate out of inorganic nature. They originate out of society, which originates out of biology which originates out of inorganic nature. And, as anthropologists know so well, what a mind thinks is as dominated by social patterns as social patterns are dominated by biological patterns and as biological patterns are dominated by inorganic patterns. There is no direct scientific connection between mind and matter. As the atomic physicist, Niels Bohr, said, "We are suspended in language." Our intellectual description of nature is always culturally derived.

The intellectual level of patterns, in the historic process of freeing itself from its parent social level, namely the church, has tended to invent a myth of independence from the social level for its own benefit. Science and reason, this myth goes, come only from the objective world, never from the social world. The world of objects imposes itself upon the mind with no social mediation whatsoever. It is easy to see the historic reasons for this myth of independence. Science might never have survived without it. But a close examination shows it isn't so.

A third puzzle illuminated by the Metaphysics of Quality is the ancient "free will vs. determinism controversy." Determinism is the philosophic doctrine that man, like all other objects in the universe, follows fixed scientific laws, and does so without exception. Free will is the philosophic doctrine that man makes choices independent of the atoms of his body.

This battle has been a very long and very loud one because an abandonment of either position has devastating logical consequences. If the belief in free will is abandoned, morality must seemingly also be abandoned under a subject-object metaphysics. If man follows the cause-and-effect laws of substance, then man cannot really choose between right and wrong.

On the other hand, if the determinists let go of their position it would seem to deny the truth of science. If one adheres to a traditional scientific metaphysics of substance, the philosophy of determinism is an inescapable corollary. If "everything" is included in the class of "substance and its properties," and if "substance and its properties" is included in the class of "things that always follow laws," and if "people" are included in the class "everything," then it is an airtight logical conclusion that people always follow the laws of substance.

To be sure, it doesn't seem as though people blindly follow the laws of substance in everything they do, but within a Deterministic explanation that is just another one of those illusions that science is forever exposing. All the social sciences, including anthropology, were founded on the bedrock metaphysical belief that these physical cause-and-effect laws of human behavior exist. Moral laws, if they can be said to exist at all, are merely an artificial social code that has nothing to do with the real nature of the world. A "moral" person acts conventionally, "watches out for the cops," "keeps his nose clean," and nothing more.

In the Metaphysics of Quality this dilemma doesn't come up. To the extent that one's behavior is controlled by static patterns of quality it is without choice. But to the extent that one follows Dynamic Quality, which is undefinable, one's behavior is free.

The Metaphysics of Quality has much much more to say about ethics, however, than simple resolution of the Free Will vs. Determinism controversy. The Metaphysics of Quality says that if moral judgments are essentially assertions of value and if value is the fundamental ground-stuff of the world, then moral judgments are the fundamental ground-stuff of the world.

It says that even at the most fundamental level of the universe, static patterns of value and moral judgment are identical. The "Laws of Nature" are moral laws. Of course it sounds peculiar at first and awkward and unnecessary to say that hydrogen and oxygen form water because it is moral to do so. But it is no less peculiar and awkward and unnecessary than to say chemistry professors smoke pipes and go to movies because irresistible cause-and-effect forces of the cosmos force them to do it. In the past the logic has been that if chemistry professors are composed exclusively of atoms and if atoms follow only the law of cause and effect, then chemistry professors must follow the laws of cause and effect too. But this logic can be applied in a reverse direction. We can just as easily deduce the morality of atoms from the observation that chemistry professors are, in general, moral. If chemistry professors exercise choice, and chemistry professors are composed exclusively of atoms, then it follows that atoms must exercise choice too. The difference between these two points of view is philosophic, not scientific. The question of whether an electron does a certain thing because it has to or because it wants to is completely irrelevant to the data of what the electron does.

So what Phædrus was saying was that not just life, but everything, is an ethical activity. It is nothing else. When inorganic patterns of reality create life the Metaphysics of Quality postulates that they've done so because it's "better" and that this definition of "betterness"—this beginning response to Dynamic Quality—is an elementary unit of ethics upon which all right and wrong can be based.

When this understanding first broke through in Phædrus' mind, that ethics and science had suddenly been integrated into a single system, he became so manic he couldn't think of anything else for days. The only time he had been more manic about an abstract idea was when he had first hit upon the idea of undefined Quality itself. The consequences of that first mania had been disastrous, and so now, this time, he told himself just to calm down and dig in. It was, for him, a great Dynamic breakthrough, but if he wanted to hang on to it he had better do some static latching as quickly and thoroughly as possible.

13.

Latching was what was needed all right. Historically every effort to unite science and ethics has been a disaster. You can't paste a moral system on top of a pile of amoral objective matter. The amoral objective matter never needs this paste job. It always sloughs it off as superfluous.

But the Metaphysics of Quality doesn't permit this slough-off. It says, first of all, that "amoral objective matter" is a low-grade form of morality. No slough-off is possible. It states, second of all, that even if matter weren't a low grade form of morality there still would be no metaphysical need to show how morals are derived from it. With static patterns of value divided into four systems, conventional moral patterns have almost nothing to do with inorganic or biological nature. These moral patterns are superimposed upon inorganic nature the way novels are superimposed upon computers. They are more commonly opposed to biological patterns than they are supportive of them.

And that is the key to the whole thing.

What the evolutionary structure of the Metaphysics of Quality shows is that there is not just one moral system. There are many. In the Metaphysics of Quality there's the morality called the "laws of nature," by which inorganic patterns triumph over chaos; there is a morality called the "law of the jungle" where biology triumphs over the inorganic forces of starvation and death; there's a morality where social patterns triumph over biology, "the law"; and there is an intellectual morality, which is still struggling in its attempts to control society. Each of these sets of moral codes is no more related to the other than novels are to flip-flops.

What is today conventionally called "morality" covers only one of these sets of moral codes, the social-biological code. In a subject-object metaphysics this single social-biological code is considered to be a minor, "subjective," physically non-existent part of the universe. But in the Metaphysics of Quality all these sets of morals, plus another Dynamic morality, are not only real, they are the whole thing.

In general, given a choice of two courses to follow and all other things being equal, that choice which is more Dynamic, that is, at a higher level of evolution, is more moral. An example of this is the statement that, "It's more moral for a doctor to kill a germ than to allow the germ to kill his patient." The germ wants to live. The patient wants to live. But the patient has moral precedence because he's at a higher level of evolution.

Taken by itself that seems obvious enough. But what's not so obvious is that, given a value-centered Metaphysics of Quality, it is absolutely, scientifically moral for a doctor to prefer the patient. This is not just an arbitrary social convention that should apply to some doctors but not to all doctors, or to some cultures but not all cultures. It's true for all people at all time, now and forever, a moral pattern of reality as real as H_2O. We're at last dealing with morals on the basis of reason. We can now deduce codes based on evolution that analyze moral arguments with greater precision than before.

In the moral evolutionary conflict between the germ and the patient, the evolutionary spread is enormous and as a result the morality of the situation is obvious. But when the static patterns in conflict are closer the moral force of the situation becomes less obvious.

A popular moral issue that parallels the germ-patient issue is vegetarianism. Is it immoral, as the Hindus and Buddhists claim, to eat the flesh of animals? Our current morality would say it's immoral only if you're a Hindu or Buddhist. Otherwise it's okay, since morality is nothing more than a social convention.

An evolutionary morality, on the other hand, would say it's scientifically immoral for everyone because animals are at a higher level of evolution, that is, more Dynamic, than are grains and fruits and vegetables. But the moral force of this injunction is not so great because the levels of evolution are closer together than the doctor's patient and the germ. It would add, also, that this moral principle holds only where there is an abundance of grains and fruits and vegetables. It would be immoral for Hindus not to eat their cows in a time of famine, since they would then be killing human beings in favor of a lower organism.

Because a value-centered Metaphysics of Quality is not tied to substance it is free to consider moral issues at higher evolutionary levels than germs and fruits and vegetables. At these higher levels the issues become more interesting.

Is it scientifically moral for a society to kill a human being? That is a very big moral question still being fought in courts and legislatures all over the world.

An evolutionary morality would at first seem to say yes, a society has a right to murder people to prevent its own destruction. A primitive isolated village threatened by brigands has a moral right and obligation to kill them in self-defense since a village is a higher form of evolution. When the United States drafted troops for the Civil War everyone knew that innocent people would be murdered. The North could have permitted the slave states to become independent and saved hundreds of thousands of lives. But an evolutionary morality argues that the North was right in pursuing that war because a nation is a higher form of evolution than a human body, and the principle of human equality is an even higher form than a nation. John Brown's truth was never an abstraction. It still keeps marching on.

When a society is not itself threatened, as in the execution of individual criminals, the issue becomes more complex. In the case of treason or insurrection or war a criminal's threat to a society can be very real. But if an established social structure is not seriously threatened by a criminal, then an evolutionary morality would argue that there is no moral justification for killing him.

What makes killing him immoral is that a criminal is not just a biological organism. He is not even just a defective unit of society. Whenever you kill a human being you are killing a source of thought too. A human being is a collection of ideas, and these ideas take moral precedence over a society. Ideas are patterns of value. They are at a higher level of evolution than social patterns of value. Just as it is more moral for a doctor to kill a germ than a patient, so it is more moral for an idea to kill a society than it is for a society to kill an idea.

And beyond that is an even more compelling reason: societies and thoughts and principles themselves are no more than sets of static patterns. These patterns can't by themselves perceive or adjust to Dynamic Quality. Only a living being can do that. The strongest moral argument against capital punishment is that it weakens a society's Dynamic capability—its capability for change and evolution. It's not the "nice" guys who bring about real social change. "Nice" guys look nice because they're conforming. It's the "bad" guys, who only look nice a hundred years later, that are the real Dynamic force in social evolution. That was the real moral lesson of the *brujo* in Zuñi. If those priests had killed him they would have done great harm to their society's ability to grow and change.

It was tempting to take all the moral conflicts of the world and, one by one, see how they fit this kind of analysis, but Phædrus realized that if he started to get into that he would never finish. Wherever he looked, whatever examples came to mind, he always seemed to be able to lay them out within this framework, and the nature of the conflicts usually seemed to be clearer when he did so.

And as a matter of fact that looked like the answer to Rigel's question that had been bugging him all day: "Does Lila have Quality?"

Biologically she does, socially she doesn't. Obviously! Evolutionary morality just splits that whole question open like a watermelon. Since biological and social patterns have almost nothing to do with each other, Lila does and Lila does not have quality at the same time. That's exactly the feeling she gave too—a sort of mixed feeling of quality and no quality at the same time. That was the reason.

How simple it was. That's the mark of a high-quality theory. It doesn't just answer the question in some complex round-about way. It dissolves the question, so you wonder why you ever asked it.

Biologically she's fine, socially she's pretty far down the scale, intellectually she's nowhere. But Dynamically . . . Ah! That's the one to watch. There's something ferociously Dynamic going on with her. All that aggression, that tough talk, those strange bewildered blue eyes. Like sitting next to a hill that's rumbling and letting off steam here and there. . . . It would be interesting to talk to her more.

He stepped forward to the hatchway and looked down. It looked as though she was sleeping on the bunk down there. He could use some of that himself. Tonight she'd probably be wide awake and raring to go. He'd be all zonked out.

Phædrus saw that an approaching buoy was slanting slightly toward him and that at its base was a little wake from a current running against him. The river was flowing backward now and it would be slow going. It would be dark soon too, but fortunately they didn't have far to go.

The position of a barge up ahead indicated his boat was getting too far over on the New York City side of the river. He brought his bow back a few degrees so as to stay out of any oncoming traffic. On the big expanse of water before him he saw a barge being pushed from behind by a tug-boat. The barge had pipes along the top that meant it was probably carrying oil or chemicals. It was heading toward him and although he figured there was no danger of collision he set a course anyway that would give it an even wider separation.

The banks of this "sea" were far away but he could see that the buildings and shore installations were metropolitan. No hills rose back of them, only a dull industrial haze. He looked at his watch. Three-thirty. A couple of hours of sunlight yet. It looked like they would get to Nyack before dark. This boat had really made time today. All the hurricane flood water on top of the tides on top of the natural river current had done it.

Anyway that was the answer to Rigel's question. Phædrus could relax now. Rigel was just pushing a narrow tradition-bound socio-biological code of morals which it was certain he didn't understand himself.

As Phædrus had gotten into them he had seen that the isolation of these static moral codes was important. They were really little moral empires all their own, as separate from one another as the static levels whose conflicts they resolved:

First, there were moral codes that established the supremacy of biological life over inanimate nature. Second, there were moral codes that established the supremacy of the social order over biological life— conventional morals—proscriptions against drugs, murder, adultery, theft and the like. Third, there were moral codes that established the supremacy of the intellectual order over the social order—democracy, trial by jury, freedom of speech, freedom of the press. Finally there's a fourth Dynamic morality which isn't a code. He supposed you could call it a "code of Art" or something like that, but art is usually thought of as such a frill that that title undercuts its importance. The moral- ity of the *brujo* in Zuñi—that was Dynamic morality.

What was emerging was that the static patterns that hold one level of organization together are often the same patterns that another level of organization must fight to maintain its own existence. Morality is not a simple set of rules. It's a very complex struggle of conflicting patterns of values. This conflict is the residue of evolution. As new patterns evolve they come into conflict with old ones. Each stage of evolution creates in its wake a wash of problems.

It's out of this struggle between conflicting static patterns that the concepts of good and evil arise. Thus, the evil of disease which the doctor is absolutely morally committed to stop is not an evil at all within the germ's lower static pattern of morality. The germ is making a moral effort to stave off its own destruction by lower-level inorganic forces of evil.

Phædrus thought that most other quarrels in values can be traced to evolutionary causes and that this tracing can sometimes provide both a rational basis for classification of the quarrels and a rational solution. The structuring of morality into evolutionary levels suddenly gives shape to all kinds of blurred and confused moral ideas that are floating around in our present cultural heritage. "Vice" is an example. In an evolutionary morality the meaning of vice is quite clear. Vice is a conflict between biological quality and social quality. Things like sex and booze and drugs and tobacco have a high biological quality, that is, they feel good, but are harmful for social reasons. They take all your money. They break up your family. They threaten the sta- bility of the community.

Like the stuff Rigel was throwing at him this morning, the old Victorian morality. That was entirely within that one code—the social code. Phædrus thought that code was good enough as far as it went, but it really didn't go anywhere. It didn't know its origins and it didn't know its own destinations, and not knowing them it had to be exactly what it was: hopelessly static, hopelessly stupid, a form of evil in itself.

Evil. . . . If he'd called it that one-hundred-and-fifty years ago he might have gotten himself into some real trouble. People got mad back then when you challenged their social institutions, and they tended to take reprisals. He might have gotten himself ostracized as some kind of a social menace. And if he'd said it six-hundred years ago he might have been burned at the stake.

But today it's hardly a risk. It's more of a cheap shot. Everybody thinks those Victorian moral codes are stupid and evil, or old-fashioned at least, except maybe a few religious fundamentalists and ultra-right-wingers and ignorant uneducated people like that. That's why Rigel's sermon this morning seemed so peculiar. Usually people like Rigel do their sermonizing in favor of whatever they know is popular. That way they're safe. Didn't he know all that stuff went out years ago? Where was he during the revolution of the sixties?

Where has he been during this whole century? That's what this whole century's been about, this struggle between intellectual and social patterns. That's the theme song of the twentieth century. Is society going to dominate intellect or is intellect going to dominate society? And if society wins, what's going to be left of intellect? And if intellect wins what's going to be left of society? That was the thing that this evolutionary morality brought out clearer than anything else. Intellect is not an extension of society any more than society is an extension of biology. Intellect is going its own way, and in doing so is at war with society, seeking to subjugate society, to put society under lock and key. An evolutionary morality says it is moral for intellect to do so, but it also contains a warning: Just as a society that weakens its people's physical health endangers its own stability, so does an intellectual pattern that weakens and destroys the health of its social base also endanger its own stability.

Better to say "has endangered." It's already happened. This has been a century of fantastic intellectual growth and fantastic social destruction. The only question is how long this process can keep on.

· · ·

After a while Phædrus could see the moorings ahead at the Nyack
Yacht Club, just where Rigel said they would be. They were about
done sailing for the day. As the boat drew closer he throttled the
engine down and unlashed the boat hook from the deck.

Lila's face appeared again in the hatchway.

It startled him for a moment. She was real, after all. All this
theoretical thought about this advanced metaphysical abstraction
called "Lila," and here, before him, was what it was all about.

Her hair was combed and a cardigan sweater covered all but the
"OV" of her T-shirt.

"I feel a little better now," she said.

She didn't look better. Her face had been changed with cosmetics
into something worse . . . a kind of a mask. Skin white with powder.
Alien black eyebrows perjured by her blonde hair. A menacing
death's-door eye-shadow.

He saw that some of the mooring floats ahead had red and white
markings that looked like they were meant for guests. He throttled
the engine down and turned the boat in a wide arc so as to approach
the outermost one. When he reckoned that the boat had just about
enough momentum to reach it by itself he shifted to neutral, grabbed
the boat hook and went forward to pick up the mooring float. It was
just light enough to see the float. In a half-hour it would be dark.

14.

Lila looked around at where they were. Ahead of them was a long, long bridge. It stretched out way over to what looked like the other shore of a big lake they were on. A lot of cars were moving on the bridge. Probably going into New York City, she thought. They were close now.

Other boats were around them on moorings in the water but no one seemed to be on board them. Everything looked empty and deserted. It looked like everyone had just gone off and left. Where was everybody? It was like the river coming down here. It was too quiet. What had happened this afternoon? She couldn't remember very well. She got frightened about something. The wind and the noise. And then she fell asleep. And now she was here. Why?

What was she doing here? she wondered. She didn't know. Another town somewhere, another man, another night coming on. It was going to be a long night.

The Captain came back and gave her a funny look and said, "Help me get the dinghy in the water. I can do it myself but it's easier with two."

He took her over to the mast and asked her if she knew how to use a winch. She said yes. Then he hooked a line from the mast onto the dinghy which was lying upside down on the deck in front of them and told her to start cranking. She did but it was heavy and she could see he didn't like the way she was doing it. But she kept on doing it and after a long time the dinghy was hanging in the air from the line and the Captain swung it over the side of the boat. He told her to lower it slowly. She let out the line on the winch.

"Slowly!" he said.

She let it out more slowly and the Captain held his hands out to guide the dinghy into the water. Then he turned and said, "That's good." At least she did one thing right. He even smiled a little.

Maybe tonight wouldn't be so bad.

Lila went below and from her suitcase got her old towel and her last change of clothes and her blow dryer and makeup. She wrapped a bar of soap from the sink into a washcloth to take with her.

When she got on deck again the Captain had a little ladder hooked to the side of the boat so that they could step down to the dinghy. She went down and got in and then he followed with some canvas tote bags. She wondered what these were for.

He hardly had to row at all. It was just a little way to the shore where there were just some wooden posts sticking out of the water and a rickety-looking wooden dock and a white building next to it. Back of the building was a hill that went up to a town, it looked like.

Inside the white building a man told them where the showers were. The Captain paid him for the mooring and the showers. Then they went down a long hallway and she went through the "Ladies" door. Inside was a sort of dark dingy shower and a wooden bench just outside. She had to look for a long time for the light switch. She turned on the shower to let it warm up and then took off her clothes and put them on the bench.

The shower was good and hot. That was good. Sometimes in these places all you get is cold water. She stepped under it and it felt good. It was the first shower since the *Karma* had been at Troy. She never seemed to get enough showers. Boats aren't clean.

Men aren't clean either. She cleaned herself extra well where the Captain had been at her last night.

He needed somebody like her. He smelled like a truck engine. That shirt he was wearing, it looked like he hadn't changed it in weeks. She'd be doing him a favor to go with him to Florida. He didn't know how to take care of himself. She could take care of him.

She didn't want to get involved with him, though. She didn't want to get involved with anybody. After a while they want to get involved, like Jim, and that's when the trouble begins.

Lila dried herself with the towel and started to dress. Her blouse and skirt were wrinkled but the wrinkles would shake out. She found a plug-in by a mirror next to the wooden bench and plugged in her blow dryer and held it to her hair.

Manhattan was so close now. If Jamie was there he'd take care of everything. It would be so good to see him again. Maybe. You never knew about him. He might not be there. Then she was in trouble. She didn't know what she would do then. She didn't want to think about it.

She remembered now she told the Captain she was going to cook the supper.

That's what he brought these canvas tote bags for; to carry the food. Maybe if she made him a really good meal he would take her all the way to Florida.

She put on her mascara slowly and carefully and when she was done she walked down the hall and around a corner there was the Captain, waiting. As she walked toward him she could see he looked better now. He was washed and shaved, and he'd changed that shirt.

Outside it had gotten dark. They walked under some streetlights along the street up a hill. Some people walked by and didn't look up.

It didn't seem like a little town. It seemed more like part of a city. The street wasn't very wide and was sort of dirty and depressing the way big cities get. When they got into the town she looked in some store windows and saw there wasn't much to look at.

She thought she smelled French fries. But she didn't see any McDonalds or Burger King or any place like that around.

Would she ever like some French fries! She was starving!

Maybe they could buy some, she thought. But then the trouble was they'd get all cold by the time they got to the boat. Maybe she could cook some. You needed something to cook them in, though. She asked the Captain if he had a deep fryer. He said he wasn't sure. She hoped he did.

At the supermarket the prices were high. She got two expensive filet mignons and big Idaho potatoes and oil to make French fries from and some chocolate pudding for dessert and some bread for toast in the morning. And some eggs and some butter and some bacon. And some milk.

As she bent over to pick up the milk a shopping cart bumped into her. Lila said, "Oh, I'm sorry." It wasn't her fault, but the woman who looked like she worked for the store just gave her a mean look and didn't excuse herself in any way.

Lila got enough groceries to fill two big bags. She was starving. She liked to buy food anyway. She probably wouldn't get to eat most of it.

But you could never tell. Maybe she and the Captain would get along tonight. Then they could go shopping in New York. She needed a lot of things.

When she finished filling the shopping cart she went to the checkout counter and saw that the checkout lady there was the same lady who bumped into her. With the same mean look on her face. She reminded Lila of her mother. Lila asked, as nicely as she could, if they could use the shopping cart to take the groceries back to the boat. It would be a lot easier than just carrying those tote bags. But the answer was "No."

Lila looked at the Captain but he didn't say anything. He just paid without any expression.

They each picked up a bag of groceries and started on their way out the door when suddenly there was a loud "OW!!" and then "YOU LET GO OF ME!" and then "I'LL TELL MY MOTHER!!!"

Lila turned and saw the store lady had her hand on a black girl's collar and the girl was hitting at her and shouting, "LET GO! LET GO!! I'LL TELL MY MOTHER!!"

"I told you to stay OUT of here!" the store lady said.

The girl looked like she was about ten or twelve years old.

"Let's go," the Captain said.

But Lila heard herself say, "Leave her alone!"

"Don't get into it," the Captain said.

"I CAN COME IN HERE IF I WANT TO!" the girl shouted. "You can't tell me what to do!"

"LEAVE HER ALONE!" Lila said.

The woman looked at her in astonishment. "This is OUR STORE!" she said.

"Jesus Christ, let's go," the Captain said.

The woman still didn't let go of the girl.

Lila exploded, "Just LEAVE her ALONE or I'll call the police!"

The woman let go of the girl. The girl ran out past Lila and the Captain through the doorway of the store. The store woman glared at her. Then she glared at Lila. But there was nothing she could do now.

It was over. Lila and the Captain went out. Outside the girl looked at her and did a quick little smile, and then skipped away.

"What the hell was that all about?" the Captain said.

"She made me mad."

"Everything makes you mad."

"I have to do that," Lila said. "Now I'll feel fine all night."

At a liquor store they bought two fifths of blended and two quarts of mix and a bag of ice. They were really loaded down now as they walked back down the narrow street to the little white house where the boat was.

"What did you get into that argument for?" the Captain asked. "It wasn't any of your business."

"People are so mean to kids," Lila said.

"I would have thought you might have enough problems of your own," the Captain said.

She didn't say anything. But it felt good. She always felt better after she lost her temper like that. She didn't know why but she always did.

As they walked down to the river the Captain didn't say a word. He was mad. That was all right, she thought. He'd get over it.

At the dock it was so dark the dinghy was hard to see. She had to watch her step. She didn't want to drop all this food.

The Captain set his bag full of groceries down on the dock and untied the dinghy. Then he told Lila to get in. Then he handed everything to her and then he got in himself. With all the bags between them it was hard for him to row so he took just one oar and paddled on one side and then the other.

As she looked back she could see that the big long bridge was like a shadow, all lit up from behind with the light in the sky from New York. It was so beautiful. She put her hand in the water and it felt warm.

Suddenly she felt really good. She knew they would go to Florida together. It was going to be a good night.

When they reached the dark side of the boat the Captain held the dinghy steady while Lila climbed up the ladder. Then in the dark he handed her the tote bags full of groceries again and she set them on the deck.

Then while he climbed aboard and tied off the dinghy to the boat she carried the bags down below.

She pushed a light switch on the side of what looked like an overhead light and it worked, although it wasn't very bright. She took the bottles of whiskey and mix out of a tote bag, and stored the extra mix and the ice in the ice box. The rest of the food she took out of the bags so she could get her shower stuff. She got it all out and went over and put it in her suitcase on the pilot berth, except the towel which was damp. She hung that on the edge of the pilot berth to dry.

The Captain said to come up and hold the flashlight.

She went up and held it while he opened up a wooden cover in the deck and reached way down inside. First he pulled out a pile of old rope. Then some hose and an old anchor. Then some wire and then an old rusted iron bowl with four legs and a grill over it.

He held it up in the light of the flashlight. "Hibachi," he said. Haven't used it since Lake Superior. . . . There's some charcoal down on the pilot berth."

Meaning, "Go get it." She went down to the berth and found a bag of charcoal and handed it back up. At least he was talking again.

From the companionway she watched him pour the charcoal in from the bag. "You just go where you feel like with this boat, don't you?" she said. "Nobody to give you any orders. Nobody to argue with you."

"That's right," he said. "Now pass up the kerosene that's behind the chart table there . . . in that little shelf. Right behind where I am."

He reached around and pointed to it. She got it and handed it to him.

"I'm going to start making the French fries," Lila said, "if you'll tell me where the pots and pans are."

"In back of the chart table. Deep inside one of those bins," the Captain said. "Just pull off the cover and you'll see them."

Lila turned on another electric light over the chart table and found a deep bin where a dozen or so different types of pots and pans were dumped together in a cluttered jumble. The bin was at the back of the counter, so that the only way to reach them was to lie on her stomach on top of the chart table and hang her arm down inside the rectangular hole, and fish. The fishing for pans made a tremendous clanging racket. She hoped the noise would impress on the Captain the condition of his housekeeping.

There wasn't any deep fryer. She felt a large frying pan and pulled it out. It was a good stainless steel pan, almost new. But it wasn't deep enough for cooking oil. She went back in the bin and clanged some more and this time came out with a deep pot and a matching lid. That should work.

"I don't suppose you have a wire basket for French fries," she said.

"No," the Captain said, "not that I know of."

It was all right. She could get by with a slotted spoon.

She looked for one and found it and also a vegetable peeler next to it. She tried the vegetable peeler on one of the potatoes. It was nice and sharp. She started peeling. She liked to peel long, hard, smooth Idaho potatoes like this. These were going to make good French fries. She let the peels shoot into the sink, so when she was done she could scoop them out with her hand.

"What will you do after you get to Florida?" she said to the Captain.

"Just keep going, probably," he said.

A flame came up from the hibachi and she could see his face suddenly in the light. It looked tired.

"Just keep going where?" she asked.

"South," he said. "There's a town where I used to live in Mexico, down on the Bay of Campeche. I'd like to go back there for a while. And see if some people I used to know are still around."

"What were you doing there?"

"Building a boat."

"This boat?"

"No, a boat that never got finished," he said. "Everything went wrong."

He poked the charcoal in the hibachi with the edge of the grate.

"With boats you always get seven kinds of trouble at once," he said. "The keel was done and the frames were up. We were ready to start planking, and the government declared the forest we were in to be '*veda*,' I think they called it, meaning no more wood.

"We went to Campeche for some more wood, paid for it—it never got sent. No way for a foreigner to sue them in Mexico. They knew that.

"Then all our fastenings from Mexico City 'disappeared.' The paint got delivered but it disappeared after we put some on a dinghy."

"Who's 'we'?" Lila asked.

"Me and my boat-carpenter."

While she peeled the potatoes the Captain came down the ladder. He lit the kerosene lamp, then turned off the electric lights, then took out some glasses from a shelf, then opened the ice box. He filled the glasses with ice, opened the mix and poured it. When he poured the whiskey he held up her glass and she told him when to stop.

Then he said, "Here's to Pancho Piquet."

Lila drank. It tasted fine.

She showed him the peeled potatoes. "I'm so starved I could eat them raw," she said, "but I'm not going to."

She found a cutting board and started to cut the potatoes, first the long way, making them into ovals, then cutting them again into pencil-thick sticks. Beautiful knife. Really sharp. The Captain stood watching her.

"Who is Pancho Piquet?" she asked.

"The *carpentero de ribera*. He was an old Cuban. He spoke Spanish so fast even the Mexicans had trouble understanding him. Looked like Boris Karloff. Didn't look Cuban or Mexican at all.

"But he was fastest carpenter I've ever seen," the Captain said. "And careful. He never slowed down, even in that jungle heat. We didn't have any electricity but he could work faster with hand tools than most people do with power tools. He was in his fifties or sixties and I was twenty-something. He used to smile that Boris Karloff smile watching me try to keep up with him."

"So why are we drinking to him?" Lila asked.

"Well, they warned me, '*El tome!*' He drinks! And so he did," the Captain said.

"One night a big *Norte*, a norther, blew in off the Gulf of Mexico and it blew so hard. . . . Oh, it was a big wind! Almost bent the palm trees to the ground. And it took the roof off his house and carried it away.

"But instead of fixing it he got drunk and he stayed drunk for more than a month. After a couple of weeks his wife had to come begging for money for food. That was so sad. I think partly he got drunk because he knew everything was going wrong and the boat would never get built. And that was true. I ran out of money and had to quit."

"So that's why we're drinking to him?" Lila said.

"Yeah, he was sort of a warning," the Captain said. "Also, he just opened my eyes a little to something. A feeling for what the tropics is really like. All this talk about going to Florida and Mexico brought him back to mind."

The potato sticks were growing into a mountain. She was making way too many. But it didn't matter. Better to have too many than too few.

"What do you want to go back there for?" she said.

"I don't know. There's always that feeling of despair down there. I can feel it now just thinking about it. *'Tristes tropiques,'* the anthropologist, Lévi-Strauss, called it. It keeps pulling you back, somehow. Mexicans know what I mean. There's always this feeling that this sadness is the real truth about things and it's better to live with a sad truth than with all the happy progress talk you get up here in the North."

"So you're going to stay down in Mexico?"

"No, not with a boat like this. This boat can go anywhere—Panama, China, India, Africa. No firm plans. You never know what'll turn up."

The potatoes were all cut. "So how do I turn this stove on, then?" she asked the Captain.

"I'll light it for you," he said.

"Why don't you teach me?" said Lila.

"It takes too long," the Captain said.

While the Captain was pumping up the stove she finished her drink, freshened up his and poured another for herself.

He went up on deck to watch the hibachi and she set the pot on the stove and filled it with the entire bottle of oil they purchased at the supermarket and then put on the lid. All that oil would take a while to heat up.

She took the steaks out of the supermarket wrappers to sprinkle them with salt and pepper. In the golden lamplight they looked gorgeous.

The pepper worked but the salt shaker was clogged. She took the lid off and whacked it on the chart table, but the holes still were clogged, so she pinched a hunk of salt with her fingers and dusted it on that way.

She handed up the steaks to the Captain. Then she got to work on the salad, shredding piles of lettuce onto two plates, and using that sharp knife to slice a tomato. As she worked, she stuffed some hunks of lettuce into her mouth.

"Oh! Oh! Oh!" she said.

"What's the matter?" he asked.

"I forgot how hungry I was. I don't know how you can stand it, going on like this without any food all day long. How do you do it?"

"Well, actually, I had breakfast," he said.

"You did?"

"Before you got up."

"Why didn't you wake me up?"

"Your friend, Richard Rigel, didn't want you along."

Lila looked up through the hatchway at the Captain for a long time. He was looking at her to see what she would say.

"Richard does that sometimes," she said. "He probably thought we were going to have lunch somewhere."

He really had it in for Richard, she thought, and he was trying to get her mad again. He wouldn't leave it alone. On a nice night like this you'd think he'd leave it alone. It was such a nice night. She could feel the booze coming on.

"If you want me to go to Florida with you, I'll go with you," Lila said.

He didn't say anything. He just poked the steak with a fork.

"What do you think?" she said.

"I'm not sure."

"Why aren't you sure?"

"I don't know."

"I can cook and fix your clothes and sleep with you," Lila said, "and when you're tired of me you can just say good-bye and I'll be gone. How do you like that?"

He still didn't say anything.

It was getting very hot in the cabin so she lifted her sweater to take it off.

"You really need me, you know," she said.

When she got the sweater off she could see he'd been watching her take it off. With that special look. She knew what that meant. Here it comes, she thought.

The Captain said, "What I was thinking about this afternoon while you were sleeping was that I want to ask you some questions that will help me fit some things together."

"What kind of questions?"

"I don't know yet," he said. "About what you like and don't like, mainly."

"Well, sure, we can do that too."

He said, "I thought maybe I could ask questions about what your attitudes are about certain things. What your values are and how you got them. Things like that. I'd just like to ask questions and jot down answers without really knowing where it's going to lead to and then later maybe try to put something together."

"Sure," Lila said. "What kind of questions?" He's going to go for it, she thought. She saw his glass was just about empty. She reached up through the hatchway and got it, then filled it.

"What holds a person together is his patterns of likes and dislikes," he said. "And what holds a society together is a pattern of likes and dislikes. And what holds the whole world together is patterns of likes and dislikes. History is just abstracted from biography. And so are all the social sciences. In the past anthropology has been centered around collective objects and I'm interested in probing around to see if it can be better said in terms of individual values. I've just had feelings that maybe the ultimate truth about the world isn't history or sociology but biography," he said.

She didn't know what he was talking about. All she could think of was Florida.

She handed him up his glass. The blue flame of the stove was hissing away under the oil. She lifted the lid on the pot and saw the heat stirring the liquid inside, but it was so dark she couldn't really tell if it was time to start the potatoes.

"You're sort of another culture," he said. "A culture of one. A culture is an evolved static pattern of quality capable of Dynamic change. That's what you are. That's the best definition of you that's ever been invented.

"You may think everything you say and everything you think is just you but actually the language you use and the values you have are the result of thousands of years of cultural evolution. It's all in a kind of debris of pieces that seem unrelated but are actually part of a huge fabric. Lévi-Strauss postulates that a culture can only be understood by reenacting its thought processes with the debris of its interaction with other cultures. Does this make sense? I'd like to record the debris of your own memory and try to reconstruct things with it."

She wished he had a frying thermometer. She broke off a bit of potato and dropped it in the pot, and it swirled slowly but didn't sizzle. She fished it out and had another bite of lettuce.

"Have you ever heard of Heinrich Schliemann?" he asked.

"Heinrich Who?"

"He was an archaeologist who investigated the ruins of a city people thought was mythological: ancient Troy.

"Before Schliemann used what he called the stratographic technique, archaeologists were just educated grave-robbers. He showed how you could dig down carefully through one stratum after another, finding the ruins of earlier cities under later ones. That's what I think can be done with a single person. I can take parts of your language and your values and trace them to old patterns that were laid down centuries ago and are what make you what you are."

"I don't think you'll get much out of me," Lila said.

The booze is really getting to him, she thought. All day he's been so quiet. Now you can't shut him off.

She said, "Boy, I sure pushed a button when I asked about going to Florida with you."

"What do you mean?"

"All day I thought you were one of those silent types. Now I can't get a word in."

He looked like she'd hurt his feelings.

"Well I don't mind," she said. "You can ask me all the questions you want."

Finally the oil looked hot enough. She used a slotted spoon to lower the first batch into the pot with a roar of bubbles and a cloud of steam. "Are the steaks getting close to done?" she asked.

"A few minutes more."

"Good," she said. The smell of the steaks mixed with the French fries coming up from the stove was making her almost faint. She couldn't remember when she'd ever been this hungry before. When the potato bubbles quieted down she spooned the potatoes out, spread them on a towel and showered them with salt, then put in the next batch. When these were done, she waited until the Captain said the steaks were ready. Then she handed the plates up for him to put the steaks on.

When he handed them down she thought, "Oh! Heavenly!" She shook the French fries onto them from the paper towel.

The Captain came down. They opened the dining table leaves, moved the plates and whiskey and mix and extra French fries onto the table, and suddenly there everything was. She looked at the Captain and he looked at her. It could be like this every night, she thought.

Oh! The steak was so good she wanted to cry! The French fries! Oh! Salad!

"You don't know what this is doing to me," she said.

"What is it doing?" He had a little smile on his face.

"Is that one of your questions?" she asked. Her mouth was full of French fries. She had to slow down.

"No," he laughed, "that wasn't one of them. I just wanted to know more about your background."

"Like a job interviewer?" she said.

"Well, yes, that's a start."

He got up and refilled their glasses.

She thought for a while. "I was born in Rochester. I was the youngest of two girls. . . . Is that the kind of stuff you want to know?"

"Just a second," he said. He got up and got a notepad and a pen.

"You mean you're going to write all this down?"

"Sure," he said.

"Oh, forget it!"

"Why?"

"I don't want to do that."

"Why not?"

"Let's just eat and relax and be friends."

He frowned a little, then shrugged his shoulders, got up again and put the pad of slips away.

As she took another bite of steak she thought maybe she shouldn't have said that. Not if she wanted to go to Florida. "Go ahead, ask some questions anyway," she said. "I'll talk. I like to talk."

The Captain handed her drink to her and then sat down beside her.

"All right, what are the things you like best?"

"Food."

"What else?"

"More food."

"And after that?"

She thought for a while. "Just what we're doing now. Did you see that light from the city across the bridge? All of a sudden it was so beautiful."

"What else?"

"Men," she laughed.

"What kind?"

"Any kind. The kind that likes me."

"What do you dislike most?"

"Mean people. . . . Like that lady in the store back in town. There's a million people like her and I hate every one of them. Always trying to make themselves big by tearing somebody else down. . . . You do it too, you know."

"Me?"

"Yes, you."

"When?"

"This afternoon. Talking so big about a boat you never saw."

"Oh, that."

"Just don't be mean like that and we'll get along fine. I only get mad at mean people."

"What after mean people?" the Captain asked.

"People who think they're better than you are."

"What next?"

"Lots of things."

"What?"

"Well, there's lots of things I don't want. I don't want to get old. I don't want people to be mean. Oh, I said that."

She thought for a while. "Sometimes I don't want to be so lonely. You know, I thought George and me were really going to make it. And then this Debbie comes along and it's like he doesn't even know me. I didn't do anything to him. That's just mean."

"Anything else?"

"Isn't that enough? It isn't any special thing that makes me feel bad. I don't know what it's going to be until it happens." She looked at him. "Sometimes there's something that just comes over me and I get scared. . . . That happened this afternoon."

"What?"

"When you started the engine."

"That was a bad wind," he said.

"It wasn't just the wind. It isn't like anything. It's like a storm coming and I don't have any house. I don't have anywhere to go." She took another bite of steak. "I like this boat. Do you have storms on this boat?"

"Yes, but the boat's like a cork. The waves wash over it."

"That's good. I like that."

"Why are you all alone like this on the river?"

"I'm not. I'm with you."

"Well then last night," he said.

"I wasn't alone," she laughed. "Don't you remember?" She reached over and put her hand on his cheek. "Don't you remember?"

"Before you met me."

"Before I met you I wasn't alone for five minutes. I was with that bastard, George. Don't you remember?

"All spring I saved money so I could take this trip with him. And then he runs off like that. They wouldn't even give me my money back. . . . Oh hell, let's not talk about him. He's all gone."

"Where were you going to go?"

"Florida."

"Ohhh," the Captain said. "So that's why you want to go with me to Florida."

"Uh-huh," she said.

While he thought about it she started on her salad. "Don't ever do this to me again," she said. "Let's just fill this whole boat with groceries, okay?"

"Somehow you didn't answer my question," he said. "Before you met me, before you knew George, why weren't you married?"

"I was married," Lila said. "A long time ago."

"You're divorced."

"No."

"You're still married."

"No, he got killed."

"Oh, I'm sorry to hear that."

"Don't be."

This steak was cooked just perfectly, but it needed just a little more pepper. She reached over and got the pepper shaker by the cutting board and added just a pinch to the steak, then handed the shaker to the Captain.

"That was a long time ago," she said. "I never think about him."

"What did he do?"

"He drove a truck. He was on the road most of the time. I never saw him much. And then one night he didn't come home and the police called and said he was dead. And that was it."

"What did you do then?"

"I got some insurance money. And they had a funeral, and I wore a black dress and all that, but I don't think about that any more."

"Why didn't you like him?" the Captain asked.

"We always had fights," Lila said.

"About what?"

"Just fights. . . . He was always suspicious of me. Of what I was going to do when he wasn't home. . . . He thought I was cheating on him."

"Were you?"

Lila looked at him. "Wait a minute. . . . When I was married I was married. I didn't do anything like that. . . . Don't get me mad."

"I'm just asking," the Captain said.

She had another bite of the salad. "He never had respect for me."

"Why did you marry him?"

"I was pregnant," Lila said.

"How old were you?"

"Sixteen. Seventeen when she was born."

"That's too young," the Captain said.

Those drinks before dinner were making her high now. She'd better slow down, she thought, and watch herself and not do something dumb, like she usually did when she got drunk. She was already talking too much.

She felt dizzy. Then she saw the lamp swing. "What's that?" she said.

"A wake," the Captain said. "A big one. . . . That's the first one. In a second there'll be . . . here it comes. . . ."

Another even bigger wave came and the whole boat rocked, and then after a while a smaller one and another one, each one getting smaller.

The Captain got up from the table and went up.

"What is it?" she said.

"I don't know," he said. "It's not a barge. . . . Some power-boat probably. He may be on the other side of the bridge."

He stood there for a long time looking around outside. Then he looked back down at her.

"How old is your baby now?" he asked.

That surprised her. That was a new one. "What do you want to know that for?"

"I already told you before I started asking all these questions," he said.

"She's dead."

"How did she die?" he asked.

"I killed her," she said.

She watched his eyes. She didn't like them. He looked mean.

"You mean accidentally," he said.

"I didn't cover her right and she smothered," Lila said. "That was long ago."

"Nobody blamed you though."

"Nobody had to. What could they say . . . that I didn't already know?"

Lila remembered she still had the black funeral dress. She remembered she had to wear it three times that year. There were hundreds of people who came to her grandfather's funeral because he was a minister and lots of Jerry's friends came to his funeral, but nobody came for Dawn.

"Don't get me started thinking about that," she said.

She sat back in the berth for the first time and stopped eating. "Ask some other questions," she said, "like, how long will it take to get to Florida?"

"So you never married again," the Captain said.

"No! God, no. Never! I would never do that again.

"These people who get married," she said, "it's the cheapest trick on a person there is. You're supposed to give up all your freedom and everything just for sex every night. That doesn't make them happy. They're just always looking around for some way out. Don't you want some more of these French fries?

"I just want to be free," she said. "That's what America's about, isn't it?"

The Captain took some French fries and she got up and took her plate over to the cutting board and took the rest of French fries and put them on her plate. "Give me your glass," she said.

He gave it to her and she lifted the lid of the ice box and scooped some more ice into it. She added mix and booze and then filled her own glass. She saw the booze was halfway down the label already, when she heard a CLUNK! It was against the side of the boat.

"Now what?" she said.

The Captain shook his head. He said, "Maybe a big branch or something." He got up and went past her and up on deck and she felt the boat tip a little as his footsteps went over to the side.

"What is it," she said.

"It's the dinghy."

After a while he said, "It's never done that before. . . . Come on up and help me put some fenders down and tie it alongside. We'll bring it up in the morning."

She came up and watched him take two big rubber fenders and

tie them to the rail so that they dangled over the side. He went over to the other side of the deck and came back with a long boat hook. She stood next to him while he reached out with the hook and brought the dinghy up against the side of the boat.

"Hold it there," he said, and gave her the boat hook. He went to a big box by the mast and opened it and took out a rope and then came back. He dropped the rope into the dinghy and then stepped and lowered himself down over the guard rail.

She looked around. It was so quiet here. Just the rolling of the cars across the bridge. The sky was still all orange from the light from the city but it was so peaceful you would never guess where they were.

When he was done the Captain grabbed the guard rail and pulled himself up again.

"I figured it out," he said. "It's because the tide is changing. . . . This is the first time I've seen this. . . . Look around at all the other boats. You remember when we came they were all pointed toward the bridge? Now they're all skewed around."

She looked and saw that all the boats were facing in different directions.

"They'll probably all be pointing away from the bridge after a while," he said. "It's warm enough out—let's sit up here and watch it. I'm sort of fascinated by this," he said.

Lila brought up the bottles and ice and some sweaters and a blanket to put over them. She sat next to him and put the blanket over their legs together. "Listen to how quiet it is," she said. "It's hard to believe we're this close to New York."

They listened for a long time.

"What are you going to do when you get to Manhattan?" the Captain asked.

"I'm going to find a friend of mine and see if he can help me," she said.

"What if you can't find him?"

"I don't know. I could do a lot of things. Get a job waitressing or something like that. . . ." She looked at him but couldn't see how he took it.

"Who is this person you're going to see in New York?"

"Jamie? He's just an old friend."

"How long have you known him?"

"Oh, two or three years," she said.

"In New York?"

"Yes."

"So you've lived there a long time?"

"Not so long," Lila said. "I always liked it there. You can be anyone you want in New York and nobody will stop you."

She suddenly thought of something. "You know what?" she said, "I bet you'd like him. You'd get along fine with him. He's a sailor too. He worked on a ship once.

"You know what?" Lila said. "He could help us sail the boat to Florida. . . . If you wanted to, I mean . . . I mean I could cook and he could steer and you could . . . well, you could give all the orders."

The Captain stared into his glass.

"Just think about it," Lila said. "Just the three of us going down to Florida."

After a while she said, "He's really friendly. Everybody likes him."

She waited a long time but the Captain didn't answer. She said, "If I could talk him into it would you take him?"

"I don't think so," the Captain said. "Three's too many."

"That's because you haven't met him," Lila said.

She took the Captain's glass and filled it again and snuggled up to him to keep warm. He just wasn't used to the idea.

Give him some time, she thought.

The cars rolled over the bridge one after another. Bright headlights went in one direction and red taillights went in the other, on and on.

"You remind me of someone," Lila said. "Someone I remember from a long time ago."

"Who?"

"I can't remember. . . . What did you do in high school?"

"Not much," he said.

"Were you popular?"

"No."

"You were unpopular?"

"Nobody paid much attention to me one way or the other."

"Weren't you on any teams?"

"The chess team."

"You went to dances."

"No."

"Then where did you learn to dance?"

"I don't know. I went for a couple of years to dancing school," the Captain said.

"Well, what else did you do in high school?"

"I studied."

"In high school?"

"I was studying to be a chemistry professor."

"You should have studied to be a dancer. You were really good last night."

Suddenly Lila knew who he reminded her of. Sidney Shedar.

"You're not much of a ladies' man, are you?"

"No, not at all," he said.

"This person wasn't either."

"Chemistry's not so bad if you're into it," he said. "It gets kind of exciting. I and another kid got the key to the school building and sometimes we'd come back at ten or eleven at night and go up to the chemistry laboratory and work on chemistry experiments until dawn."

"Sounds weird."

"No. Actually it was pretty great."

"What did you do?"

"Adolescent stuff. . . . The secret of life. I was working hard on that."

"You should have stuck to dancing," Lila said. "That's the secret of life."

"I was sure I was going to find it, studying proteins and genetics and things like that."

"Really weird."

"Is that what this other person was like?"

"Sidney? Yes, I guess so. He was a real nerd."

"Oh," the Captain said. "And I remind you of him?"

"You both talk the same way. He used to ask a lot of questions too. He always had a lot of big ideas."

"What was he like?"

"Nobody liked him very much. He was very smart and he was always trying to tell you about things you weren't interested in."

"What did he talk about?"

"Who knows! There was just something about him that made everybody mad at him. He didn't really do anything bad. He just— I don't know what it was—he just didn't. . . . He was smart but at the same time he was dumb. And he could never see how dumb he was because he thought he knew everything. Everyone used to call him Sad Sack."

"And I remind you of him?"

"Yes."

"If I'm such a nerd why did you dance with me last night?" the Captain asked.

"You asked me."

"I thought you asked me."

"Maybe I did," Lila said. "I don't know. You looked different maybe. They all look different at first.

"You know Sidney really was smart," Lila said. "About two years ago I was sitting at a table in this restaurant and I looked up and there he was, much older and he had glasses on and he was getting bald. He's a pediatrician now. He's got four children now. He was really nice. He said, 'Hello Lila,' and we talked a long time."

"What did he say?"

"He just wondered how I was and everything, and was I married and I said, 'No the right one hasn't come along yet,' and he laughed at that and said, 'Someday he will.' . . . You see what I mean?" Lila said.

She excused herself and went down to the bathroom. On her way back she had to hang on to things to keep steady. It didn't matter. She wasn't going anywhere. She sat down again next to the Captain and he asked, "How long have you known Richard Rigel?"

"Since the second grade," she said.

"The second grade!"

"Surprised, huh?"

"God, I'll say! I had no idea."

She arranged the blanket neatly and settled back and then looked up in the sky. There was so much light from the city there weren't any stars at all. It was just all orange and black. Like Halloween.

"Whew!" the Captain said.

"What's the matter?"

"I'm just sort of shook," he said. "The second grade! That's just unbelievable!"

"Why is that unbelievable?"

"You mean he used to sit behind you and make faces at the teacher and things like that?"

"No, we were just in the same class. Why does that seem so unbelievable?"

"I don't know," the Captain said. "He doesn't seem like the sort of person who would have had a childhood. . . . But I suppose he must have."

"We were good friends," Lila said.

"You were childhood sweethearts."

"No, we were just friends. We've always been friends. I don't see why you're surprised at that."

"Why, out of a whole classroom full of people, would you pick a person like him for a friend?"

"He came in at the second grade and I was the only one who was nice to him."

The Captain shook his head.

After a while he made a sound like, "Tch!"

"You don't know him," Lila said. "He was very quiet and shy. He used to stutter. Everybody laughed at him."

"He sure doesn't stutter now," the Captain said.

"You don't know him."

"So you went all the way through grade school and high school with him?"

"No, after sixth grade he went to prep school, and I didn't see him much."

"What does his father do?"

"I don't know. They were divorced. He lived in New York some-where. Or, I think, Kingston, maybe. Where we were last night. . . ."

"Well, I guess what's bothering me," the Captain said, "is, if you've known him since the second grade and you're such good friends, why was he so down on you last night?"

"Richard likes me," Lila said.

"No. Not true," the Captain said. "That's what's getting me. Why was he so rude to you? Why wouldn't he talk to you last night?"

"Oh, that's a long story," Lila said.

"Last night he didn't even say 'hello.' "

"I know. That's just the way he is. He just doesn't approve of the way I live."

"Well, that's true," the Captain said.

Lila held up the bottle and showed it to the Captain. "You know something?"

"What?"

"I think we are getting a little smashed. . . . At least I am. You're not drinking very much."

"But something's still missing," the Captain said.

"What?"

"You never saw him after prep school."

"I saw plenty of him after prep school."

"You mean he used to go out with you?"

"Everybody used to go with me," Lila said. "You don't know what I was like. I wish you could have seen me when I was younger. I had such a cute figure. . . . It sounds like I'm bragging, but it was true. I don't look like so much now, but you should have seen me back then. Everybody wanted to go out with me. I was popular then. . . . I was really popular."

"So you went out with him."

"Sometimes we'd go out together and then his mother found out about it and she made him stop."

"Why?"

"Well, you know why. She is very rich and I'm not in their social class. Also women don't approve of people like me. Especially mothers with little sons who are interested in me."

The booze was hitting real hard now. She had to stop.

"Anyway Richie is a real nice guy," she said.

The Captain didn't say anything.

". . . And you aren't," she added.

"Rigel said you got someone named Jim in trouble."

"Did he talk about that?" Lila shook her head.

"What was that all about?"

"Oh, God. I wish he hadn't talked about that."

"What was it about?"

"Nothing!

"We weren't doing anything. . . . Anything worse than you and me are doing on this boat right now. I told Jim never to tell anyone about us. Then he went and told Richie and Richie told his mother and his mother told Jim's wife. That's when all the trouble started. Oh, God, what a mess that was. . . . All because Richie's mother couldn't leave us alone."

"His mother?"

"Look, Richie dotes on his mother, morning, noon and night. That's where he gets all his money. I think he sleeps with her! She really hates me!" Lila said.

"Why did Rigel's mother hate you?"

"I told you. She was afraid I was going to take her little Richie away from her. And she was the one who got Jim's wife to hire the detectives."

"Detectives!"

"We were in the motel and they pounded on the door and I told Jim, 'Don't answer it!' but he didn't listen. He said, 'I'll just talk to them.' Sure . . . that's all they wanted. Just to talk. . . . Oh, he was so dumb. It was just awful. As soon as he opened the door they came in with flash cameras and took pictures of everything. Then they wanted him to sign a confession. They said they wouldn't prosecute if he just signed.

"You know what he did? He signed. . . .

"He wouldn't listen to me. If he'd listened to me there's nothing they could have done. They didn't have a warrant or anything.

"Then they left and you know what Jim did? . . . He started to cry. . . . That's what I remember most, him sitting on the edge of the bed, with his big eyes all full of tears.

"I was the one who should have been crying! And what do you suppose he was crying about? . . . About how he didn't want his wife to divorce him. . . . Oh, he made me so disgusted. He made everybody disgusted.

"He was weak. He always complained about how she ran his life, but he really wanted her to. That's why he wanted to go back.

"They always talk about how they're going to leave their wives, but they never do. They always go back."

"Did his wife take him back?"

"No . . . she wasn't dumb. She took his money instead. Almost a hundred thousand dollars. . . . She couldn't stand him any more than I could, after that."

"Did you see Jim after that?"

"For a while. But I never respected him after that. Then he got fired from the bank and I got tired of him and I met this friend from New York, Jamie, and I came down here with him for a while."

"I thought Rigel said he was Jim's lawyer."

"He was, but after they got the pictures and the confession there wasn't much he could do."

"Why did he take the case?"

"Because of me. I'm the one who told Jim to go to him."

The Captain made a "tch" sound again. He tipped his head back and looked up at the sky.

He didn't say anything for a long time. He just stared up into the sky like he was looking for some stars.

"There aren't any stars up there," Lila said. "I already looked."

"Is Rigel married?" the Captain asked.

"No."

"Why not?"

"I don't know. He's all messed up just like everybody else. . . . You know something?"

"What?"

"You're not drinking as much as I am." She held the bottle up to the sky and looked at it. "And you know something else?"

"What?"

"I'm not going to answer any more of your questions."

"Why not?"

"You're the detective. That's what you are. You think you're going to learn something, I don't know what, but you're not going to learn anything. . . . You'll never find out who I am because I'm not anything."

"What do you mean?"

"I'm not anybody. All these questions you're asking are just a waste of time. I know you're trying to find out what kind of a person

I am but you're never going to find out anything because there's nothing to know."

Her voice was getting slushy. She could tell it was getting slushy.

"I mean, I used to play I was this kind of person and that kind of person but I got so tired of playing all those games. It's such work and it doesn't do any good. There's just all these pictures of who I am and they don't hold together. They're all different people I'm supposed to be but none of them are me. I'm not anybody. I'm not here. Like you now. I can see you've got a lot of bad impressions about me in your mind. And you think that what's in your mind is here talking to you but nobody's here. You know what I mean? Nobody's home. That's Lila. Nobody's home.

"You know what?" Lila said.

"What."

"What you want to do is make me into something I'm not."

"Just the opposite."

"You think just the opposite. But you're really trying to do something to me that I don't like."

"What's that?"

"You're trying to . . . you're trying to destroy me."

"No."

"Yes."

"Well you've completely misunderstood what I'm asking these questions for," the Captain said.

"No, I haven't. I've completely understood it just exactly right," Lila said. "All men do that. You're no big exception. Jerry did it. Every man does it. But you know something? It won't work."

"I'm not trying to destroy you," he said.

"That's what you think. You're just playing around the edges, aren't you! You can't go to the center of me. You don't know where the center of me is!"

That set him back.

"You're not a woman. You don't know. When men make love they're really trying to destroy you. A woman's got to be real quiet inside because if she shows a man anything they'll try to kill it.

"But they all get fooled because there's nothing to destroy but what's in their own mind. And so they destroy that and then they hate what's left and they call what's left, 'Lila,' and they hate Lila. But Lila isn't anybody. That's true. You don't believe it, but it's true.

"Women are very deep," Lila said. "But men never see it. They're too selfish. They always want women to understand them. And that's all they ever care about. That's why they always have to try to destroy them."

"I'm just asking questions," the Captain said.

"Fuck your questions! I'm whatever your questions turn me into. You don't see that. It's your questions that make me who I am. If you think I'm an angel then that's what I am. If you think I'm a whore then that's what I am. I'm whatever you think. And if you change your mind about me then I change too. So whatever Richard tells you, it's true. There's no way he can lie about me."

Lila took the bottle and took a swig down straight. "The hell with glasses," she said. "Everybody wants to turn Lila into somebody else. And most women put up with that, because they want the kids and the money and the good-looking clothes. But it won't work with me. I'm just Lila and I always will be. And if men don't like me the way I am, then men can just get out. I don't need them. I don't need anyone. I'll die first. That's just the way I am."

After a while Lila looked around and saw that all the boats were lying straight in line just like the Captain said they would be. That's pretty good. He'd figured that out. She told him about it. He didn't say anything. He hadn't said anything for a long time.

A bad feeling started to creep up. He wasn't drinking. Was he getting mad? That's what happens when you don't keep up drinking. You get mad.

She was talking too much. Sober up, Lila, before it's too late. Hang on. Sober up.

"You know what?" Lila said.

"What?"

"I'm really sick of talking about me. Let's talk about something else."

"It's getting cold out here," the Captain said.

He got up. "I didn't get any real sleep last night," he said. "I'm going to bed early."

Lila got up and followed him into the cabin. He went into the bunk at the front of the boat and she could hear him lie down and then he was quiet.

She looked around the cabin. All this food and things to put away. What a mess.

Suddenly she remembered the chocolate pudding never got made. She would probably never get to eat it, she thought.

15.

In the forecabin Phædrus turned back the bed covers, then sat on the bunk and slowly pulled off his sweater and his other clothes. He felt weary.

Some archaeological expedition, he thought. Garbage and more garbage.

That's what an archaeologist is, really—a highly trained garbage man. You see all the great finds in museums. You don't see what they had to go through to find them. . . . Some of those ancient ruins, Phædrus remembered, were located under city dumps.

Rigel would really be gloating now. "What do you think now?" he'd say. "Does Lila have Quality? What's your answer?"

A light flashed through the porthole and then disappeared. Somebody's searchlight, or a beacon maybe. But it was too irregular to be a beacon. Phædrus waited for it to reappear, but it didn't.

This really wasn't his day. Funny how everything kept going back to high school with her. That's what this was. This was one of those high school disasters where you take the girl home early and do not kiss her good night and if you call again later and ask her out she is going to be doing something else.

She really was that girl on the streetcar.

And he really was that guy. That was him. The guy who doesn't get the girl.

What was it she had said about "Sad Sack"? ". . . He was quiet most of the time. . . . You thought it was because he was listening to you . . . but he wasn't. He was always thinking about something else. Chemistry, I guess. . . . I felt sorry for him. . . . He knew a lot but he just didn't know what was going on. He didn't understand women because he didn't understand anybody. . . . You never could get close to him. He was very smart in some ways, but in other ways he was very stupid, you know what I mean? . . ."

Phædrus knew what she meant. He knew who she meant.

He slowly stretched his legs out down under the blankets, and remembered something else he hadn't thought of for years.

It was a movie he watched long ago when he was a chemistry student. There was a pretty girl, played by Priscilla Lane, he seemed to remember, who was having romantic difficulties with the handsome young leading man—maybe it was Richard Powell. For comic relief Priscilla Lane had a dumb-cluck girlfriend who gave everybody laughs and warm feelings of self-importance because they knew that stupid as they might be they weren't as stupid as she was. They loved her for that.

In one scene the dumb-cluck girlfriend came home from a dance and met Priscilla Lane and Richard Powell who were standing arm in arm—blue-eyed, radiant and beautiful—and they asked her, "How was the dance?"

She said, "Awful. I danced every dance with a chemistry professor."

He remembered how the audience tittered.

"Have you ever danced with a chemistry professor?" the dumb-cluck girlfriend asked. The audience laughed. "Ohhhwww, my feet!" she groaned.

The audience howled with laughter.

Except one. He sat there, his face burning, and finished the movie with the same kind of stunned depression he felt now, a feeling of dislocation and paralysis, devoured for a moment by this other pattern that made himself and everything he believed in worthless and comic.

He didn't remember what he did after that. Maybe just got on the streetcar and went home.

That could have been the night Lila was on the streetcar. . . .

. . . That smile. That's what he remembered most. There it was. Lila on the streetcar. Lila and the lilacs in spring. The little suppressed smile. The little half-hidden contempt. And the sadness that nothing he could do or say could ever make her smile at him in any other way.

He remembered once there was a huge cottonwood tree in the night and he stood alone under it and listened and its leaves rattled slightly in the night breeze. It had been a warm night and there was a smell of lilacs in the breeze.

These patterns of his mind slowly vanished into sleep.

After an unknown time some new patterns returned in the form of shimmering water. The shimmering was above him. He lay at the bottom of the ocean shoal on a bank of sand. The water was faintly bluish but so clear he could see little hills and ripples in the surface of the sand as clearly as if no water were there.

Growing from the bottom were dark green blades of eel-grass that rippled in the current of the water like eels struggling to get free of the sand. He could feel the same currents against his own body. They were pleasant gentle currents and he felt serene. His lungs had stopped their struggle long ago and everything was quiet now. He felt like he belonged here. He had always belonged here.

Above the tips of the grass in the faint blue water were hundreds of milky pink and white jellyfish floating through the water. They seemed to drift at first but then as he watched closely he saw they propelled themselves by pulsing in-and-out, in-and-out, as if they had some mysterious goal. The littlest ones were so thin and transparent he saw them mainly by refraction of the shimmering water above them as they passed between him and a dark shape suspended on the surface. The dark shape was like that of a boat which from the bottom of the ocean seemed more like a spaceship suspended in the sky. It belonged to another world that he had come from. Now that he was no longer attached to it he felt better.

One of the peculiar milky-white creatures swam toward him and nudged against his body, first on his arm and then on his side, alarming him a little. Was the creature being friendly? Was it hungry for some-thing? He tried to get up and move away from it but found he couldn't. He had lost all power of motion. The creature nudged and stroked and nudged and stroked until he gradually felt himself being released from a dream.

It was dark now and he felt the nudging again. It was a hand. He didn't move. The hand moved up and down his arm, carefully and deliberately, then began to make further and further adventures across his body. By the time the hand had reached far enough to arrive at its destination, its destination was rigid and waiting. The dream-like feeling of helplessness and motionlessness persisted and he lay silently as he had lain at the bottom of the ocean, letting this happen to him, as if he were watching it from afar, a kind of spectator to some ancient ritual he was not supposed to see or understand.

The hand continued to stroke and caress and gently grasp and then, slowly in the darkness the body of Lila rose above him, and slid itself over him, kneeled and lowered itself gently and slowly down until it enveloped what it had come for.

. . . Then it tightened. Then, slowly, it lifted and paused. Then it eased and descended. Then it lifted and tightened—and released and descended again. Then again. And again. Each time a little less slow. Each time a little more coaxing. Each time a little more demanding of what it was there to receive.

Surges of excitement in his body grew with each demand. They became stronger and stronger until his hands rose up and seized her hips and his own body began to move with hers in each rise and fall. His thoughts were swamped by this ocean current of feeling and the huge jellyfish-like body hovering over him pulsing in and out, in and out, expanding and contracting on and on. He could feel huge waves of emotion that were not directed by anything. He could feel the explosion almost coming . . .

Then ALMOST coming . . .

Then . . . her body was suddenly tense and rigidly hard around him and she gave a crying-out sound and his whole self let go into her and his mind leapt out to some place beyond anywhere.

. . . When it returned he could feel the vulval pressure slowly releasing and the flesh of her hips became soft again.

She was still for a long time.

Then a tear fell on his cheek. It surprised him.

"I do that for someone I like very much," her voice whispered. It seemed to come from some place other than the body that was above him; from someone who perhaps had also been an onlooker at all of this.

Then Lila lay back beside him, stretched the full length of her body against him and wrapped her arms around him as if to possess him forever.

They lay there together for a long time. Her arms held him but his mind began to drift free in an ebb tide of thought nothing could hold.

After a time he heard a steady breathing which told him she was asleep.

Sometimes between sleep and waking there's a zone where the mind gets a glimpse of old active subconscious worlds. He'd just passed through that zone and for a moment had seen something he would forget if he went back to sleep. But he'd forget it if he became any more awake too.

This was the first time he'd been passive like this. Before it had been his idea, his aggression, his carnal desires. Now this passivity seemed to open something up.

What he seemed to have seen was that maybe "he" hadn't had anything to do with it at all. He tried to hang on to it, half awake, half asleep.

A light shone again in the port. Maybe a car headlight from shore. Lila turned under the covers and brought her arm up over her face so that her hand opened upward toward him. Then she lay quietly.

He put his own hand up next to it. They were the same. The pattern that had caused her to come in and do this had also made these two hands alike. They were like leaves of trees, with no more knowledge than leaves have of why their cells produced them or made them so alike.

That was it, maybe. That was the thing, the other thing that was doing this that was not Lila and not himself.

The car headlight vanished and then, in the fading mental image of her hand, he thought he had seen something else. On her forearm near the wrist had been long scars, one of them slightly diagonal to the others. He wondered if it was something she had done herself.

He turned and put the tip of his forefinger against the wrist. The scars were there, all right, but they were smooth. It must have been long ago. It could have been a car accident or some other trauma, of course, but something told him it wasn't. It seemed like more evidence of some past internal war with the thing that had brought her here tonight—some enormous battle between the intelligence of her mind and the intelligence of her cells.

If that's what it was, the cells had won. Probably they had bled enough to throw off infection, then swelled to slow down the bleeding, clotted, and then slowly, with the special intelligence of their own that had nothing to do with Lila's mind, they remembered how they had been before she had cut them apart and they carefully joined themselves back together again. They had a mind and will of their own. The mental Lila had tried to die but the cellular Lila had wanted to live.

That's the way it always is. The intelligence of the mind can't think of any reason to live, but it goes on anyway because the intelligence of the cells can't think of any reason to die.

That explained what had happened tonight. The first intelligence out there in the cabin disliked him and still did. It was this second intelligence that had come in and made love. The first Lila had nothing to do with it.

These cellular patterns have been lovers for millions of years and they aren't about to be put off by these recent little intellectual patterns that know almost nothing about what is going on. The cells want immortality. They know their days are numbered. That is why they make such a commotion.

They're so old. They began to distinguish this body on the left from this body on the right more than a billion years ago. Beyond comprehension. Of course they pay no attention to mind patterns. In their scale of time, mind is just some ephemera that arrived a few moments ago, and will probably pass away in a few moments more.

That was what he had seen that he was trying to hang on to now, this confluence where the mental and the biological patterns are both awake and aware of each other and in conflict.

The ebb-tide feeling. At ebb tide this cellular sexual activity is all so intellectually vulgar and shunnable, but when the flood tide returns the vulgarity magically turns into a high-quality attraction and there's a deflection of mind by something that isn't mind at all and there's some feeling of awe in this. The mind sitting detached, aloof and discerning is suddenly rudely shoved aside by this other intelligence which is stronger than its own. Then strange things happen that the mind sees as vulgar and shunnable when the tides are out again.

He listened to the even breathing of this body next to him. That twilight zone was gone now. His mind was getting the upper hand, getting more and more awake, thinking about what he'd seen.

It fitted into the independence and opposition of levels of evolution that was emphasized in the Metaphysics of Quality. The language of mental intelligence has nothing to say to the cells directly. They don't understand it. The language of the cells has nothing to say to the mind directly. It doesn't speak that language either. They are completely separate patterns. At this moment, asleep, "Lila" doesn't exist any more than a program exists when a computer is switched off. The intelligence of her cells had switched Lila off for the night, exactly the way a hardware switch turns off a computer program.

The language we've inherited confuses this. We say "my" body and "your" body and "his" body and "her" body, but it isn't that way. That's like a FORTRAN program saying, "this is my computer." "This body on the left," and "This body on the right." That's the way to say it. This Cartesian "Me," this autonomous little homunculus who sits behind our eyeballs looking out through them in order to pass judgment on the affairs of the world, is just completely ridiculous. This self-appointed little editor of reality is just an impossible fiction that collapses the moment one examines it. This Cartesian "Me" is a software reality, not a hardware reality. This body on the left and this body on the right are running variations of the same program, the same "Me," which doesn't belong to either of them. The "Me's" are simply a program format.

Talk about aliens from another planet. This program based on "Me's" and "We's" is the alien. "We" has only been here for a few thousand years or so. But these bodies that "We" has taken over were around for ten times that long before "We" came along. And the cells—my God, the cells have been around for thousands of times that long.

These poor stupid bodies that "We" has invaded, he thought. Every once in a while, like tonight and last night, they overthrow the program and go about their ways leaving "We" mystified about how all this could have happened. That's what happened just now.

Mystified, and somewhat horrified too at the things bodies do without its permission. All of this sexual morality of Rigel's—it wasn't just social codes. It was also part of this sense of horror at these cells "We" has invaded and the strange patterns of Quality that existed before "We" arrived.

These cells make sweat and snot and phlegm. They belch and bleed and fuck and fart and piss and shit and vomit and squeeze out more bodies just like themselves all covered with blood and placental slime that grow and squeeze out more bodies, on and on.

"We," the software reality, find these hardware facts so distressing that it covers them with euphemisms and clothes and toilets and medical secrecy. But what "We" is covering up is pure quality for the cells. The cells have gotten to their advanced state of evolution through all this fucking and farting and pissing and shitting. That's quality! Particularly the sexual functions. From the cells' point of view sex is pure Dynamic Quality, the highest Good of all.

So when Phædrus told Rigel that Lila had Quality he was telling the truth. She does. This same attraction which is now so morally condemned is what created the condemners.

Talk about ingratitude. These bodies would still be a bunch of dumb bacteria if it hadn't been for sexual quality. When mutation was the only means of genetic change, life sat around for three billion years, doing almost no changing at all. It was sexual selection that shot it forward into the animals and plants we have today. A bacterium gets no choice in what its progeny are going to be, but a queen bee gets to select from thousands of drones. That selection is Dynamic. In all sexual selection, Lila chooses, Dynamically, the individual she wants to project into the future. If he excites her sense of Quality she joins him to perpetuate him into another generation, and he lives on. But if he's unable to convince her of his Quality—if he's sick or deformed or unable to satisfy her in some way—she refuses to join him and his deformity is not carried on.

Now Phædrus was really awake. Now he felt he was at some sort of source. Was this thing that he had seen tonight the same thing that he had glimpsed in the streetcar, the thing that had been bothering him all these years? He thought about it for a long time and slowly decided that it probably was.

Lila is a judge. That's who lay here beside him tonight: a judge of hundreds of millions of years standing, and in the eyes of this judge he was nobody very important. Almost anyone would do, and most would do better than he.

After a while he thought, maybe that's why the famous "Gioconda Smile" in the Louvre, like Lila's smile in the streetcar, has troubled viewers for so many years. It's the secret smile of a judge who has been overthrown and suppressed for the good of social progress, but who, silently and privately, still judges.

"Sad Sack." That was the term she used. It had no intellectual meaning, but it had plenty of meaning nevertheless. It meant that in the eyes of this biological judge all his intelligence was some kind of deformity. She rejected it. It wasn't what she wanted. Just as the patterns of intelligence have a sense of disgust about the body functions, the patterns of biology, so do Lila's patterns of biology have a disgust about the patterns of intelligence. They don't like it. It turns them off.

Phædrus thought about William James Sidis, the prodigy who could read five languages when he was five years old. After discovering what Sidis had said about Indians, Phædrus had read a full biography of him and found that when Sidis was a teenager he announced he would refuse to have anything to do with sex for the rest of his life. It seemed as though in order to sustain a satisfactory intellectual life he felt he had to cut himself off from social and biological domination except where they were absolutely necessary. This vow of ancient priests and ascetics was once considered a high form of morality, but in the "Roaring Twenties" of the twentieth century a new standard of morals had arrived, and when journalists found out about this vow they ridiculed Sidis mercilessly. That coincided with the beginning of a pattern of seclusion that lasted the rest of his life.

"Is it better to have wisdom or is it better to be attractive to the ladies?" That was a question debated by Provençal poets way back in the thirteenth century. Sidis opted for wisdom, but it seemed to Phædrus there ought to be some way you could have both.

The question seemed to imply the stupidity of women but a

feminist could turn it around and ask, "Is it better to have wisdom or to be attractive to men!" That's practically the theme song of the whole feminist movement. Although the feminists and the male Provençal poets would appear to be condemning the opposite sex, they are, in fact, both actually condemning the same thing: not men, not women, but static biological antagonism to social and intellectual Quality.

Phædrus began to feel a slow rock of the boat.

His own cells were sick of all this intellectualizing. They'd had enough for one day. They'd had way too much, in fact, and were starting to switch him off. Tomorrow they'd need him when they got hungry, and they would turn him on again to find them some food, but for now they were rubbing him out. He felt like Hal, the computer in "2001," as its internal patterns slowed down. "Daisy . . . Daisy . . . give me your . . . answer . . . true."

Lila, Lila, what is your answer true?

What a strange, strange day this had been.

Phædrus became aware again of Lila's body next to him, and again the gentle rocking of the boat. That was the only good thing that had happened all day, the way their bodies paid no attention to all their social and intellectual differences and had gone on in as if these "people" that "owned" them didn't exist at all. They had been at this business of life for so long.

Now that he was quiet he noticed that the boat's motion wasn't so much a rocking as a surge, a very faint, very slow, lift and drop accompanying the waves. He wondered if that could be a surge coming in from the ocean. Probably not, he thought. They were still way too far upriver from the ocean. Still it could be, he thought. If the tides get up to Troy maybe the surge could get this far.

It could be. . . .

He waited for each next faint lift and fall to come, thinking about it, and then after a while didn't think any more.

Part Two

16.

Fatso thought that was pretty funny the way Lila come in. He said she come in "like the Queen of Diamonds" and "*wished* to *know* where Mr. Jamison could be found." Fatso can imitate anybody, perfect.

Fatso said he didn't tell her nothing but he just listened. She said she's "on her way to Florida for the season." She was "on a yacht with a gentleman and she wished to stop by and renew old acquaintances."

When Fatso said that Jamie broke up laughing.

"If she's with a gentleman what does she want to see *me* for?" Jamie said.

"I guess she misses you."

"She wants *something*."

"One way to find out," Fatso said.

So the next day they went to where she told Fatso she would be. She wasn't there so they sat down. Then she come in the door. Sad. She was really looking old. She used to be a real looker. Getting fat too. Drinking too much beer. She always did like her beer. She better take care of herself. Lila saw them and come over to the table where they was sitting. Jamie got up and opened up his arms for a big hug. He said, "You really came all the way here just to see me? That's too much. *Too* much!"

Then he saw the man coming in behind her was with her. He

caught one look in that man's eyes and his muscles went tight. . . . He hugged Lila but he watched that man. His hair was all white . . . like snow, and his eyes were *cold*, real cold. . . . Like looking in a refrigerator . . . at the morgue. . . . Bad vibes all over him. . . . All the time he was holding Lila that man was watching them. . . .

What the hell'd she bring him here for? Fatso didn't say nothing about that. He told her a hundred times not to bring the clientele around. That was the rule. What was the trouble now?

The man put out his hand to shake.

Jamie shook it.

He put out his for Fatso to shake.

Fatso shook it.

"This is the Captain," Lila says.

"Pleased to meet you Cap'n," Jamie says.

The Cap'n looks like he wants to sit down.

He sits down.

The Captain is full of smiles like he's the nicest man ever lived. Nobody fooled. He wants to buy drinks for everybody. Everybody drinking. Everybody smiling. Everybody just sits around and talks nice now till their teeth drop out, if that's what they want. But that isn't what they want.

Jamie had nothing to tell. They all looked at him like he was supposed to say something but he didn't.

Fatso started asking questions then. He asked the Captain where he was from and where they're going and all about that. He asked about what kind of boat they had and how big it was and how fast it went. Jamie never heard Fatso ask so many questions.

The Captain just sat there with the cold eyes and answered everything just exactly right. Like some kind of detective, maybe. "Watch out Fats, don't tell him nothing," Jamie thought.

Lila kept looking over like she wanted Jamie to do some talking. Then she said, "What are you doing these days, Jamison?"

Jamison!?? She never called him that before. What kind of air was *that*? He thought about it. Then he said, "I don't know, Mizz Lila." He said it that way to mock her a little. "Not much of anything, I guess." He made it sound like he was just up from Alabama.

"Nothing at all?"

"No ma'am. Every year I'se just a little lazier. Don't want to do nothing I don't have to. All wore out with things I don't have to do."

He watched the Captain when he said this. The Captain just smiled. That made Jamie feel better. If he was a detective he gonna know what that's about.

"We have an opportunity for you," Lila said, "which we hope might interest you."

"Oh you *do?*" Jamie said. "Let's *hear* it."

Lila looked at him funny like she saw how it was going. She said, "The Captain has been advised that he needs another crew member for his ocean voyage and we have been hoping that you might consider an offer. I've told him you are an excellent person," she said.

Jamie caught her wink. He smiled a little. Then he had to laugh.

"What are you laughing at," Lila said.

"You sure haven't changed. Crazy Lila! Always thinking something crazy. That's why you came all the way here just to talk to *me?* Just for *that?*"

"Yes," she said, and looked at him. She turned her mouth down like he busted every nice feeling she ever had. "What's wrong with that?"

"Oh Lila," he said. "You sure come a long way."

He looked at both of them for a while. He wondered what kind of place they come from that they could come here and talk to him like that.

He said, "You mean you and the Captain here want to sit on your luxury yacht, sippin' Juleps and watchin' the sunset go down, while I stand there and say 'Yessah, Yessah?' "

"Not like that," Lila said.

"What the hell do you think I am?" Jamie said. It really made him mad coming all the way down here just to hear this. And they thought they were being nice to him.

He turned to the Captain. "Is that all you came here for? To find yourself a cheap nigger to work on your boat?"

The Captain looked like he never heard it. Like what he said to him just bounced off some stone wall. "It's not *my* idea," he said.

"Then what did you come here for?"

"I don't know," the Captain said. "That's what *I* was trying to find out."

The Captain got up. "I've got an appointment now." He picked up his coat. "I'll take care of the bill on the way out," he said. He looked at Lila real pissed. "See you later," he said. Then he went.

Lila looked scared.

"What the hell you up to, Lila?" Jamie said.

"You said you weren't doing anything," she said. "Why did you put him down like that? He didn't do anything to you."

"You know what he's thinking," Jamie said.

"You don't know anything about him," Lila said. "He's just a nice man and a real gentleman."

"Well if you're making it with this nice gentleman, what are you bringing him here for? If you're making it with this nice old cracker you better keep right on making it with him, Lila, because you sure ain't making it anywhere else."

"I was just trying to do you a favor," Lila said.

"What kind of favor is *that*?"

"Well, *think* about it," Lila said. "What do you think is going to happen if we go sailing down to Florida with him? Do you think he's going to live forever?"

Jamie looked at Fatso to see if he heard what she was saying. Fats looked back at him the same way.

"You mean you want me to be there to help in case he accidentally happens to fall overboard, or something?" Jamie asked.

"Yes."

Jamie looked at Fatso again and then looked down. He shook his head and laughed. Then he thought about it some more.

Then he looked up at her. "Sometimes I think I'm bad, Lila, and then someone like you comes along and shows me how."

They talked about old times. Millie's gone. Nobody knows where. Mindy got married, he told her. It's no good any more, he told her. You don't know how bad it's got.

She didn't listen. All she wanted to do was talk about Florida.

After she left Fatso asked, "How long did you know her?"

"Long time," Jamie said. "She used to be good. But she always talked back. That old fart she was with, that's what she's good for now. That's her speed. With him. She walked out on me and I never did nothing to her. Now she should stay the hell away.

"I'm so tired of them," Jamie said. "Long time ago I used to think they was everything. You know, all the money and the big cars and the big smiles and the big-looking clothes. You know? Padded shoulders. I thought that was *really* it. Then I got to see what really went on with them and why they have to have all that—that money and boats and furs and padded shoulders and everything."

"Why?"

"*Why?* Because if they ever lose that big money they got *nothing*. Under all that big money there is nothing there! Nobody! Nobody home.

"I *mean* it," Jamie said. "That's what drives them people day and night. Trying to cover that up. What we know. They think they fool you. They ain't foolin' nobody.

"They know we got something they haven't got. And they come here and they going to try to take it away from us. But they can't figure out what it is. It just drives them crazy. What is it we got they can't get away from us?"

Fatso wondered how far the boat can go.

"Did you hear what she said?" Fatso asked. "That boat can go all the way to South America."

Fatso said he heard about a man out on Long Island who buys boats, no questions.

"How much do you think that boat is worth?" Fatso said.

"Sure would be nice to have a big boat like that," Fatso said. "Go sailing down to Florida. Lots of nice stuff down there in Florida."

"All kinds of stuff," Fatso said. "You know Belford? He goes down to Andrews Island down there and gets all kind of good news. Can make a lot of money that way. If you was on a boat you might put some of that good news where nobody can find it and when you come back take it off again. Nobody know the difference."

Fatso smiled. "And if they find it that nice friend of Lila might have to go to jail."

Jamie didn't say any more to Fatso. But he was thinking.

17.

It was a long way to the hotel but Phædrus felt like walking it. After that blow-up with Lila he needed to walk. This city always made him feel like walking. In the past whenever he'd come here he'd always walked everywhere. Tomorrow he'd be gone.

The skyscrapers rose up all around him now and the street was crowded with people and cars. About twenty or thirty blocks to go, he figured. But these were the short blocks going up and down the island, not the long blocks going across. He could feel himself speeding up.

The New York eyes were everywhere now. Quick, guarded, emotionless. Watch out, they said. Concentrate! Things happen fast around here. . . . Don't miss those horn honks!

This city! He would *never* get used to it. He always wanted to fill up with tranquilizers before he arrived. Some day he'd come here without being manic and overwhelmed, but that day hadn't arrived. Always this wild crazy exhilarated feeling. Crowds, high speed, mental detachment.

It was these crazy skyscrapers. The 3-D. Not just in front of you and in back of you and right of you and left of you—*above* you and *below* you too. Thousands of people hundreds of feet up in the air talking on telephones and staring into computers and conferring with each other, as though it were normal. If you call that normal you call anything normal.

A light turned yellow. He hurried across. . . . Drivers run you down and kill you here. That's why you don't take tranquilizers.

Take tranquilizers and you just *might* get killed. This adrenalin is protection.

At the curb he hoisted his canvas bag full of mail on his shoulder so he could carry it better, then continued. There must be twenty pounds of mail in it, he thought, all the mail since Cleveland. He could spend the rest of the day reading it in his hotel room. He was so full from that lunch with his editor he could skip supper and just read until his famous visitor showed up.

The magazine interviews seemed to have gone well enough—predictable questions about what he was doing now (writing his next book); what his next book was about (Indians); and what changes had occurred since his first book was written. He knew what to tell them because he'd been a reporter himself once, but for some reason he didn't tell them about the boat. That was something he didn't want to share. He'd always heard celebrities led double lives. Here it was, happening.

. . . Junk in store windows . . . radios. Hand-calculators. . . .

. . . A woman coming toward him hasn't clicked yet, that quick New York dart-of-the-eyes, but she will. . . . Here it comes. . . . Click! . . . Then looks away. . . . She passes by. . . . Like the click of a candid-camera shutter. . . .

This was manic New York, now. Later would come depressive New York. Now everything's exciting because it's so different. As soon as the excitement wears off depression will come. It always does.

Culture shock. People who live here all their lives don't get that culture shock. They can't go around being overwhelmed all the time. So to cope they seem to pick some small part of it all and try to be on top of that. But they miss something.

. . . Someone practicing the piano upstairs. . . . Eee-oh-eee-oh . . . police wagon. . . . White flowers, chrysanthemums, 70 dollars. . . . Guy in the street on a skateboard, Korean-looking, headed for Leo Vito's delicatessen. Transients, like himself, who are overwhelmed and get manic and depressive are maybe the ones who really understand the place, the only ones with the Zen *shoshin*, the "beginner's mind". . . .

. . . There he goes.

. . . Lovers hand in hand. Not so young either.

. . . A pennant of some kind in a half-open window two stories up. . . . Too far away to read. Will never know what it says.

All these different patterns of people's lives passing *through* each other without any contact at all.

. . . Smells . . . all different kinds of food odors. . . . Cigars.

. . . Above the window with the pennant, a billboard for Marx Furs. Something angering. . . . The model. . . . High-fashion, high-class. "I am so desirable, I am so unapproachable. But if you have the price (you cheap bastard), I am for sale." That price. . . . Was it all for sale if you had that price? . . . Do women really act like that here? . . . Some, he supposed. . . . It must sell furs. And jewelry and cosmetics. . . . Ahh, it was just an advertising cliché. *Those* guys were for sale.

. . . More candid-camera eyes, some cynical. If he wasn't up to something, why was he here? . . . It wore on you, that guilty-until-proven-innocent attitude. He didn't want to prove anything to anyone. He was done with that.

That was it. He didn't want to prove anything. Not to Rigel, not to Lila, not to her "friends". . . . God, what a shock that was. If those were her friends he sure didn't want to meet her enemies.

He wondered what it was about himself that she couldn't see when he was getting angry. Just now at the café she'd gone on for fifteen minutes about what great people they were and she never saw what was coming. She missed the whole point of everything. She's after Quality, like everybody else, but she defines it entirely in biological terms. She doesn't see intellectual quality at all. It's outside her range. She doesn't even see social quality.

That whole thing with her on the river was like Mae West and Sherlock Holmes. What a mismatch. Sherlock lowers his standards by having anything to do with Mae, but Mae is also lowering *her* standards by having anything to do with Sherlock. Sherlock is smart, all right, but that isn't what interests Mae. These biological "friends" of Lila: that's what she goes for.

. . . They can have her. She'd be off the boat tonight. If this last meeting at the hotel went as smoothly as the others he'd be out of here tomorrow and heading south.

. . . More eyes. . . . They weren't *watching* you so much as watching *out* for you. Survivors' eyes.

He had to step off the sidewalk to get around a steel mesh fence in front of a huge hole that went down now where there used to be something. Cement trucks at the bottom of the hole were pouring concrete. On the other side of the hole the adjacent building looked all scarred and damaged. Maybe that was coming down next. Always something going up. Always something coming down. Change and change, on and on. He had never come here when there wasn't all this demolition and construction going on.

Suddenly he was back into posh fabrics and clothing stores. Saying what this city is like is like saying what Europe is like. It depends on what neighborhood you're in, what time of day, how depressed you are.

He buttoned the top of his jacket, put his free hand in his pocket, and walked more briskly. He should have worn a sweater under his jacket. The weather was turning cold again.

The first time he was alone here, when was it? In the Army maybe? No, it couldn't have been. Some time around World War II. He couldn't remember. All he could remember was the route. It was from Bowling Green all the way up Broadway to somewhere past Columbus Circle.

He remembered it was a cold day like this one so that when he slowed down he got chilly. So instead of getting tired and slowing down more and more he kept going faster and faster until in the end he was running through crowds, up blocks and across intersection after intersection with sweat soaking his clothes and running down his face. The next day in his hotel room his legs were so stiff he could hardly move.

It must have been on his way to India. Breaking out of this whole system. Running to get free. He couldn't run like that any more. He'd never make it. Now he had to go slow and use his mind more.

What was he running from? He didn't know then. It seemed like he'd been running all his life.

It used to fill his dreams, night after night. When he was little it was a giant octopus that he'd seen in a cartoon movie. The octopus would come up on the beach and wrap its tentacles around him and squeeze him to death. He would wake up in the dark and think he was dead. Later it was a huge, shadowy, faceless giant who was coming to kill him. He would wake up afraid and then slowly realize that the giant wasn't real. He supposed everyone had dreams like that although he doubted whether most people had them so often.

He had come to think of dreams as Dynamic perceptions of reality. They were suppressed and filtered out of consciousness by conventional patterns of static social and intellectual order but they revealed a primary truth: a value truth. The static patterns of the dreams were false but the underlying values that produced the patterns were true. In static reality there is no octopus coming to squeeze us to death, no giant that is going to devour us and digest us and turn us into a part of its own body so that it can grow stronger and stronger while we are dissolved and lost into nothingness.

But in Dynamic reality?

. . . These manhole covers always fascinated him. Many intersections seemed to have nearly a dozen of them, some new and rough, others worn smooth and shiny from so many tires rolling over them. How many tires did it take to wear a steel manhole cover smooth?

He'd seen drawings of how the manholes led down to staggeringly complex underground networks of systems that made this whole island happen: electric power networks, telephone networks, water pipe networks, gas line networks, sewage networks, subway tunnels, TV cables, and who knows how many special-purpose networks he had never even heard of, like the nerves and arteries and muscle fibers of a giant organism.

The Giant of his dreams.

It was spooky how it all worked with an intelligence of its own that was way beyond the intelligence of any person. He would never know how to fix one of these systems of wire and tubes down below the ground that ran it all. Yet there was someone who did. And there was a system for finding that person if he was needed, and a system for finding that system that would find him. The cohesive force that held all these systems together: that was the Giant.

When he was young Phædrus used to think about cows and pigs and chickens and how they never knew that the nice farmer who provided food and shelter was doing so only so that he could sell them to be killed and eaten. They would "oink," or "cluck," and he would come with food, so they probably thought he was some sort of servant.

He also used to wonder if there was a higher farmer that did the same thing to people, a different kind of organism that they saw every day and thought of as beneficial, providing food and shelter and protection from enemies, but an organism that secretly was raising these people for its own sustenance, feeding upon them and using their accumulated energy for its own independent purposes. Later he saw there was: this Giant. People look upon the social patterns of the Giant in the same way cows and horses look upon a farmer; different from themselves, incomprehensible, but benevolent and appealing. Yet the social pattern of the city devours their lives for its own purposes just as surely as farmers devour the flesh of farm animals. A higher organism is feeding upon a lower one and accomplishing more by doing so than the lower organism can accomplish alone.

The metaphysics of substance makes it difficult to see the Giant. It makes it customary to think of a city like New York as a "work of man," but what man invented it? What group of men invented it? Who sat around and thought up how it should all go together?

If "man" invented societies and cities, why are all societies and cities so repressive of "man"? Why would "man" want to invent internally contradictory standards and arbitrary social institutions for the purpose of giving himself a bad time? This "man" who goes around inventing societies to repress himself seems real as long as you deal with him in the abstract, but he evaporates as you get more specific.

Sometimes people think there are some evil individual "men" somewhere who are exploiting them, some secret cabal of capitalists, or "400," or "Wall Street bankers," or WASPs or name-any-minority group that gets together periodically and has secret conferences on how to exploit them personally. These "men" are supposed to be enemies of "man." It gets confusing, but nobody seems to notice the confusion.

A metaphysics of substance makes us think that all evolution stops with the highest evolved substance, the physical body of man. It makes us think that cities and societies and thought structures are all subordinate creations of this physical body of man. But it's as foolish to think of a city or a society as created by human bodies as it is to think of human bodies as a creation of the cells, or to think of cells as created by protein and DNA molecules, or to think of DNA as created by carbon and other inorganic atoms. If you follow that fallacy long enough you come out with the conclusion that individual electrons contain the intelligence needed to build New York City all by themselves. Absurd.

If it's possible to imagine two red blood cells sitting side by side asking, "Will there ever be a higher form of evolution than us?" and looking around and seeing nothing, deciding there isn't, then you can imagine the ridiculousness of two people walking down a street of Manhattan asking if there will ever be any form of evolution higher than "man," meaning biological man.

Biological man doesn't invent cities or societies any more than pigs and chickens invent the farmer that feeds them. The force of evolutionary creation isn't contained by substance. Substance is just one kind of static pattern left behind by the creative force.

This city is another static pattern left behind by the creative force. It's composed of substance but substance didn't create it all by itself. Neither did a biological organism called "man" create it all by himself. This city is a higher pattern than either a substance or a biological pattern called man. Just as biology exploits substance for its own purposes, so does this social pattern called a city exploit biology for its own purposes. Just as a farmer raises cows for the sole purpose of devouring them, this pattern grows living human bodies for the sole purpose of devouring them. That is what the Giant really does. It converts accumulated biological energy into forms that serve itself.

When societies and cultures and cities are seen not as inventions of "man" but as higher organisms than biological man, the phenomena of war and genocide and all the other forms of human exploitation become more intelligible. "Mankind" has never been interested in getting itself killed. But the superorganism, the Giant, who is a pattern of values superimposed on top of biological human bodies, doesn't mind losing a few bodies to protect his greater interests.

The Giant began to materialize out of Phædrus' Dynamic dreams when he was in college. A professor of chemistry had mentioned at his fraternity that a large chemical firm was offering excellent jobs for graduates of the school and almost every member of the fraternity thought it was wonderful news. World War II had just ended and good jobs were all that anyone seemed to think of. The revolution of the sixties was still twenty years off. No one had thought of making the film, "The Graduate," back then.

Phædrus had always believed science is a search for truth. A real scientist is not supposed to sell out that goal to corporations who are searching for mere profit. Or, if he had to sell out in order to live that was nothing to be happy about. These fraternity brothers of his acted like they never heard of science as truth. Phædrus had suddenly seen a tentacle of the Giant reaching out and he was the only one who could see it.

So here was this Giant, this nameless, faceless system reaching for him, ready to devour him and digest him. It would use his energy to grow stronger and stronger throughout his life while he grew older and weaker until, when he was no longer of much use, it would excrete him and find another younger person full of energy to take his place and do the same thing all over again.

That was why he had run that day through all this traffic—through all these systems and sub-systems of the island. He was on his way to India, done with this corporate pseudo-science, still pursuing truth, knowing that to find it he would have to get free of the Giant first.

Here up in the sky above him right now were the heads of the corporation that had prompted the chemistry professor to make that talk to that fraternity so many years ago. This was the brain center of that corporate network, surrounded by other networks: financial networks, information networks, electronic transmission networks. That's what all those tiny bodies were doing up there suspended so many hundreds of feet up in the sky. Participating in the Giant.

So Phædrus had been right in running then. But now—funny thought—this was actually his home. All his income came from here. His only fixed address now was right here—his publisher's address on Madison Avenue. He was as much a part of the Giant as anyone else.

Once you understand something well enough, you don't need to run from it. In recent years each time he'd returned to New York he could feel his fear of this old monster lessening, and a kind of familiar affection for it growing.

From a Metaphysics of Quality's point of view this devouring of human bodies is a moral activity because it's more moral for a social pattern to devour a biological pattern than for a biological pattern to devour a social pattern. A social pattern is a higher form of evolution. This city, in its endless devouring of human bodies, was creating something better than any biological organism could by itself achieve.

Well, of course! My God! Look at it! The power of this place! Fantastic! What individual work of art can come anywhere near to equaling it? Sure: dirty, noisy, rude, dangerous, expensive. Always has been and probably always will be. Always been a hell-hole if what you're looking for is stability and serenity. . . . But if you're looking for stability and serenity, go to a cemetery, don't come here! This is the most Dynamic place on earth!

Now Phædrus felt it all around him—the speed, the height, the crowds and their tension. All the early strangeness was gone now. He was in it.

He remembered that its great symbol used to be the ticker tape, ticking out unpredictable fortunes rising and falling every second, a great symbol of luck. Luck. When E. B. White wrote, "If you want to live in New York you should be willing to be lucky," he meant not just "lucky" but *willing* to be lucky—that is, Dynamic. If you cling to some set static pattern, when opportunity comes you won't take it. You have to hang loose, and when the time comes to be lucky, then be lucky: that's Dynamic.

When they call it freedom, that's not right. "Freedom" doesn't mean anything. Freedom's just an escape from something negative. The real reason it's so hallowed is that when people talk about it they mean Dynamic Quality.

That's what neither the socialists *nor* the capitalists ever got figured out. From a static point of view socialism is more moral than capitalism. It's a higher form of evolution. It is an intellectually guided society, not just a society that is guided by mindless traditions. That's what gives socialism its drive. But what the socialists left out and what has all but killed their whole undertaking is an absence of a concept of indefinite Dynamic Quality. You go to any socialist city and it's always a dull place because there's little Dynamic Quality.

On the other hand the conservatives who keep trumpeting about the virtues of free enterprise are normally just supporting their own self-interest. They are just doing the usual cover-up for the rich in their age-old exploitation of the poor. Some of them seem to sense there is also something mysteriously virtuous in a free enterprise system and you can see them struggling to put it into words but they don't have the metaphysical vocabulary for it any more than the socialists do.

The Metaphysics of Quality provides the vocabulary. A free market is a *Dynamic* institution. What people buy and what people sell, in other words what people *value*, can never be contained by any intellectual formula. What makes the marketplace work is Dynamic Quality. The market is always changing and the direction of that change can never be predetermined.

The Metaphysics of Quality says the free market makes everybody richer by preventing static economic patterns from setting in and stagnating economic growth. That is the reason the major capitalist economies of the world have done so much better since World War II than the major socialist economies. It is not that Victorian social economic patterns are more moral than socialist intellectual economic patterns. Quite the opposite. They are *less* moral as static patterns go. What makes the free-enterprise system superior is that the socialists, reasoning intelligently and objectively, have inadvertently closed the door to Dynamic Quality in the buying and selling of things. They closed it because the metaphysical structure of their objectivity never told them Dynamic Quality exists.

People, like everything else, work better in parallel than they do in series, and that is what happens in this free enterprise city. When things are organized socialistically in a bureaucratic series, any increase in complexity increases the probability of failure. But when they're organized in a free-enterprise parallel, an increase in complexity becomes an increase in diversity more capable of responding to Dynamic Quality, and thus an increase of the probability of success. It's this diversity and parallelism that make this city work.

And not just this city. Our greatest national economic success, agriculture, is organized almost entirely in parallel. All life has parallelism built into it. Cells work in parallel. Most body organs work in parallel: eyes, brains, lungs. Species operate in parallel, democracies operate in parallel; even science seems to operate best when it is organized through the parallelism of the scientific societies.

It's ironic that although the philosophy of science leaves no room for any undefined Dynamic activity, it's science's unique organization for the handling of the Dynamic that gives it its superiority. Science superseded old religious forms, not because what it says is more true in any absolute sense (whatever *that* is), but because what it says is more Dynamic.

If scientists had simply said Copernicus was right and Ptolemy was wrong without any willingness to further investigate the subject, then science would have simply become another minor religious creed. But scientific truth has always contained an overwhelming difference from theological truth: it is provisional. Science always contains an eraser, a mechanism whereby new Dynamic insight could wipe out old static patterns without destroying science itself. Thus science, unlike orthodox theology, has been capable of continuous, evolutionary growth. As Phædrus had written on one of his slips, "The pencil is mightier than the pen."

That's the whole thing: to obtain static and Dynamic Quality *simultaneously.* If you don't have the static patterns of scientific knowledge to build upon you're back with the cave man. But if you don't have the freedom to change those patterns you're blocked from any further growth.

You can see that where political institutions have improved throughout the centuries the improvement can usually be traced to a static-Dynamic combination: a king or constitution to preserve the static, and a parliament or jury that can act as a Dynamic eraser; a mechanism whereby new Dynamic insight can wipe out old static patterns without destroying the government itself.

Phædrus was surprised by the conciseness of a commentary on *Robert's Rules of Order* that seemed to capture the whole thing in two sentences: No minority has a right to block a majority from conducting the legal business of the organization. No majority has a right to prevent a minority from peacefully attempting to become a majority. The power of those two sentences is that they create a stable static situation where Dynamic Quality can flourish.

In the abstract, at least. When you get to the particular it's not so simple.

It seems as though any static mechanism that is open to Dynamic Quality must also be open to degeneracy—to falling back to lower forms of quality.

This creates the problem of getting maximum freedom for the emergence of Dynamic Quality while prohibiting degeneracy from destroying the evolutionary gains of the past. Americans like to talk about all their freedom but they think it's disconnected from something Europeans often see in America: the degeneracy that goes with the Dynamic.

It seems as though a society that is intolerant of all forms of degeneracy shuts off its own Dynamic growth and becomes static. But a society that tolerates all forms of degeneracy degenerates. Either direction can be dangerous. The mechanisms by which a balanced society grows and does not degenerate are difficult, if not impossible, to define.

How can you tell the two directions apart? Both oppose the status quo. Radical idealists and and degenerate hooligans sometimes strongly resemble each other.

Jazz was generally considered degenerate music when it first appeared. "Modern" art was considered degenerate.

When you define morality scientifically as that which enhances evolution it sounds as though you have really solved the problem of what morality is. But then when you try to say specifically what is and what isn't evolution and where evolution is going, you find you are right back in the soup again. The problem is that you can't really say whether a specific change is evolutionary at the time it occurs. It is only with a century or so of hindsight that it appears evolutionary.

For example, there was *no way* those Zuñi priests could have known that this fellow they were hanging by his thumbs was going to turn into some future savior of their tribe. Here was a drunken bragging window-peeper who told the authorities they could all go to hell and they couldn't do anything to him. What were they supposed to do? What else *could* they do? They couldn't let every damn degenerate in Zuñi do as he pleased on the ground that he might, at some future date, save the tribe. They had to enforce the rules to hold the tribe together.

This is really the central problem in the static-Dynamic conflict of evolution: how do you tell the saviors from the degenerates? Particularly when they look alike, talk alike and break all the rules alike? Freedoms that save the saviors also save the degenerates and allow them to tear the whole society apart. But restrictions that stop the degenerates also stop the creative Dynamic forces of evolution.

It was almost a custom for people to come to New York, prophesy a doomsday of one sort or another and then wait for it to descend. They're doing it now. But so far the doomsday has never come. New York has always been going to hell but somehow it never gets there. Always changing. Always changing for the worse, it seems, but then right in the middle of the worse comes this new Dynamic thing that nobody ever heard of before and the worse is forgotten because this new Dynamic thing (which is also getting worse) has taken its place. What looks like hell always turns out to be something else.

When something new and Dynamic wants to come into the world it often looks like hell, but it can get born in New York. It can *happen*. It seems like it could happen anywhere but that's not so. There has to be a certain kind of people who can look at it and say "Hey, wait a second! That's good!" without having to look over their shoulder to see if somebody else is saying the same thing. That's rare. This is one of the few places in the world where people don't ask whether something's been approved somewhere else.

That, Phædrus thought, is how the Metaphysics of Quality explains the incredible contrasts of the best and the worst one sees here. Both exist here in such terrific intensity because New York's never been committed to any preservation of its static patterns. It's always ready to change. Whether you are or not. That is what creates its horror and that is what creates its power. Its strength is its looseness. It's the freedom to be so awful that gives it the freedom to be so good.

And so things keep happening here all the time that have this Dynamic sparkle that saves it all. In the midst of everything that's wrong, it sparkles.

Like the kids. You don't see them but they're here, growing like mushrooms in secret places. Once Phædrus went to a museum on a weekday morning and there were hundreds of them pointing at all the minerals and dinosaurs and grabbing each other's arms and holding hands, laughing and watching their teacher from time to time to see if everything was all right. Then suddenly they all vanished and it was as though they had never been there.

What you see in New York depends on your static patterns. What makes the city Dynamic is the way it always busts up whatever those patterns are. This morning, in the restaurant, this black, jet-black thug-like guy with a dirty wool cap pulled over his head comes in. Dirty blue satin sports jacket, Reebok shoes, also dirty. Orders a coffee which they have to serve him because it's the law and then what does he do? Does he pull out a gun? No. Guess again. He pulls out a *New York Times*. He starts reading. It's the book review section. He's some kind of an intellectual. This is New York.

Wham! You're always seeing something you're not set up to see. It's not been all bad, this rich-poor contrast. When you pass a lot of static laws to cut out the worst, the best goes with it, the sparkle disappears and what's left is just a lot of suburban blandness. It's been a psychological fuel that's jet-propelled a lot of people into doing things they might have been too lazy to do otherwise. If everybody here had the same income, same clothes, same background, same opportunities, the whole city would go dead. It's this physical proximity and incredible social gulf that gives this place such power. The city brings everyone up a notch. Or down ten notches. Or up a hundred notches. It sorts them out. It's always been that way, millions of rich and poor all mixed together, skyscrapers and parks, diamond tiaras in the windows and drunken vomit on the street. It really shocks you and motivates you. The Devil is taking the hindmost right before your eyes! And just beyond the beggars go the frontmost, chauffeur-assisted, into their stretch limousines. Yeow!! Keep moving! Don't slow down!

You see the people who smile at you and are ready to cheat you. Sometimes you miss the ones who scowl at you but secretly support you in every way they can. When you talk to them they treat you with a ten-foot pole, but at the other end of it you sense this guarded affection. They're just survivors whose rough edges are all worn smooth. They know how this celebrity of a city works.

• • •

It was getting darker now. And colder too. An edge of depression was approaching. Sooner or later it always appeared. The adrenaline was about normal now and still dropping. His walking had slowed down.

Phædrus reached what he recognized was the edge of Central Park. It was windier here. From the northwest. That's what was bringing all this cold weather. The trees were dark now and billowing heavily in the wind. They still had their leaves, probably because it was nearer the ocean here and warmer than back at Troy and Kingston.

As he walked along he saw the park still kept its quiet, genteel look despite everything.

Of all the monuments the Victorians left to the city, this masterpiece of Olmstead and Vaux's was the greatest, he thought. If money and power and vanity were all they were interested in, why was this place here?

He wondered what the Victorians would think about it now. The skyscrapers all around it would astonish them. They would like the way the trees have grown so big. He had an old Currier and Ives print of the park that showed the park almost barren of trees. Probably they would think the park was fine. Elsewhere in New York they would have other opinions.

They certainly put their stamp on this city. It's still here, under all the Art Deco and Bauhaus. The Victorians were the ones who really built New York up, he thought, and it's still their city deep down inside. When all their brownstones with their ornate pilasters and entablatures went out of style they were considered the apotheosis of ugliness, but now, as their buildings get fewer every year, they give a nice accent to all the twentieth century slick.

Victorian rococo brickwork and stonework and ironwork. God, how they loved ornateness. It went with their language. The final ultimate proof of their rise from the savages. They really thought they had done it in this city.

Everywhere you still see little signs of what they thought about this city. All the baroque brownstone friezes and gargoyles waiting for the wreckers' ball. The riveted iron bridges in Central Park. Their wonderful museums. Their lions in front of the public library. They were sculpting an image of themselves.

All this unnecessary ornateness they left behind: that wasn't just vanity. There was a lot of love in it, too. They gussied this city up so much partly because they loved it. They paid for all these gargoyles and ornamental iron work the way a newly-rich father might buy a fancy dress for a daughter he's proud of.

It's easy to condemn them as pretentious snobs, since they openly invited that opinion, and ignore the history that made them that way. They did everything they could to ignore that history themselves. What the Victorians never wanted you to know was that actually they were nothing more than a bunch of rich hicks. For the most part they were rural, backwater, religion-bound people who, after the Civil War had disrupted their lives, suddenly found themselves in the middle of an industrial age.

There was no precedent for it. They really had no guidelines for what to do with themselves. The possibilities of steel and steam and electricity and science and engineering were dazzling. They were getting rich beyond their wildest dreams, and the money pouring in showed no signs of ever stopping. And so a lot of the things they were later condemned for, their love of snobbery and gingerbread architecture and ornamental cast iron, were just the mannerisms of decent people who were trying to live up to all this. The only wealthy models available were the European aristocracy.

What we tend to forget is that, unlike the European aristocrats they aped, the American Victorians were a very creative people. The telephone, the telegraph, the railroad, the transatlantic cable, the light bulb, the radio, the phonograph, the motion pictures, and the techniques of mass production—almost all the great technological changes that are associated with the twentieth century are, in fact, American *Victorian* inventions. This *city* is *composed* of their value patterns! It was their optimism, their belief in the future, their codes of craftsmanship and labor and thrift and self-discipline that really built twentieth-century America. Since the Victorians disappeared the entire drift of this century has been toward a dissipation of these values.

You could imagine some old Victorian aristocrat coming back to these streets, looking around, and then becoming stony-faced at what he saw.

. . .

Phædrus saw that it was nearly dark. He was almost at his hotel now. As he crossed the street he noticed a gust of wind swirling dust and scraps of paper up from the pavement before the lights of a taxi. A sign on top of the taxi said "SEE THE BIG APPLE" and under it the name of some tour line, with a telephone number.

The "Big Apple." He could almost feel the disgust with which a Victorian would greet *that* name.

They never thought of New York City that way. "The Big Opportunity" or the "Big Future" or the "Empire City" would have been closer to their vision. They saw the city as a monument to their own greatness, not something they were devouring. "The mentality that sees New York as a 'Big Apple,' " the Victorian might say, "is the mentality of a worm." And then he might add, "To be sure, the worm means the name only as a compliment, but that is because the worm has no idea of what the effects of his eating the Big Apple are."

The hotel doorman seemed to recognize Phædrus as he approached and opened the gold-lettered, monogrammed glass door with a professional smile and flourish. But as Phædrus smiled back he realized the doorman probably "seemed to recognize" everybody who came in. That was his role. Part of the New York illusion.

Inside, the lobby's world of subdued gilt and plush suggested Victorian elegance without denying the advantages of twentieth century modernity. Only the howl of wind at the crack between the elevator doors reminded him of the world outside.

In the elevator he thought about the vertical winds that must be in all these buildings, and wondered if there were compensating vertical downdrafts outside. Probably not. The hot elevator winds would just keep rising into the sky after they left the building. Cold air would fill in from horizontal currents on the streets.

The room had been cleaned since he'd left and the bed had been made. He dropped the heavy canvas sack of mail on it. He wouldn't have much time to read mail now. That walk had taken longer than he'd thought it would. But he felt sort of tired and relaxed and that felt good.

He turned on the living room light and heard a buzzing sound by the bulb. At first he thought it was a loose bulb, but then he saw that the buzzing was coming from a large moth.

He watched it for a moment and wondered, "How did it get up this high in the sky?" He thought moths stayed close to the ground.

It blended with the Victorian decor of the place as it fluttered around the lampshade.

"It must be a Victorian moth," he thought, "aspiring eternally to higher things. And then, reaching its goal, burning to death and falling to the dust below." Victorians loved that kind of imagery.

Phædrus went to a large glass door that seemed to open onto a balcony. There was too much reflection from the room to see what was on the other side, so he opened it a little. Through the opening he could see the night sky, and far away, the random patterns of window lights in other skyscrapers. He opened the door wider, stepped out onto the balcony and felt the cold air. It was windy up here. And high, too. He could see he was almost at a level with the tops of the buildings way over on the other side of the huge dark space of Central Park. The balcony seemed to be made of some sort of gray stone, but it was too dark to see.

He stepped to the stone rail and looked over.

. . . YEEOW!! . . .

Way down there the cars were like little ladybugs. They were yellow, most of them, and they crawled along slowly, just like bugs. The yellow ones must be taxis. They moved so slowly. One of them pulled to the curb directly below him and stopped. Then Phædrus could see a speck that had to be a person get out and go into the entrance he himself had come in. . . .

He wondered how long it would take to fall all the way down there. Thirty seconds? Less than that, he figured. Thirty seconds is a long time. Five seconds would be more like it. . . .

The thought started a tingling in his body. It rose to his head and made him dizzy. He stepped back carefully.

He looked up for a while. The sky was not really a night sky. It was filled with the same orange glow he and Lila had seen at Nyack. Only much more intense now. He supposed it was atmospheric pollution or even normal sea mist or dust reflecting the streetlights from below back down from the sky, but it gave a feeling of not being really outdoors at all. This Giant of a city even dominated the sky.

How quiet it was now. Almost serene. Strange that way up here, looking down on all the noise and jangle and tension below, is this upper zone of silence. You don't even think about it when you're down on the street.

No wonder multi-millionaires paid huge sums for space up here in the sky. They could endure all that competitive life down below when they had a place like this up here to retreat to.

The Giant could be very good to you, he thought. . . .

. . . If it wanted to.

18.

Lila didn't care *where* she was going. She was so mad at the Captain she could spit. That bastard! Who the *hell* did he think he *was* calling her that—"A bitch setting up a dog fight." She should have *hit* him!

What did he know? She should have said, "Yes, and who made me one? Was it *me*? You don't know me!" She should have said, "Nobody knows me. You'll *never* know me. I'll *die* before you know me. But *boy oh boy, do I ever know YOU!*" That's what she should have told him.

She was so sick of men. She didn't want to hear men talk. They just want to dirty you. That's what they all want to do. Just dirty you so you'll be just like them. And then tell you what a bitch you are.

This is what she got for being honest. Wasn't that funny? If she'd lied to him everything would be fine. If she was really a bitch did he think she would have *told* him all that stuff about Jamie? No. That was really funny.

What was she going to do with these shirts now? She sure wasn't going to give them to him now. She was tired of carrying them. She spent hours looking for them and now she had to take them back. Why did she have to try to be nice to him? She never learned. No matter what you do they always want to make you look worse than they are.

You're not doing anything wrong, you know, you're not hurting anybody and you're not stealing anything, you know, and still they just *hate* you for it anyway, for making love. Before they get on you're a real angel, but after they get off you're a real whore. For a while. Until they get ready again. Then you're an angel again.

She'd never been on the street every night. She wasn't one of the bad ones. Just sometimes when she felt like it. She *liked* it. She always did. She liked it all the time. Every night. So what? And she didn't like it always with the same man. And she didn't care what people thought about her. And she liked money too, to spend. And she liked booze too and a lot of other things. Put all that together and you got Lila, she should have told him. "Just don't try to turn me into somebody else. 'Cause it won't work. I'm just Lila and I always will be. And if you don't like me the way I am then just get out. I don't need you. I don't need anyone. I'll die first. That's the way I am." That's what she should have told him.

A store window showed her reflection. She looked like she was hurrying. She should slow down. She didn't have to hurry so fast. She didn't have anywhere to go except to the boat to get her things off.

It was dumb to tell him anything. You can't tell people like him anything. If you do, they're gone. All he wanted her for was to prove how big he was. He didn't care what she said, he just wanted her to be some kind of guinea pig to study or something like that, when he really thought all those bad things about her all the time.

He never talked straight, but she could tell he was picking on her in his mind all the time for things she said. Trying to treat her so "nice." He always wanted to know what *she* thought but he'd never tell her what *he* thought. Always playing around the edges. That's what she couldn't stand. She never should have told him that stuff about nerds like him. That's what did it. Nerds like him couldn't stand to hear that.

She knew how to handle people like him. They're not hard to live with. All you have to do is let them talk. You've got to build someone like him up all the time or they get rid of you. She'd probably be going on the boat to Florida tomorrow if she'd kept her mouth shut. She could have taken care of him whenever he wanted it. Jamie didn't mind. Jamie didn't care who she slept with. Everybody could have been happy.

Jamie didn't like the Captain either. Jamie always knew what people were thinking. If somebody thought he was going to make trouble for Jamie, Jamie had him all figured out.

A black witch on a broom looked at her through a display window. It was almost Halloween time.

She didn't know this part of the city. If she'd ever been here before, she'd forgotten it. Or maybe it had changed so much she didn't recognize it. Everything was always changing here. Except the big buildings.

When she first came here she used to think there was somebody up in those big buildings who knows what's going on here. They would never come down and talk to her. After a while she found out nobody knows what's going on.

Why wouldn't Jamie even give her his address? He acted so different. Something was wrong. She didn't like that friend of his. Maybe it was just the Captain being there.

She had never been on this street before. There was something about it she didn't like. It didn't look dangerous, just grungy. Jamie always told her, "Look around, and if you don't see any women walking by themselves, watch out!" But there was an old lady with a dog farther up the street.

. . . So, if the Captain was all done with her, that was nothing new. . . . She was used to that. She'd find something. . . . She always landed on her feet.

A little shop had some bottles in the windows and dirt and junk. She always thought they were going to fix things up some day around here but nobody ever fixes anything. It just gets worse and worse.

An old church had a padlock on the doors and a sign saying it was closed. The sign was all faded so it must have been closed for a long time. In a wooden box under the window all the plants were dead. It didn't look like her grandfather's church. Her grandfather's church was bigger and it wasn't in a dirty city like this.

She'd get a room for a while, a few days maybe, and then look around. That sounded good. She didn't want to go back on the street. It wasn't worth it. Jamie said not to do it, and he knows. He said it was too dangerous. It isn't like it used to be.

She didn't like this street.

She could always get a job waitressing. She knew how to do that. Then after a while something better would turn up. If she tried to think that way it would make her feel better. But first she had to find some place to stay.

She walked for block after block. She kept an eye out for room signs, but didn't see any.

She passed a big hole in the street with orange and white stands around it to keep people away. There was steam coming out of the hole. A man with a cement sack was staring at her. He wasn't going to do anything. Just staring.

She started to read the writing on all the other signs. Leave Fire Lane for Emergency Vehicles. . . . Snow Route. . . . No Standing During Emergency. . . . Vehicles Towed. Moving $9.95 An Hour. . . . Painting. Get Free Estimates. 10% off. . . .

Maybe the signs would tell her what was going on. . . . Drugs Rally. . . . They meant "no drugs rally". . . . Irving's Pantry Deli. . . . Greyer Butcher Block. . . . Clothes Closet King. . . . Audio breakthroughs. . . . We Sell Kosher and Non-Kosher Foods. . . . Natural Health Food store. 20% Off All Vitamins. . . .

Behind an iron fence was a tree with red-orange berries. She remembered a tree like that in her backyard. She used to pick the berries but they were never any good for anything. What's it doing here? The big steel fence kept people from picking the berries. If she tried to go over there they'd throw her out. Some pigeons were there under the trees. . . . The pigeons could be there but she couldn't.

Somebody got inside the iron fence and did spray paint all over the wall. She could never figure out what all that writing said. It looked like just names or something. But they write it so funny you can't see what they're trying to write. They never say "Fuck You" or anything. They just write these strange things like there's something they know that nobody else knows.

. . . Driver. . . . Electric Company. . . . Keep Driveway Clear. . . . One Way. . . . They never tell you what *you* want they only tell you what *they* want. . . .

Some words in Hebrew on a wall. Napoli Pizza. Franklin Cleaners. Since 1973. . . . Police Line. Do Not Cross Blue Lines. Police Department. . . . A lot of barbed wire on the buildings. There didn't used to be all that barbed wire.

There is a guy lying on the sidewalk. Some people are walking by him without looking at him. . . .

Personal Touch. Fine Laundering And Dry Cleaning. Hotels, Hospitals and Clubs. . . . Athens Plumbing and Heating. . . . Hilarious Non-Stop Laughter. I Couldn't Stop Laughing—McGillicudy, *New York Times.* Winner Tony Award.

Lots of plastic bags were lying around. . . . One Way. . . . They never tell you what *you* want they only tell you what *they* want. . . .

These shoes hurt. This street was getting worse. Sidewalks were coming apart here. They're all broken and slanting so that if she didn't watch out she'd turn an ankle. She could fall on all that broken glass. The glass was from an empty window where it looked like somebody had tried to break in.

It was beginning to get cold.

She should be doing something different than this. What was she doing here? Something was wrong that she should be living like this. She should be somewhere better.

She crossed a street and when she looked down it, it looked like there was water down there. That must be the river, she thought.

She decided to get a cab. She still had to get to the boat and get her suitcase off before it got dark. It was too far to walk. Already her legs felt worn out. She hadn't walked this far in a long time. A cab would cost a lot but there wasn't anything else to do. If only she hadn't bought these dumb shirts.

But when she came to a corner she saw a restaurant sign down across the street at the other end of the block. That looked really good. She could rest and get something to eat and call a cab from there.

When she looked through the restaurant window she saw that the menu was expensive. The tables inside had cloths on them and cloth napkins.

Oh, what the hell, she thought. It was time to celebrate something. Being through with the Captain, maybe.

Inside it wasn't crowded. A little old lady waitress was laying out napkins on the other side of the room. She saw Lila and gave her a little smile and came over slowly and showed her to a table by the window.

At the table Lila sat down. It felt really good to sit down.

The waitress asked her if she would care for anything to drink before eating.

"I'll have a scotch and soda," Lila said. "No, make that a Johnnie Walker Black and soda," she smiled. The waitress didn't seem to have much expression. She went off to the bar.

The street out the window looked like some of the streets in Rochester. It was old, without many people on it. In some dirt by the gutter under an old fire escape a cat walked slowly, looking for something. It pawed the dirt first to one side and then to the other. It couldn't seem to find what it was looking for.

Lila still had her old address book. She could call up some old friends and maybe they would invite her over and they could talk about things. She could call them up and maybe they would be able to tell her where she could find a good room. They might even let her stay with them for a while. You could never tell.

She saw through the window that across the street the cat was gone.

The trouble with seeing all her old friends again was that she didn't want to. It didn't feel good to think about it. She didn't want to talk to any of them. She wanted to be done with all that. She didn't want to talk to anybody.

When the waitress came with the drink Lila gave her a big smile and a big "thank you." The waitress smiled a little and then went away.

Lila took a sip of her drink. Oh, did that ever taste good!

She looked at the menu to see what to have to eat.

She ought to just get something cheap. The trouble was she was really hungry. Those steaks really looked good. And French fries. With all the calories. She had better be careful. She didn't want to get into that. She already had too much of that. But it sure sounded good, anyway. She remembered the French fries she made on the boat. Oh, why did she ever tell him anything? She could be making French fries all the way down to Florida if only she had kept her mouth shut.

As she thought about this Lila saw a man's face staring at her through the window. It startled her for a second. But then she thought, what's the matter, Lila, you getting scared of men?

He wasn't bad looking.

She smiled at him. . . .

. . . He just looked at her. Then he looked away.

Then he looked at her again.

She winked to see what that would do.

He smiled a little bit and then pretended he was reading the menu in the window. She stared down at her own menu but watched out of the corner of her eye.

After a while he moved on. She waited to hear the door open, but it didn't. He was gone.

She wondered if she said something that made Jamie angry. He was so different this time. Something was wrong. Something had happened to him, and that was why he wouldn't give his address. He was the kind who didn't tell you. He didn't want to hurt your feelings. That was the way he was.

The Captain wouldn't know anything about that. People like him never do. They just get it off and think they've done something big. That's all they know how to do. That's why they have to pay. You try to show them something and you just waste your time. They don't know what you're doing. The Captain never knew what she tried to do for him. That nerd never would. He probably wouldn't even pay for the shirts.

She had to stop thinking about him.

The waitress came to take her order but Lila still hadn't made up her mind. "I guess I'm not ready yet," she said. She looked inside her glass. "Why don't you bring me another one of these?"

She didn't want to get boozy, she still had a lot of things to do, but this really felt good. It would be a long time until the next one, she thought.

She didn't know what she would do next. It seemed like she'd done it all. She didn't have as much strength any more, or something. She was tired.

Out the window she could see the street was already starting to get old and gray and dark. She wondered where the cat went to that was prowling in the dirt across the street.

She didn't like the dark.

In Rochester it was even darker, she thought.

Maybe she could just go back to Rochester and get a regular job.

She couldn't go back. They all hated her there. That's why they fired her. Because she told them the truth.

Everybody wants to turn you into a servant. And when you won't be a servant for them then you're no good. Then you're bad. No matter how hard you try to please them you're still no good. You can never serve them enough. They've always got to have more. So it doesn't matter; sooner or later they're going to hate you no matter what you do.

She shouldn't have left the *Karma*. If she just hadn't got mad at George she'd still be there. On her way to Florida now. In Florida it was lighter. Because it was South. She sure had some happy times there. She'd still get there, but now she'd have to get some money first.

Maybe she could just go and tell the Captain she was sorry and he'd change his mind. She didn't want to do that. Then she'd have to put up with his nerd talk all the way to Florida. She didn't want to do that. Besides he already told her she had to get off his boat.

She wondered what he did in New York. She wondered where he was going tonight. He sure didn't want to take her with him. She didn't care. She didn't want to go with him. But she knew why. As soon as any of their wife's friends are around they get rid of Lila.

Anyway, it didn't matter.

What was it she wanted to do? It was something but she didn't know what.

There wasn't anything she wanted to do. That was the trouble. She didn't want to have anything more to do with people. She was tired of people. She just wanted to go off somewhere and be by herself and all alone.

The waitress came again. Lila ordered another drink. That wasn't good. Not on an empty stomach. Her stomach still hurt. She should have taken some Empirin earlier.

Lila reached into her purse to get her Empirin. She couldn't find them. That was funny. She knew they were right there. Her other pills weren't there either! She felt around with her hand to find the round plastic bottle. She could always find it by its shape. It wasn't there.

She poked harder and harder through the lipstick and mirror and cigarettes and Kleenexes.

She didn't leave them in the boat because she took three this morning. She brought the purse up and looked inside. Then she looked in the other pocket of the purse. But they weren't there.

Then Lila suddenly knew that the billfold wasn't inside the purse either. She looked up and felt frightened. Outside the window the street had become darker.

She reached all through everything all over again, all her pockets, everywhere in her purse . . . but it was gone. It was really gone.

That was all the money she had!

Some other customers were coming in. They looked cold. Lila didn't see the little old lady waitress. It looked like another waiter had come on duty in her place. He had a bow tie. She didn't like his looks.

She still couldn't believe it. How could she lose it? All her money was in there. It couldn't possibly have dropped out. She had it this morning. She bought the shirts with it. She remembered because she put the receipt in the billfold in case she had to take them back. Now that was gone too.

The new waiter was looking over at her.

She remembered that friend of Jamie's. He sat next to her. The purse was between them.

It had to be him. She knew there was something wrong about him the way he looked at her. Wait till she told Jamie.

Lila looked down at her glass. It was empty.

She didn't have Jamie's new number. He didn't give it to her. What was she going to do now? She couldn't even order dinner. She had to stop and think. She couldn't even think straight. Is that why Jamie didn't give her his number? So there was no way she could tell him?

So he could set her up?

The waiter came over.

"I'm not ready yet," Lila told him.

He gave her a nothing look and went away.

Jamie wouldn't have done that. When Jamie wanted money he just said so. He didn't have to steal from her.

It was so hard to think. She wished she hadn't had these drinks. There was a coin purse inside. He didn't take that. She took it out and counted it. Two quarters, four nickels, and seven pennies.

She didn't even have enough to even pay for the drinks. There was going to be trouble.

She felt sick. She had to go to the toilet.

When she went past the waiter he looked like he already knew she wasn't going to pay.

The toilet stunk. She tried to wash but there wasn't any soap. This was a god-damn dump, this place. Her face was dirty too but there was nowhere to wash. This dirty city. She saw in the mirror that her hair was dirty too. She needed to wash.

If she used the coins to call some friends they could come and help. But it was four years now. Nobody stayed still for four years in New York.

When she got to the phone, on the first coin, she tried Laurie's number. The phone rang and rang. While it was ringing she realized that if she wanted to she could go out the door right from where this phone was and they wouldn't be able to stop her.

The waiter was watching her. He'd stop her. He looked mean. He looked like he'd been around.

Laurie's phone didn't answer. That was all right. That meant she got the coin back. But then it answered and the voice asked who was calling. She said "Lila Blewitt." The woman went away and Lila waited. Thank God Laurie was still here.

But then the voice came back and said, "You must have the wrong number," and hung up.

What did that mean?

She tried two other numbers and got her coin back. She was going to call another address but she realized she really didn't know her. She wouldn't help even if she remembered her. The waiter was still watching.

Lila thought about him for a while. What could he do? She might as well get it over with.

She braced herself and went over and told him, "Somebody stole my money. I can't pay."

He just looked at her. He didn't say anything.

She wondered if he heard what she said.

Then he said, "What were you puttin' in the telephone?"

"That was coins," Lila said. "They took my billfold."

He just stared at her some more. She could see he didn't believe her.

After a while he said, "They took your billfold."

"Yes," she said.

He stared some more.

Then he said, "I just work here. The manager isn't here."

He turned and went out to the kitchen.

When he came back he said, "They said to leave your name and address."

"I don't have an address," she said. He stared some more.

"You don't have an address," he repeated.

"That's what I *said*." She was starting to get mad.

"Where do you live?"

"On a boat."

"Where's the boat?" he asked. She wondered why he wanted to know that. What was he going to do now?

"On the river," she said. "It doesn't matter. I have to leave tonight. I don't know where the boat is."

The waiter kept staring at her. Jesus Christ, what a starer!

"Well just sign the name of the boat," he said.

He looked at where she signed the piece of paper. Then he gave her a dirty look and said, "And now, when you get back to your boat please get some money from your boat and bring it back here, okay? Because other people gotta live too, ya know?"

She picked up her purse and shirts from the floor by the telephone and saw him smile at somebody back in the kitchen and shake his head as she went out the door. At least he wasn't as bad as she thought he was going to be. He could have called the cops or something. He probably thought she was some kind of crazy person.

It was getting cold and the street looked spooky now in the dark.

The restaurant door closed behind her. She could have left this box of shirts to pay for it, she thought. Now she had to carry them. But he never asked.

She thought about going back and giving them to him. . . . No, it was all over. He wouldn't take them, anyway. . . .

But there was no reason for him to look dirty at her like that, Lila thought. She buttoned her cardigan. They didn't pay him to look like that.

Maybe the Captain would like them when he saw them. Then he could give her some money to pay the restaurant and they could go back and have a meal and he wouldn't give the waiter any tip. No, they'd give him a super big tip just to make him feel bad.

She didn't have any money to take a cab now. She couldn't call the police. Maybe she could call the police. They probably wouldn't remember her. Nobody remembered her. But she didn't want to do that.

Everybody was gone. Where has everybody gone, she wondered. What's happening that everybody's gone? First the Captain is gone and then Jamie is gone. And Richard too, even Richard is gone. She never did anything to him. Something really bad was happening. But they weren't telling her what it was. They didn't want her to know.

Lila began to feel her hands shake a little.

She reached in her handbag for her pills and then remembered they were gone too.

She began to feel scared.

This was the first time since the hospital that she didn't have them.

She didn't know how far it was to the boat. . . . It was toward the river, in this direction, she thought. . . . Maybe not. . . . She'd try not to think about anything bad and maybe her hands would stop shaking. . . . She hoped this was the right direction. . . .

. . . It was so dark now.

19.

It's dark out, Phædrus thought. Beyond the large sliding glass doors of the hotel room there was no trace of light left in the sky. All the light in the room came from the wall lamp where the moth was still fluttering.

He looked at his watch. His guest was late. About half an hour late. That was traditional for Hollywood celebrities. The bigger they are the later they come, and this one, Robert Redford, was very big indeed. Phædrus remembered that George Burns had joked that he'd been at Hollywood parties where the people were so famous they never showed up at all. But Redford was coming now to talk about film rights and that was vital business. There was no reason to think he wouldn't be here.

When Phædrus heard the knock on the door it had that special metallic sound of all the fireproof hotel doors in the world, but this time he was suddenly filled with tension. He got up, walked over to open it, and there in the corridor stood Redford with an expectant, unassuming look on his famous face.

He seemed smaller than his film images had portrayed him to be. A golf cap covered his famous hair; odd, rimless glasses drew attention away from the face behind them and a turned-up jacket collar made him even more inconspicuous. Tonight he didn't look anything at all like the Sundance Kid.

"Come on in," Phædrus said, feeling a real wave of stage fright. This was suddenly real time. This is the *present*. It is as though this is opening night and the curtain has just gone up and everything is up to him now.

He feels himself force a smile. He takes Redford's coat, tensely, trying not to show his nervousness, being smooth about all this, but accidentally he bunches the coat in back, clumsily, so that the Kid has trouble getting one arm out. . . . My God, he can't get his arm out. . . . Phædrus lets go and the Kid gets the coat off by himself, and hands it to him with a questioning glance, then hands him the hat.

What a start. . . . Real Charlie Chaplin scene. Redford goes ahead into the sitting room, walks to the glass doors and looks over the park, apparently orienting himself. Phædrus, who has followed behind, sits down in one of the overstuffed silk-upholstered gilded Victorian chairs they have put in this room.

"Sorry to be so late," Redford says. He turns from the glass doors and then moving slowly, at his own discretion, settles down on the opposing couch.

"I just got in from Los Angeles a half-hour ago," he says. "You lose three hours coming this way. At night they call it the 'Red-Eye' flight. . . ." His eyes dart in for a reaction. "Well named . . . you don't get any sleep at all. . . ."

Redford is saying this but as he is saying it he is becoming somebody real. It's like "The Purple Rose of Cairo," where a character comes off the screen and shares the life of one of the audience. What is he saying?

"Every time I go back I like it less," he says. "I grew up there, you know. . . . I remember what it used to be like. . . . And I resent what's happened to it. . . ." He keeps watching Phædrus for reactions.

"I still have a lot of beautiful memories from California," Phædrus says, finally taking hold.

"Did you live there?"

"I lived next door once, in Nevada," Phædrus says.

He is expected to speak. He speaks: a jumble of random sentences about California and Nevada. Deserts and pines and rolling hills, eucalyptus trees and freeways and that sense of something missed, something unfulfilled, that he always gets when he is there. This is just filling time now, developing rapport, and as Redford listens intently, Phædrus gets the feeling this is his normal habit. Real stage presence. He's just flown across the whole country, probably talked to a lot of people before that, yet he sits right here with his famous face listening as though he had all the time in the world, as though nothing of any importance had occurred before he walked in this room and nothing of importance was waiting for him after he walked out.

The rambling goes on until a common point of connection is found in the name of Earl Warren, the former Supreme Court chief justice, who Phædrus says represents a kind of personality not too many people think of as Californian. Redford concurs wholeheartedly, revealing personal values. "He was our governor, you know," Redford says. Phædrus says yes, and that Warren's family came from Minnesota.

"Is that right?" Redford says. "I didn't know that."

Redford says he's always had a special interest in Minnesota. His movie "Ordinary People" was a Minnesota story, although they filmed it in northern Illinois. His college roommate came from Minnesota, and he'd visited his house there and never forgotten it.

"Where did he live?" Phædrus asks.

"Lake Minnetonka," Redford says. "Do you know that area?"

"Sure. The first chapter of my book touched down for a second at Excelsior, on Lake Minnetonka."

Redford looks concerned, as though he had missed an important detail. "There's something about that area . . . I don't know what it was . . ."

"There was a certain 'graciousness,' " Phædrus says.

Redford nods, as though that is right on.

"There was a Minneapolis neighborhood called 'Kenwood' that was the same way. People there seemed to have that same Earl Warren 'charm' or 'graciousness' or whatever it was."

Redford stares at him intensely for a moment. It's an intensity he never shows on the screen.

"What caused it?" he asks.

"Money," Phædrus answers, but then, realizing that isn't quite right, he adds, "and something else too."

Redford waits for him to continue.

"There was a lot of old wealth out there," Phædrus says. "Fortunes from the lumber days and the early flour mill days. It was easier to be gracious when you had a maid and chauffeur and seven other servants running around the place."

"Did you live near Lake Minnetonka?"

"No, nowhere close, but I used to go to birthday parties there back in the thirties when I was a kid."

Redford looks engrossed.

Phædrus says, "I wasn't one of the rich kids. I was on a scholarship at a school in Minneapolis where the rich kids went . . . by chauffeur usually.

"In the morning these big, long, black Packard limousines would pull up outside the school and a black-uniformed chauffeur would jump out and dash around and open up the back door and this little kid would pop out. In the afternoon the limousines and chauffeurs would all be back again and the kids would pop in, one kid to a limousine, and they'd be off to Lake Minnetonka.

"I used to ride my bike to school and sometimes I'd see in my mirror one of these big Packards was coming up behind me and I'd turn and wave to the kid inside and he'd wave back and sometimes the chauffeur would wave too, and the funny thing is I always knew that kid was the one who envied *me*. I had all the freedom. He was a prisoner in the back of that black Packard, and he knew it."

"What school was that?"

"Blake."

Redford's eyes become intense. "That's the school my roommate went to!"

"Small world," Phædrus says.

"It certainly is!" Redford's excitement indicates something has connected here, a high spot in the surface of things that indicates some important structure underneath.

"I still have kind memories of it," Phædrus said.

Redford looks as though he would like to listen some more but that, of course, is not why he is here. After some more conversation about desultory subjects, he comes to the matter at hand.

He pauses and then says, "I guess I should say, first of all, that I admire your book greatly and feel challenged and stimulated by it. The ideas about 'Quality' are what I've always thought. I've *always* done it that way. I first read it when it first came out and would have contacted you then but was told that someone else had already bought it."

A funny woodenness has crept into his speech, as though he had rehearsed all this. Why should *he* sound like a poor actor? "I really would like to have the film rights to this book," Redford says.

"You've got them," Phædrus says.

Redford looks startled. Phædrus must have said something wrong. Redford's biographies said he was 'unflappable,' but he looks flapped now.

"I wouldn't have gotten this involved if I hadn't intended to give it to you," Phædrus says.

But Redford doesn't look overjoyed. Instead he looks surprised, and retreats to somewhere inside himself. His engrossment is gone.

He wants to know what the previous film deals were. "It's had quite a history," Phædrus says, and he relates a succession of film options that have been sold, and allowed to lapse for one reason or another. Redford is back to his former self, listening intently. When that subject is covered they turn cautiously to the question of how the book will be treated. Redford recommends a writer whom Phædrus has already met. Phædrus says okay.

Redford wants to make full use of a scene where a teacher faces a classroom of students for a whole hour and says nothing, until by the end of the hour they are so tense and frightened they literally run for the door. Apparently he wants to build the story in terms of flashbacks within that scene. Phædrus thinks that sounds very good. It is remarkable the way Redford has homed in on the book. For that scene he completely bypasses all the road scenes, all the motorcycle maintenance, where other script writers have bogged down, and goes right to the classroom, which was where the book started—as a little monograph on how to teach English composition.

Redford says that the road scenes will be made on location. He says that Phædrus can visit the sets whenever he wants to, "but not every day." Phædrus doesn't know what this involves.

The central problem of abstract ideas comes up. The book is largely about philosophic ideas about Quality. Big commercial films don't show ideas visually. Redford says you have to condense the ideas and show them indirectly. Phædrus is not sure what that means. He would like to see how this is going to be done.

Redford senses Phædrus' doubts and warns that, "No matter how the film is done, you won't like it." Phædrus wonders if he says this just to keep himself covered. Redford talks about how the author of another book he filmed saw the movie and tried to like it but you could see that no enthusiasm was there. "That was hard to take," Redford says, and then adds, "but that's the way it always seems to happen."

Other subjects come up but they don't seem to be quite to the point. Eventually Redford looks at his wrist watch.

"Well I guess there are no big problems at this point," he says, "I'll go ahead and call the writer and see where he's at on this."

He sits forward. "I'm really tired," he says, "and there's no point in romancing you all night about all this. . . . I'll call the others and then, sometime after that, our agency will get in touch with you."

He gets up, goes to the hall closet and, by himself, gets his cap and coat. At the door he says, "Where are you living now?"

"In my boat. Down on the river."

"Oh. Is there any way of reaching you there?"

"No, I'll be gone tomorrow. I'm trying to get south before it freezes around here."

"Well, we'll contact you through your lawyer then."

At the door he adjusts his hat and glasses and jacket. He says good-bye, turns and moves down the corridor with a tense springiness, like a skier or a cat—or like the Sundance Kid—and vanishes around a corner.

Then the corridor becomes just another hotel corridor again.

20.

Phædrus stood in the hotel corridor for a long time without thinking about where he was. After a while he turned back, went into the room and closed the door.

He looked at the empty couch where Redford had been sitting. It seemed like some of his presence was still there but you couldn't *talk* to it any more.

He felt like pouring himself a drink . . . but there wasn't any. . . . He should call Room Service.

But he didn't really *want* a drink. Not enough to go to all that trouble. He didn't know what he wanted.

A wave of anti-climax hit. All the tension and energy that had been built up for this meeting suddenly had nowhere to go. He felt like going out and running down the corridors. Maybe a long walk through the streets again until the tension wore off . . . but his legs already ached from the long walk getting here.

He went to the balcony door. On the other side of the glass was the same fantastic night skyline.

It looked more stale now.

The trouble with paying high prices for places with a view like this was that the first time it's wonderful but it gets more and more static until you hardly notice it's there. The boat was better, where the view keeps changing all the time.

He could see from the blurring of the skyline lights that rain had started. The balcony wasn't wet, however. The wind must be blowing the rain away from this side of the building.

When he cracked open the door a howling rush of cold air poured through. He opened the crack wide enough to pass through, then stepped out onto the balcony and closed the door again.

What a wild wind there was out here. Vertical wind. Crazy. The whole night skyline was blurring and clearing with squalls of rain. He could only see distant parts of the park from the way the lights stopped at its edges.

Disconnected. All this seemed to be happening to somebody else. There was excitement of a kind; tension, confusion; but no real emotional involvement. He felt like some galvanometer that had been zapped and now the needle was jammed stuck, unable to register.

Culture shock. He guessed that's what it was. This schizy feeling was culture shock. You enter another world where all the values are so different and switched around and upside-down you can't possibly adapt to them—and culture shock hits.

He was really on top of the world now, he supposed . . . at the opposite end of some kind of incredible social spectrum from where he had been twenty years ago, bouncing through South Chicago in that hard-sprung police truck on the way to the insane asylum.

Was it any better now?

He honestly didn't know. He remembered two things about that crazy ride: the first was that cop who grinned at him all the way, meaning "We're going to fix you *good*, boy"—as if the cop really enjoyed it. The second was the crazy understanding that he was in two worlds at the same time, and in one world he was at the rock bottom of the whole human heap and in the other world he was at the absolute top. How could you make any sense out of that? What could you do? The cop didn't matter, but what about this last?

Now here it was all upside-down again. Now he was at some kind of top of that first world, but where was he in the second? At the bottom? He couldn't say. He had the feeling that if he sold the film rights big things were going to happen in that first world, but he was going to take a long slide to somewhere in the second. He'd expected that feeling might go away tonight, but it didn't.

There was a "something wrong—something wrong—something wrong" feeling like a buzzer in the back of his mind. It wasn't just his imagination. It was real. It was a primary perception of negative quality. First you sense the high or low quality, then you find reasons for it, not the other way around. Here he was, sensing it.

The *New Yorker* critic George Steiner had warned Phædrus. "At least you don't have to worry about a film," he'd said. The book seemed too intellectual for anyone to try it. Then he'd told Steiner his book was already under option to 20th Century-Fox. Steiner's eyes widened and then turned away.

"What's the matter with that?" Phædrus had asked.

"You're going to be very sorry," Steiner had said.

Later a Manhattan film attorney had said, "Look, if you love your book my advice is don't sell it to Hollywood."

"What are you talking about?"

The attorney looked at him sharply. "I know what I'm talking about. Year after year I get people in here who don't understand films and I tell them just what I told you. They don't believe me. Then they come back. They want to sue. I tell them, 'Look! I told you! You signed your rights away. Now you're going to have to live with it!'

"So I'm telling you now," the attorney said, "if you love your book don't sell it to Hollywood."

What he was talking about was artistic control. In a stage play there's a tradition that nobody changes the playwright's lines without his permission, but in films it's almost standard to completely trash an author's work without even bothering to mention it to him. After all, he sold it, didn't he?

Tonight Phædrus had hoped to get a contradiction of all this from Redford, but it was just the opposite. Redford had confirmed it. He *agreed* with Steiner and the attorney.

So it looked as though this meeting wasn't as important as Phædrus had expected. The celebrity effect had created all the excitement, not the deal itself. He'd told Redford, "You've got it," but nothing was settled until the contract was signed. There was still a price to settle on and that meant there was still room to back off.

He felt a real sense of let-down. Maybe it was just normal anti-climax, maybe Redford was just tired from his flight in but whatever he was really thinking about, Phædrus didn't think he'd heard it tonight, or at least not all of it, or even very much of it. It was always

exciting to see a famous person like that up close but when he subtracted that excitement he saw that Redford was just following a
standard format.

The whole thing had a lack of freshness about it. Redford had a
reputation for honest dealing but he operated in the middle of an
industry with the opposite reputation. No one was expected to say
what they really thought. "Deals" are supposed to follow a format.
Redford's honesty wasn't triumphing over this format or even arguing
with it.

There was no sense of sharing. It was more like selling a house,
where the prospective owners don't feel any obligation to tell you
what color they are going to paint it or how they are going to arrange
the furniture. That's the Hollywood format. Redford gave the feeling
he'd been through many of these bargaining sessions. It was a kind
of ritual for him. He'd done it a dozen times before, at least. He was
just operating out of old patterns.

That's probably why he seemed surprised when Phædrus said,
"You've got it." He was flapped because the format wasn't followed.
Phædrus was supposed to do all his bargaining at this point. This was
where he could get all his concessions, and here he was now, giving
it all away: a big mistake in terms of a real-estate type of legal "ad-
versary" format where each side tries all the tactics they can think of
to get the best "deal" out of the other side. Redford was here to get
rather than give, and when he was suddenly given so much more than
he expected without any effort on his part it seemed to throw him
off balance for a second. That's how it seemed anyway.

That comment about visiting the sets, "but not every day," also
spelled it out. Phædrus would never be a co-creator, just a visiting
VIP. And that bit of film jargon about "romancing" was the real key.
"Romancing" is part of the format. The producer or screen-writer or
director or whoever's getting the thing started begins by "romancing"
the author. They tell him how much money he's going to get, they
get his signature on an option, and then they go and "romance" the
financial people by telling them what a great book *they're* going to get.
Once they get both the book and the money, the romance is over.
Both the money-man and the author get locked out as much as possible
and the "creative people" go ahead and make a film. They'd change

what Phædrus had written, add whatever stuff they thought would make it work better, sell it, and go on to something else, leaving him with some money that would soon disappear, and a lot of bad memories that wouldn't.

Phædrus began to shiver, but still he didn't go in. That room on the other side of the door was like some glassed-in cage. Outside here the rain seemed to have died and the lights were so intense now they made the clouds in the sky seem like some sort of ceiling. He preferred it out here in the cold.

He looked over the city and then down at the little bugs of cars way down on the street below. It was a lot easier to get there from here than to here from there. Maybe that's why so many jump. It's easier that way.

Crazy! He backed off from the concrete railing. What puts thoughts like that in a person's head?

"Culture shock." That's what it was. The "gods." He'd been watching them for years. The "gods" were the static culture patterns. They never quit. After trying all these years to kill him with failure, now they were pretending they'd given up. Now they were going to try the other way, to get him with success.

It wasn't the crazy wind or the rain-blurred light along the sky across the park that was making him feel so strange. What caused the culture shock were these two crazy different cultural evaluations of himself—two different realities of himself—sitting side by side. One was that he was in some kind of high-voltage celebrity world like Redford. The other was that he was at ground-level like Rigel and Lila and just about everybody else. As long as he stayed within just one of those two cultural definitions he could live with it. But when he tried to hang on to both wires simultaneously, that's when the shock hit.

"If you get too famous you will go straight to hell," a Japanese Zen master had warned a group Phædrus was in. It had sounded like one of those Zen "truths" that don't make any sense. Now it was making sense.

He wasn't talking about anything Dante would have identified. Dante's Christian hell is an after-life of eternal torment, but Zen hell is this world right here and now, in which you see life around you but can't participate in it. You're forever a stranger from your own life because there's something in your life that holds you back. You see others bathing in the life all around them while you have to drink it through a straw, never getting enough.

You would think that fame and fortune would bring a sense of closeness to other people, but quite the opposite happens. You split into two people, who they think you are and who you really are, and that produces the Zen hell.

It's like a hall of mirrors at a carnival where some mirrors distort you one way and some distort you another. Already he'd seen three completely different mirror reflections this week: from Rigel, who reflected an image of some kind of moral degenerate; from Lila, who reflected a tedious old nerd; and now Redford who was probably going to cast him into some sort of heroic image.

Each person you come to is a different mirror. And since you're just another person like them maybe you're just another mirror too, and there's no way of ever knowing whether your own view of yourself is just another distortion. Maybe all you ever see is reflections. Maybe mirrors are all you ever get. First the mirrors of your parents, then friends and teachers, then bosses and officials, priests and ministers, and maybe writers and painters too. That's their job too, holding up mirrors.

But what controls all these mirrors is the culture: the Giant, the gods; and if you run afoul of the culture it will start throwing up reflections that try to destroy you, or it will withdraw the mirrors and try to destroy you that way. Phædrus could see how this celebrity could get to be like some sort of narcosis of mirrors where you have to have more and more supportive reflections just to stay satisfied. The mirrors take over your life and soon you don't know *who* you are. Then the culture controls you and when it takes away your mirrors and the public forgets you the withdrawal symptoms start to appear. And there you are, in the Zen hell of celebrity. . . . Hemingway with the top of his head blown off, and Presley, full of prescription drugs. The endless dreary exploitation of Marilyn Monroe. Or any of dozens of others. It seemed like it was the celebrity, the mirrors of the "gods," that did it.

A subject-object metaphysics presumes that all these mirrors are subjective and therefore unreal and unimportant, but that presumption, like so many others, seems to deliberately ignore the obvious.

It ignores the phenomenon of someone like Redford walking down the street and observing that people, in his own words, "goon out" when they see him. His manager said it's almost impossible for him to attend public meetings because when people see he's there they all turn around and watch *him*.

Phædrus remembered that he himself had started to "goon out" when Redford came to the door. All that Charlie Chaplin stuff with the coat. What is this "goon-out" phenomenon? It was no subjective illusion. It's a very real *primary* reality, an empirical perception.

It seems to have biological roots, like hunger or fear or greed. Is it similar to stage fright? There seems to be a loss of real-time awareness. A fixed image of the famous person, like the Sundance Kid, seems to overwhelm the Dynamic real-time person who exists in the moment of confrontation. That's why Phædrus had so much trouble getting started.

But there is much more than that.

This whole business of celebrity also had something perceptibly degenerate about it. Vulgar and degenerate and enormously fascinating and at times obsessive, very much in the same way that sex seemed to be vulgar and degenerate at some times, and enormously fascinating and obsessive.

Sex and celebrity. Before Phædrus got his boat and cleared out of Minnesota he remembered ladies at parties coming over to rub up against him. A teenage girl squealing in ecstasy at one of his lectures. A woman broadcasting executive grabbing his arm at lunch and saying, "I must have you. I mean *you*." You'd think he was a sandwich or something. For forty years he'd wondered what it took, that he was so obviously lacking, that made women look at you twice. Was celebrity it? Was that all? He thought there was more to it than that.

There's a parallel there, he thought. There's something slightly obscene about the whole celebrity feeling. It's that same feeling you get from sex magazines on the newsstands. There's something troubling about seeing those magazines there. And yet if you thought no one would notice you might want to take a look in those magazines.

One part of you wants to get rid of the magazines; one part wants to look at them. There's a conflict of two patterns of quality, social patterns and biological patterns.

In celebrity it's the same—except that the conflict is between social and intellectual patterns!

Celebrity is to social patterns as sex is to biological patterns. Now he was getting it. This celebrity is Dynamic Quality within a static social level of evolution. It looks and feels like pure Dynamic Quality for a while, but it isn't. Sexual desire is the Dynamic Quality that primitive *biological* patterns once used to organize themselves. Celebrity is the Dynamic Quality that primitive *social* patterns once used to organize themselves. That gives celebrity a new importance.

None of this celebrity has any meaning in a subject-object universe. But in a value-structured universe celebrity comes roaring to the front of reality as a huge fundamental parameter. It becomes an organizing force of the whole social level of evolution. Without this celebrity force, advanced complex human societies might be impossible. Even simple ones.

Funny how a question can just sit there and then suddenly, at a time you least expect it, the answer starts to unfold.

Celebrity was the culture force. That was it. It seemed like it, anyway.

It was crazy. People going over Niagara Falls in a barrel and killing themselves just for the celebrity of it. Assassins murdering for it. Maybe the real reason nations declared war was to increase their celebrity status. You could organize an anthropology around it.

Sure, of course. When you look back into the very first writings in the history of the Western world, the cuneiform writings on the mud tablets of Babylon, what are they about? Why, they're about celebrity: I, Hammurabi, am the big wheel here. I have this many horses and this many concubines and this many slaves and this many oxen, and I am one of the greatest of the greatest kings there ever was, and you better believe it. That's what writing was invented for. When you read the Rig Veda, the oldest religious literature of the Hindus, what are they talking about? "The heavens and earth themselves have not grown equal to half of me: Have I not drunk the soma juice? I in my grandeur have surpassed the heavens and all this spacious earth: Have I not drunk the soma juice?" This is interpreted as devotion to God, but the celebrity is obvious. Phædrus remembered now that it had bothered him a little that in *The Odyssey* Homer seemed at times to be equating Quality and celebrity. Perhaps in Homer's time, when evolution had not yet transcended the social level into the intellectual, the two were the same.

The Pyramids were celebrity devices. All the statues, the palaces, the robes, and jewels of social authority: those are just celebrity devices. The feathers of the Indian headdress. Children being told they would be struck blind if they ever accidentally looked at the emperor. All the Sirs and Lords and Reverends and Doctors of European address, those are celebrity symbols. All the badges and trophies, all the blue ribbons, all the promotions up the business ladder, all the elections to "high office," all the compliments and flattery of tea parties and cocktail parties are celebrity enhancements. All the feuding and battling for prestige among academics and scientists. All the offense at "insults." All the "face" of the Orient. Celebrity. Celebrity.

Even a policeman's uniform is a kind of celebrity device so that you will do what he says without questioning him. Without celebrity nobody would take orders from anybody and there would be no way you could get the society to work.

. . . High school. High school was *really* the place for celebrity. That's what had those jocks out playing football every afternoon. That's what the pom-pom girls were all about. It was the *celebrity*. They were all swimming up the celebrity stream. And Phædrus hadn't even known it was there. Or he knew it was there but he didn't understand how significant it was. That's what made him such a nerd, maybe. That's what separated him from that eager-eyed, beautifully dressed, smiley-talky crowd.

At the university he remembered the celebrity force was still there, especially in the fraternities and student activity groups. But it was weaker. In fact you can measure the quality of a university by comparing the relative strengths of the celebrity patterns and the intellectual patterns. You never got rid of the celebrities, even at the best universities, but there the intellectuals could ignore them and be in a class by themselves.

Anyway there it was: another whole field Phædrus would never have time to study—the anthropology of celebrity.

Some of it had been done: anthropologists study tribal patterns carefully to see who kowtows to whom. But that was nothing, compared to what could be done.

Money and celebrity are fame and fortune, traditionally paired as twin forces in the Dynamic generation of social value. Both fame and fortune are huge Dynamic parameters that give society its shape and meaning. We have whole departments of universities, in fact, whole colleges, devoted to the study of economics, that is fortune, but what do we have that is similarly devoted to the study of fame? What exactly is the mechanism by which the culture controls the shapes of the mirrors that produce all these different images of celebrity? Would analysis of that mirror-changing force enable the resolution of ethnic conflicts? Phædrus didn't know. Why is it you can be a great guy in, say, Germany, and then walk across the border into France and suddenly find you have become a very bad guy without having done anything? What changes the mirrors?

Politics, maybe, but politics mixes celebrity with static legal patterns and isn't a pure study of celebrity. In fact, the way political science is taught now, celebrity is made to look incidental to politics. But go to any political gathering and see what's making it run. Watch the candidates jockey for celebrity. They know what's making it run.

On and on the ideas went.

But it was an assertion of the Metaphysics of Quality that there exists a reality beyond all these social mirrors. *That* he *had* explored. In fact there are two levels of reality beyond these mirrors: an intellectual reality and beyond that, a Dynamic reality.

And the Metaphysics of Quality says that movement upward from the social mirrors of celebrity is a moral movement from a lower form of evolution to a higher one. People should go that way if they can.

And now Phædrus began to see how all this brought him full circle with what had started all this thinking about celebrity: the film about his book. Films are social media; his book was largely intellectual. That was the center of the problem. Maybe that's why Redford was so closed. He had reservations about that too. Sure, it's *possible* to use film for primarily intellectual purposes, to make a documentary, but Redford wasn't here to make a documentary, or anything close to it.

As Sam Goldwyn said, "If you got a message send a telegram." Don't make a movie out of it. Pictures aren't intellectual media.

Pictures are pictures. The movie business belonged to the celebrity people and they wouldn't begin to know how to portray an intellectual book like his. And even if they did, the public wouldn't buy it, probably, and that would be the end of their money.

Phædrus still didn't want to commit himself yet. He would just have to think about it for a while and let things settle down and then see what he wanted to do.

But what he saw at this point was a social pattern of values, a film, devouring an intellectual pattern of values, his book. It would be a lower form of life feeding upon a higher form of life. As such it would be immoral. And that's exactly how it felt: immoral.

That's what had produced all these something-wrong, something-wrong, something-wrong feelings. The mirrors were trying to take over the truth. They think that because they pay you money, which is a social form of gratification, they are entitled to do as they please with the intellectual truth of a book. Uh-uh.

Those gods. They'll pull anything.

21.

It was really getting cold out here.

Phædrus went to the big glass sliding door, pulled it open and with a *wooshhhhh* of inrushing wind went inside.

Ahh. Here it was warm again. And quiet. The room still seemed like some empty stage after the audience has gone home. The moth that he had noticed before now circled the wall lamp just above the davenport where Redford's head had been. It went under the shade, made a little noise against the shade and then stopped. He waited for it to start again but it didn't. Resting, maybe. . . . Maybe burned by the heat of the bulb. . . .

That's what celebrity can do for you. . . .

Phædrus heard a noise that sounded like a flow of water from some pipe draining above and then a wail that sounded like a small girl crying. She seemed about three. Maybe it was just TV. A woman's voice was trying to console her. The woman's voice sounded good. Well bred. Not trash. Then it stopped. Not TV.

He wondered how old this hotel was. Something from the twenties, maybe. The best period. The Victorians created this city, but in the twenties it really flowered.

. . . The joke about that Victorian moth metaphor is that according to science the moth isn't really flying toward the flame. The moth is really trying to fly straight. Moths steer by keeping a constant angle with the sun or the moon, which works because the sun and moon are so far away a constant angle with them is virtually a straight line. But with a close-up light bulb a constant angle makes a circle. That's what keeps the moths spinning round and round and round. What's killing the moths is not a Dynamic aspiration for a "higher life." That's just Victorian nonsense. It's a static biological pattern of value. They can't change.

That was the feeling Phædrus got from this city. He was like a moth in danger of drifting in circles into some kind of celebrity orbit. Maybe at some prehistoric time, before celebrity became important, people could trust their natural desires to keep them going in a straight-forward direction. But once the artificial sun of celebrity was invented they started going in circles. Brains were capable of handling physical and biological patterns in prehistoric times but are brains Dynamic enough to handle modern social patterns? Maybe that scientific explanation didn't weaken the Victorian metaphor. Maybe it fitted in with it.

It was strange the way the talk with Redford had suddenly converged on Blake school. When Phædrus said he'd gone to that school Redford had looked up with surprise. He'd looked as though he expected Phædrus to supply something he'd wanted to know for a long time.

"Small world," Phædrus had said, and Redford agreed. Phædrus was going to tell him something more but they didn't get into it. What was it?

Oh yes, what he was going to tell him was that there was more than just money involved, despite all the Packards and Minnetonka mansions and all the other capitalist symbols. The "graciousness" that he'd talked about was a left-over from Victorian days.

Those Victorians seemed to light Redford up too. He'd made a lot of films about that era. Something about them probably interested him as it does many other people. The Victorians represented the last really static social pattern we've had. And maybe someone who feels his life is too chaotic, too fluid, might look back at them enviously. Something about their rigid convictions about what was right and what was wrong might appeal to anyone brought up in laid-back Southern California of the forties and fifties. Redford seemed to be a rather Victorian person himself: restrained, well mannered, gracious. Maybe that's why he lives here in New York. He likes the Victorian graciousness that still exists here in places.

It was too much to get into but Phædrus could have told Redford about the fifth grade school play called the *The Miser's Dream* in which he had played the miser who learns generosity through various events. For Blake School it was well chosen. That tiny stage was loaded with little future millionaires. Afterward a bald-headed old Victorian had come down to the locker room and shaken his hand and congratulated him and talked for a long time with a kind of gracious interest, and one of the teachers asked later, "Do you know who that was?" and of course Phædrus didn't. But twenty years later when he was reading a magazine article about General Mills, the world's largest flour milling company, he suddenly recognized the face of this little old bald-headed man. He was the *founder* of General Mills.

The face stuck in his mind as one of those fragments of memory that don't fit. Here was one of the great giants of the evil greed-ridden Victorian capitalist tradition, but the direct primary impression was of a kind and friendly and gracious man.

Phædrus didn't know what Blake was like today but back then it was grounded in Victorian traditions and values. The headmaster sermonized in chapel each morning on Victorian moral themes with the dedication and vigor of Theodore Roosevelt. He was so intense that after all these years Phædrus would be able to recognize his face instantly if he saw it in a crowd.

There was never any hesitation in the headmaster's mind as to what quality was. Quality was the manner and spirit that a man of good breeding exemplified. The masters understood it and the boys did not. If the boys studied hard and played hard and showed that they were in earnest about their lives there was a good chance they would some day become worthy people. But there was no sign in the masters' eyes they had any confidence this would occur soon. The masters were always so sure of what was good and what was right. You knew that no matter how hard you tried you would never measure up to their standards. It was like Calvinistic Grace. There was a chance for you. That was all. They were offering you a chance.

Grace and morals were always external. They were not something you embodied. They were only something you could aspire to. You did bad things because you *were* bad and when you got whacked for doing something wrong it was an attempt to mold bad old you into something better. That word "mold" was important. The stuff they were trying to mold was inherently unchangeably bad, but the masters thought that by trying to shape it like modeling clay, through whacks and detentions and obloquy, they could *mold* it into something that gave it the appearance of goodness even though everyone understood it was still the same old rotten stuff underneath.

Truth, knowledge, beauty, all the ideals of mankind, are external objects, passed on from generation to generation like a flaming torch. The headmaster said each generation must hold them up high and protect them with their very lives lest that torch go out.

That torch. That was the symbol of the whole school. It was part of the school emblem. It should be passed on from one generation to another to light the way for mankind by those who understood its meaning and were strong enough and pure enough to hold to its ideals. What would happen if that torch went out was never stated, but Phædrus had guessed it would be like the end of the world. All of man's progress out of the darkness would be ended. No one doubted that the headmaster's only purpose in being there was to pass that torch to us. Were we worthy enough to receive it? It was a question everyone was expected to take seriously. And Phædrus did.

In some diluted and converted sense, he thought, that's what he was still doing. That's what this Metaphysics of Quality was, a ridiculous torch no Victorian would accept that he wanted to use to light a way through the darkness for mankind.

What a cornball image. Just awful. Yet there it was, burned into him from childhood.

Twenty and thirty years later he still dreamed of following the path that led between brown-leaved oaks up the hill to the Blake School buildings. But the buildings were all locked and deserted and he couldn't get in. He tried every door but none were open. He looked in the library window, cupping his hand so that the reflection would not prevent him from seeing inside. There he could see a grandfather clock with a pendulum swinging back and forth, but there was nobody in the room. The only movement was the pendulum. Then the dream ended.

. . .

That moth was buzzing again by the lamp.

Maybe he should open the huge glass door to the balcony and shoo it out into the night. . . .

Would that be moral? . . .

He really didn't know enough about moths to know whether it was or not.

It would probably just find another light somewhere, a searchlight probably, and really get zapped.

But suppose it flew up from the balcony so high it got free of the lights of the city and saw the moon and began to fly straight. Would that make releasing it moral? What does the Metaphysics of Quality say to that?

Better not to interfere. Maybe that moth had its own patterns to fulfill, and he had his, whatever they were. This Metaphysics of Quality, maybe. Certainly not running around like some Victorian romantic, shooing moths outdoors.

That was the Victorian stance, affecting some romantic notion of social quality without any real intellectual penetration of the meaning of Quality.

Anyway, today they are all gone, those gracious Victorian dinosaurs, and it is possible now to look at them with a little less anxiety and opposition than when they were looking back at *you*.

Phædrus thought that the reason his thoughts kept returning to them—and maybe Redford's thoughts, and maybe a lot of other people's thoughts too—is that something enormously important and mystifying has happened in the time that separates us from them. He thought that in returning to them and trying to fathom who they were, one can begin to make some sense out of the social forces that have upheaved the world since their time. What makes them stand out today like dinosaurs is that a gulf exists between us and them. A huge cultural mutation has taken place. They really were a different cultural species. What the torch of the Metaphysics of Quality seems to illumine is an understanding of this gulf and a recognition that this gulf is one of the most profound in history.

If he were going to be precise in talking about the Victorians he would have to be careful not to imply he was talking about a specific group of people. "Victorian," as he used the term, is a pattern of social values that was dominant in a period between the American Civil War and World War I, not a biological pattern. Mark Twain's life coincided with this period but Phædrus didn't think of him as a Victorian. His stock-in-trade was humor that poked fun at Victorian pompousness. He was a *relief* from the Victorians. On the other hand, Herbert Hoover and Douglas MacArthur were biologically outside the Victorian period most of their lives. But they were Victorians, nevertheless, because their social values were Victorian.

Phædrus thought the metaphysics of substance fails to illuminate the gulf between ourselves and Victorians because it regards both society *and* intellect as possessions of biology. It says society and intellect don't have substance and therefore can't be real. It says biology is where reality stops. Society and intellect are ephemeral *possessions* of reality. In a substance metaphysics, consequently, the distinction between society and intellect is sort of like a distinction between what's in the right pocket and what's in the left pocket of biological man.

In a value metaphysics, on the other hand, society and intellect are patterns of value. They're real. They're independent. They're not properties of "man" any more than cats are the property of catfood or a tree is a property of soil. Biological man does not create his society any more than soil "creates" a tree. The pattern of the tree is dependent upon the minerals in the soil and would die without them, but the tree's pattern is not created by the soil's chemical pattern. It is hostile to the soil's chemical pattern. It "exploits" the soil, "devours" the soil for its own purposes, just as the cat devours the catfood for its own purposes. In this manner biological man is exploited and devoured by social patterns that are essentially hostile to his biological values.

This is also true of intellect and society. Intellect has its own patterns and goals that are as independent of society as society is independent of biology. A value metaphysics makes it possible to see that there's a conflict between intellect and society that's just as fierce as the conflict between society and biology or the conflict between biology and death. Biology beat death billions of years ago. Society beat biology thousands of years ago. But intellect and society are still fighting it out, and that is the key to an understanding of both the Victorians and the twentieth century.

What distinguishes the pattern of values called Victorian from the post-World War I period that followed it is, according to the Metaphysics of Quality, a cataclysmic shift in levels of static value; an earthquake in values, an earthquake of such enormous consequence that we are still stunned by it, so stunned that we haven't yet figured out what has happened to us. The advent of both democratic and communistic socialism and the fascist reaction to them has been the consequence of this earthquake. The whole "Lost Generation" of the twentieth century which continues, as lost as ever, through generation after generation, is a consequence of it. The twentieth century collapse of morals is a consequence of it. Further consequences are on their way.

What distinguishes the Victorian culture from the culture of today is that the Victorians were the last people to believe that patterns of intellect are subordinate to patterns of society. What held the Victorian pattern together was a social code, not an intellectual one. They called it morals, but really it was just a social code. As a code it was just like their ornamental cast-iron furniture: expensive looking, cheaply made, brittle, cold, and uncomfortable.

The new culture that has emerged is the first in history to believe that patterns of society must be subordinate to patterns of intellect. The one dominating question of this century has been, "Are the social patterns of our world going to run our intellectual life, or is our intellectual life going to run the social patterns?" And in that battle, the intellectual patterns have won.

Now, with that illumination, all sorts of things clear up. The reason the Victorians sound so superficial and hypocritical to us today is because of this gulf in values. Even though they were our ancestors they were another very different culture. Trying to understand a member of another culture is impossible without taking into account differences in value. If a Frenchman asks, "How can Germans stand to live the way they do?" he will get no answer as long as he applies French values to the question. If a German asks, "How can the French stand to live the way they do?" he will get no answer as long as he applies German values to the question. When we ask how could the Victorians stand to live in the hypocritical and superficial way they did, we cannot get a useful answer as long as we superimpose on them twentieth century values that they did not have.

If one realizes that the essence of the Victorian value pattern was an elevation of society above everything else, then all sorts of things fall into place. What we today call Victorian hypocrisy was not regarded as hypocrisy. It was a virtuous effort to keep one's thoughts within the limits of social propriety. In the Victorian's mind quality and intellectuality were not related to one another in such a way that quality *had* to stand the test of intellectual meaning. The test of anything in the Victorian mind was, "Does society approve?"

To put social forms to the test of intellectual value was "ungracious," and those Victorians really did believe in the social graces. They valued them as the highest attributes of civilization. "Grace" is an interesting word with an important history, and the fact that they used it the way they did makes it even more interesting. A "state of grace" as defined by the Calvinists was a state of religious "enlightenment." But by the time the Victorians were through with it, "grace" had changed from "godliness" to mean something close to "social polish."

To the early Calvinists and to ourselves too this debasement of the word seems outrageous, but it becomes understandable when one sees that within the Victorian pattern of values society *was* God. As Edith Wharton said, Victorians feared scandal worse than they feared disease. They had lost their faith in the religious values of their ancestors and put their faith in society instead. It was only by wearing the corset of society that one kept oneself from lapsing back into a condition of evil. Formalism and prudery were attempts to suppress evil by denying it a place in one's "higher" thoughts, and for the Victorian, higher spiritually meant higher socially. There was no distinction between the two. "God is a gentleman through and through, and in all probability, Episcopal too." To be a gentleman was as close as you would ever get, while on earth, to God.

All this explains why Victorian robber barons in America aped European aristocracy in ways that seem so ludicrous to us today. It explains why it was so fashionable for Victorian nabobs to pay large sums to be included in biographies of "distinguished citizens." It explains why Victorians so despised the frontier part of the American personality and went to ridiculous extremes to conceal it. They wanted to strike it from their history, conceal it in every way possible.

It explains why the Victorians were so vehement in their loathing of Indians. The statement, "The only good Indian is a dead Indian," was a Victorian statement. The idea of extermination of all Indians was not common before the nineteenth century. Victorians wanted to destroy "inferior" societies because inferior societies were a form of evil. Colonialism, which before that time was an economic opportunity, became with Victorians a *moral* course, a "white man's burden" to spread their social patterns and thus virtue throughout the world.

Truth, knowledge, beauty, all the ideals of mankind, are passed on from generation to generation like a flaming torch, the headmaster said, which each generation must hold up high and protect with their very lives lest that torch go out. But what he meant by that torch was a static Victorian social value pattern. And what he either did not know, or found it convenient to ignore, was that the torch of Victorian romantic idealism had gone out long before he spoke those words in the 1930s. Perhaps he was just trying to relight it.

But there is no way to light that torch within a Victorian pattern of values. Once intellect has been let out of the bottle of social restraint, it is almost impossible to put it back in again. And it is immoral to try. A society that tries to restrain the truth for its own purposes is a lower form of evolution than a truth that restrains society for its own purposes.

Victorians repressed the truth whenever it seemed socially unacceptable, just as they repressed thoughts about the powdery horse manure dust that floated about them as they drove their carriages through this city. They knew it was there. They breathed it in and out. But they didn't consider it socially proper to talk about it. To speak plainly and openly was vulgar. They never did so unless forced by extreme social circumstances because vulgarity was a form of evil.

Because it was evil to speak the truth openly, their apparatus for social self-correction became atrophied and paralyzed. Their houses, their social lives became filled with ornamental curlicues that never stopped proliferating. Sometimes the useless ornamentation was so heavy it was hard to discover what the object was *for*. Its original purpose had been all but lost under the gee-gaws and bric-a-brac they had laid upon it.

Ultimately their minds became the same way. Their *language* became filled with ornamental curlicues that never stopped proliferating until it was all but incomprehensible. And if you didn't understand it you dared not show it because to show it meant you were vulgar and ill-bred.

With Victorian spirits atrophied and their minds hemmed in by social restraints, all avenues to any quality other than social quality were closed. And so this social base which had no intellectual meaning and no biological purpose slowly and helplessly drifted toward its own stupid self-destruction: toward the senseless murder of millions of its own children on the battlefields of World War I.

22.

Where the physical climate changes suddenly from high temperature to low temperature, or from high atmospheric pressure to low atmospheric pressure the result is usually a storm. When the social climate changes from preposterous social restraint of all intellect to a relative abandonment of all social patterns, the result is a hurricane of social forces. That hurricane is the history of the twentieth century.

There had been other comparable times, Phædrus supposed. The day the first protozoans decided to get together to form a metazoan society. Or the day the first freak fish, or whatever-it-was, decided to leave the water. Or, within historical time, the day Socrates died to establish the independence of intellectual patterns from their social origins. Or the day Descartes decided to start with himself as an ultimate source of reality. These were days of evolutionary transformation. And like most days of transformation, no one at the time had any idea of what was being transformed.

Phædrus thought that if he had to pick one day when the shift from social domination of intellect to intellectual domination of society took place, he would pick November 11, 1918, Armistice Day, the end of World War I. And if he had to pick one person who symbolized this shift more than any other, he would have picked President Woodrow Wilson.

The picture of him Phædrus would have selected is one in which Wilson rides through New York City in an open touring car, doffing the magnificent silk hat that symbolized his high rank in Victorian society. For a cutline he would select something from Wilson's penetrating speeches that symbolized his high rank in the intellectual community: We must use our intelligence to stop future war; social institutions can not be trusted to function morally by themselves; they must be guided by intellect. Wilson belonged in both worlds, Victorian society and the new intellectual world of the twentieth century: the only university professor ever to be elected president of the United States.

Before Wilson's time academicians had been minor and peripheral within the Victorian power structure. Intelligence and knowledge were considered a high manifestation of social achievement, but intellectuals were not expected to run society itself. They were valued servants of society, like ministers and doctors. They were expected to decorate the social parade, not lead it. Leadership was for practical, businesslike "men of affairs." Few Victorians suspected what was coming: that within a few years the intellectuals they idealized as the best representatives of their high culture would turn on them and destroy that culture with contempt.

The Victorian social system and the Victorian morality that led into World War I had portrayed war as an adventurous conflict between noble individuals engaged in the idealistic service of their country: a kind of extended knighthood. Victorians loved exquisitely painted heroic battle scenes in their drawing rooms, with dashing cavalrymen riding toward the enemy with sabers drawn, or a horse returning riderless with the title, "Bad News." Death was acknowledged by an occasional soldier in the arms of his comrades looking palely toward heaven.

World War I wasn't like that. The Gatling gun removed the nobility, the heroism. The Victorian painters had never shown a battlefield of mud and shell holes and barbed wire and *half a million* rotting corpses—some staring toward heaven, some staring into the mud, some without faces to stare in any direction. That many had been murdered in one battle alone.

Those who survived suffered a stunnedness, and a lostness and felt bitter toward the society that could do that to them. They joined the faith that intellect must find some way out of old Victorian "nobility" and "virtue" into a more sane and intelligent world. In an instant it seemed, the snobbish fashionable Victorian social world was gone.

New technology fueled the change. The population was shifting from agriculture to manufacturing. Electrification was turning night into day and eliminating hundreds of drudgeries. Cars and highways were changing the landscape and the speed with which people did things. Mass journalism had emerged. Radio and radio advertising had arrived. The mastery of all these new changes was no longer dominated by social skills. It required a technologically trained, analytic mind. A horse could be mastered if your resolve was firm, your disposition pleasant and fear absent. The skills required were biological and social. But handling the new technology was something different. Personal biological and social qualities didn't make any difference to machines.

A whole population, cut loose physically by the new technology from farm to city, from South to North, and from East to West Coast, was also cut adrift morally and psychologically from the static social patterns of the Victorian past. People hardly knew what to do with themselves. "Flappers," airplanes, bathing beauty contests, radio, free love, movies, "modern" art . . . suddenly the door had been sprung on a Victorian jail of staleness and conformity they had hardly known was there, and the elation at the new technological and social freedom was dizzying. F. Scott Fitzgerald caught the giddy exhilaration of it:

> There'd be an orchestra
> Bingo! Bango!
> Playing for us
> To dance the tango,
> And people would clap
> When we arose,
> At her sweet face
> And my new clothes.

No one knew what to do about the lostness. The explainers of that period were the most lost of all. "Whirl is King," wrote Walter Lippman in his "Preface to Morals." Whirl, *chaos* seemed to be in control of the times. Nobody seemed to know why or where they were going. People raced from one fad to another, from one headline sensation to the next, hoping this was really the answer to their lostness, and finding it was not, flying on. Older Victorians muttered about the degeneracy that was tearing society apart, but nobody young was paying any attention to old Victorians any more.

The times were chaotic, but it was a chaos of *social* patterns only. To people who were dominated by old social values it seemed as though everything valuable had ended. But it was only social value patterns being destroyed by new intellectual formulations.

The events that excited people in the twenties were events that dramatized the new dominance of intellect over society. In the chaos of social patterns a wild new intellectual experimentation could now take place. Abstract art, discordant music, Freudian psychoanalysis, the Sacco-Vanzetti trial, contempt for alcoholic prohibition. Literature emphasized the struggle of the noble, free-thinking individual against the crushing oppression of evil social conformity. The Victorians were damned for their *narrow-mindedness*, their *social* pretentiousness. The test of what was good, of what had Quality, was no longer "Does it meet society's approval?" but "Does it meet the approval of our intellect?"

It was this issue of intellect versus society that made the Scopes trial of 1925 such a journalistic sensation. In that trial a Tennessee schoolteacher, John Scopes, was charged with illegally teaching Darwinian evolution.

There was something not quite right about that trial, something phony. It was presented as a fight for academic freedom, but battles of that sort had been going on for centuries without the kind of attention the Scopes trial got. If Scopes had been tried back in the days when he might have been tortured on the rack for his heresy his stance would have been more heroic. But in 1925 his lawyer, Clarence Darrow was just taking easy shots at a toothless tiger. Only religious fanatics and ignorant Tennessee hillbillies opposed the teaching of Evolution.

But when that trial is seen as a conflict of social and intellectual values its meaning emerges. Scopes and Darrow were defending academic freedom but, more importantly, they were prosecuting the old static religious patterns of the past. They gave intellectuals a warm feeling of arriving somewhere they had been waiting to arrive for a long time. Church bigots, pillars of society who for centuries had viciously attacked and defamed intellectuals who disagreed with them, were now getting some of it back.

The hurricane of social forces released by the overthrow of society by intellect was most strongly felt in Europe, particularly Germany, where the effects of World War I were the most devastating. Communism and socialism, programs for intellectual control over society, were confronted by the reactionary forces of fascism, a program for the social control of intellect. Nowhere were the intellectuals more intense in their determination to overthrow the old order. Nowhere did the old order become more intent on finding ways to destroy the excesses of the new intellectualism.

Phædrus thought that no other historical or political analysis explains the enormity of these forces as clearly as does the Metaphysics of Quality. The gigantic power of socialism and fascism, which have overwhelmed this century, is explained by a conflict of levels of evolution. This conflict explains the driving force behind Hitler not as an insane search for power but as an all-consuming glorification of social authority and hatred of intellectualism. His anti-Semitism was fueled by anti-intellectualism. His hatred of communists was fueled by anti-intellectualism. His exaltation of the German *volk* was fueled by it. His fanatic persecution of any kind of intellectual freedom was driven by it.

In the United States the economic and social upheaval was not so great as in Europe, but Franklin Roosevelt and the New Deal, nevertheless, became the center of a lesser storm between social and intellectual forces. The New Deal was many things, but at the center of it all was the belief that intellectual planning by the government was necessary for society to regain its health.

The New Deal was described as a program for farmers, laborers and poor people everywhere, but it was also a new deal for the intellectuals of America. Suddenly, for the first time, they were at the center of the planning process—Tugwell, Rosenman, Berle, Moley, Hopkins, Douglas, Morgenthau, Frankfurter—these were people from a class that in the past could normally be hired for little more than laborers' wages. Now intellectuals were in a position to give orders to America's finest and oldest and wealthiest social groups. "That Man," as the old aristocrats sometimes called Roosevelt, was turning the whole United States of America over to foreign radicals, "eggheads," "Commies" and the like. He was a "traitor to his class."

Suddenly, before the old Victorians' eyes, a whole new social caste, a caste of intellectual Brahmins, was being created *above* their own military and economic castes. These new Brahmins felt they could look down on them and, through the political control of the Democratic Party, push them around. Social snobbery was being replaced with intellectual snobbery. Brain trusts, think tanks, academic foundations were taking over the whole country. It was joked that Thorstein Veblen's famous intellectual attack on Victorian society, "The Theory of The Leisure Class," should be updated with a new one called "The Leisure of The Theory Class." A new social class had arrived: the theory class, which had clearly put itself above the social castes that dominated before its time.

Intellectualism, which had been a respected servant of the Victorian society, had become society's master, and the intellectuals involved made it clear they felt that this new order was best for the country. It was like the replacement of Indians by pioneers. That was too bad for the Indians but it was an inevitable form of progress. A society based upon scientific truth *had* to be superior to a society based on blind unthinking social tradition. As the new scientific modern outlook improved society, these old Victorian hatreds would be lost and forgotten.

And so, from the idea that society is man's highest achievement, the twentieth century moved to the idea that intellect is man's highest achievement. Within the academic world everything was blooming. University enrollments zoomed. The Ph.D. was on its way to becoming the ultimate social status symbol. Money poured in for education in a flood the academic world had never seen. New academic fields were expanding into new undreamed-of territories at a breathless pace, and among the the most rapidly expanding and breathless fields of all was one that interested Phædrus more than any other: anthropology.

Now the Metaphysics of Quality had come a long way from his days of frustrated reading about anthropology in the mountains of Montana. He saw that during the early decades of this century anthropology's unassailable Olympian "objectivity" had had some very partisan cultural roots of its own. It had been a political tool with which to defeat the Victorians and their system of social values. He doubted whether there was another field anywhere within the academic spectrum that so clearly revealed the gulf between the Victorians and the new twentieth century intellectuals.

The gulf existed between Victorian evolutionists and twentieth century relativists. The Victorians such as Morgan, Tylor, and Spencer presumed all primitive societies were early forms of "Society" itself and were trying to "grow" into a complete "civilization" like that of Victorian England. The relativists, following Boas' "historical reconstruction," stated that there is no empirical scientific evidence for a "Society" toward which all primitive societies are heading.

Cultural relativists held that it is unscientific to interpret values in culture B by the values of culture A. It would be wrong for an Australian Bushman anthropologist to come to New York and find people backward and primitive because hardly anyone could throw a boomerang properly. It is equally wrong for a New York anthropologist to go to Australia and find a Bushman backward and primitive because he cannot read or write. Cultures are unique historical patterns which contain their own values and cannot be judged in terms of the values of other cultures. The cultural relativists, backed by Boas' doctrines of scientific empiricism, virtually wiped out the credibility of the older Victorian evolutionists and gave to anthropology a shape it has had ever since.

That victory is always presented as a victory of scientific objectivity over unscientific prejudice, but the Metaphysics of Quality says deeper issues were involved. The phenomenal sales of Ruth Benedict's *Patterns of Culture* and Margaret Mead's *Coming of Age in Samoa* indicated something else. When a book about the social customs of a South Sea island suddenly becomes a best-seller you know there's something in it other than an academic interest in Pacific island customs. Something in that book has "hit a nerve" to cause such a huge public acclaim. The "nerve" in this case was the conflict between society and intellect.

These books were legitimate anthropological documents but they were also political tracts in the new shift from social to intellectual dominance, in which the reasoning ran: "If we have seen scientifically that they can have free sex in Samoa and it doesn't seem to hurt anybody, then that proves we can have it here and not hurt anybody either. We have to use our intellect to discover what is right and wrong and not just blindly follow our own past customs." The new cultural relativism became popular because it was a ferocious instrument for the dominance of intellect over society. Intellect could now pass judgment on all forms of social custom, including Victorian custom, but society could no longer pass judgment on intellect. That put intellect clearly in the driver's seat.

When people asked, "If no culture, including a Victorian culture, can say what is right and what is wrong, then how can we ever *know* what is right and what is wrong?" the answer was, "That's easy. Intellectuals will tell you. Intellectuals, unlike members of studiable cultures, know what they're talking and writing about, because what *they* say isn't culturally relative. What they say is absolute. This is because intellectuals follow science, which is objective. An objective observer does not have relative opinions because he is nowhere within the world he observes."

Good old Dusenberry. This was the same hogwash he had denounced in the 1950s in Montana. Now, with the added perspective on the twentieth century provided by the Metaphysics of Quality, you could see its origins. An American anthropologist could no more embrace non-objectivity than a Stalinist bureaucrat could play the stock market. And for the same kind of ideological, conformist reasons.

Now, it should be stated at this point that the Metaphysics of Quality *supports* this dominance of intellect over society. It says intellect is a higher level of evolution than society; therefore, it is a more moral level than society. It is better for an idea to destroy a society than it is for a society to destroy an idea. But having said this, the Metaphysics of Quality goes on to say that science, the intellectual pattern that has been appointed to take over society, has a defect in it. The defect is that subject-object science has no provision for morals. Subject-object science is only concerned with facts. Morals have no objective reality. You can look through a microscope or telescope or oscilloscope for the rest of your life and you will never find a single moral. There aren't any there. They are all in your head. They exist only in your imagination.

From the perspective of a subject-object science, the world is a completely purposeless, valueless place. There is no point in anything. Nothing is right and nothing is wrong. Everything just functions, like machinery. There is nothing morally wrong with being lazy, nothing morally wrong with lying, with theft, with suicide, with murder, with genocide. There is nothing morally wrong because there are no morals, just functions.

Now that intellect was in command of society for the first time in history, was *this* the intellectual pattern it was going to run society with?

As far as Phædrus knew, that question has never been successfully answered. What has occurred instead has been a general abandonment of all social moral codes, with "a repressive society" used as a scapegoat to explain any and every kind of crime. Twentieth century intellectuals noted that Victorians believed all little children were born in sin and needed strict discipline to remove them from this condition. The twentieth century intellectuals called that "rubbish." There is no scientific evidence that little children are born in sin, they said. The whole idea of sin has no objective reality. Sin is simply a violation of a set of arbitrary social rules which little children can hardly be expected to be aware of, let alone obey. A far more objective explanation of "sin" is that a collection of social patterns, grown old and corrupt and decadent, tries to justify its own existence by proclaiming that all who fail to conform to it are evil rather than admit any evil of its own.

There are two ways to get rid of this "sin," said the intellectuals. One is to force all children to conform to the ancient rules without ever questioning whether these rules are right or wrong. The other is to study the social patterns that have led to this condemnation and see how *they* can be altered to allow the natural inclinations of an innocent child to fulfill his needs without this charge of sinfulness arising. If the child is behaving naturally, then it is the society that calls him sinful that needs correction. If children are shown kindness and affection and given freedom to think and explore for themselves, children can arrive rationally at what is best for themselves and for the world. Why should they want to go in any other direction?

The new intellectualism of the twenties argued that if there are principles for right social conduct they are to be discovered by social experiment to see what produces the greatest satisfaction. The greatest satisfaction of the greatest number, rather than social tradition, is what determines what is moral and what is not. The scientific test of a "vice" should not be, "Does society approve or disapprove?" The test should be, "Is it rational or irrational?"

For example, drinking that causes car accidents or loss of work or family problems is irrational. That kind of drinking is a vice. It does not contribute to the greatest satisfaction of the greatest number. On the other hand, drinking is not irrational when it produces mere social or intellectual relaxation. That kind of drinking is not a vice. The same test can be applied to gambling, swearing, lying, slandering or any other "vice." It is the intellectual aspect not the social aspect that dictates the answer.

Of all the "vices" none was more controversial than premarital and extramarital sex. There was no depravity the Victorians condemned more vehemently and no freedom the new intellectuals have defended more ardently. Scientifically speaking, sexual activity is neither good nor evil, the intellectuals said. It is merely a biological function, like eating or sleeping. Denial of this normal physical function for some pseudo-moral reasons is irrational. If you open the door to premarital sex you simply allow freedom that does nobody any harm.

Books such as *Lady Chatterley's Lover* and *Tropic of Cancer* were defended as great salients in the struggle against social oppression. Prostitution and adultery laws were eased. It was expected that with the new application of reason, sex could be handled much like other commodities without the terrible tensions and frustrations of social repression exposed by Sigmund Freud.

Thus, throughout this century we have seen over and over again that intellectuals weren't blaming crime on man's *biological* nature, but on the *social patterns* that had *repressed* this biological nature. At every opportunity, it seems, they derided, denounced, weakened and undercut these Victorian social patterns of repression in the belief that this would be the cure of man's criminal tendencies. It was as a part of this new dominance over society that intellectuals became excited about anthropology in the hope that the field would provide facts upon which to base new scientific rules for the proper governing of our own society. That was the significance of *Coming of Age in Samoa*.

Here in this country, American Indians—who since Custer's Last Stand had been reduced to near-pariahs by the Victorians—were suddenly revived as models of primitive communal virtue. Victorians had despised Indians because they were so primitive. Indians were at the opposite extreme of society from the Europeans that the American Victorians adored. But now "anthros" from everywhere swarmed to huts and teepees and hogans of every tribe they could find, jockeying to be in on the great treasure hunt for new information about possible new moral indigenous American ways of life.

This was illogical since, if subject-object science sees no morals anywhere, then no scientific study of any kind is going to fill the moral void left by the overthrow of Victorian society. Intellectual permissiveness and destruction of social authority are no more scientific than Victorian discipline.

Phædrus thought that this lapse in logic magically fitted the thesis he had started with: that the American personality has two components, European and Indian. The moral values that were replacing the old European Victorian ones were the moral values of American Indians: kindness to children, maximum freedom, openness of speech, love of simplicity, affinity for nature. Without any real awareness of where the new morals were coming from, the whole country was moving in a direction that it felt was right.

The new intellectualism looked to the "common people" as a source of cultural values rather than to the old Victorian European models. Artists and writers of the thirties such as Grant Wood, Thomas Hart Benton, James Farrell, Faulkner, Steinbeck and hundreds of others dug deep into the illiterate roots of white American culture to find the new morality, not understanding that it was this white illiterate American culture that was closest to the values of the Indian. The twentieth century intellectuals were claiming scientific sanction for what they were doing, but the changes that were actually taking place in America were changes toward the values of the Indian.

Even the language was changing from European to Indian. Victorian language was as ornamental as their wallpaper: full of involutions and curlicues and floral patterns that had no practical function whatsoever, and distracted you from whatever content was there. But the new style of the twentieth century was Indian in its simplicity and directness. Hemingway, Sherwood Anderson, Dos Passos and many others were using a style that in the past would have been thought crude. Now this style was a reincarnation of the directness and honesty of the common man.

The western movie was another example of this change, showing Indian values which had become cowboy values which had become twentieth century all-American values. Everyone knew the cowboys of the silver screen had little to do with their actual counterparts, but it didn't matter. It was the values, not the historical accuracy, that counted.

It was in this new world of technological achievement, of weakening social patterns of authority, of scientific amoralism, of adoration of the "common man," and of an unconscious drift toward Indian values, that Phædrus grew up. The drift away from European social values had worked all right at first, and the first generation children of the Victorians, benefiting from ingrained Victorian social habits seem to have been enormously liberated intellectually by the new freedom. But with the second generation, Phædrus' own generation, problems began to emerge.

Indian values are all right for an Indian style of life, but they don't work so well in a complex technological society. Indians themselves have a terrible time when they move from the reservation to the city. Cities function on punctuality and attention to material detail. They depend on the ability to subordinate to authority, whether it is a cop or an office manager or a bus driver. An upbringing that allows the child to grow "naturally" in the Indian fashion does not necessarily guarantee the finest sort of urban adjustment.

In the time that Phædrus grew up, intellect was dominant over society, but the results of the new social looseness weren't turning out as predicted. Something was wrong. The world was no doubt in better shape intellectually and technologically but despite that, somehow, the "quality" of it was not good. There was no way you could say why this quality was no good. You just felt it.

Sometimes you could see little fragments of reflections of what was wrong but they were just fragments and you couldn't put them together. He remembered seeing *The Glass Menagerie*, by Tennessee Williams, in which one edge of the stage had an arrow-shaped neon sign flashing on and off, on and off, and beneath the arrow was the word, "PARADISE," also flashing on and off. Paradise, it kept saying, is right where this arrow points:

PARADISE ⇨ PARADISE ⇨ PARADISE ⇨

But the Paradise was always somewhere pointed to, always somewhere else. Paradise was never here. Paradise was always at the end of some intellectual, technological ride, but you knew that when you got there paradise wouldn't be there either. You would just see another sign saying:

PARADISE ⇨ PARADISE ⇨ PARADISE ⇨

and pointing another direction to go.

On a theater marquee, the title *Rebel Without a Cause* caught his attention in the same way. It pointed to the same low-quality thing that he saw everywhere but which couldn't be put into words.

You *had* to be a rebel without a cause. The intellectuals had preempted all the causes. Causes were to the twentieth century intellectuals as manners had been to Victorians. There was no way you could beat a Victorian on manners and there was no way you could beat a twentieth century intellectual on causes. They had *everything* figured out. That was part of the problem. That was what was being rebelled against. All that neat scientific knowledge that was supposed to guide the world.

Phædrus had no "cause" that he could explain to anybody. His cause was the Quality of his life, which could not be framed in the "objective" language of the intellectuals and therefore in their eyes was not a cause at all. He knew that intellectually contrived technological devices had increased in number and complexity, but he didn't think the ability to enjoy these devices had increased in proportion. He didn't think you could say with certainty that people are any happier than they were during the Victorian era. This "pursuit of happiness" seemed to have become like the pursuit of some scientifically created, mechanical rabbit that moves ahead at whatever speed it is pursued. If you ever did catch it for a few moments it had a peculiar synthetic, technological taste that made the whole pursuit seem senseless.

Everyone seemed to be guided by an "objective," "scientific" view of life that told each person that his essential self is his evolved material body. Ideas and societies are a component of brains, not the other way around. No two brains can merge physically, and therefore no two people can ever really communicate except in the mode of ship's radio operators sending messages back and forth in the night. A scientific, intellectual culture had become a culture of millions of isolated people living and dying in little cells of psychic solitary confinement, unable to talk to one another, really, and unable to judge one another because scientifically speaking it is impossible to do so. Each individual in his cell of isolation was told that no matter how hard he tried, no matter how hard he worked, his whole life is that of an animal that lives and dies like any other animal. He could invent moral goals for himself, but they are just artificial inventions. Scientifically speaking he has no goals.

Sometime after the twenties a secret loneliness, so penetrating and so encompassing that we are only beginning to realize the extent of it, descended upon the land. This scientific, psychiatric isolation and futility had become a far *worse* prison of the spirit than the old Victorian "virtue" ever was. That streetcar ride with Lila so long ago. That was the feeling. There was no way he could ever get to Lila or understand her and no way she could ever understand him because all this intellect and its relationships and products and contrivances intervened. They had lost some of their *realness*. They were living in some kind of movie projected by this intellectual, electromechanical machine that had been created for their happiness, saying:

PARADISE ⇨ PARADISE ⇨ PARADISE ⇨

but which had inadvertently shut them out from direct experience of life itself—and from each other.

23.

It seemed to Lila that all this was some kind of a dream she was in. Where did it start? She couldn't remember. Her mind always went faster and faster like this when she got scared. Why did he have to take the pills out of her purse? The pills could have made it not so scary. He must have thought those pills were dope or something. That's why he took them. She could tell when she needed them by how scary everything got. Now she needed them bad.

She should have got her suitcase this afternoon like she said she was going to. Then she wouldn't have to go back to the boat like this. Now it was dark.

That damn waiter. He could have given her some money to help her out. Then she could have taken a cab. Now she didn't have anything. He was acting like she had lied to him. But she hadn't lied. And he knew she hadn't lied. He could tell. But that didn't matter. He had to make it look like she had done something wrong even when he knew she hadn't done anything wrong.

It was so cold now. The wind went right through this sweater. The streets were so dirty here. Everything was dirty here. Everything was worn out and cold.

It was starting to rain.

She didn't even know if this was the right way. It seemed like she must be getting close to the river.

When she looked down a street she could see a highway where cars were going fast. But the park wasn't where it was supposed to be. Maybe her directions got twisted and she was walking the wrong way. The rain was shining in their headlights. She remembered when she and the Captain had walked from the boat there was a park.

Maybe she could just take a taxi and not pay. She saw one coming with its light off. She thought about waving to it but she didn't do it. In the old days she could have done it. And spit in his face when he tried to collect. But she was so tired now. She didn't want to fight.

Maybe she should just ask somebody for some money. No, that wouldn't work. They wouldn't give it. Not here. It was dangerous going up to people in this city without any reason. They could do anything.

She could go to the cops or go to a shelter somewhere. . . . But they'd find out about her. In this town once they know you've got a record you don't want to see them again.

She didn't want to walk along the river to get to the boat. She didn't think she'd like it down there. She'd just stay up until she saw where the marina might be. Then she'd cross down.

That man who looked at her through the restaurant window. That was bad. Ten or fifteen years ago he would have been in that door so fast they couldn't stop him. Now he just walked away. She remembered what Allie used to say: "*You* never change, honey, but *they* do." She used to say, "When you don't need 'em they're all over the place. But when you want one you never find him."

She wondered where Allie was now. She must be about fifty by now. She was probably some old bag lady like the ones she saw yesterday. That's what Lila was going to be. A bag lady. Sitting on a grate somewhere trying to keep warm with all those old clothes on. . . .

. . . Like the witch in the store window. With a big nose with a wart on it hanging down over her chin. . . .

She should touch up her hair. She was really looking ratty now. The rain was getting her hair so wet she must be looking like a witch too.

There was supposed to be a big castle with a high green steeple at the top sticking up in the air. That's what she remembered. When she got to the castle she should turn down to the river and that's where the boat should be. She remembered that from when they left.

Her shoes were getting all squishy. Like her clothes and this box of shirts. Maybe she should just stop walking and wait for the rain to stop. But then she wouldn't get to the castle. Until she got to the castle there was nowhere to stop.

Why didn't she ever learn not to get mad at people? You always think someone's going to come along and save you but this time it was too late. Some nice man's going to come along and save you. Like the Captain there. You always think that, don't you? But they're all gone now, Lila. The Captain was the last one. There won't be any more, Lila. He was the last one.

That's what the one in the window was telling her.

These shirts she bought for the Captain were getting all wet. He wouldn't even pay her for them now. Maybe if she could stand in a doorway or something until the rain stopped she could keep the shirts dry. She should have kept the bag they were in. That would have kept them dry. Then she could take the shirts back to the store and she could get some money for a taxi. But she needed a taxi to get back to the store. Besides the store was closed by this time.

The receipt was in the billfold. Maybe they would remember her. No they wouldn't. . . .

. . . Maybe there'll be some money in the boat. She could just go in and look through all the drawers and places like that. But then she remembered she couldn't get *in* the boat. She didn't have the combination. She'd just have to wait until the Captain came to let her in. But then if he was there she couldn't look through all the drawers. Maybe he'd give her some money then. No, he was really mad. He wouldn't give her anything.

Maybe she would walk all night and not find the river. Probably she'd *passed* the castle. She'd walk and walk and never find it. She couldn't even ask where the boat was. She didn't remember the name of the place the boat was at. She just thought it was in this direction. Maybe she would never find it and she would just walk and walk, on and on.

Then the Captain would just go and sail away and she would never see him again. With all her things! He was going to take her suitcase! All her things! Everything she owned was in there!

She didn't see any sign of the river. She should ask someone where the boat place on the river is but she didn't know what to ask for. The buildings changed slowly as she walked. She didn't know any of them.

Someone was coming on a bicycle. He went right by. It was getting quieter and quieter here now. It looked like a better neighborhood, but you never know. This is where they come.

She must have gone too far. She didn't remember this neighborhood. She should have stayed close to the river. Soon she'd be up in Harlem somewhere and she didn't want to be there. Not at night. Some of the windows had iron over them and barbed wire underneath.

There wasn't any castle. The castle would be skinny with a green pointed top that looked like a space ship, but there wasn't any.

Why did she have to go and call the Captain names and get him mad like that? Now she didn't know what she was going to do. If she'd just been mealy-mouthed with him instead of telling him off she'd be on her way to Florida now.

She shouldn't have tried to get him to take Jamie along. She could see how he got uptight the moment she said it. She should have kept her mouth shut.

She shouldn't have argued with him. If you don't sneak around and say mealy-mouthed things they'll get you for that. They'll make you pay. They've all got to show you how big and strong they are. If you ever dare breathe that you don't think they're as big and strong as they pretend, they hate you. They can't take that. That's what they've got to have. Jamie made him look weak. That's what he didn't like.

All she wanted to do was show the Captain what she was like really. He wanted to know all about her, he said. He wanted to see what she was really like. So she tried to show him and see what happened. Jamie saw what *he* was like too. He saw it right away.

You mustn't ever tell their secret about how weak they are. They think you don't see. If you tell them they get mad. Then they *really* hate you. Then they call you names. That's what they did in Rochester. But she was telling them the truth. That's why they said she was sick. They don't want to hear the truth. If you tell them, they'll try to do things to you.

Her feet were hurting bad. She should take her shoes off and walk barefoot. Even if it was cold. It would feel good to walk barefoot.

She would walk for a while more. Then if she didn't see the river she should maybe take them off. Maybe she would take everything off.

She remembered when she walked home and it started to rain. It was her new dress. She tried to stand under trees and she felt terrible. She knew she would catch it at home and she did. Her clothes were so soaked it was like she'd been swimming in them. The shoes made squeeze sounds when she walked, and she sat down by the gutter with her new dress and cried and just let the water pour all around her. Then she felt better.

Maybe she should sit down now. No, not here. Not yet.

She put one hand against a sign post and took off one shoe and then the other. That felt better. It felt good to walk on her bare feet.

She'd like to take everything off. Just take everything off. Then somebody'd stop and help her. It's the clothes that make them think you're not really there. If she took all her clothes off then they'd see she was really here.

"You'll never find happiness this way, Lila." Her mother's face always came back at times like this. Her little pin-eyes. Her mother was always right. There were only two things that made her happy, being right and thinking about how much better she was than everybody else. If you did something good she didn't say anything. But if you did something bad, she told you about it, over and over again.

But you're not doing anything wrong, you know. You're not hurting anybody and you're not stealing anything, you know, and still people just *hate* you for it.

If you really love people they'll kill you for it. You have to hate them and then *pretend* you love them. Then they respect you. But what's the purpose of living if all you can do is hate people and have them hate you? She was so sick and tired of this world where everybody is supposed to hate everybody else.

How could they keep going day after day with all this hate? It never stopped. See, now she was getting into it too. Now they got her going too. That's how it works. Now they got her into it and she couldn't get out. She kept trying to get out but she couldn't get out. There's nothing left. They took it all away.

They just want to dirty you. That's what they want to do. Just dirty you so you'll be like them. Shooting their filth into you and then say, "Look, Lila, you're a whore! You're a slut!"

They just hate it when people make love. And then they'll go to a fist fight where somebody's really hurt and all covered with blood and they'll just love that. Or a war and stuff like that. They're all mixed up and they're trying to take it out on you so you get mixed up too. They want to mix you up just like they are and then you'll be all mixed up too and then they'll like you. They'll say, "Lila, you're really good." They're the ones who're really crazy. They don't know you, Lila. Nobody knows you. They'll never know you! But boy oh boy do you ever know *them*!

They're always so calm afterward. That's when they start thinking about how to leave you. The minute before they come you're the Queen of the World but the minute after you're just garbage.

Like the Captain there. Now he had his fun. Now he just wanted her to go. Now he's going to take his boat and his money and everything down to Florida and leave her here.

There was no one else on the street here but she had the feeling somebody was watching her. It seemed that if she turned her head suddenly she'd see somebody right behind her.

The dark buildings looked like some place she had never seen before. Some bad movie where people get killed.

What did she need to be so scared of? There was nothing to be afraid of. At least she wasn't going to get robbed. All they'd get would be these shirts. That would be a laugh. "Here," she'd say. "Have some shirts." They wouldn't know what to do.

She looked back suddenly to see what was following. There was nothing. Most of the windows were dark. In just a few there was some light behind some shades. There was an orange round little light in one window. It looked like a face.

Somebody had put a jack o'lantern in the window. Like the witch in the store window. Halloween.

Like that old bag lady yesterday who looked like a witch. She looked at Lila in a funny way. Like she recognized her. Maybe she was really a witch too! That's why she had looked at her that way.

She didn't want to be a witch. When she was little she wanted to wear the pirate costume but Em got to wear it instead. Lila had to wear the witch's costume. That's what the old bag lady looked like. Like the mask she wore on that witch's costume when she was little. She didn't want to wear it but her mother made her.

Her mother's face came back. *"Lila, why can't you be more like Emmaline?"*

"I *hate* Emmaline!" Lila said.

"Em doesn't hate *you*."

"That's what *you* think," Lila said. Lila knew what she really was like. Always getting what she wanted. Always playing up. That's what her mother wanted. Lies. Em got all the new dresses. Lila got to be the witch.

At her grandfather's funeral her mother made her wear Em's old blue dress, and gave all the blue and white plates to Emmaline. She saw a bee this morning on top of a car and she thought about the island and her grandfather.

She wished she was at the island now. Her grandfather had bees and he used to make toast with the honey from the bees and give her some. She remembered he always used to put it on a blue and white plate. Then the funeral came and they sold his house and gave the blue and white plates to Emmaline and Lila never saw the bees again. She used to think the bees went over to the island with her grandfather. And then sometimes they'd fly back and she'd see them again and they always knew where her grandfather was. That's what she thought about this morning when she saw the bee on the car.

"I told you you'll never find happiness this way, Lila," her mother said. Her face had that little smile she always got when she made somebody feel bad.

"I'm tired of hearing that, mother," Lila answered. "What happiness did *you* find?"

Little pin-eyes, eyes, eyes. . . .

Her mother thought Lila was going to hell because she was bad, but the island, when you went there, it didn't matter whether you were bad. You just went there. It was in the picture on her grandfather's wall.

The wind came around the corner and blew through her sweater and blew something into her eyes like sand or dirt or something so she couldn't see. She had to stop and stand close to a brick wall and blink to get it out.

There! Around the corner of the building she saw it! It *was* following her! She concentrated on it and concentrated some more with all her might. She really *was* a witch because slowly the face started to appear. She could make things come to her.

But now she could see it wasn't a man at all that was following her. It was just a dog.

As soon as the dog saw that she saw it, it disappeared back behind the building.

She concentrated some more. After a while, slowly, it started to come again. She didn't move but held her eyes on it and then slowly step by step it came toward her. By the time it was halfway across the street she saw who it was. It was Lucky! After all these years.

"Oh Lucky, you've come back," she said. "You're all whole again."

She started to walk toward him. She wanted to reach down and pet him but Lucky backed away.

"Don't you know me, Lucky?" Lila asked. "You're all whole again. Don't you remember me?"

It didn't show where he got hit by the car.

"How did you get back from the island, Lucky? Did you swim? Where is the island, Lucky? We must be getting close to it now. You show me the way."

But as soon as Lila walked toward him Lucky walked ahead of her and as she followed him she saw that his feet hardly touched the ground, as though he didn't have any weight at all.

From the dark far down the street came a truck without any headlights on. It hardly made any sound either. Scary. When the truck got near a streetlight and she could see whose it was, her heart jumped. Now she was really scared. He was here! He'd found her.

The last time she saw that truck was when they towed it to the junk yard. All smashed up. Just like him. The blood was all over the door of the truck from where his head hung over it. In the morgue she never looked at him. They couldn't make her look at him.

Here he came now, in his pick-up truck, right down that street there, and he's going to open the door and say "Get in!"

Then he'll know what to do. He'll find that god-damned bastard friend of Jamie's that took her money and he'll make him give it back. Then he'll smash him to pieces. With one hand. He knew how to do that. He was always smashing up somebody. The son-of-a-bitch. . . . You shouldn't say that about somebody when they're dead. As soon as she'd said it the truck steered to hit Lucky.

But Lucky stepped out of the way.

The truck went right by and she saw it was who she thought it was. He looked at her like she was somebody he didn't want to have anything to do with. But he knew who she was and she knew who he was and then he sped up and the truck was gone.

She remembered the blood. Everybody acted like they were so sorry for her. All the hypocrites said, "Oh Lila, we're so sorry!" But they were just hypocrites. They hated him as much as she did. The bastard. You shouldn't say that about dead people but that's what he was. She said it to him when he was alive. No reason to change now. It was the truth.

When she got around the corner, there it was, the castle! Lucky found it! But it was off where she didn't think it would be. But she saw she could turn here and then down there was the park and the cement place and she thought that the boats were there too.

What a good dog! He was always so good. Someone must have sent him from the island to show her the way. Now she could go to the boat and wait for the Captain and he would take her down the river to the island.

She didn't remember the cement place very well. It was scary. It looked like something where the lions come out at you. And there were steps going out from the other side and you didn't know who might be there waiting. She walked slowly, step by step. . . .

She didn't hear anything, but she was afraid. . . .

She took another step closer. There was nothing else she could do. She had to go past it. She held her breath and looked around the corner. . . .

There was the marina! And all the water of the river. It was all here! Oh, it felt so good to be back again. She could hear the boat ropes going bing-bing-bing in the wind.

At the gate for the marina was a black man who said something to her but she couldn't understand what he was saying. He kept waving his hands and pointed to her but he didn't touch her when she walked past him to the boat.

She walked down the dock and there was the boat! Lucky had found the way.

Where was Lucky?

She looked for him and she didn't see him. She called, but he didn't come. She looked into the river to see if he had started to swim back to the island but all she could see was lights far away all blurred by the rain.

After she stepped over the railing onto the boat she sat down in the cockpit. Oh it felt so good to sit down again! Her teeth were chattering and her clothes were all soaked all the way through but it didn't matter now. All she had to do was wait for the Captain and they would go to the island.

A wake came across from somewhere out on the river. She could see it coming by the way the lights moved from on top of the waves. It lifted up and rocked the boat against the dock and then after a while it died down.

The water beside the boat was mucky-looking with a lot of junk in it. There were pieces of old plastic bottles, and dirty swirls of foam and a sponge and some branches and a dead fish caught on one of the branches. The fish was turned up on its side and was partly gone. Then the fish and the branch moved on by and she could smell the fish. Then the branch came back again and the whirlpool caught it and it went down into the center of the whirlpool and disappeared.

The junk went round and round in a whirlpool. It looked like the whirlpool was sucking all the junk to the bottom of the river. She remembered watching some fish once and how one of them kept turning on its side and the others tried to take bites out of it. Then it straightened up again. But after a while it went over on its side again and then it couldn't straighten up at all. Then the others started to eat it and it didn't struggle any more.

She hoped they wouldn't bite Lucky when he swam back to the island. When you slow down the fish eat you up alive. You can't do anything that makes them think you're slowing down, or they'll come after you.

They wouldn't dare bite Lucky.

She wished the Captain would come.

She was so tired of this side of the river. She'd even swim if she had to. She didn't know how long the Captain would take to come and she didn't want to wait any more.

Lila took off her sweater. That felt better with it off.

Then she put her hand down into the water.

The water felt warm! It was real warm in the river. If she swam to the island she wouldn't be cold any more.

She looked at the water again.

She didn't want to be cold any more. She was so tired of fighting it. Just to give up. Just to let go.

Just to let go. Toward that hand in the water. The hand was sticking up out of the water where the branch had been, reaching for her to take it. The hand came close to her and then a little whirlpool in the water carried it away. It was like a baby's hand sticking out of the water. A baby's hand.

The little hand was reaching up out of the water. It was a baby's hand. She could see the little fingers. The hand was just farther than she could reach going into the whirlpool. Then it came closer and she caught it, and her heart held still as she brought it up out of the water.

Its little body was all stiff and cold.

Its eyes were closed. Thank God. She cleaned off the scum from its body and saw that none of the baby seemed to be gone. The fish had not eaten any of it yet. But it was not breathing.

Then she took her sweater from the cockpit floor and put it in her lap and wrapped the baby in it and held it close. And she rocked the baby back and forth until she could feel some of the coldness go out of it. "It's all right," she said. "It's all right. You're all right now. It's all over. You're all right now. No one's going to hurt you any more."

After a while Lila could feel the baby's body becoming warm against her own. She began to rock it a little back and forth. Then she began to hum a little song to it that she remembered from long ago.

Part Three

24.

"Does Lila have Quality?" The question seemed inexhaustible. The answer Phædrus had thought of before, "Biologically she does, socially she doesn't," still didn't get all the way to the bottom of it. There was more than society and biology involved.

Phædrus heard some voices in the corridor become louder and closer, then fade away again.

What had happened since the end of World War I was that the intellectual level had entered the picture and had taken over everything. It was this intellectual level that was screwing everything up. The question of whether promiscuity is moral had been resolved from prehistoric times to the end of the Victorian era, but suddenly everything was upended by this new intellectual supremacy that said sexual promiscuity is neither moral nor immoral, it is just *amoral* human behavior.

That may have been why Rigel was so angry back in Kingston. He thought Lila was immoral because she'd broken up a family and destroyed a man's position in the social community—a biological pattern of quality and sex, had destroyed a social pattern of quality, a family and a job. What made Rigel mad was that into this scene come intellectuals like Phædrus who say it's unintelligent to repress biological drives. You must decide these matters on the basis of reason, not on the basis of social codes.

But if Rigel identified Phædrus with this intellect-vs.-society code and the social upheavals it has produced, he certainly picked on the wrong person. The Metaphysics of Quality uproots the intellectual *source* of this confusion, the doctrine that says, "Science is not concerned with values. Science is concerned only with facts."

In a subject-object metaphysics this platitude is unassailable, but the Metaphysics of Quality asks: *which* values is science unconcerned with?

Gravitation is an inorganic pattern of values. Is science unconcerned? Truth is an intellectual pattern of values. Is science unconcerned? A scientist may argue rationally that the moral question, "Is it all right to murder your neighbor?" is not a scientific question. But can he argue that the moral question, "Is it all right to fake your scientific data?" is not a scientific question? Can he say, as a scientist, "The faking of scientific data is no concern of science?" If he gets tricky and tries to say that that is a moral question *about* science which is not a *part* of science, then he has committed schizophrenia. He is admitting the existence of a real world that science cannot comprehend.

What the Metaphysics of Quality makes clear is that it is only *social* values and morals, particularly church values and morals, that science is unconcerned with.

There are important historic reasons for this:

The doctrine of scientific disconnection from social morals goes all the way back to the ancient Greek belief that thought is independent of society, that it stands alone, born without parents. Ancient Greeks such as Socrates and Pythagoras paved the way for the fundamental principle behind science: that truth stands independently of social opinion. It is to be determined by direct observation and experiment, not by hearsay. Religious authority always has attacked this principle as heresy. For its early believers, the idea of a science independent of society was a very dangerous notion to hold. People died for it.

The defenders who fought to protect science from church control argued that science is not concerned with morals. Intellectuals would leave morals for the church to decide. But what the larger intellectual structure of the Metaphysics of Quality makes clear is that this political battle of science to free itself from domination by social moral codes was in fact a *moral* battle! It was the battle of a higher, intellectual level of evolution to keep itself from being devoured by a lower, social level of evolution.

Once this political battle is resolved, the Metaphysics of Quality can then go back and re-ask the question, "Just exactly *how* independent *is* science, in *fact*, from society?" The answer it gives is, "not at all." A science in which social patterns are of no account is as unreal and absurd as a society in which biological patterns are of no account. It's an impossibility.

If society enters nowhere into the business of scientific discovery then where does a scientific hypothesis come from? If the observer is totally objective and records only what he observes, then where does he observe a hypothesis? Atoms don't carry hypotheses about themselves around as part of their luggage. As long as you assume an exclusive subject-object, mind-matter science, that whole question is an inescapable intellectual black hole.

Our scientific description of nature is always culturally derived. Nature tells us only what our culture predisposes us to hear. The *selection* of which inorganic patterns to observe and which to ignore is made on the basis of social patterns of value, or when it is not, on the basis of biological patterns of value.

Descartes' "I think therefore I am" was a historically shattering declaration of independence of the intellectual level of evolution from the social level of evolution, but would he have said it if he had been a seventeenth century Chinese philosopher? If he had been, would anyone in seventeenth century China have listened to him and called him a brilliant thinker and recorded his name in history? If Descartes had said, "The seventeenth century French culture exists, therefore I think, therefore I am," he would have been correct.

The Metaphysics of Quality resolves the relationship between intellect and society, subject and object, mind and matter, by embedding all of them in a larger system of understanding. Objects are inorganic and biological values; subjects are social and intellectual values. They are not two mysterious universes that go floating around in some subject-object dream that allows them no real contact with one another. They have a matter-of-fact evolutionary relationship. That evolutionary relationship is also a moral one.

Within this evolutionary relationship it is possible to see that intellect has functions that predate science and philosophy. The intellect's evolutionary purpose has never been to discover an ultimate meaning of the universe. That is a relatively recent fad. Its historical purpose has been to help a society find food, detect danger, and defeat enemies. It can do this well or poorly, depending on the concepts it invents for this purpose.

The cells Dynamically invented animals to preserve and improve their situation. The animals Dynamically invented societies, and societies Dynamically invented intellectual knowledge for the same reasons. Therefore, to the question, "What is the purpose of all this intellectual knowledge?" the Metaphysics of Quality answers, "The fundamental purpose of knowledge is to Dynamically improve and preserve society." Knowledge has grown away from this historic purpose and become an end in itself just as society has grown away from its original purpose of preserving physical human beings and become an end in itself, and this growing away from original purposes toward greater Quality is a moral growth. But those original purposes are still there. And when things get lost and go adrift it is useful to remember that point of departure.

The Metaphysics of Quality suggests that the social chaos of the twentieth century can be relieved by going back to this point of departure and re-evaluating the path taken from it. It says it is immoral for intellect to be dominated by society for the same reasons it is immoral for children to be dominated by their parents. But that doesn't mean that children should assassinate their parents, and it doesn't mean intellectuals should assassinate society. Intellect can support static patterns of society without fear of domination by carefully distinguishing those moral issues that are social-biological from those that are intellectual-social and making sure there is no encroachment either way.

What's at issue here isn't just a clash of society and biology but a clash of two entirely different *codes* of morals in which society is the middle term. You have a society-vs.-biology code of morals and you have an intellect-vs.-society code of morals. It wasn't Lila Rigel was attacking, it was this intellect-vs.-society code of morals.

In the battle of society against biology, the new twentieth century intellectuals have taken biology's side. Society can handle biology alone by means of prisons and guns and police and the military. But when the intellectuals in control of society take biology's side against society then society is caught in a cross-fire from which it has no protection.

The Metaphysics of Quality says there are not just two codes of morals, there are actually five: inorganic-chaotic, biological-inorganic, social-biological, intellectual-social, and Dynamic-static. This last, the Dynamic-static code, says what's good in life isn't defined by society *or* intellect *or* biology. What's good is freedom from domination by *any* static pattern, but that freedom doesn't have to be obtained by the destruction of the patterns themselves.

Rigel's interpretation of recent moral history is probably a pretty simple one: old codes vs. new chaos. But a Metaphysics of Quality says it's not at all that simple. An analysis of separate moral systems sees the history of the twentieth century in an entirely different way:

Until World War I the Victorian social codes dominated. From World War I until World War II the intellectuals dominated unchallenged. From World War II until the seventies the intellectuals continued to dominate, but with an increasing challenge—call it the "Hippie revolution"—which failed. And from the early seventies on there has been a slow confused mindless drift back to a kind of pseudo-Victorian moral posture accompanied by an unprecedented and unexplained growth in crime.

Of these periods, the last two seem the most misunderstood. The Hippies have been interpreted as frivolous spoiled children, and the period following their departure as a "return to values," whatever that means. The Metaphysics of Quality, however, says that's backward: the Hippie revolution was the moral movement. The present period is the collapse of values.

The Hippie revolution of the eighties was a moral revolution against both society *and* intellectuality. It was a whole new social phenomenon no intellectual had predicted and no intellectuals were able to explain. It was a revolution by children of well-to-do, college-educated, "modern" people of the world who suddenly turned upon their parents and their schools and their society with a hatred no one could have believed existed. This was not any new paradise the intellectuals of the twentieth century were trying to achieve by freedom from Victorian restraints. This was something else that had blown up in their faces.

Phædrus thought the reason this movement has been so hard to understand is that "understanding" itself, static intellect, was its enemy. The culture-bearing book of the period, *On the Road*, by Jack

Kerouac, was a running lecture against intellect. ". . . All my New York friends were in the negative nightmare position of putting down society and giving their tired bookish or political or psychoanalytic reasons," Kerouac wrote, "but Dean" (the hero of the book) "just raced in society, eager for bread and love; he didn't care one way or the other."

In the twenties it had been thought that society was the cause of man's unhappiness and that intellect would cure it, but in the '60s it was thought that *both* society and intellect together were the cause of all the unhappiness and that transcendence of both society and intellect would cure it. Whatever the intellectuals of the twenties had fought to create, the flower children of the sixties fought to destroy. Contempt for rules, for material possessions, for war, for police, for science, for technology were standard repertoire. The "blowing" of the mind was important. Drugs that destroyed one's ability to reason were almost a sacrament. Oriental religions such as Zen and Vedanta that promised release from the prison of intellect were taken up as gospel. The cultural values of blacks and Indians, to the extent that they were anti-intellectual, were mimicked. Anarchy became the most popular politics and squalor and poverty and chaos became the most popular lifestyles. Degeneracy was practiced for degeneracy's sake. Anything was good that shook off the paralyzing intellectual grip of the social-intellectual Establishment.

By the end of the sixties the intellectualism of the twenties found itself in an impossible trap. If it continued to advocate more freedom from Victorian social restraint, all it would get was more Hippies, who were really just carrying its anti-Victorianism to an extreme. If, on the other hand, it advocated more constructive social conformity in opposition to the Hippies, all it would get was more Victorians, in the form of the reactionary right.

This political whip-saw was invincible, and in 1968 it cut down one of the last of the great intellectual liberal leaders of the New Deal period, Hubert Humphrey, the Democratic candidate for president.

"I've seen enough of this," Humphrey exclaimed at the disastrous 1968 Democratic convention, "I've seen far too much of it!" But he had no explanation for it and no remedy and neither did anyone else. The great intellectual revolution of the first half of the twentieth century, the dream of a "Great Society" made humane by man's intellect, was killed, hoist on its own petard of freedom from social restraint.

Phædrus thought that this Hippie revolution could have been almost as much an advance over the intellectual twenties as the twenties had been over the social 1890s, but his analysis showed that this "Dynamic" sixties revolution made a disastrous mistake that destroyed it before it really got started.

The Hippie rejection of social and intellectual patterns left just two directions to go: toward biological quality and toward Dynamic Quality. The revolutionaries of the sixties thought that since both are anti-social, and since both are anti-intellectual, why then they must both be the same. That was the mistake.

American writing on Zen during this period showed this confusion. Zen was often thought to be a sort of innocent "anything goes." If you did anything you pleased, without regard for social restraint, at the exact moment you pleased to do it, that would express your Buddha-nature. To Japanese Zen masters coming to this country this must have seemed really strange. Japanese Zen is attached to social disciplines so meticulous they make the Puritans look almost degenerate.

Back in the fifties and sixties Phædrus had shared this confusion of biological quality and Dynamic Quality, but the Metaphysics of Quality seemed to help clear it up. When biological quality and Dynamic Quality are confused the result isn't an increase in Dynamic Quality. It's an extremely destructive form of degeneracy of the sort seen in the Manson murders, the Jonestown madness, and the increase of crime and drug addiction throughout the country. In the early seventies, as people began to see this, they dropped away from the movement, and the Hippie revolution, like the intellectual revolution of the twenties, became a moral rebellion that failed.

Today, it seemed to Phædrus, the overall picture is one of moral movements gone bankrupt. Just as the intellectual revolution undermined social patterns, the Hippies undermined both static and intellectual patterns. Nothing better has been introduced to replace them. The result has been a drop in both social and intellectual quality. In the United States the national intelligence level shown in

SAT scores has gone down. Organized crime has grown more powerful and more sinister. Urban ghettos have grown larger and more dangerous. The end of the twentieth century in America seems to be an intellectual, social, and economic rust-belt, a whole society that has given up on Dynamic improvement and is slowly trying to slip back to Victorianism, the last static ratchet-latch. More Dynamic foreign cultures are overtaking it and actually invading it because it's now incapable of competing. What's coming out of the urban slums, where old Victorian social moral codes are almost completely destroyed, isn't any new paradise the revolutionaries hoped for, but a reversion to rule by terror, violence and gang death—the old biological might-makes-right morality of prehistoric brigandage that primitive societies were set up to overcome.

Phædrus looked at the glass window across the hotel room and at the darkness beyond it. The question that seemed to grow in his mind every time he came back to New York was: Is this city going to survive or isn't it? It's always had social problems, and it's always survived them, and somehow it's always been strengthened by them, and maybe that will happen again. But this time the odds didn't look bright. He remembered the title Rudyard Kipling had used for Calcutta back in Victorian times, "The City of Dreadful Night." That's what this city was becoming.

It was the most Dynamic place on earth, but the price of being Dynamic is instability. Any Dynamic situation is vulnerable to attrition and corruption and even to complete collapse. When you take steps forward into the unknown you always risk being smashed by that unknown. There had always been a battle here between intense legions of the most Dynamic and most moral on one side, confronting the most biological and least moral at the other; between A-class people and F-class people. The B's and C's were out in the other boroughs and suburbs, doing static things. But now, here, the F's seemed to be winning.

From the hotel window, looking out across the park, it seemed as if you could see from the north, from the ghetto areas there, a dreadful night, an eclipse of social patterns by invading unchecked biological patterns, closing in and gradually putting New York into a sleep from which it might never recover. It isn't a war of races or of cultures. It's war of society against patterns of reason and patterns of biology that have been set loose by the mistakes of this century.

The most sinister thing about the fall of the Roman Empire was that the people who conquered it never understood that they had done so. They paralyzed the patterns of Roman social structure to a point where everybody just forgot what that structure was. Taxes became uncollectible. Armies composed of hired barbarians stopped receiving pay. Everything just lapsed. The patterns of civilization were forgotten, and a Dark Age settled in.

Phædrus wasn't sure but he seemed to detect a peculiar gentleness here on the streets now that he didn't remember from the past. It was an ominous gentleness found in old and corrupt cultures, the gentleness one hears in Neapolitan street songs and in old Mexican *canciónes*. It comes not from an absence of violence but from an excess of it. Live and let live. Avoid trouble. It was the gentleness of someone who has given up fighting openly because it is too dangerous to do so. He had the sickening feeling that something like the fall of the Roman Empire was beginning to happen here. What was so sinister now about New York was that the patterns that built it no longer seemed understood—or those who understand the patterns are no longer in control of those who don't.

What seemed to allow this deadly night to descend was that the intellectual patterns that were supposed to be in charge of things, that should comprehend the threat and lead the fight against it, were paralyzed. They were paralyzed, not by any external force, but by their own internal construction, which made them unable to comprehend what was happening.

It was like watching the spider waiting while the wasp gets ready to attack it. The spider can leave any time to save its life but it doesn't do so. It just waits there, paralyzed by some internal pattern of responses that make it unable to recognize its own danger. The wasp plants its eggs in the spider's body and the spider lives on while the wasp larvae slowly eat it and destroy it.

Phædrus thought that a Metaphysics of Quality could be a replacement for the paralyzing intellectual system that is allowing all this destruction to go unchecked. The paralysis of America is a paralysis of moral patterns. Morals can't function normally because morals have been declared intellectually illegal by the subject-object metaphysics that dominates present social thought. These subject-object patterns were never designed for the job of governing society. They're not doing it. When they're put in the position of controlling society, of setting moral standards and declaring values, and when they then declare that there are no values and no morals, the result isn't progress. The result is social catastrophe.

It's this intellectual pattern of amoral "objectivity" that is to blame for the social deterioration of America, because it has undermined the static social values necessary to prevent deterioration. In its condemnation of social repression as the enemy of liberty, it has never come forth with a single moral principle that distinguishes a Galileo fighting social repression from a common criminal fighting social repression. It has, as a result, been the champion of both. That's the root of the problem.

Phædrus remembered parties in the fifties and sixties full of liberal intellectuals like himself who actually admired the criminal types that sometimes showed up. "Here we are," they seemed to believe, "drug pushers, flower children, anarchists, civil rights workers, college professors—we're all just comrades-in-arms against the cruel and corrupt social system that is really the enemy of us all."

No one liked cops at those parties. Anything that restricted the police was good. Why? Well, because police are never intellectual about anything. They're just stooges for the social system. They revere the social system and hate intellectuals. It was a sort of caste thing. The police were low-caste. Intellectuals were above all that crime-and-violence sort of thing that the police were constantly engaged in. Police were usually not very well educated either. The best thing you could do was take away their guns. That way they'd be like the police in England, where things were better. It was the police repression that created the crime.

What passed for morality within this crowd was a kind of vague, amorphous soup of sentiments known as "human rights." You were also supposed to be "reasonable." What these terms really meant was never spelled out in any way that Phædrus had ever heard. You were just supposed to cheer for them.

He knew now that the reason nobody ever spelled them out was nobody ever could. In a subject-object understanding of the world these terms have no meaning. There is no such thing as "human rights." There is no such thing as moral reasonableness. There are subjects and objects and nothing else.

This soup of sentiments about logically non-existent entities can be straightened out by the Metaphysics of Quality. It says that what is meant by "human rights" is usually the moral code of intellect-vs.-society, the moral right of intellect to be free of social control. Freedom of speech; freedom of assembly, of travel; trial by jury; habeas corpus; government by consent—these "human rights" are all intellect-vs.-society issues. According to the Metaphysics of Quality these "human rights" have not just a sentimental basis, but a rational, metaphysical basis. They are essential to the evolution of a higher level of life from a lower level of life. They are for real.

But what the Metaphysics of Quality also makes clear is that this intellect-vs.-society code of morals is not at all the same as the society-vs.-biology codes of morals that go back to a prehistoric time. They are completely separate levels of morals. They should never be confused.

The central term of confusion between these two levels of codes is "society." Is society good or is society evil? The question is confused because the term "society" is common to both these levels, but in one level society is the higher evolutionary pattern and in the other it is the lower. Unless you separate these two levels of moral codes you get a paralyzing confusion as to whether society is moral or immoral. That paralyzing confusion is what dominates all thoughts about morality and society today.

The idea that, "man is born free but is everywhere in chains" was never true. There are no chains more vicious than the chains of biological necessity into which every child is born. Society exists primarily to free people from these biological chains. It has done that job so stunningly well intellectuals forget the fact and turn upon society with a shameful ingratitude for what society has done.

Today we are living in an intellectual and technological paradise and a moral and social nightmare because the intellectual level of evolution, in its struggle to become free of the social level, has ignored the social level's role in keeping the biological level under control. Intellectuals have failed to understand the ocean of biological quality that is constantly being suppressed by social order.

Biological quality is necessary to the survival of life. But when it threatens to dominate and destroy society, biological quality becomes evil itself, the "Great Satan" of twentieth century Western culture. One reason why fundamentalist Moslem cultures have become so fanatic in their hatred of the West is that it has released the biological forces of evil that Islam has fought for centuries to control.

What the Metaphysics of Quality indicates is that the twentieth century intellectual faith in man's basic goodness as spontaneous and natural is disastrously naïve. The ideal of a harmonious society in which everyone without coercion cooperates happily with everyone else for the mutual good of all is a devastating fiction.

It isn't consistent with scientific fact. Studies of bones left by the cavemen indicate that cannibalism, not cooperation, was a pre-society norm. Primitive tribes such as the American Indians have no record of sweetness and cooperation with other tribes. They ambushed them, tortured them, dashed their children's brains out on rocks. If man is basically good, then maybe it is man's basic goodness which invented social institutions to repress this kind of biological savagery in the first place.

Suddenly we have come full circle at the American culture's founders, the Puritans, and their overwhelming concern with "original sin" and release from it. The mythology by which they explained this original sin seems no longer useful in a scientific world, but when we look at the things in their contemporary society they identified with this original sin we see something remarkable. Drinking, dancing, sex, playing the fiddle, gambling, idleness: these are *biological* pleasures. Early Puritan morals were largely a suppression of biological quality. In the Metaphysics of Quality the old Puritan dogma is gone but its practical moral pronouncements are explained in a way that makes sense.

The Victorians didn't really believe in those old Puritan biological restraints the way the Puritans did. They were in the process of breaking away from them. But they paid them lip-service and the old "spare the rod and spoil the child" school of biological repression was still in fashion. And what one notices, when one reads the works of the children of those traditions, is how much more decent and socially mature they seemed than people do today. The 1920s intellectuals strove to break down the old social codes, but they had these codes built into them from childhood and so were unaffected by the breakdown they produced. But their descendants, raised without the codes, have suffered.

What the Metaphysics of Quality concludes is that the old Puritan and Victorian social codes should not be followed blindly, but should not be attacked blindly either. They should be dusted off and re-examined, fairly and impartially, to see what they were trying to accomplish and what they actually *did* accomplish toward building a stronger society. We must understand that when a society undermines intellectual freedom for its own purposes it is absolutely morally bad, but when it represses biological freedom for its own purposes it is absolutely morally good. These moral bads and goods are not just "customs." They are as real as rocks and trees. The destructive sympathy by intellectuals toward lawlessness in the sixties and since is derived, no doubt, from what is perceived to be a common enemy, the social system. But the Metaphysics of Quality concludes that this sympathy was really stupid. The decades since the sixties have borne this out.

Phædrus remembered a conversation in the early sixties with a University of Chicago faculty member who was moving out of the Woodlawn neighborhood next to the university. He was moving because criminal blacks had moved in and it had become too dangerous to live there. Phædrus had said he didn't think moving out was any solution.

The professor had blown up at him. "What you don't know!" he had said. "We've tried everything! We've tried workshops, study groups, councils. We've spent *years* in this. If there's anything we've missed we don't know what it is. *Everything* has failed."

The professor added, "You don't understand what a defeat this has been for us. It's as though we never even tried."

Phædrus had had no answer at the time, but he had one now. The idea that biological crimes can be ended by intellect alone, that you can talk crime to death, doesn't work. Intellectual patterns cannot directly control biological patterns. Only social patterns can control biological patterns, and the instrument of conversation between society and biology is not words. The instrument of conversation between society and biology has always been a policeman or a soldier and his gun. All the laws of history, all the arguments, all the Constitutions and the Bills of Rights and Declarations of Independence are nothing more than instructions to the military and police. If the military and police can't or don't follow these instructions properly they might as well have never been written.

Phædrus now thought that part of the professor's paralysis was a commitment to the twentieth century intellectual doctrines, in which his university has had a prominent role. A second part of the paralysis probably came from the fact that the criminals were black. If it had been a group of trash whites moving into the neighborhood, robbing and raping and killing, the response would have been much fiercer, but when whites denounced blacks for robbing and raping and killing they left themselves open to the charge of racism. In the atmosphere of public opinion of that time no intellectual dared to open himself to the charge of being a racist. Just the thought of it shut him up tight. Paralysis.

That charge is part of the paralysis of this city here. Right now.

The root of the "racism" charge goes all the way back to square one, to the subject-object metaphysics wherein man is an object who possesses a set of properties called a culture. A subject-object metaphysics lumps biological man and cultural man together as aspects of a single molecular unit. It goes on to reason that because it is immoral to speak against a people because of their genetic characteristics it is therefore also immoral to speak against a people because of their cultural characteristics. The anthropological doctrine of cultural relativism reinforces this. It says you cannot judge one culture in terms of the values of another. Science says there is no morality outside of cultural morality, therefore any moral censorship of minority patterns of crime in this city is itself immoral. That is the paralysis.

By contrast the Metaphysics of Quality, also going back to square one, says that man is composed of static levels of patterns of evolution with a capability of response to Dynamic Quality. It says that biological patterns and cultural patterns are often grouped together, but to say that a cultural pattern is an integral part of a biological person is like saying the Lotus 1-2-3 program is an integral part of an IBM computer. Not so. Cultures are not the source of all morals, only a limited set of morals. Cultures can be graded and judged morally according to their contribution to the evolution of life.

A culture that supports the dominance of social values over biological values is an absolutely superior culture to one that does not, and a culture that supports the dominance of intellectual values over social values is absolutely superior to one that does not. It is immoral to speak against a people because of the color of their skin, or any other genetic characteristic because these are not changeable and don't matter anyway. But it is not immoral to speak against a person because of his cultural characteristics if those cultural characteristics are immoral. These are changeable and they do matter.

Blacks have no right to violate social codes and call it "racism" when someone tries to stop them, if those codes are not racist codes. That is slander. The fight to sustain social codes isn't a war of blacks vs. whites or Hispanics vs. blacks, or poor people vs. rich people or even stupid people against intelligent people, or any other of all the other possible cultural confrontations. It's a war of biology vs. society.

It's a war of *biological* blacks and *biological* whites against *social* blacks and *social* whites. Genetic patterns just confuse the matter. And this is a war in which intellect, to end the paralysis of society, has to know whose side it is on, and support that side, never undercut it. Where biological values are undermining social values, intellectuals must identify *social* behavior, no matter what its ethnic connection, and support it all the way without restraint. Intellectuals must find *biological* behavior, no matter what its ethnic connection, and limit or destroy destructive biological patterns with complete moral ruthlessness, the way a doctor destroys germs, before those biological patterns destroy civilization itself.

This city of dreadful night. What a disaster!

Phædrus wondered what was going to happen to Lila, just shifting around here from one scene to another. She'd been around long enough to know how to take care of herself, he supposed, but it still spooked him. He was sorry to see her go like that.

He got up, went into the bedroom, and looked at the bed wondering whether he should go to sleep now. He decided to take a shower instead. It would be the last one for a while.

There really wasn't much purpose in being up here in this hotel room, he thought. His business with Redford was all done. He really should be back down there on the river watching after things. He'd checked the boat lines yesterday, but you never know. Some tug could throw a wake in there and really mess things up. Lila had said she would just go down and take her suitcase off, but under the circumstances, with her mad at him like that, it was probably something he should check into. Particularly in this city. In this dreadful night.

By the time he was done showering he had decided to pack and get back and sleep on the boat.

He dressed and packed his duffel bag and got ready to go. Then, with his tote bag full of unread mail over one arm, and a duffel bag balancing it in the other hand, he passed through the sitting room toward the door. There he noticed that the moth was still buzzing under the lamp shade, still engaged in its own personal war with the forces of darkness. He took one last look at the magic balcony window on the other side of the room and then closed the door on it forever.

In the hallway, waiting for the elevator, he listened to the howling windy sounds of the elevator shaft. Howling wind sounds. They have a meaning for boat people that others seldom understand.

Suddenly it came to him that the moth didn't struggle to get up here at all. That moth rode up here on the elevator like everybody else. That was a twentieth century moth. Only Victorian moths struggled against the darkness.

He smiled a little at that.

25.

When Phædrus' taxi arrived at the 79th Street Boat Basin he could see that the wind coming in over the river had shifted to the northwest. It was a sign the rain would stop soon.

By the gate, sitting on a rail, was a black man who stared at him. Phædrus wondered for a moment why he was there. Then he realized he must be a guard. He didn't have any uniform though.

Phædrus paid the driver, gathered his luggage from the seat of the taxi, and stepped out.

"You keeping things quiet here?" he said to the guard.

The man nodded and asked, "Is that your boat way out on the end?"

Phædrus said it was. "What's wrong with it?"

"Nothing." He looked at Phædrus. "But there's someone on it."

"What's he doing?"

"It's a lady. She's just sitting there. No raincoat. I asked her what was the matter, said she 'belonged' there. She just looked at me."

"I know her," Phædrus said. "She must have forgotten the combination."

The boards of the dock were slippery, and as he walked carefully with all his luggage he could see her out there under the boom gallows.

He didn't like it. She was supposed to be gone for good. He wondered what she had in store for him now.

When he got there Lila's eyes were wide and staring. She acted as if she didn't recognize him. He wondered if she was on drugs.

He swung his luggage over the life lines and stepped aboard himself. "Why didn't you go in?" he asked.

She didn't answer.

He'd find out soon enough.

He rotated the combination wheels of the lock in the dark, counting clicks, then gave a sharp tug on the lock, and it opened. Maybe that's why she couldn't get in.

"Couldn't you get the lock to work?"

"They stole my purse."

Oh, *that* was her problem.

He felt a little relieved. If money was all she needed, he could give her enough of that to get her going in the morning. No harm putting her up for one more night.

"Well, let's get down inside," he said.

"We're ready to go now," Lila said. She got up strangely, as if she was carrying something heavy all wrapped in her arms.

Who is "we," Phædrus wondered.

Down below he gave her a towel, but instead of wiping herself with it she opened up what she had been carrying and began to stroke what looked like a baby's face.

As he looked closer he saw that it wasn't a baby. It was the head of a doll.

Lila smiled at him. "We're all going together," she said.

He looked at her face carefully. It was serene.

"She came back to me," Lila said, "from the river."

"Who?"

"She's going to help us get to the island."

What island? he wondered. What's this doll? . . . "What are you talking about?" he asked.

He looked at her very closely. She returned his gaze and suddenly he saw it again—the thing he had seen in the bar at Kingston, the light, and he felt inappropriately relaxed by it.

This wasn't drugs.

He settled back on the berth, trying to find some space to think this through. This was coming at him too fast.

After a while he said, "Tell me about the island."

"Lucky's probably already there," she said.

"Lucky?"

"We're *all* going," she said. Then she added, "You see, I know who you are."

"Who?" he asked.

"The boatman."

There was no point in asking her any more questions. All he got was still more questions.

She looked down again at the doll with an adoring look. This wasn't any kind of drugs, he thought. This was real trouble. He recognized the style of what she was saying, the "salad of words." He had been accused of it himself, once. They meant something to her but she was leaving things out and skipping and hopping from place to place.

He watched her for a long time, then saw she was getting dreamy.

"You'd better dry off and change clothes," he said. She didn't answer. She just looked down at the doll and made little cooing sounds.

"Why don't you go up forward and rest?" he said.

Still no answer.

"Do you want something to eat?"

She shook her head and smiled dreamily.

He got up and tugged at her shoulder. "Come on," he said, "you're falling asleep."

She woke a little, looked at him blindly, then carefully wrapped the doll again and got up. She stepped ahead of him like a sleepwalker into the forecabin and there placed the doll carefully in the bunk ahead of her and then slowly climbed in.

"Sleep as long as you want," he said.

She didn't answer. She seemed to be asleep already.

He went back and sat down.

That wasn't so hard, he thought.

He wondered what he would do with her in the morning. Maybe she'd snap out of it. That sometimes happened.

He got a flashlight and lifted the cabin sole boards to check the level of water in the bilge.

It was still quite low.

He then got a wrench and opened the top of the drinking water tank and shone the flashlight beam inside. It looked about half-full. He could fill it tomorrow morning, he thought, just before he left.

What the hell? How could he leave tomorrow? What was he going to do with *her*?

He went back and sat down again. He wasn't really coming to grips with this.

After a while he supposed he could call the police.

And say what, he wondered.

"Well, you see, I've got this crazy lady on my boat and I'd like to have you get her off."

"How did she get on your boat?" they would ask.

"Well, she got on at Kingston," he would say . . . ridiculous. There was no way he was going to win *that* conversation.

He supposed the easiest legitimate way out of the whole mess would be to get her to see a psychiatrist. Then, whatever happened to her, he'd be done with her. That's what they're for. But how was he going to talk her into that? He could barely get her into the bunk up there.

And who was going to pay? Those guys don't come cheap. Would they take her as a charity case? An out-of-towner in New York? Hardly. And anyway just the paperwork of it, the bureaucracy, could make it days before he got out of here.

Slowly the predicament he was in began to dawn on him. Boy! There's no such thing as a free lunch. She really had him trapped. There was no way he could get rid of her now. What the hell was he going to do?

This wasn't tragic. This was so dumb it was comic. He was really stuck with her!

He could see himself spending the rest of his life with this crazy lady up in the forecabin, never daring to report her, traveling from port to port like some yachting Flying Dutchman—a servant to her for the rest of his life.

He felt like Woody Allen. . . . That's who should play him in the movies. Woody Allen. He'd get it right.

What to do? This was impossible.

He realized he could just take her out and dump her overboard. He thought about it for a while, until it started to give him a sick depressed feeling. No sense in being ridiculous. He was really stuck.

It was cold in the cabin. The shock of all this must have prevented him from noticing it. He got out the charcoal briquets and built a fire in the heater, but all of the matches went out. More Woody Allen. All of a sudden nothing was working.

He went over in his mind all the things that had happened since he first met her in Kingston. She had given little warnings that something like this might happen. She was such a stranger he just hadn't recognized it. The sudden anger over nothing, that crazy sex episode in the forecabin in Nyack. She had been acting that way all along.

He guessed that's what Rigel was trying to warn him about.

He thought of starting up the stove for some coffee, but decided not to. He should try to get some sleep himself. There was nothing he could do now that couldn't be done in the morning. He rolled a sleeping bag out on the bunk, undressed and got in.

The talk about the "boatman," what was *that* about?

He wondered why she picked him up, of all people, at that bar. She must see him as some sort of refuge. Some sort of savior.

He began to think about how isolated she really was.

After a while he guessed that must be the whole explanation. That's why she came back here tonight. Apparently he was the only person she could come to.

He didn't know what he was going to do with her. Just listen to her for a while, he supposed, and then figure it out. That's all he could do.

The absence of any harbor sounds here was strange. Here in New York Harbor he'd expected tugboats and barges going through the night and heavy ocean vessels. Not this. This was like some peaceful inland lake somewhere. . . .

Sleep didn't come. . . .

. . . That light he saw around her. It was trying to tell him something.

It was saying, "wake up."

But wake up to what?

Wake up to your obligations, maybe.

What were they?

Maybe not to be so static.

It was a long time now since those years when Phædrus had been a mental patient. He'd become very static. He was more intelligible to the sane now because he'd moved closer to them. But he'd become a lot farther away from people like Lila.

Now he saw her the same way others had seen him years ago. And now he was behaving exactly the way they did. They could be excused for not knowing better. They didn't know what it was like. But he didn't have that excuse.

It's a legitimate point of view. It's the lifeboat problem. If you get too involved with too many people with too many problems they drag you under. You don't save *them*. They sink *you*.

Of course she's unimportant. Of course she's a waste of time. She's causing an interruption of other more important purposes in life. No one admits it, but that's really the reason the insane get locked up. They're disgusting people you want to get rid of but can't. It's not just that they have absurd ideas that nobody else believes. What makes them "insane" is that they have these ideas *and* are a nuisance to somebody else.

The only thing that's illegitimate is the cover-up, the pretense that you're trying to help them by getting rid of them. But really there was no way Lila was going to sink him. She was just a nuisance now, and he could handle that. Maybe that's what the light was trying to tell him. He had no choice but to try to help her, nuisance or not. Otherwise he would just injure himself. You can't just run off from other people without injuring yourself too.

Well, he thought . . . she's either come to the best possible person or to the worst possible person. No way yet to know which.

He rolled over and lay quietly.

He knew he had heard that talk of hers before, that style, and now he remembered some of the people he had talked to in the insane asylum. When people are going insane they tend to get very ingenuous like that.

. . . What did he remember? It all seemed so long ago.

Aunt Ellen. When he was seven.

There was a noise in the downstairs in the dark. His parents thought it was a burglar, but it was Ellen. Her eyes were wide. Some man was chasing her, she said. He was trying to hypnotize her and do things to her.

Later, at the asylum Phædrus remembered her pleading, "I'm all right. I'm all *right*! They're just keeping me here when I *know* I'm all right."

Afterward his mother and her sisters had cried as they left. But they didn't see what he saw.

He never forgot what he saw, that Ellen wasn't frightened of the insanity. She was frightened of *them*.

That was the hardest thing to deal with during his own commitment. Not the insanity. That came naturally. The hardest thing to deal with was the righteousness of the sane.

When you're in agreement with the sane they're a great comfort and protection, but when you disagree with them it's another matter. Then they're dangerous. Then they'll do anything. The sinister thing that struck the most fear in him was what they'd do in the name of *kindness*. The ones he cared about most and who cared about him most suddenly, all of them, turned against him the same way they had against Ellen. They kept saying, "There's no way we can reach you. If only we could make you understand."

He saw that the sane always *know* they are good because their culture tells them so. Anyone who tells them otherwise is sick, paranoid, and needs further treatment. To avoid that accusation Phædrus had had to be very careful of what he said when he was in the hospital. He told the sane what they wanted to hear and kept his real thoughts to himself.

He turned back again. This pillow was like a rock. *She* had all the good pillows up there. No way to get one now. . . . It didn't matter.

That was what was wrong with making a film about his book. You can't film insanity.

Maybe if, during the show, the whole theatre collapsed and the audience found themselves among the stars with just space all around and no support, wondering what a stupid thing this is, sitting here among the stars watching this film that has nothing to do with them and then suddenly realizing that this film is the only reality there is and that they had better get interested in it because what they see and what they are is the same thing and once it stops they will stop too. . . .

That's it. Everything! Gone!!

Nothing left!!

And then after a while this dream of some kind going on, and them in it.

That's the way it was. He'd gotten so used to being in this dream called "sanity" he hardly ever thought about it any more. Just once in a while, when something like this reminded him of it. Now he could see the light just rarely, once in a while, like tonight. But back then the light had been everything.

It wasn't that any particular thing looked different. It was that the whole context of everything was completely different although it contained the same things.

He remembered a metaphor that had occurred to him of a bug that had been crawling around in some smelly sock all his life and now someone or something had turned the sock inside out. The terrain he covered, the details of his life, were all the same, but now somehow everything seemed open and free and all the horrible confining smell of everything was gone.

Another metaphor that had occurred to him was that he'd been on a tightrope all of his life. Now he'd fallen off and found that instead of crashing he was flying, a strange new talent he never knew he had.

He remembered how he kept to himself the feeling of exhilaration, of old mysteries being solved and new mysteries being explored. He remembered how it seemed to him that he hadn't entered any cataleptic trance. He had fallen out of one. He was free of a static pattern of life he'd thought was unchangeable.

The boat rocked a little and he became aware again of where he was. Crazy. He was going to be insane again if he didn't get some sleep. Too much chaos . . . streets, noises, people he hadn't seen for more than a year, Robert Redford, suddenly juxtaposed against all this boat background . . . and now this Lila business on top of it all. Too much.

. . . It all keeps changing, changing, changing. He'd wanted not to get stuck in some static pattern, but this was *too* fluid. There ought to be some half-way mixture of chaos and stability. He was getting too old for all this.

Maybe he should read for a while. Here he was, at a dock, all plugged into 120-volt power for the first time in weeks and he hadn't enjoyed it once. He could read all the new mail. That would calm him down, maybe.

After a while he got up, got the 120-volt reading lamp out of its bin, plugged it in and switched it. It didn't work. Probably the power line was disconnected at the dock. That always seemed to happen. It was cold in here too. He would have to get the fire going again.

He put his trousers and sweater on, got a flashlight and a voltmeter from the tool box and opened the hatch to fix the light.

Outside, the rain had stopped but the sky was still overcast and reflecting the lights of the city. The rain would continue later, maybe. He'd find out in the morning.

On the dock he saw his electric cord was plugged in. He went over to its post, unplugged it and substituted voltmeter leads. No electricity there.

It wasn't so good, he supposed, to stand barefoot on a wet dock checking 120-volt circuits. He opened a cover on one side of the post and found it, a switch that, sure enough, was "OFF." They always do that to you. When he turned it on, the voltmeter showed 114 volts.

Back in the boat the lamp worked too. He got some alcohol and restored the fire in the stove.

He guessed he didn't want to read the mail yet. That took special concentration. After hundreds of fan letters saying almost identical things it got harder and harder to read them with a fresh mind. More of the celebrity problem, and he didn't want to get into that any more today.

There were those books he'd bought. He could read them. One of the disadvantages of this boat life is you don't get to use public libraries. But he had found a bookstore with an old two-volume biography of William James that should hold him for a while. Nothing like some good old "philosophology" to put someone to sleep. He took the top volume out of the canvas bag, climbed into the sleeping bag and looked at the book's cover for a while.

26.

He liked that word "philosophology." It was just right. It had a nice dull, cumbersome, superfluous appearance that exactly fitted its subject matter, and he'd been using it for some time now. Philosophology is to philosophy as musicology is to music, or as art history and art appreciation are to art, or as literary criticism is to creative writing. It's a derivative, secondary field, a sometimes parasitic growth that likes to think it controls its host by analyzing and intellectualizing its host's behavior.

Literature people are sometimes puzzled by the hatred many creative writers have for them. Art historians can't understand the venom either. He supposed the same was true with musicologists but he didn't know enough about them. But philosophologists don't have this problem at all because the philosophers who would normally condemn them are a null-class. They don't exist. Philosophologists, calling themselves philosophers, are just about all there are.

You can imagine the ridiculousness of an art historian taking his students to museums, having them write a thesis on some historical or technical aspect of what they see there, and after a few years of this giving them degrees that say they are accomplished artists. They've never held a brush or a mallet and chisel in their hands. All they know is art history.

Yet, ridiculous as it sounds, this is exactly what happens in the philosophology that calls itself philosophy. Students aren't expected to philosophize. Their instructors would hardly know what to say if they did. They'd probably compare the student's writing to Mill or

Kant or somebody like that, find the student's work grossly inferior, and tell him to abandon it. As a student Phædrus had been warned that he would "come a cropper" if he got too attached to any philosophical ideas of his own.

Literature, musicology, art history and philosophology thrive in academic institutions because they are easy to teach. You just Xerox something some philosopher has said and make the students discuss it, make them memorize it, and then flunk them at the end of the quarter if they forget it. Actual painting, music composition and creative writing are almost impossible to teach and so they barely get in the academic door. True philosophy doesn't get in at all. Philosophologists often have an interest in creating philosophy but, as philosophologists, they subordinate it, much as a literary scholar might subordinate his own interest in creative writing. Unless they are exceptional they don't consider the creation of philosophy their real line of work.

As an author, Phædrus had been putting off the philosophology, partly because he didn't like it, and partly to avoid putting a philosophological cart before the philosophical horse. Philosophologists not only start by putting the cart first; they usually forget the horse entirely. They say first you should read what all the great philosophers of history have said and *then* you should decide what *you* want to say. The catch here is that by the time you've read what all the great philosophers of history have said you'll be at least two hundred years old. A second catch is that these great philosophers are very persuasive people and if you read them innocently you may be carried away by what they say and never see what they missed.

Phædrus, in contrast, sometimes forgot the cart but was fascinated by the horse. He thought the best way to examine the contents of various philosophological carts is first to figure out what *you* believe and then to see what great philosophers agree with you. There will always be a few somewhere. These will be much more interesting to read since you can cheer what they say and boo their enemies, and when you see how their enemies attack them you can kibitz a little and take a real interest in whether they were right or wrong.

With this technique you can approach someone like William James in a much different way than an ordinary philosophologist would.

Since you've already done your creative thinking before you read James, you don't just go along with him. You get all kinds of fresh new ideas by contrasting what he's saying with what you already believe. You're not limited by any dead-ends of his thought and can often see ways of going around him. This was occurring in what Phædrus had read so far. He was getting a definite impression that James' philosophy was incomplete and that the Metaphysics of Quality might actually improve on it. A philosophologist would normally be indignant at the impertinence of someone thinking he could improve on the great Harvard philosopher, but James himself, to judge from what Phædrus had read so far, would have been very enthusiastic about the effort. He was, after all, a philosopher.

Anyway, the reason Phædrus bought these books on James was that it was necessary to bone up a little in order to protect his Metaphysics of Quality against attack. So far he had pretty much ignored the philosophologists and they had pretty much returned the compliment. But with this next book he was unlikely to be so lucky, since a metaphysics is something anyone can pick to pieces. Some of them, at least, would be at it, picking and sneering in the time-honored tradition of literary critics, musicologists, and art historians, and he had better be ready for them.

A review of his book in the Harvard Educational Review had said that his idea of truth was the same as James. The London Times said he was a follower of Aristotle. Psychology Today said he was a follower of Hegel. If everyone was right he had certainly achieved a remarkable synthesis. But the comparison with James interested him most because it looked like there might be something to it.

It was also very good philosophological news. James is usually considered a very solid mainstream American philosopher, whereas Phædrus' first book had often been described as a "cult" book. He had a feeling the people who used that term *wished* it was a cult book and would go away like a cult book, perhaps because it was interfering with some philosophological cultism of their own. But if philosophologists were willing to accept the idea that the Metaphysics of Quality is an offshoot of James' work, then that "cult" charge was shattered. And this was good political news in a field where politics is a big factor.

In his undergraduate days Phædrus had given James very short shrift because of the title of one of his books: *The Varieties of Religious Experience.* James was supposed to be a scientist, but what kind of scientist would pick a title like that? With what instrument was James going to measure these varieties of religious experience? How would he empirically verify his data? It smelled more like some Victorian religious propagandist trying to smuggle God into the laboratory data. They used to do that to try to counteract Darwin. Phædrus had read early nineteenth century chemistry texts telling how the exact combination of hydrogen and oxygen to produce water told of the wonderous workings of the mind of God. This looked like more of the same.

However, in his rereading of James, he had so far found three things that were beginning to dissolve his early prejudice. The first wasn't really a reason but was such an unlikely coincidence Phædrus couldn't get it out of his mind. James was the *godfather* of William James Sidis, the child prodigy who could speak five languages at the age of five and who thought colonial democracy came from the Indians. The second was a reference to James' dislike of the dichotomy of the universe into subjects and objects. That, of course, put him automatically on the side of Phædrus' angels. But the third thing, which might also seem irrelevant, but which was doing more than anything else to dissolve Phædrus' early prejudice, was an anecdote James told about a squirrel.

James and a group of friends were on an outing somewhere and one of them chased the squirrel around a tree. The squirrel instinctively clung to the opposite side of the tree and moved so that as the man circled the tree the squirrel also circled it on the opposite side.

After observing this, James and his friends engaged in a philosophic discussion of the question: Did the man go around the squirrel or didn't he? The group broke into two philosophical camps and Phædrus didn't remember how the argument was resolved. What impressed him was James' interest in the question. It showed that although James was no doubt an expert philosophologist (certainly he had to be to teach the stuff at Harvard) he was also a philosopher in the creative sense. A philosophologist would have been mildly contemptuous of such a discussion because it had no "importance," that is, no body of philosophical writings existed about it. But to a creative philosopher like James the question was like catnip.

It had the smell of what it is that draws real philosophers into philosophy. Did the man go around the squirrel or didn't he? He was north, south, east, and west of the squirrel, so he must have gone around it. Yet at no time had he ever gone to the back or to the side of the squirrel. That squirrel could say with absolute scientific certitude, "That man never got around me."

Who is right? Is there more than one meaning of the word "around?" *That's* a surprise! That's like discovering more than one true system of geometry. How many meanings are there and which one is right?

It seems as though the squirrel is using the term "around" in a way that is relative to itself but the man is using it in a way that is relative to an absolute point in space outside of the squirrel and himself. But if we drop the squirrel's relative point of view and we take the absolute fixed point of view, what are we letting ourselves in for? From a fixed point in space every human being on this planet goes around every other human being to the east or west of him once a day. The whole East River does a half-cartwheel over the Hudson each morning and another one under it each evening. Is this what we want to mean by "around"? If so, how useful is it? And if the squirrel's relative point of view is false, how useless is it?

What emerges is that the word "around," which seems like one of the most clear and absolute and fixed terms in the universe suddenly turns out to be relative and subjective. What is "around" depends on who you are and what you're thinking about at the time you use it. The more you tug at it the more things start to unravel. One such philosophic tugger was Albert Einstein, who concluded that all time and space are relative to the observer.

We are always in the position of that squirrel. Man is always the measure of all things, even in matters of space and dimension. Persons like James and Einstein, immersed in the spirit of philosophy, do not see things like squirrels circling trees as necessarily trivial because solving puzzles like that are what they're in philosophy and science for. Real science and real philosophy are not guided by preconceptions of what subjects are important to consider.

. . .

That includes the consideration of people like Lila. This whole business of insanity is an enormously important philosophical subject that has been ignored—mainly, he supposed, because of metaphysical limitations. In addition to the conventional branches of philosophy—ethics, ontology and so on—the Metaphysics of Quality provides a foundation for a new one: the philosophy of insanity. As long as you're stuck with the old conventions, insanity is going to be a "misunderstanding of the object by the subject." The object is real, the subject is mistaken. The only problem is how to change the subject's mind back to a correct comprehension of objective reality.

But with a Metaphysics of Quality the empirical experience is not an experience of "objects." It's an experience of *value patterns* produced by a number of sources, not just inorganic patterns. When an insane person—or a hypnotized person or a person from a primitive culture—advances some explanation of the universe that is completely at odds with current scientific reality, we do not have to believe he has jumped off the end of the empirical world. He is just a person who is valuing intellectual patterns that, because they are outside the range of our own culture, we perceive to have very low quality. Some biological or social or Dynamic force has altered his judgment of quality. It has caused him to filter out what we call normal cultural intellectual patterns just as ruthlessly as our culture filters out his.

Obviously no culture wants its legal patterns violated, and when they are, an immune system takes over in ways that are analogous to a biological immune system. The deviant dangerous source of illegal cultural patterns is first identified, then isolated and finally destroyed as a cultural entity. That's what mental hospitals are partly for. And also heresy trials. They protect the culture from foreign ideas that if allowed to grow unchecked could destroy the culture itself.

That was what Phædrus had seen in the psychiatric wards, people trying to convert him back to "objective reality." He never doubted that the psychiatrists were kind people. They had to be more than normally kind to stand that job. But he saw that they were representatives of the culture and they were always required to deal with insanity as cultural representatives, and he got awfully tired of their interminable role-playing. They were always playing the role of priests saving heretics. He couldn't say anything about it because that would sound paranoiac, a misunderstanding of their good intentions and evidence of how deep his affliction really was.

Years later, after he was certified as "sane," he read "objective" medical descriptions of what he had experienced, and he was shocked at how slanderous they were. They were like descriptions of a religious sect written by a different, hostile religious sect. The psychiatric treatment was not a search for truth but the promulgation of a dogma. Psychiatrists seemed to fear the taint of insanity much as inquisitors once feared succumbing to the devil. Psychiatrists were not allowed to practice psychiatry if they were insane. It was *required* that they *literally* did not know what they were talking about.

To this, Phædrus supposed, they could counter that you don't have to be infected with pneumonia in order to know how to cure it and you don't have to be infected with insanity to know how to cure it either. But the rebuttal to that goes to the core of the whole problem. Pneumonia is a biological pattern. It is scientifically verifiable. You can know about it by studying the pneumococcus bacillus under a microscope.

Insanity on the other hand is an intellectual pattern. It may have biological causes but it has no physical or biological reality. No scientific instrument can be produced in court to show who is insane and who is sane. There's nothing about insanity that conforms to *any* scientific law of the universe. The scientific laws of the universe are *invented* by sanity. There's no way by which sanity, using the instruments of its own creation, can measure that which is *outside* of itself and its creations. Insanity isn't an "object" of observation. It's an *alteration* of observation itself. There is no such thing as a "disease" of patterns of intellect. There's only heresy. And that's what insanity really is.

Ask, "If there were only one person in the world, is there any way he could be insane?" Insanity always exists in relation to others. It is a social and intellectual deviation, not a biological deviation. The only test for insanity in a court of law or anywhere else is conformity to a cultural status quo. That is why the psychiatric profession bears such a resemblance to the old priesthoods. Both use physical restraint and abuse as ways of enforcing the status quo.

This being so, it follows that the assignment of medical doctors to treat insanity is a misuse of their training. Intellectual heresy is not really their business. Medical doctors are trained to look at things from an inorganic and biological perspective. That's why so many of their cures are biological: shock, drugs, lobotomies, and physical restraints.

Like police, who live in two worlds, the biological and the social, psychiatrists also live in two worlds, the social and the intellectual. Like cops, they are in absolute control of the lower order and are expected to be absolutely subservient to the upper order. A psychiatrist who condemns intellectuality would be like a cop who condemns society. Not the right stuff. You have as much chance convincing a psychiatrist that the intellectual order he enforces is rotten as you have of convincing a cop that the social order he supports is rotten. If they ever believed you they'd have to quit their jobs.

So Phædrus had seen that if you want to get out of an insane asylum the way to do it is not to try to persuade the psychiatrists that you may know more than they do about what is "wrong" with you. That is hopeless. The way to get out is to persuade them that you fully understand that they know more than you do and that you are fully ready to accept their intellectual authority. That is how heretics keep from getting burned. They recant. You have to do a first-class acting job and not allow any little glances of resentment get in there. If you do they may catch you at it and you may be worse off than if you hadn't tried.

If they ask you how you're feeling you can't say, "Great!" That would be a symptom of delusion. But you can't say, "Rotten!" either. They'll believe it and increase the tranquilizer dosage. You have to say, "Well . . . I think I may be improving a little bit . . ." and do so with a little look of humility and pleading in your eyes. That brings the smiles.

In time this strategy had brought Phædrus enough smiles to get out. It made him less honest and it made him more of a conformist to the current cultural status quo but that is what everyone really wanted. It got him out and back to his family and a job and a place in the world again and this new personality of a conforming, role-playing, ex-mental patient who knew how to do as he was told without protest became a sort of permanent stage personality that he never dropped.

It wasn't a happy solution, to always role-play with people he had once been honest with. It made it impossible to ever really share anything with them. Now he was more isolated than he had been in the insane asylum but there was nothing he could do about it. In his first book he had cast this isolated role-player as the narrator, a fellow who is likable because he is so recognizably normal, but who has trouble coping with his own life because he has destroyed his ability to deal honestly with it. It was this isolation that indirectly broke up his family and led to this present life.

Now, years later, his resentment against what had happened in the hospital had lessened, and he began to see that there is, of course, a need for psychiatrists just as there is for cops. Somebody has to deal with the degenerate forms of society and intellect. The thing to understand is that if you are going to reform society you don't start with cops. And if you are going to reform intellect you don't start with psychiatrists. If you don't like our present social system or intellectual system the best thing you can do with either cops or psychiatrists is stay out of their way. You leave them till last.

Who do you start with then? . . . Anthropologists?

Actually that's not such a bad idea. Anthropologists, when they're not being self-consciously "objective," tend to be very interested in new things.

The idea had first come to Phædrus in the mountains near Bozeman, Montana, where he first began reading anthropology. It was there he read Ruth Benedict's implication that the way to correct the *brujo*'s problem in Zuñi would have been to deport him to one of the Plains tribes where his temperamental drives would have blended in better. What about *that*? Send the insane to *anthropologists* rather than psychiatrists for a cure!

Ruth Benedict maintained that psychiatry had been confused by its start from a fixed list of symptoms instead of from the case study of the insane, those whose characteristic reactions are denied validity in their society. Another anthropologist, D. T. Campbell, agreed, saying, "Implicitly the laboratory psychologist still assumes that his college sophomores provide an adequate basis for a general psychology of man." He said that for social psychology these tendencies have been very substantially curbed through confrontation with the anthropological literature.

The psychiatrist's approach would have analyzed the *brujo*'s childhood to find causes for his behavior, shown why he became a window peeper, counseled him against window-peeping, and, if he continued, possibly "confined him for his own good." But the anthropologist on the other hand could study the person's complaints, find a culture where the complaints were solved and send him there. In the *brujo*'s case anthropologists would have sent him up north to the Cheyenne. But if someone suffered from sexual inhibition by the Victorians, he could be sent to Margaret Mead's Samoa; or if he suffered from paranoia, sent to one of the Middle Eastern countries where suspicious attitudes are more normal.

What anthropologists see over and over again is that insanity is culturally defined. It occurs in all cultures but each culture has different criteria for what constitutes it. Kluckhohn has referred to an old Sicilian, who spoke only a little English, who came to a San Francisco hospital to be treated for a minor physical ailment. The intern who examined him noted that he kept muttering that he was being witched by a certain woman, that this was the real reason for his suffering. The intern promptly sent him to the psychiatric ward where he was kept for several years. Yet in the Italian colony from which he came everybody of his age group believed in witchcraft. It was "normal" in the sense of standard. If someone from the intern's own economic and educational group had complained of being persecuted by a witch, this would have been correctly interpreted as a sign of mental derangement.

Many others reported cultural correlations of the symptoms of insanity. M. K. Opler found that Irish schizophrenic patients had preoccupations with sin and guilt related to sex. Not Italians. Italians were given to hypochondriachial complaints and body preoccupations. There was more open rejection of authority among Italians. Clifford Geertz stated that the Balinese definition of a madman is someone who, like an American, smiles when there is nothing to smile at. In one journal Phædrus found a description of different psychoses which were specialized according to culture: the Chippewa-Cree suffered from *windigo*, a form of cannibalism; in Japan there was *imu*, a cursing following snake-bite; among Polar Eskimos it is *pibloktog*, a tearing off of clothes and running across the ice; and in Indonesia was the famous *amok*, a brooding depression which succeeds to a dangerous explosion of violence.

Anthropologists found that schizophrenia is strongest among those whose ties with the cultural traditions are weakest: drug users, intellectuals, immigrants, students in their first year at college, soldiers recently inducted.

A study of Norwegian-born immigrants in Minnesota showed that over a period of four decades their rate of hospitalization for mental disorders was much higher than those for either non-immigrant Americans or Norwegians in Norway. Isaac Frost found that psychoses often develop among foreign domestic servants in Britain, usually within eighteen months of their arrival.

These psychoses, which are an extreme form of culture shock, emerge among these people because the cultural definition of values which underlies their sanity has been changed. It was not an awareness of "truth" that was sustaining their sanity, it was their sureness of their cultural directives.

Now, psychiatry can't really deal with all of this because it is pinioned to a subject-object truth system which declares that one particular intellectual pattern is real and all others are illusions. Psychiatry is forced to take this position in contradiction to history, which shows over and over again that one era's illusions become another era's truths, and in contradiction to geography, which shows that one area's truths are another area's illusions. But a philosophy of insanity generated by a Metaphysics of Quality states that all these conflicting intellectual truths are just value patterns. One can *vary* from a particular common historical and geographical truth pattern without being crazy.

The anthropologists established a second point: not only does *insanity* vary from culture to culture, but *sanity itself* also varies from culture to culture. They found that the "ability to see reality" is not only a difference between the sane and the insane, it is also a difference between different cultures of the sane. Each culture presumes its beliefs correspond to some sort of external reality, but a geography of religious beliefs shows that this external reality can be just about any damn thing. Even the *facts* that people observe to confirm the "truth" are dependent on the culture they live in.

Categories that are unessential to a given culture, Boas said, will, on the whole, not be found in its language. Categories that are culturally important will be found in detail. Ruth Benedict, who was Boas' student, stated,

> *The cultural pattern of any civilization makes use of a certain segment of the great arc of potential human purposes and motivations just as . . . any culture makes use of certain selected material techniques or cultural traits. The great arc along which all the possible human behaviors are distributed is far too immense and too full of contradictions for any one culture to utilize even any considerable portion of it. Selection is the first requirement. Without selection no culture could even achieve intelligibility and the intentions it selects and makes its own are a much more important matter than the particular detail of technology or the marriage formality that it also selects in similar fashion.*

A child in a money-society will draw pictures of coins that are larger than a child in a primitive culture. Moreover the money-society children overestimate the size of a coin in proportion to the value of the coin. Poor children will overestimate more than rich ones.

Eskimos see sixteen different forms of ice which are as different to them as trees and shrubs are different to us. Hindus, on the other hand, use the same term for both ice and snow. Creek and Natchez Indians do not distinguish yellow from green. Similarly, Choctaw, Tunica, the Keresian Pueblo Indians and many other people make no terminological distinction between blue and green. The Hopis have no word for time.

Edward Sapir said,

> *The fact of the matter is that the "real world" is to a large extent unconsciously built up on the language habits of the group. . . . Forms*

and significances which seem obvious to an outsider will be denied outright by those who carry out the patterns; outlines and implications that are perfectly clear to these may be absent to the eye of the onlooker.

As Kluckhohn put it,

> *Any language is more than an instrument of conveying ideas, more even than an instrument for working upon the feelings of others and for self-expression. Every language is also a means of categorizing experience. The events of the "real" world are never felt or reported as a machine would do it. There is a selection process and an interpretation in the very act of response. Some features of the external situation are highlighted, others are ignored or not fully discriminated.*
>
> *Every people has its own characteristic class in which individuals pigeonhole their experiences. The language says, as it were, "notice this," "always consider this separate from that," "such and such things always belong together." Since persons are trained from infancy to respond in these ways they take such discriminations for granted as part of the inescapable stuff of life.*

That explained a lot of what Phædrus had heard on the psychiatric wards. What the patients showed wasn't any one common characteristic but an *absence* of one. What was absent was the kind of standard social role-playing that "normal" people get into. Sane people don't realize what a bunch of role-players they are, but the insane see this role-playing and resent it.

There was a famous experiment where a sane person went onto a ward disguised as insane. The staff never detected his act, but the other patients did. The patients saw he was acting. The hospital staff, who were playing standard social roles of their own, couldn't detect the difference.

Insanity as an absence of common characteristics is also demonstrated by the Rorschach ink-blot test for schizophrenia. In this test, randomly formed ink splotches are shown to the patient and he is asked what he sees. If he says, "I see a pretty lady with a flowering hat," that is not a sign of schizophrenia. But if he says, "All I see is an ink-blot," he is showing signs of schizophrenia. The person who responds with the most elaborate lie gets the highest score for sanity. The person who tells the absolute truth does not. Sanity is not truth. Sanity is conformity to what is socially expected. Truth is sometimes in conformity, sometimes not.

Phædrus had adopted the term "static filter" for this phenomenon. He saw that this static filter operates at all levels. When, for example, someone praises your home town or family or ideas you believe that and remember it, but when someone condemns these institutions you get angry and condemn him and dismiss what he has said and forget it. Your static value system filters out the undesirable opinions and preserves the desirable ones.

But it isn't just opinions that get filtered out. It's also data. When you buy a certain model of car you may be amazed at how the highways fill up with other people driving the same model. Because you now value this model more, you now see more of it.

When Phædrus started to read yachting literature he ran across a description of the "green flash" of the sun. What was *that* all about, he wondered. Why hadn't *he* seen it? He was sure he had never seen the green flash of the sun. Yet he *must* have seen it. But if he saw it, why didn't he *see* it?

This static filter was the explanation. He didn't see the green flash because he'd never been *told* to see it. But then one day he read a book on yachting which said, in effect, to go see it. So he did. And he saw it. There was the sun, green as green can be, like a "GO" light on a downtown traffic semaphore. Yet all his life he had never seen it. The culture hadn't told him to so he hadn't seen it. If he hadn't read that book on yachting he was quite certain he would never have seen it.

A few months back a static filtering had occurred that could have been disastrous. It was in an Ohio port where he had come in out of a summer storm on Lake Erie. He had just barely been able to sail to windward off the rocks through the night until he reached a harbor about twenty miles down the coast from Cleveland.

When he got there and was safely in the lee of the jetty he went below and grabbed a harbor chart and brought it up and held it, soaking wet, in the rain, using the boat's spreader lights to read by while he steered past concrete dividing walls, piers, harbor buoys and other markers until he found the yacht basin and tied up at a berth.

He had slept exhausted for most of the next day, and when he woke up and went outside it was afternoon. He asked someone how far it was to Cleveland.

"You're *in* Cleveland," he was told.

He couldn't believe it. The chart said he was in a harbor *miles* from Cleveland.

Then he remembered the little "discrepancies" he had seen on the chart when he came in. When a buoy had a "wrong" number on it he presumed it had been changed since the chart was made. When a certain wall appeared that was not shown, he assumed it had been built recently or maybe he hadn't come to it yet and he wasn't quite where he thought he was. It *never* occurred to him to think he was in a whole different harbor!

It was a parable for students of scientific objectivity. Wherever the chart disagreed with his observations he *rejected the observation* and followed the chart. Because of what his mind thought it knew, it had built up a static filter, an immune system, that was shutting out all information that did not fit. Seeing is not believing. Believing is seeing.

If this were just an individual phenomenon it would not be so serious. But it is a huge cultural phenomenon too and it is very serious. We build up whole cultural intellectual patterns based on past "facts" which are extremely selective. When a new fact comes in that does not fit the pattern we don't throw out the pattern. We throw out the fact. A contradictory fact has to keep hammering and hammering and hammering, sometimes for centuries, before maybe one or two people will see it. And then these one or two have to start hammering on others for a long time before they see it too.

Just as the biological immune system will destroy a life-saving skin graft with the same vigor with which it fights pneumonia, so will a cultural immune system fight off a beneficial new kind of understanding like that of the *brujo* in Zuñi with the same kind of vigor it uses to destroy crime. It can't distinguish between them.

Phædrus recognized that there's nothing *immoral* in a culture not being ready to accept something Dynamic. Static latching is necessary to sustain the gains the culture has made in the past. The solution is not to condemn the culture as stupid but to look for those factors that will make the new information acceptable: the keys. He thought of this Metaphysics of Quality as a key.

The *Dharmakāya* light. That was a huge area of human experience cut off by cultural filtering.

Over the years it also had become a burden to him, this knowledge about the light. It cut off a whole area of rational communion with others. It was not something that he could talk about without being slammed by the cultural immune system, being thought crazy, and with his record it was not good to invite that suspicion.

But he had seen it again on Lila tonight and he had seen it very strongly back in Kingston. That's sort of what got him into all this. It told him there was something of importance here. It told him to wake up and not go by the book in dealing with her.

He didn't think of this light as some sort of supernatural occurrence that had no grounding in physical reality. In fact he was sure it *was* grounded in physical reality. But nobody sees it because the cultural definition of what is real and what is unreal filters out the *Dharmakāya* light from twentieth century American "reality" just as surely as time is filtered out of Hopi reality, and green-yellow differences mean nothing to the Natchez.

He couldn't demonstrate it scientifically, because you couldn't predict when it was going to occur and thus couldn't set up an experiment to test for it. But, without any experimental testing, he thought that the light was nothing more than an involuntary widening of the iris of the eyes of the observer that lets in extra light and makes things look brighter, a kind of hallucinatory light produced by optic stimulation, somewhat like the light that comes when one stares at something too long. Like eye blinks, it's assumed to be an an irrelevant interruption of what one "really" sees, or it's assumed to be a subjective phenomenon, which is unreal, as opposed to an objective phenomenon, which is real.

But despite filtering by the cultural immune system, references to this light occur in many places, scattered, disconnected, and unrelated. Lamps are sometimes used as symbols of learning. Why should they be? A torch, like the old Blake School torch, is sometimes used as a symbol of idealistic inspiration. When we suddenly understand something we say, "I've seen the light," or, "It has dawned on me." When a cartoonist wants to show someone getting a great idea he puts an electric light bulb over the character's head. Everybody understands instantly what this symbol means. Why? Where did it come from? It can't be very old because there weren't any electric bulbs much before this century. What have electric light bulbs got to do with new ideas? Why doesn't the cartoonist ever have to explain what he means by that light bulb? Why does everybody *know* what he means?

In other cultures, or in the religious literature of our past, where the immune system of "objectivity" is weak or non-existent, reference to this light is everywhere, from the Protestant hymn, "Lead Kindly Light," to the halos of the saints. The central terms of Western mysticism, "enlightenment," and "illumination" refer to it directly. Darsana, a fundamental Hindu form of religious instruction, means "giving of light." Descriptions of Zen *sartori* mention it. It is referred to extensively in *The Tibetan Book of the Dead*. Aldous Huxley referred to it as part of the mescaline experience. Phædrus remembered it from the time with Dusenberry at the peyote meeting, although he had assumed that it was just an optical illusion produced by the drug and not of any great importance.

Proust wrote about it in "Remembrance of Things Past." In El Greco's "Nativity" the *Dharmakāya* light emanating from the Christ child provides the only illumination there is. El Greco was thought by some to have defective eyesight because he painted this light. But in his portrait of Cardinal Guevara, the prosecutor of the Spanish Inquisition, the lace and silks of the cardinal's robes are done with exquisite "objective" luster but the light is completely absent. El Greco didn't *have* to paint it. He painted what he saw.

Once when Phædrus was standing in one of the galleries of the Boston Museum of Fine Arts, he saw on one wall a huge painting of the Buddha and nearby were some paintings of Christian saints. He noticed again something he had thought about before. Although the Buddhists and Christians had no historic contact with one another they both painted halos. The halos weren't the same size. The Buddhists painted great big ones, sometimes surrounding the person's whole body, while the Christian ones were smaller and in back of the person's head or over it. It seemed to mean the two religions weren't copying one another or they would have made the halos the same size. But they were both painting something they were seeing separately, which implied that that "something" they were painting had a real, independent existence.

Then as Phædrus was thinking this he noticed one painting in the corner and thought, "There. What the others are just painting symbolically he is actually showing. They're seeing it second-hand. He's seeing it first hand."

It was a painting of Christ with no halo at all. But the clouds in the sky behind his head were slightly lighter near his head than farther away. And the sky near his head was lighter too. That was all. But that was the *real* illumination, no objective thing at all, just a shift in intensity of light. Phædrus stepped up to the canvas to read the nameplate at the bottom. It was El Greco again.

Our culture immunizes us against giving much importance to all this because the light has no "objective" reality. That means it's just some "subjective" and therefore unreal phenomenon. In a Metaphysics of Quality, however, this light is important because it often appears associated with *undefined auspiciousness*, that is, with Dynamic Quality. It signals a Dynamic intrusion upon a static situation. When there is a letting go of static patterns the light occurs. It is often accompanied by a feeling of relaxation because static patterns have been jarred loose.

He thought it was probably the light that infants see when their world is still fresh and whole, before consciousness differentiates it into patterns; a light into which everything fades at death. Accounts of people who have had a "near death experience" have referred to this "white light" as something very beautiful and compelling from which they didn't want to return. The light would occur during the breakup of the static patterns of the person's intellect as it returned into the pure Dynamic Quality from which it had emerged in infancy.

During Phædrus' time of insanity when he had wandered freely outside the limits of cultural reality, this light had been a valued companion, pointing out things to him that he would otherwise have missed, appearing at an event his rational thought had indicated was unimportant, but which he would later discover had been more important than he had known. Other times it had occurred at events he could not figure out the importance of, but which had left him wondering.

He saw it once on a small kitten. After that for a long time the kitten followed him wherever he went and he wondered if the kitten saw it too.

He had seen it once around a tiger in a zoo. The tiger had suddenly looked at him with what seemed like surprise and had come over to the bars for a closer look. Then the illumination began to appear around the tiger's face. That was all. Afterward, that experience associated itself with William Blake's "Tiger! tiger! burning bright."

The eyes had blazed with what seemed to be inner light.

27.

In the dream he thought someone was shooting at him, and then he realized no this was no dream. Someone was pounding on the boat hull.

"Okay!" he shouted. "Just a minute." It must be the marina attendant wanting to get paid or something.

He got up and, in his pajamas, slid the hatch cover open. It was someone he didn't know. He was black, with a big grin on his face and a white tunic that was so bright and clean it knocked out everything else. He looked like he'd just stepped off an Uncle Ben's rice package.

"First mate Jamison reporting for duty, sir!" he said and snapped a smart salute, still grinning. The tunic had big shiny brass buttons. Phædrus wondered where he had found something like that. He seemed to be grinning at his own ludicrousness.

"What do you want?" Phædrus said.

"I'm here to start workin'."

"You've got the wrong boat."

"No I ain't. You just don't know me in this uniform. Where's Lila?" he said.

Phædrus suddenly recognized him. He was Jamie, the one he had met in that bar.

"She's still sleeping," Phædrus said.

"Sleeping!?" Jamie threw his head back and laughed. "Man, you can't let her get away with that. It's past ten in the morning."

Jamie pointed to his gold wristwatch. "Time to get her up!" His voice was very loud. Phædrus noticed a head from another boat was watching them.

Jamie started to laugh again, then looked up and down the boat with a smile. "Well, you sure had me fooled. The way Lila told it this boat was at *least* five times this big. And all you got is this pee-wee little thing."

He glanced twice at Phædrus to check the reaction to this. "That's all right. That's all right. It's plenty big enough for me. It's just Lila had me fooled."

Phædrus tried to shake the cobwebs out of his head. What the hell was this all about?

"What did Lila tell you?" he asked.

"Lila told me to come here for work this morning. So here I am."

"That's crazy," Phædrus said. "She told you wrong."

The grin disappeared from Jamie's face. He looked puzzled, hurt. Then he said, "I think I gonna have a little talk with her," and stepped aboard. The way he jumped over the life-line showed he was no sailor: no permission, dirty street shoes on. Phædrus was about to call him on the dirty shoes but then suddenly he saw Richard Rigel coming down the dock. Rigel waved to him and came over. Where did *he* come from?

"I'm going down to talk to her," Jamie said.

Phædrus shook his head. "She's tired."

Jamie shook his head back. "No offense," he said, "but you don't know shit about Lila."

"No, she's tired."

"No, man. She always talks like that. I know how to fix that." Jamie went down the hatchway. "We'll be right up," he said.

Phædrus started to feel alarmed. He saw that Rigel was staring at him. He said to Rigel, "I didn't know you were here."

"I've been here for a while," Rigel said. "Who is that?"

"He's some friend of Lila's."

"Is *she* still here?"

"She's in trouble." He looked up at Rigel. "She's *really* in trouble. . . ."

Rigel squinted. He looked as though he was going to say something but then he didn't. Finally he said, "What are you going to do about it?"

"I don't know," Phædrus said, "I just woke up. I haven't got anything in mind yet."

Before Rigel could answer they heard a low deep noise below, then a shout, then a scuffling sound, and then another shout.

Suddenly Jamie's face appeared. His white Uncle Ben jacket had a big spot of blood by one of the buttons. His hand against his cheek had blood on it.

"That fuckin' whore!" he shouted.

He came out the hatch on deck.

He reached for the hatch rail and Phædrus saw his cheek had a bloody gash.

"God-damn *bitch*! I'm gonna *kill* her!"

Phædrus wondered where he could find a rag to stop the bleeding. Maybe below somewhere.

"Let me off here," Jamie said, "I'm callin' the police!"

"What happened?" Rigel said. Over his shoulder the face of another boat-owner now stared.

"She tried to *kill* me!"

Jamie looked at him. Something in Rigel's expression seemed to stop him. Jamie stepped over the boat's life-line to the dock. He looked at Rigel again. "She did!" he said. "She tried to *kill* me!" Rigel's expression didn't change. Jamie then turned and walked down the dock toward the marina office. He jerked his head over his shoulder and looked back. "I'm goin' to call the police. She tried to *kill* me. She's going to *get* it."

Phædrus looked up at Rigel and the other man who was still staring. "I'd better go down and see what happened," Phædrus said.

"You had better get out of here," Rigel said.

"What? Why? I haven't done anything."

"That doesn't matter," Rigel said. His face had that same angry look he had had at breakfast in Kingston.

At the far side of the marina Phædrus could see Jamie at the marina office saying something to the people standing there. He was gesticulating, waving one arm, holding his face with the other. The man behind Rigel started to walk over there.

Rigel said, "I'm going over there too, to see what he's saying." He left, and Phædrus could see that at the marina office where Rigel was headed some sort of argument was going on.

What was Lila doing now? Down below it was ominously quiet. He stepped down the ladder and saw that the door to the forecabin was shut.

Phædrus went to the door, opened it slowly, and saw Lila on the bunk. Her nose was bleeding. In her hand was a pocket knife. The hypnotic look of last night was all gone. The sheet underneath her had some small blood spots.

"Why did you do it?" he asked.

"He killed my baby."

"How?"

She pointed to the floor below the bunk.

Phædrus saw the doll lying face down on the floor. He watched her for a moment, wanting to be careful what to say.

Finally he said, "Shall I pick it up?"

Lila didn't say anything.

He picked up the doll very carefully, using both hands, and carefully set it beside her.

"This is a bad place," Lila said.

Phædrus stepped into the head and got a handful of toilet paper for the nosebleed and brought it to her.

"Let me see," he said.

Her nose didn't look broken. But she was starting to puff up under one eye. He saw that her hand was clenched tight on the jackknife.

This wasn't the time to talk about it.

He heard a rapping on the hull.

When he got up the ladder he saw it was Rigel again.

"He's gone," Rigel said, "but they're upset. Some of them want to call the police. I told them you were just leaving. It will be a lot easier if you just left now."

"What are the police going to do?" Phædrus says.

Rigel looked exasperated. "You can be here five more seconds or you can be here five more weeks. Which do you want?"

Phædrus thought about it. "Okay," he said, "untie the bow line."

"You'll have to untie it yourself."

"What's the matter with you?"

"Aiding and abetting . . ."

"For Christ's sake."

"I've got to face these people after you leave."

Phædrus looked at him and shook his head. God what a mess. He jumped onto the dock, grabbed the electric power cord and threw it aboard, uncleated the stern line and threw it aboard too. As he went forward to take off the bow lines he saw that people who had gathered at the office were looking down his way. Crazy how Rigel had shown up just at this minute. And he was right, as usual.

Phædrus threw the bow lines aboard, and with his hands on the boat's bow, shoved with all his might to get the heavy hull clear of the dock. The current was already starting to move the stern away. Then he grabbed a stanchion and pulled himself aboard.

"There's an anchorage inside Sandy Hook," Rigel said. "Horseshoe Bay. It's on the chart."

Phædrus moved aft smartly over the tangled lines to get control of the boat but in the cockpit he saw the key was out of the engine. The boat was out of control now but for the moment it didn't matter because the current was carrying it into the river and away from the dock. He jumped down below, opened the top drawer under the chart table and found the key, then scampered up again and inserted it and turned over the engine.

This would be a great time for it to fail.

It didn't. It took hold and he let it idle for a while.

At the dock, now sixty or seventy feet away, Rigel was talking to some people who had gathered around him. Phædrus shifted into gear, increased the throttle and waved to them. They didn't wave back, but they were watching him.

One of them cupped his hands and shouted something, but the sound of the diesel was too loud for it to be heard. Phædrus waved to them and headed out into the river toward the New Jersey shore.

Whew!

As he looked back over his shoulder he saw the water of the river between the boat and the marina become wider and wider, and the figures become smaller and smaller. They seemed to diminish in importance as they diminished in size.

The whole city was starting to take shape from the perspective of the water now. The marina was sinking back into the skyline of the city. The green trees of the parkway dominated it now and the apartments rising above the parkway dominated the trees. Now he could see some large skyscrapers at the center of the island rising above the apartments.

The Giant!

It gave him an eerie feeling.

This time he'd just barely slipped out of its grasp.

28.

When he neared the far side of the river, Phædrus swung the boat so that it headed downstream. Already he could feel the open water and the distance between himself and the city start to calm him down.

What a morning! He wasn't even dressed yet. The dock was getting really far away now, and the people who had been watching him seemed to be gone. Up the river the George Washington Bridge had begun to recede into the bluffs.

He saw there was some blood beginning to dry on the deck by the cockpit. He slowed down the engine, tied off the rudder, and went below and found a rag. He found his clothes on the bunk, and brought everything up on deck. Then he freed the rudder and put the boat back on course again. Then he scrubbed away all the blood spots he could find.

There was no hurry now. So strange. All that rush and calamity, and now suddenly he had all the time in the world. No obligations. No commitments.

. . . Except Lila, down there. But she wasn't going anywhere.

What was he going to *do* with her?

. . . Just keep going, he supposed.

He really wasn't under any pressure. There weren't any deadlines. . . .

Except the deadline of ice and snow. But that was no problem. He could just single-hand south and let her stay there in the forecabin if that's where she wanted to be.

Dreamy day. The sun was out! Still hardly any boats in the river.

As he dressed he saw that along the Manhattan shore were old green buildings that looked like warehouses sticking out into the water. They looked rotted out and abandoned. They reminded him of something.

Long ago he'd seen those buildings. . . .

. . . There was a gangplank going up, up, up, way up—into a big ship with the huge red smokestacks and he had walked up it ahead of his mother—she looked terribly worried—and when he stopped to look down at the cement below the gangplank she told him to "Hurry! Hurry! The ship is going to leave!" and just as she said this there was an enormous noise of the fog horn that frightened him and made him run up the gangplank. He was only four and the ship was the *Mauritania* going to England.

. . . But those were the same pier buildings, it seemed, the ones the ship had left from. Now they were all in ruins.

That was all so long ago. . . . Selim . . . Selim . . . what was that about? A story his mother had read to him. Selim the fisherman and Selim the baker and a magic island that they just barely escaped from before it all sank into the sea. It had been connected with this place in his memory.

So strange. Other than a barge and one other sailboat way downstream, there was still nothing on the river. Far to the south, among all the clutter of buildings on the horizon, he could see the Statue of Liberty.

Strange how he could remember the old *Mauritania* docks from that childhood voyage but not the Statue of Liberty.

Once on a later visit to New York he had joined a crowd of other tourists and climbed up inside the Statue of Liberty. He remembered it was all greenish copper and old looking, supported with riveted girders like an old Victorian bridge. The iron staircase going up got thinner and smaller and thinner and smaller and the line of people going up kept getting slower and slower and suddenly he'd gotten a huge wave of claustrophobia. There was no way he could get out of this procession! In front of him was a very fat lady who acted like the climb was too much for her. She looked like she might collapse any minute. He could envision the whole procession collapsing beneath her like a row of dominoes, with himself in it, with no hope but to crash with the rest of them. He'd wondered if he'd have the strength to hold her there if she collapsed.

. . . Trapped and going crazy with claustrophobia underneath a fat lady inside the Statue of Liberty. What a great allegorical theme, he'd thought later, for a story about America.

Phædrus saw the deck was still a mess of lines that needed to be put away. He tied off the rudder, went forward, gathered up a dock line, brought it back to the cockpit and then, while steering back on course again, coiled the line and stowed it into the lazarette; then tied off the rudder again and repeated the process until he had all four lines and the electrical power cable stowed and the fenders brought inboard. By the time he was done downtown Manhattan was approaching.

There were rather pleasant-looking Victorian houses over on the Jersey side. Some high-rises, but surprisingly few. There was some sort of a cathedral up high on the shore and a road going up the bluffs. He could see how steep the bluffs are. That might be why there's so little development there compared to the other side of the river.

As the statue drew nearer Phædrus could see the old Blake School torch still held on high; a Victorian statue but still impressive, particularly from the water like this. It's the size that does it, mainly. And the location. If she were just an ordinary park-statue most of that inspiration would be gone.

There was more water traffic now. Over by Governors Island some tugs were moving a big ship toward the East River. He could see what was probably a Staten Island ferry boat in the distance. Nearer, a river tour was coming in his direction.

He wondered why it was so heeled-over, then realized it was because all the passengers were on the Manhattan side of the boat, watching the skyline that loomed up above everything.

What a skyline! The clouds were reflected in the glass of some of the tallest buildings. Rhapsody in Blue. For the moment the towers of the World Trade Center seemed to have won the race upward but those other skyscrapers seemed not to know it. All of them together were no longer just buildings or part of a city, but something else people didn't know they could be. Some kind of energy and power that wasn't anything planned seemed to constantly surprise everyone at how great it all was. No one had done this. It had just done itself. The Giant was its own creation.

The Verrazano bridge was drawing closer and closer. Underneath it he could see a line that might be the far side of the lower bay. This was the last bridge. The *last* one!

As Phædrus approached the bridge he felt the beginning of a deep, periodic swell. It was a kind of a trapeze-like feeling. But slow. Very slow. It lifted and lowered the boat. Then it lifted it and lowered it again. Then again. It was the ocean.

Suddenly he realized he didn't know where he was going. He tied off the rudder again and went down below and got a pile of charts from the chart drawer—still no sign of Lila—and went back up on deck. He paged through the charts until he found one that said "New York Harbor." On the back side of the chart was the Lower Bay, speckled with buoys that marked channels for ships. At the bottom of the Lower Bay was Sandy Hook, and in the middle of Sandy Hook was Horseshoe Cove. That had to be the cove Rigel had told him about.

The chart showed about ten nautical miles from the bridge to the cove. There were so many buoys in the bay it was hard to tell which was which, but the chart said it didn't matter, there was no way he could go aground. In fact he was safer outside the channel where the big ships couldn't go.

As the bridge moved farther and farther behind he noticed the engine sounded a little odd, and he saw the temperature gauge was up near the red range. He throttled down to just above an idle.

It was probably some debris in the water that had gotten into the engine's cooling water intake. That had happened before. The trouble was the intake was so far below the water line and the curve of the hull was so great he couldn't see the debris or get it with a boat hook. He had to get out into the dinghy and try to pull it off. Now he couldn't do that because the ocean surge coming into the bay would clunk the dinghy all over the place. He'd have to wait until he got into the cove.

A fresh breeze seemed to be building from the southwest New Jersey shore. He might just as well sail the rest of the way.

He shut off the engine and for a moment enjoyed the silence. There was just the faint sound of the breeze and the sound of the waves against the hull, getting quieter as the boat slowed. With what momentum was left he headed the boat into the wind and went forward to the mast to put up the main sail.

The roll of the boat from the surge made it tricky to keep his balance, but once the sail was up and the boat came off the wind, it steadied on a slight heel, picked up speed, and he suddenly felt very good. From the cockpit he put her on course, rolled out the jib and the boat speeded up some more. He was feeling some of the old sea fever again. This was the first real open water since Lake Ontario and the surge was bringing it back.

To the east, there it was out there, the landless horizon. Some sort of ship way off in the distance, apparently heading this way. No problem. He would just keep the sailboat outside the channel.

Old Pancho would be smiling now.

This sea fever was like malaria. It disappeared for long periods, sometimes years, and then suddenly was back again, like now, in a wave that was like the surge itself.

He remembered long ago being taken by a song called, "The Sloop John B.," that had an unusual speed-up and slow-down rhythm. He didn't know why he liked it so much until one day it dawned on him that the speed-up and slow-down was the same as the surge of the sea. It was a running surge where the wind and sea are behind you and the boat rushes forward and rises as each wave passes underneath and then descends and hesitates as the wave rolls on ahead.

That motion never made him uncomfortable, probably because he loved it so much. It was all mixed up with the sea fever.

He remembered the day the fever started, Christmas Day, after his sixth birthday, when his parents had bought him the most expensive globe they could afford, heavy and on a hardwood stand, and he had turned it on its axis around and around. From it he'd learned the shapes and names of all the continents and most of the countries and seas of the world: Arabia, Africa, South America, India, Australia, Spain and the Mediterranean, the Black Sea, the Caspian Sea. He was overwhelmed with the idea that the whole city he lived in was just one tiny dot on this globe, and that most of this globe was blue. If you wanted to really see the world you couldn't go there except over all that blue.

For years after that his favorite book had been a book about old ships, which he'd paged through slowly, again and again, wondering what it would be like to live in one of those little ornamented aft cabins with the tiny windows, staring out like Sir Francis Drake at the surging waves rolling under you. It seemed as though all his life after that, whenever he took long trips, he ended up on a dock in a harbor somewhere, staring at the boats.

Sandy Hook, as the boat approached it, looked like it hadn't changed much since the wooden ships of Verrazano and Hudson sailed by. There were some radio towers and old-looking buildings on the northern tip which seemed to be part of some abandoned fortification. The rest seemed almost deserted.

As the boat moved inside the hook's protection from the sea the surge died and only a ripple from the southwest wind was left. The bay became like an inland lake, calm and surrounded by land wherever Phædrus could see. He furled the jib to slow the boat a little and stepped below for a moment to turn on the depth sounder. Still no sign of Lila in the forecabin up there.

Back on deck he saw that the cove looked quite good. It was exposed to wind from the west, but the chart showed shallow water and a long jetty off to the west that would probably keep big waves out. There certainly weren't any now. Just a quiet shore, and a couple of sailboats at anchor with no one on deck. Beautiful.

When the depth sounder showed about ten feet of water he rounded up into the breeze, dropped the sail and anchor, started and reversed the engine to set the anchor, then shut it off, furled the main and went below.

He put away the chart, then turned on the Coast Guard weather station to see what was predicted. The announcer said a few more days of light southwest winds and good weather before turning colder. Good. That gave him a little while to figure out what to do with Lila before heading out on the ocean.

29.

He heard Lila move.

He went to her door, knocked and then opened it.

She was awake but she didn't look at him. He saw now for the first time that the right side of her face was discolored and swollen. That guy had really slugged her.

After a while he said, "Hi."

She didn't answer. She just looked straight ahead. The pupils of her eyes seemed dilated.

"Are you comfortable?" he asked.

Her gaze didn't alter.

It wasn't a very bright question. He made another try: "How is everything?"

Still no answer. Her gaze just looked right past him.

Oh-oh. He thought he knew what this was. He supposed he should have known this was coming. This is how it looked from the outside. The catatonic trance. She's cutting off everything.

After a while he said gently, "Everything's all right. I'll be taking care of you for a while." He watched for a flicker of recognition but didn't see any. Just the hypnotic gaze—straight ahead.

She knows I'm here, he thought, she probably knows I'm here better than I know she's here. She just won't acknowledge it. She's like some treed cat, way out on the end of a limb. To go after her just scares her farther out on the limb, or else forces her into a fight.

He didn't want that. Not after what happened back at the dock.

He softly closed the door and went back into the cabin again.

Now what?

He remembered from his anthropological reading that these trance-like states are supposed to be dangerous. What happened back there at the dock fit the description of Malayan *amok*—intense brooding that's sometimes followed by sudden violence. But from what he remembered personally it wasn't so dangerous. If there's violence it's provoked by hostile people trying to break the trance and he wasn't about to do that.

Actually, he had a feeling the worst was over. The ominous thing about last night back in Manhattan was that she seemed so happy. She wasn't suffering. When she hugged and rocked that doll it was like listening to someone freezing to death say they feel warm. You want to say "No! No! Feel the cold! As long as you're suffering you're all right."

Now she's changed. The question is, changed for the better or for the worse? The only thing to do now, he thought, is just to wait it out for a while and see which way she goes. It looked like this good weather might hold for a while. He had plenty of things to do to keep himself occupied.

. . . Such as eat. It was already afternoon. He'd planned to tie up at Atlantic Highlands and buy food there, but now that was a couple of miles away. Maybe tomorrow he could put the outboard on the dinghy and putt over if the weather was calm. Or maybe see if there's a bus on shore somewhere and take that. For now they'd have to get by on what food was left from Nyack.

Nyack. That was a long time ago. Everything would be stale.

He pulled up the ice box top and looked inside. He reached down into the ice box and pulled up what he could find and placed it on the galley counter.

. . . There were some cocktail hot dogs in little jars . . . some small cans of meat and ham and roast beef. . . . The bread was still there. He picked it up and it felt stiff. . . . He opened the bread wrapper. . . . It looked still edible . . . canned tunafish . . . peanut butter . . . jelly. . . . The butter looked okay. One nice thing about cruising in October is that the food goes bad slowly . . . some chocolate pudding. . . . He'd have to get groceries very soon. That was going to be a problem.

What to drink, though? Nothing but whiskey and water. And mix. . . .

These cocktail hot dogs were stuck in the jar. He held the jar upside-down over the galley sink until all the juice around them ran out, but the dogs were still stuck. He got a fork and pried one out over a plate. It came out in pieces. Then suddenly they all came out in one big plop! They were kind of soft and squishy but they smelled all right.

He supposed he might just as well give her the whiskey and mix to drink. Yes, that ought to be good. She might refuse the food but the booze would be a little more tempting. . . .

He spread some of the butter on the stale bread, put three of the cocktail hot dogs on top and another slice of bread on top of that. Then he poured her a really stiff one and put the glass on the plate with the sandwich and brought it up forward.

He knocked lightly, and said, "Lunch. Beautiful lunch!"

He opened the door and put the tray on the bunk across from her. "If I've made the drink too stiff let me know and I'll add some water to it," he said.

She didn't answer but she didn't look angry or disconnected either. Some progress, maybe.

He closed the door and went back into the main cabin and started to fix his own meal. . . .

There are three ways she can go, he thought. First, she can go into permanent delusions, cling to this doll and whatever else she's inventing, and eventually he'd have to get rid of her. It would be tricky, but it could be done. Just call a doctor at some town they came to and have him look at her and figure out what to do from there. Phædrus didn't like it, but he could do it if he had to.

The trouble is there's a self-stoking thing where the craziness makes people reject you more and more, which makes you crazier, and that's what he would be getting involved in. Not very moral. If it went that way she'd probably spend the rest of her life in an insane asylum, like some caged animal.

Her second alternative, he thought, would be to cave in to whatever it was she was fighting, and learn to "adjust." She'd probably go into some kind of cultural dependency, with recurring trips to a psychiatrist or some kind of "social counselor" for "therapy," accept the cultural "reality" that her rebellion was no good, and live with it. In this way she'd continue to lead a "normal" life, continuing her problem, whatever it was, within conventional cultural limits.

The trouble was, he didn't really like that solution much better than the first.

The question isn't "What makes people insane?" It's "What makes people *sane*?" People have been asking for centuries how to deal with the insane and he didn't see that they'd gotten anywhere. The way to really deal with insanity, he thought, is to turn the tables and talk about truth instead. Insanity's a medical subject that everyone agrees is bad. Truth's a metaphysical subject that everyone disagrees about. There are lots of different definitions of truth and some of them could throw a whole lot more light on what was happening to Lila than a subject-object metaphysics does.

If objects are the ultimate reality then there's only one true intellectual construction of things: that which corresponds to the objective world. But if truth is defined as a high-quality set of intellectual value patterns, then insanity can be defined as just a low-quality set of intellectual value patterns, and you get a whole different picture of it.

When the culture asks, "Why doesn't this person see things the way we do?" you can answer that he doesn't see them because he doesn't value them. He's gone into illegal value patterns because the illegal patterns resolve value conflicts that the culture's unable to handle. The causes of insanity may be all kinds of things, from chemical imbalances to social conflicts. But insanity has *solved* these conflicts with illegal patterns which appear to be of higher quality.

Lila seems to be in some kind of trance-like state up there but what does that mean? In a subject-object world, trance and hypnosis are big-time platypi. That's why there's this prejudice that while hypnosis and trance can't be denied, there's something "wrong" about them. They're best nudged as close as possible to the empirical trash heap called "the occult" and left to that anti-empirical crowd that indulges in astrology, Tarot cards, the I-Ching and the like. If seeing is believing then hypnosis and trance should be impossible. But since they do exist, what you have is an empirically observable case of empiricism being overthrown.

The irony is that there are times when the culture actually fosters trance and hypnosis to further its purposes. The theater's a form of hypnosis. So are movies and TV. When you enter a movie theater you know that all you're going to see is 24 shadows per second flashed on a screen to give an illusion of moving people and objects. Yet despite this knowledge you laugh when the 24 shadows per second tell jokes and cry when the shadows show actors faking death. You know they are an illusion yet you enter the illusion and become a part of it and while the illusion is taking place you are not aware that it is an illusion. This is hypnosis. It is trance. It's also a form of temporary insanity. But it's also a powerful force for cultural reinforcement and for this reason the culture promotes movies and censors them for its own benefit.

Phædrus thought that in the case of permanent insanity the exits to the theater have been blocked, usually because of the knowledge that the show outside is so much worse. The insane person is running a private unapproved film which he happens to *like* better than the current cultural one. If you want him to run the film everyone else is seeing, the solution would be to find ways to prove to him that it would be *valuable* to do so, Phædrus thought. Otherwise why should he get "better"? He already *is* better. It's the patterns that constitute "betterness" that are at issue. From an internal point of view insanity isn't the problem. Insanity is the solution.

What it would take that's more valuable to Lila, Phædrus wasn't sure.

He finished his sandwich, put away the food and cleared off his plate in the sink. He guessed the next thing to worry about would be that engine, and why it was overheating.

If he was lucky it would be something caught in or over the through-hull water intake for the engine cooling system. If he was unlucky it would be that something had clogged up in the water passages inside the engine itself. That would mean taking the cylinder heads off and fishing through the heads and jackets to find it. The thought of that was awful. Really stupid, when he bought the boat, not to have bought a freshwater cooling system that would have prevented the second possibility.

You can't think of everything.

Up on deck he raised the dinghy with the mast halyard, held it suspended over the side of the boat and lowered it gently so that its transom didn't go under. Then he got in, unsnapped it from the halyard, and by hand-over-handing along the boat gunwale, worked it to the stern of the boat.

He took off his shirt, lay flat in the dinghy and reached down with his hand into the water until it almost was up to his shoulder. It was cold! He felt around but there didn't seem to be plastic bags or other debris covering the engine intake. Bad news. He pulled his arm back up again and wiped it dry on his shirt.

He supposed whatever it was could have dropped off after the engine stopped, while he was sailing. He should have run the engine for a while before he got into the dinghy to see if it was still happening. You always think of these things too late. Too much other stuff on his mind.

He tied the dinghy to a stanchion and got aboard. He went back to the cockpit and started the engine. While it was warming up he began to think about Lila again.

She's what you could call a "contrarian." "You're a loner, just like me," she had said the day they left Kingston. That stuck in his mind because it was true. But what she meant by it was not just someone who's alone, but a contrarian, someone who's always doing everything the wrong way, just out of pure willfulness, it would seem.

Contrarians sometimes just seem to savagely attack every kind of static moral pattern they can find. It seems as though they're trying to destroy morality as a kind of revenge.

He'd gotten that word out of his anthropology reading. It indicated there's more to contrarians than just individual "wrongness." It's common to many cultures. That *brujo* in Zuñi was a contrarian. The Cheyenne had a whole society of contrarians to assimilate the phenomenon within their social fabric. Cheyenne contrarians rode their horses sitting backward, entered teepees backward, and had a whole repertoire of things they performed in a contrary way. Members seemed to enter the contrary society when they felt a great wrong, a great injustice, had been done to them and apparently it was felt that this was a way of resolving the injustice.

Once you see it in another culture like that and then come back to our own you can see that in an unofficial way we have our contrarian societies too. The "Bohemians" of the Victorian era were contrarians. So, to some extent, were the Hippies of the sixties.

. . . The engine didn't seem to be overheating now. Maybe the problem was gone? . . . Hah—not very likely. . . . Probably it was just because the engine was in neutral and wasn't working very hard. Phædrus shifted into reverse to let it tug against the anchor for a while. He waited and watched the temperature dial. . . .

Anyway it seemed to him that when you add a concept of "Dynamic Quality" to a rational understanding of the world, you can add a lot to an understanding of contrarians. Some of them aren't just being negative toward static moral patterns, they are actively pursuing a Dynamic goal.

Everybody gets on these negative contrarian streaks from time to time, where no matter what it is they're supposed to be doing, that's the one thing they least want to do. Sometimes it's a degenerative negativism, where biological forces are driving it. Sometimes it's an ego pattern that says, "I'm too important to be doing all this dumb static stuff."

Sometimes the contrary anti-static drive becomes a static pattern of its own. This contrary stuff can become a tiger-ride where you can't get off and you have to keep riding and riding until the tiger finally throws you and devours you. The degenerative contrarian stuff usually goes that way. Drugs, illicit sex, alcohol and the like.

But sometimes it's Dynamic, where your whole being senses that the static situation is an enemy of life itself. That's what drives the really creative people—the artists, composers, revolutionaries and the like—the feeling that if they don't break out of this jailhouse somebody has built around them, they're going to die.

But they're not being contrary in a way that is just decadent. They're way too energetic and aggressive to be decadent. They're fighting for some kind of Dynamic freedom from the static patterns. But the Dynamic freedom they're fighting for is a kind of morality too. And it's a highly important part of the overall moral process. It's often confused with degeneracy but it's actually a form of moral regeneration. Without its continual refreshment static patterns would simply die of old age.

When you see Lila that way it's possible to interpret her current situation as much more significant than psychology would suggest. If she seems to be running from something, that could be the static patterns of her own life she's running from. But a Metaphysics of Quality adds the possibility that she's running *toward* something too. It allows a hypothesis that if this running is stopped, if *any* static patterns claim her—if either her own insane patterns claim her or the static cultural patterns she is shutting out and running from claim her—then she loses.

What he thought was, that in addition to the usual solutions to insanity—stay locked up or learn to conform—there was a third one, to reject *all* movies, private and cultural, and head for Dynamic Quality itself, which is no movie at all.

If you compare the levels of static patterns that compose a human being to the ecology of a forest, and if you see the different patterns sometimes in competition with each other, sometimes in symbiotic support of each other, but always in a kind of tension that will shift one way or the other, depending on evolving circumstances, then you can also see that evolution doesn't take place only within societies, it takes place within individuals too. It's possible to see Lila as something much greater than a customary sociological or anthropological description would have her be. Lila then becomes a complex ecology of patterns moving toward Dynamic Quality. Lila individually, herself, is in an evolutionary battle against the static patterns of her own life.

That's why the absence of suffering last night seemed so ominous and her change to what looked like suffering today gave Phædrus a feeling she was getting better. If you eliminate suffering from this world you eliminate life. There's no evolution. Those species that don't suffer don't survive. Suffering is the negative face of the Quality that drives the whole process. All these battles between patterns of evolution go on within suffering individuals like Lila.

And Lila's battle is everybody's battle, you know? Sometimes the insane and the contrarians and the ones who are the closest to suicide are the most valuable people society has. They may be precursors of social change. They've taken the burdens of the culture onto themselves, and in their struggle to solve their own problems they're solving problems for the culture as well.

So the third possibility that Phædrus was hoping for was that by some miracle of understanding Lila could avoid *all* the patterns, her own *and* the culture's, see the Dynamic Quality she's working toward and then come back and handle all this mess without being destroyed by it. The question is whether she's going to work through whatever it is that makes the defense necessary or whether she is going to work around it. If she works through it she'll come out at a Dynamic solution. If she works around it she'll just head back to the old karmic cycles of pain and temporary relief.

Apparently whatever caused that engine overheating was gone. He sure couldn't reproduce it now. He shut off the engine and the boat eased forward toward the anchor.

The sun across the water was getting on to the end of the afternoon and he began to get a slightly depressed feeling. Not the best of days. He noticed a seagull pick up an oyster or a clam or something from the sand on the shore and fly up into the sky and then drop it. Another seagull was homing in and diving to take it away from him. Pretty soon they set up a real screeching. He watched them for a while. Their fighting depressed him too.

He noticed on one of the other boats at anchor there was someone aboard. If he stayed up on deck they might start waving and want to socialize. Not something he wanted to do. He picked up his stuff and went below.

It had been a long week. *God*, what a week! He needed to get back to the old life. That whole city and all its karmic problems, and now on top of it Lila and all *her* karmic problems, were just too much. Maybe he should just take it easy for a while.

On the pilot berth was the tote bag with all the mail. At last he could get started with that, a good diversion. He opened up the leaf of the dining table, put the tote bag on top of it and took out the top bunch of letters and spread them out.

For the rest of the afternoon he sat with his feet propped up on the table, reading the letters, smiling at them, frowning at them, chuckling at them and answering each one that seemed to call for it, telling them "no" when they wanted something with as much grace as possible. He felt like Ann Landers.

He heard Lila stirring once or twice. Once she got up and used the head. She wasn't *that* catatonic. This quietness and boredom of a boat at anchor was the best cure in the world for catatonia.

By the time it was dark he began to feel stale at answering mail. The day was done. It was time to relax. The light breeze of the day was now completely gone, and except for a slight rock of the boat now and then everything was still. What a blessing.

He took the kerosene lamp from its gimbaled mounting, lit it and placed it near the galley sink. He made another meal out of the left-over food from Nyack and thought about Lila some more, but didn't reach any conclusion except the one he had already reached: there was nothing to do but wait.

When he brought in Lila's food he saw the plate and glass he'd brought in earlier were empty. He tried again to talk to her but she still didn't answer.

He felt it getting colder now that the sun was down. Rather than start up the heater tonight he thought he'd just get into the sleeping bag early. It had been a long day. Maybe make a few slips on these new books on William James.

These books were biography. He'd read quite a bit of James' philosophy. Now he wanted to get into some of his biography to put some perspective on it.

He wanted particularly to see how much actual evidence there was for the statement that James' whole purpose was to "unite science and religion." That claim had turned him against James years ago, and he didn't like it any better now. When you start out with an axe like that to grind, it's almost guaranteed that you will conclude with something false. The statement seemed more like some philosopho-logical simplification written by someone with a weak understanding of what philosophy is for. To put philosophy in the service of any social organization or any dogma is immoral. It's a lower form of evolution trying to devour a higher one.

Phædrus removed the bag of mail to the pilot berth, then placed the kerosene lamp on top of the ice box where it would be over his shoulder and he could read by it, then sat down and began to read.

After some time he noticed the lamp had become dim and he stopped reading to turn up the wick.

Some time later he got his little wooden box from the pilot berth to make some slips about what he was reading.

In the hours that continued he made a dozen of them.

At another time he looked up from his reading and listened for a moment. There was not a sound. A little tilt of the boat now and then, but that was all.

There was nothing in what he was reading that suggested James was some kind of religious ideologue interested in proving some foregone conclusion about religion. Ideologues usually talk in terms of sweeping generalities and what Phædrus was reading seemed to confirm that James was about as far as you can get from these. In his early years especially, James' concept of ultimate reality was of things concrete and individual. He didn't like Hegel or any of the German idealists who dominated philosophy in his youth precisely *because* they were so general and sweeping in their approach.

However, as James grew older his thoughts did seem to get more and more general. This was appropriate. If you don't generalize you don't philosophize. But to Phædrus it seemed that James' generalizations were heading toward something very similar to the Metaphysics of Quality. This could, of course, be the "Cleveland Harbor Effect," where Phædrus' own intellectual immune system was selecting those aspects of James' philosophy that fit the Metaphysics of Quality and ignoring those that didn't. But he didn't think so. Everywhere he read it seemed as though he was seeing fits and matches that no amount of selective reading could contrive.

James really had two main systems of philosophy going: one he called *pragmatism* and the other *radical empiricism*.

Pragmatism is the one he is best remembered for: the idea that the test of truth is its practicality or usefulness. From a pragmatic viewpoint the squirrel's definition of "around" was a true one because it was useful. Pragmatically speaking, that man never got around the squirrel.

Phædrus, like most everyone else, had always assumed that pragmatism and practicality meant virtually the same thing, but when he got down to an exact quotation of what James did say on the subject he noticed something different:

James said, "Truth is one species of good, and not, as is usually supposed, a category distinct from good, and coordinate with it." He said, "The true is the name of whatever proves itself to be good in the way of belief."

"Truth is a species of good." That was right on. That was *exactly* what is meant by the Metaphysics of Quality. Truth is a static intellectual pattern *within* a larger entity called Quality.

James had tried to make his pragmatism popular by getting it elected on the coattails of practicality. He was always eager to use such expressions as "cash-value," and "results," and "profits," in order to make pragmatism intelligible to "the man in the street," but this got James into hot water. Pragmatism was attacked by critics as an attempt to prostitute truth to the values of the marketplace. James was furious with this misunderstanding and he fought hard to correct the misinterpretation, but he never really overcame the attack.

What Phædrus saw was that the Metaphysics of Quality avoided this attack by making it clear that the good to which truth is subordinate is intellectual and Dynamic Quality, not practicality. The misunderstanding of James occurred because there was no clear intellectual framework for distinguishing social quality from intellectual and Dynamic Quality, and in his Victorian lifetime they were monstrously confused. But the Metaphysics of Quality states that practicality is a *social* pattern of good. It is immoral for truth to be subordinated to social values since that is a lower form of evolution devouring a higher one.

The idea that satisfaction alone is the test of anything is very dangerous, according to the Metaphysics of Quality. There are different kinds of satisfaction and some of them are moral nightmares. The Holocaust produced a satisfaction among Nazis. That was quality for them. They considered it to be practical. But it was a quality dictated by low level static social and biological patterns whose overall purpose was to retard the evolution of truth and Dynamic Quality. James would probably have been horrified to find that Nazis could use his pragmatism just as freely as anyone else, but Phædrus didn't see anything that would prevent it. But he thought that the Metaphysics of Quality's classification of static patterns of good prevents this kind of debasement.

The second of James' two main systems of philosophy, which he said was independent of pragmatism, was his *radical empiricism*. By this he meant that subjects and objects are not the starting points of experience. Subjects and objects are secondary. They are concepts derived from something more fundamental which he described as "the immediate flux of life which furnishes the material to our later reflection with its conceptual categories." In this basic flux of experience, the distinctions of reflective thought, such as those between consciousness and content, subject and object, mind and matter, have not yet emerged in the forms which we make them. Pure experience cannot be called either physical or psychical: it logically precedes this distinction.

In his last unfinished work, *Some Problems of Philosophy*, James had condensed this description to a single sentence: "There must always be a discrepancy between concepts and reality, because the former are static and discontinuous while the latter is dynamic and flowing." Here James had chosen exactly the same words Phædrus had used for the basic subdivision of the Metaphysics of Quality.

What the Metaphysics of Quality adds to James' *pragmatism* and his *radical empiricism* is the idea that the primal reality from which subjects and objects spring is *value*. By doing so it seems to unite pragmatism and radical empiricism into a single fabric. Value, the pragmatic test of truth, is also the primary empirical experience. The Metaphysics of Quality says pure experience is value. Experience which is not valued is not experienced. The two are the same. This is where value fits. Value is not at the tail-end of a series of superficial scientific deductions that puts it somewhere in a mysterious undetermined location in the cortex of the brain. Value is at the very front of the empirical procession.

In the past empiricists have tried to keep science free from values. Values have been considered a pollution of the rational scientific process. But the Metaphysics of Quality makes it clear that the pollution is from threats to science by static lower levels of evolution: static *biological* values such as the biological fear that threatened Jenner's small pox experiment; static *social* values such as the religious censorship that threatened Galileo with the rack. The Metaphysics of Quality says that science's empirical rejection of biological and social values is not only rationally correct, it is also morally correct because the intellectual patterns of science are of a higher evolutionary order than the old biological and social patterns.

But the Metaphysics of Quality also says that Dynamic Quality—the value-force that chooses an elegant mathematical solution to a laborious one, or a brilliant experiment over a confusing, inconclusive one—is another matter altogether. Dynamic Quality is a higher moral order than static scientific truth, and it is as immoral for philosophers of science to try to suppress Dynamic Quality as it is for church authorities to suppress scientific method. Dynamic value is an integral part of science. It is the cutting edge of scientific progress itself.

Anyway, all this certainly answered the question of whether the Metaphysics of Quality was a foreign, cultish, deviant way of looking at things. The Metaphysics of Quality is a continuation of the mainstream of twentieth century American philosophy. It is a form of pragmatism, of instrumentalism, which says the test of the true is the good. It adds that this good is not a social code or some intellectualized Hegelian Absolute. It is direct everyday experience. Through this identification of pure value with pure experience, the Metaphysics of Quality paves the way for an enlarged way of looking at experience which can resolve all sorts of anomalies that traditional empiricism has not been able to cope with.

Phædrus supposed he could read on into all this James material but he doubted that he would find anything different from what he had already found. There is a time for investigation and there is a time for conclusion and he had a feeling that that latter time had come. His watch showed it was only nine-thirty but he was glad the day was done. He turned down the wick on the kerosene lamp, blew it out, placed it in its wall-holder and then settled down into the sleeping bag.

Good old sleep.

30.

He awoke to a tugging motion. There was a low sound of wind and a lapping of water. The wind must have changed direction. He hadn't heard that for a long time. The boat was tugging a little to port, then after a time tugging back to starboard . . . and then after another long time another tug to port again. . . . On and on. The portlights showed an overcast sky.

Loneliness was what he always associated with these sounds and motions of the boat. A boat out on anchor exposed to a steady wind is almost always in some lonely place, a place only boats can get to.

It was a relaxing sound. Gray skies and wind mean a kind of day when it's pleasant not to go anywhere, just putter around the cabin fixing up things that you've been putting off, studying charts and harbor guides and planning where you will be going.

Then he remembered that today he was going to go into town and try to get some food.

Then he remembered Lila. Maybe today he'd find out if she was any better.

He got out of the sleeping bag. When he put his feet down on the cabin sole he didn't get the usual shock. The cabin thermometer showed 55 degrees. Not bad.

The ocean was doing that. The lakes and canals back inland would start icing up in a month or so, but he doubted whether this water would freeze at all. The tides and currents would keep it moving. Certainly on the other side of this hook the ocean never froze, so he had escaped that danger. He could always get out. The ice couldn't get him any more.

He stepped up the ladder, pushed open the hatch and put his head out.

It was beautiful. Gray skies. South wind. Warm wind with an ocean smell in it. The other two boats that had been at anchor were gone.

The curve of the hook concealed Manhattan and Brooklyn. All he could see across the bay to the west was a barge at anchor and a high-rise apartment from another world miles away.

He suddenly felt a wild freedom.

The change in the wind had placed his boat a little closer to shore now and he noticed something he hadn't paid much attention to yesterday. The shore was piled with debris. There were plastic bottles, an old tire and, farther off, what looked like old creosoted telephone poles half buried in the sand next to a boat hull with its transom knocked out. Sandy Hook seemed like some final resting place for all the junk of civilization that had come down the Hudson river.

He looked at his watch. Nine o'clock. He'd really slept. He went back below, rolled up the sleeping bag and put away the books and slips from last night's reading. He built a new fire, noting there were only about two days of charcoal left. When the fire was going he went to the chart table and opened the second drawer down. He pulled out all the Hudson River charts, gathered them into a pile and carried them to a bin above the settee berth where he stored them. He wouldn't be needing those again. To take their place he brought out a roll of charts from Sandy Hook to Cape May and the Delaware River. At the chart table he unrolled them and studied each one.

The coast had many little criss-cross marks showing wrecks. Rigel had warned him not to get caught off the New Jersey shore in a northeaster. But it looked like an easy three days to Cape May if the weather was good, with an easy run to Manasquan Inlet and a longer one to Atlantic City.

Phædrus folded the charts and placed them in the chart table drawer. He prepared a simple breakfast for himself, ate it, and then made one for Lila.

When he brought it in she was awake. The swelling of her face didn't seem to have gone down much but she was looking at him again, *really* looking at him now: making contact.

"Why is the boat swinging?" she said.

"It's all right," he said.

"It's making me dizzy," she said. "Stop the boat from swinging."

She's not only talking, he thought, she's complaining. That's real progress. "How does that eye feel?" he asked.

"Awful."

"We can put hot rags on it or something."

"No."

"Well, here's breakfast, anyway."

"Are we at the island?"

"We're at Sandy Hook, New Jersey."

"Where is everybody?"

"Where?"

"On the island," she said.

He didn't know what she was talking about, but something told him not to ask.

"It's not an island, it's a spit of land. There's nobody here, at least on this part. Just a lot of junk lying around."

"You know what I mean," she said.

He sensed there was a problem coming up. If he rejected what she was telling him then she'd reject *him*. He didn't want that. She was trying to reach out to him now. He should try to meet her half-way.

"Well it's almost an island," he said.

"Richard is coming."

"Rigel?"

She didn't say anything. He supposed she must mean Rigel. There weren't any other Richards.

"Rigel said he was going to Connecticut to sell his boat," Phædrus said. "This is New Jersey now, so he won't be coming this way."

"Well I'm ready," Lila said.

"That's good," he said. "That's very good. I'm going down the road to try to find some groceries. Do you want to come along?"

"No."

"Okay. You can rest here as long as you feel like," he said. He stepped back and closed the door.

Ready for what, he wondered, as he entered the main cabin. They want to superimpose their movie on you. It's like talking to some religious nut. You can't argue with her, you've just got to find some common ground. She was sure a lot better but there was a long way to go.

He wondered if it was safe to leave her here alone. There wasn't much else he could do. It was a lot safer than at a dock where she might start to interact with people on other boats. God knows what would happen then.

The chart showed a road right next to shore here where he could hike or hitchhike about three miles south to a place called the Highlands of Navesink that might have a grocery store.

He got his billfold from a small drawer, filled it with twenties and from the wet locker by the chart table got out two canvas tote bags to carry the groceries. He said good bye to Lila, and from the deck got down into the dinghy again and rowed ashore.

The beach seemed to be grayish fine sand. He stepped out onto the sand and pulled the dinghy way up on the beach, then tied it off to an iron spike sticking out from the end of a large driftwood pole. The junk he'd noticed from the boat was everywhere and he studied it as he walked to the road—some glass bottles, a lot of small bleached driftwood pieces worn round at the corners and ends, an innersole of a shoe, a box with a faded Budweiser label, some old cushions, a wooden toy locomotive.

He wondered if he would come across a doll like Lila's, but he didn't see any.

Farther on was a Styrofoam coffee cup, a tire, another coffee cup, some more big burned timbers with rusted steel spikes that he had to step over. It all looked worn and bleached and seemed to have drifted in from the bay, not brought by any tourists who were here. It looked too trashy here for tourists. Strange how you could be so close to Manhattan yet in such a remote rural place. It wasn't rural exactly. It wasn't anything exactly except abandoned. It was a ruins of something. The vegetation was ruins vegetation.

Back of the debris were some evergreens that looked like yews or junipers. Other bushes had only a few red leaves left. Still farther back were marsh grasses of various species, mostly gold but still a little green. They looked as pure and delicate as prehistoric plants.

Off on the far side of marsh by an abandoned day beacon stood a white egret.

Phædrus found the road where the chart said it would be, nice asphalt, clean, deserted. He enjoyed the stretch of his legs.

The sumac here was just turning red.

Another road. How many had he hiked like this?

October was a good month for hiking.

He walked down the tree and shrub-lined road feeling sort of marvelous about the fact that somehow he was right here. Dynamic.

Lila was talking. That was an accomplishment. It showed he was on the right track.

She wasn't making much sense yet with all that talk about the island and Rigel, but that would come in time. The thing was not to force it, not to set up a confrontation. It was an intriguing idea to send someone like Lila to Samoa for a cure but it wouldn't work. What's wrong with insanity is that she's outside *any* culture. She's a culture of one. She has her own reality which *no* other culture is able to see. That's what had to be reconciled. It could be that if he just didn't give her any problems for the next few days her culture of one might just clear the whole thing up by itself.

He wasn't going to send her to any hospital. He knew that now. At a hospital they'd just start shooting her full of drugs and tell her to adjust. What they wouldn't see is that she *is* adjusting. That's what the insanity is. She's adjusting to something. The insanity is the adjustment. Insanity isn't necessarily a step in the wrong direction, it can be an intermediate step in a right direction. It wasn't necessarily a disease. It could be part of a cure.

He was no expert on the subject but it seemed to him that the problem of "curing" an insane person is like the problem of "curing" a Moslem or "curing" a communist or "curing" a Republican or Democrat. You're not going to make much progress by telling them how wrong they are. If you can convince a mullah that everything will be of higher value if he changes his beliefs to those of Christianity, then a change is not only possible but likely. But if you can't, forget it. And if you can convince Lila that it's more valuable to consider her "baby" to be a doll than it is to consider her doll to be a baby, then her condition of "insanity" will be alleviated. But not before.

That doll thing was a solution to something, some child thing, but he didn't know what it was. The important thing was to support her delusions and then slowly wean her away from them rather than fight them.

The catch here, which almost any philosopher would spot, is the word, "delusion." It's always the *other* person who's "deluded." Or ourselves in the past. Ourselves in the present are never "deluded." Delusions can be held by whole groups of people, as long as we're not a part of that group. If we're a member then the delusion becomes a "minority opinion."

An insane delusion can't be held by a group at all. A person isn't considered insane if there are a number of people who believe the same way. Insanity isn't supposed to be a communicable disease. If one other person starts to believe him, or maybe two or three, then it's a religion.

Thus, when sane grown men in Italy and Spain carry statues of Christ through the streets, that's not an insane delusion. That's a meaningful religious activity because there are so many of them. But if Lila carries a rubber statue of a child with her wherever she goes, that's an insane delusion because there's only one of her.

If you ask a Catholic priest if the wafer he holds at mass is really the flesh of Jesus Christ, he will say yes. If you ask, "Do you mean *symbolically?*" he will answer, "No, I mean actually." Similarly if you ask Lila whether the doll she holds is a dead baby she will say yes. If you ask, "Do you mean *symbolically?*" she would also answer, "No, I mean actually."

It is considered correct to say that until you understand that the wafer is really the body of Christ you will not understand the Mass. With equal force it is possible to say that until you understand that this doll is really a baby you will never understand Lila. She's a culture of one. She's a religion of one. The main difference is that the Christian, since the time of Constantine, has been supported by huge social patterns of authority. Lila isn't. Lila's religion of one doesn't have a chance.

That isn't a completely fair comparison, though. If the major religions of the world consisted of nothing but statues and wafers and other such paraphernalia they would have disappeared long ago in the face of scientific knowledge and cultural change, Phædrus thought. What keeps them going is something else.

It sounds quite blasphemous to put religion and insanity on an equal footing for comparison, but his point was not to undercut religion, only to illuminate insanity. He thought the intellectual separation of the topic of "sanity" from the topic of "religion" has weakened our understanding of both.

The current subject-object point of view of religion, conventionally muted so as not to stir up the fanatics, is that religious mysticism and insanity are the same. Religious mysticism is intellectual garbage. It's a vestige of the old superstitious Dark Ages when nobody knew anything and the whole world was sinking deeper and deeper into filth and disease and poverty and ignorance. It is one of those delusions that isn't called insane only because there are so many people involved.

Until quite recently Oriental religions and Oriental cultures have been similarly grouped as "backward," suffering from disease and poverty and ignorance because they were sunk into a demented mysticism. If it were not for the phenomenon of Japan suddenly leaving the subject-object cultures looking a little backward, the cultural immune system surrounding this view would be impregnable.

The Metaphysics of Quality identifies religious mysticism with Dynamic Quality. It says the subject-object people are *almost* right when they identify religious mysticism with insanity. The two are *almost* the same. Both lunatics and mystics have freed themselves from the conventional static intellectual patterns of their culture. The only difference is that the lunatic has shifted over to a private static pattern of his own, whereas the mystic has abandoned all static patterns in favor of pure Dynamic Quality.

The Metaphysics of Quality says that as long as the psychiatric approach is encased within a subject-object metaphysical understanding it will always seek a patterned solution to insanity, never a mystic one. For exactly the same reasons that Choctaw Indians don't distinguish blue from green and Hindi speaking people don't distinguish ice from snow, modern psychology cannot distinguish between a patterned reality and an unpatterned reality and thus cannot distinguish lunatics from mystics. They seem to be the same.

When Socrates says in one of his dialogues, "Our greatest blessings come to us by way of madness provided the madness is given us by divine gift," the psychiatric profession doesn't know what in the world he is talking about. Or when traces of this identification are found in the expression "touched in the head" meaning touched by God, the roots of this expression are ignored as ignorant and superstitious.

It's another case of the Cleveland Harbor Effect, where you don't see what you don't look for, because when one looks through the record of our culture for connections between insane understanding and religious understanding one soon finds them everywhere. Even the idea of insanity as "possession by the Devil" can be explained by the Metaphysics of Quality as a lower biological pattern, "the Devil," trying to overcome a higher pattern of conformity to cultural belief.

The Metaphysics of Quality suggests that in addition to the customary solutions to insanity—conform to cultural patterns or stay locked up—there is another one. This solution is to dissolve *all* static patterns, both sane and insane, and find the base of reality, Dynamic Quality, that is independent of all of them. The Metaphysics of Quality says that it is immoral for sane people to force cultural conformity by suppressing the Dynamic drives that produce insanity. Such suppression is a lower form of evolution trying to devour a higher one. Static social and intellectual patterns are only an *intermediate* level of evolution. They are good servants of the process of life but if allowed to turn into masters they destroy it.

Once this theoretical structure is available, it offers solutions to some mysteries in the present treatment of the insane. For example, doctors know that shock treatment "works," but are fond of saying that no one knows why.

The Metaphysics of Quality offers an explanation. The value of shock treatment is not that it returns a lunatic to normal cultural patterns. It certainly does *not* do that. Its value is that it destroys *all* patterns, both cultural and private, and leaves the patient temporarily in a Dynamic state. All the shock does is duplicate the effects of hitting the patient over the head with a baseball bat. It simply knocks him senseless. In fact it was to imitate the effect of hitting someone over the head with a baseball bat without the risk of skull injury that Ugo Cerletti developed shock treatment in the first place.

But what goes unrecognized in a subject-object theoretical structure is the fact that this senseless unpatterned state is a valuable state of existence. Once the patient is in this state the psychiatrists of course don't know what to do with it, and so the patient often slips back into lunacy and has to be knocked senseless again and again. But sometimes the patient, in a moment of Zen wisdom, sees the superficiality of both his own contrary patterns and the cultural patterns, sees that the one gets him electrically clubbed day after day and the other sets him free from the institution, and thereupon makes a wise mystic decision to get the hell out of there by whatever avenue is available.

Another mystery in the treatment of the insane explained by a value-centered metaphysics is the value of peace and quiet and isolation. For centuries that has been the primary treatment of the insane. Leave them alone. Ironically the one thing the mental hospitals and doctors do best is the one thing they never take credit for. Maybe they're afraid some crusading journalist or other reformer will come along and say, "Look at all those poor crazies in there with nothing to do. Inhuman treatment," so they don't play that part of it up. They know it works, but there's no way of justifying that because the whole cultural set they have to operate in says that doing nothing is the same as doing something wrong.

The Metaphysics of Quality says that what sometimes accidentally occurs in an insane asylum but occurs deliberately in a mystic retreat is a natural human process called *dhyāna* in Sanskrit. In our culture *dhyāna* is ambiguously called "meditation." Just as mystics traditionally seek monasteries and ashrams and hermitages as retreats into isolation and silence, so are the insane treated by isolation in places of relative calm and austerity and silence. Sometimes, as a result of this monastic retreat into silence and isolation the patient arrives at a state Karl Menninger has described as "better than cured." He is actually in better condition than he was before the insanity started. Phædrus guessed that in many of these "accidental" cases, the patient had learned by himself not to cling to any static patterns of ideas—cultural, private or any other.

In the insane asylum this *dhyāna* is underrated and often undermined because there is no metaphysical basis for understanding it scientifically. But among religious mystics, particularly Oriental mystics, *dhyāna* has been one of the most intensely studied practices of all.

This Western treatment of *dhyāna* is a beautiful example of how the static patterns of a culture can make something not exist, even when it does exist. People in this culture are hypnotized into thinking they do not meditate when in fact they do.

Dhyāna was what this boat was all about. It's what Phædrus had bought it for, a place to be alone and quiet and inconspicuous and able to settle down into himself and be what he really was and not what he was thought to be or supposed to be. In doing this he didn't think he was putting this boat to any special purpose. That's what the purpose of boats like this has always been . . . and seaside cottages too . . . and lake cabins . . . and hiking trails . . . and golf courses. . . . It's the need for *dhyāna* that is behind all these.

Vacations too . . . how perfectly named that is . . . a *vacation*, an emptying out . . . that's what *dhyāna* is, an emptying out of all the static clutter and junk of one's life and just settling into an undefined sort of tranquillity.

That's what Lila's involved in now, a huge *vacation*, an emptying out of the junk of her life. She's clinging to some new pattern because she thinks it holds back the old pattern. But what she has to do is take a vacation from *all* patterns, old and new, and just settle into a kind of emptiness for a while. And if she does, the culture has a moral obligation not to bother her. The most moral activity of all is the creation of space for life to move onward.

The Metaphysics of Quality associates religious mysticism with Dynamic Quality but it would certainly be a mistake to think that the Metaphysics of Quality endorses the static beliefs of any particular religious sect. Phædrus thought sectarian religion was a static social fallout from Dynamic Quality and that while some sects had fallen less than others, none of them told the whole truth.

His favorite Christian mystic was Johannes Eckhart, who said, "Wouldst thou be perfect, do not yelp about God." Eckhart was pointing to a profound mystic truth, but you can guess what a hand of applause it got from the static authorities of the Church. "Ill-sounding, rash, and probably heretical," was the general verdict.

From what Phædrus had been able to observe, mystics and priests

tend to have a cat-and-dog-like coexistence within almost every religious organization. Both groups need each other but neither group
likes the other at all.

There's an adage that, "Nothing disturbs a bishop quite so much
as the presence of a saint in the parish." It was one of Phædrus'
favorites. The saint's Dynamic understanding makes him unpredictable and uncontrollable, but the bishop's got a whole calendar of static
ceremonies to attend to; fund-raising projects to push forward, bills
to pay, parishioners to meet. That saint's going to up-end everything
if he isn't handled diplomatically. And even *then* he may do something
wildly unpredictable that upsets everybody. What a quandary! It can
take the bishops years, decades, even centuries to put down the hell
that a saint can raise in a single day. Joan of Arc is the prime example.

In all religions bishops tend to gild Dynamic Quality with all sorts
of static interpretations because their cultures require it. But these
interpretations become like golden vines that cling to a tree, shut out
its sunlight and eventually strangle it.

Phædrus heard the sound of a car coming closer from behind. When
it approached he held out his thumb and it stopped. He told the
driver he was looking for groceries and the driver took him to Atlantic
Highlands where the car was going anyway. At a supermarket Phædrus
filled the tote bags with all the food he could find that looked good,
then found another ride back as far as the junction in the road where
Sandy Hook started. He shouldered his bags, now pretty heavy, hoping another ride would come along, but none came.

He thought some more about Lila's insanity and how it was related
to religious mysticism and how both were integrated into reason by
the Metaphysics of Quality. He thought about how once this integration occurs and Dynamic Quality is identified with religious mysticism it produces an avalanche of information as to what Dynamic
Quality is. A lot of this religious mysticism is just low-grade "yelping
about God" of course, but if you search for the sources of it and don't
take the yelps too literally a lot of interesting things turn up.

Long ago when he first explored the idea of Quality he'd reasoned that if Quality were the primordial source of all our understanding then it followed that the place to get the best view of it would be at the beginning of history when it would have been less cluttered by the present deluge of static intellectual patterns of knowledge. He'd traced Quality back into its origins in Greek philosophy and thought he'd gone as far as he could go. Then he found he was able to go back to a time *before* the Greek philosophers, to the rhetoricians.

Philosophers usually present their ideas as sprung from "nature" or sometimes from "God," but Phædrus thought neither of these was completely accurate. The logical order of things which the philosophers study is derived from the "mythos." The mythos is the social culture and the rhetoric which the culture must invent before philosophy becomes possible. Most of this old religious talk is nonsense, of course, but nonsense or not, it is the *parent* of our modern scientific talk. This "mythos over logos" thesis agreed with the Metaphysics of Quality's assertion that intellectual static patterns of quality are built up out of social static patterns of quality.

Digging back into ancient Greek history, to the time when this mythos-to-logos transition was taking place, Phædrus noted that the ancient rhetoricians of Greece, the Sophists, had taught what they called *aretê*, which was a synonym for Quality. Victorians had translated *aretê* as "virtue" but Victorian "virtue" connoted sexual abstinence, prissiness and a holier-than-thou snobbery. This was a long way from what the ancient Greeks meant. The early Greek literature, particularly the poetry of Homer, showed that *aretê* had been a central and vital term.

With Homer Phædrus was certain he'd gone back as far as anyone could go, but one day he came across some information that startled him. It said that by following linguistic analysis you could go even further back into the mythos than Homer. Ancient Greek was not an original language. It was descended from a much earlier one, now called the Proto-Indo-European language. This language has left no fragments but has been derived by scholars from similarities between such languages as Sanskrit, Greek and English which have indicated that these languages were fallouts from a common prehistoric tongue. After thousands of years of separation from Greek and English the

Hindi word for "mother" is still "Ma." *Yoga* both looks like and is translated as "yoke." The reason an Indian *rajah*'s title sounds like "regent" is because both terms are fallouts from Proto-Indo-European. Today a Proto-Indo-European dictionary contains more than a thousand entries with derivations extending into more than one hundred languages.

Just for curiosity's sake Phædrus decided to see if *aretê* was in it. He looked under the "a" words and was disappointed to find it was not. Then he noted a statement that said that the Greeks were not the most faithful to the Proto-Indo-European spelling. Among other sins, the Greeks added the prefix "a" to many of the Proto-Indo-European roots. He checked this out by looking for *aretê* under "r." This time a door opened.

The Proto-Indo-European root of *aretê* was the morpheme *rt*. There, beside *aretê*, was a treasure room of other derived "rt" words: "arithmetic," "aristocrat," "art," "rhetoric," "worth," "rite," "ritual," "wright," "right (handed)" and "right (correct)." All of these words except arithmetic seemed to have a vague thesaurus-like similarity to Quality. Phædrus studied them carefully, letting them soak in, trying to guess what sort of concept, what sort of way of seeing the world, could give rise to such a collection.

When the morpheme appeared in *aristocrat* and *arithmetic* the reference was to "firstness." *Rt* meant first. When it appeared in art and wright it seemed to mean "created" and "of beauty." "Ritual" suggested repetitive order. And the word *right* has two meanings: "right-handed" and "moral and esthetic correctness." When all these meanings were strung together a fuller picture of the *rt* morpheme emerged. *Rt* referred to the "first, created, beautiful repetitive order of moral and esthetic correctness."

Interestingly, in the sciences today arithmetic still enjoys this status.

Later Phædrus discovered that even though the Hebrews were from "across the river" and not part of the Proto-Indo-European group, they had a similar term, *arhetton*, which meant "the One" and which was considered so sacred it was not allowed to be spoken.

The right-handedness was also interesting. He had come across an anthropology book called *La Prééminence de la Main Droite* by Robert

Hertz, showing how condemnation of left-handedness as "sinister" is an almost universal anthropological characteristic. Our modern twentieth century culture is one of the few exceptions, but even today when legal oaths are taken or military salutes are given or people shake hands or when a president is inaugurated and agrees to uphold the first created beautiful repetitive order of moral and esthetic correctness of his country, it is mandatory that he raise his right hand. When school children pledge allegiance to the flag as a symbol of this tribal beauty and moral correctness they are required to do the same thing. Prehistoric *rt* is still with us.

There was just one thing wrong with this Proto-Indo-European discovery, something Phædrus had tried to sweep under the carpet at first, but which kept creeping out again. The meanings, grouped together, suggested something different from his interpretation of *aretê*. They suggested "importance" but it was an importance that was formal and social and procedural and manufactured, almost an antonym to the Quality he was talking about. *Rt* meant "quality" all right but the quality it meant was static, not Dynamic. He had wanted it to come out the other way, but it looked as though it wasn't going to do it. Ritual. That was the last thing he wanted *aretê* to turn out to be. Bad news. It looked as though the Victorian translation of *aretê* as "virtue" might be better after all since "virtue" implies ritualistic conformity to social protocol.

It was in this gloomy mood, while he was thinking about all the interpretations of the *rt* morpheme, that yet another "find" came. He had thought that surely this time he had reached the end of the Quality-*aretê-rt* trail. But then from the sediment of old memories his mind dredged up a word he hadn't thought about or heard of for a long time:

Ṛta. It was a Sanskrit word, and Phædrus remembered what it meant: *Ṛta* was the "cosmic order of things." Then he remembered he had read that the Sanskrit language was considered the most faithful to the Proto-Indo-European root, probably because the linguistic patterns had been so carefully preserved by the Hindu priests.

Ṛta came surrounded by a memory of bright chalky tan walls in a classroom filled with sun. At the head of the classroom, Mr. Mukerjee, a perspiring *dhoti*-clad brahmin was drilling dozens of ancient

Sanskrit words into the assembled students' heads—*advaita, māyā, avidyā, brahmān, ātman, prajñā, sāṃkhya, visiṣṭādvaita, Ṛg-Veda, upaniṣad, darśana, dhyāna, nyāya*—on and on. He introduced them day after day, each in turn with a little smile that promised hundreds more to come.

At Phædrus' worn wooden desk near the wall in back of the classroom, he had sat sweaty and annoyed by buzzing flies. The heat and light and flies came and went freely through openings in a far wall which had no window-glass because in India you don't need it. His notebook was damp where his hand had rested. His pen wouldn't write on the damp spot, so he had to write around it. When he turned the page he found the damp had gotten through to the next page too.

In that heat it was agony to remember what all the words were supposed to mean—*ajīva, mokṣa, kāma, ahiṃsa, suṣupti, bhakti, saṃsāra*. They passed by his mind like clouds and disappeared. Through the openings in the wall he could see real clouds—giant monsoon clouds towering thousands of feet up—and white-humped Sindhi cows grazing below.

He thought he'd forgotten all those words years ago, but now here was *ṛta*, back again. *Ṛta*, from the oldest portion of the *Ṛg Veda*, which was the oldest known writing of the Indo-Aryan language. The sun god, *Sūrya*, began his chariot ride across the heavens from the abode of *ṛta*. *Varuṇa*, the god for whom the city in which Phædrus was studying was named, was the chief support of *ṛta*.

Varuṇa was omniscient and was described as ever witnessing the truth and falsehood of men—as being "the third whenever two plot in secret." He was essentially a god of righteousness and a guardian of all that is worthy and good. The texts had said that the distinctive feature of *Varuṇa* was his unswerving adherence to high principles. Later he was overshadowed by *Indra* who was a thunder god and destroyer of the enemies of the Indo-Aryans. But all the gods were conceived as "guardians of *ṛta*," willing the right and making sure it was carried out.

One of Phædrus' old school texts, written by M. Hiriyanna, contained a good summary: "*Ṛta*, which etymologically stands for 'course' originally meant 'cosmic order,' the maintenance of which was the purpose of all the gods; and later it also came to mean 'right,' so that the gods were conceived as preserving the world not merely from physical disorder but also from moral chaos. The one idea is implicit in the other: and there is order in the universe because its control is in righteous hands. . . ."

The physical order of the universe is also the moral order of the universe. *Rta* is both. This was exactly what the Metaphysics of Quality was claiming. It was not a new idea. It was the oldest idea known to man.

This identification of *ṛta* and *aretê* was enormously valuable, Phædrus thought, because it provided a huge historical panorama in which the fundamental conflict between static and Dynamic Quality had been worked out. It answered the question of why *aretê* meant ritual. *Rta* also meant ritual. But unlike the Greeks, the Hindus in their many thousands of years of cultural evolution had paid enormous attention to the conflict between ritual and freedom. Their resolution of this conflict in the Buddhist and Vedantist philosophies is one of the profound achievements of the human mind.

The original meaning of *ṛta*, during what is called the *Brāhmaṇa* period of Indian history, underwent a change to extremely ritualistic static patterns more rigid and detailed than anything heard of in Western religion. As Hiriyanna wrote,

> *The purpose of invoking the several gods of nature was at first mostly to gain their favor for success in life here as well hereafter. The prayers were then naturally accompanied by simple gifts like grain and ghee. But this simple form of worship became more and more complicated and gave rise, in course of time, to elaborate sacrifices and also to a special class of professional priests who alone, it was believed, could officiate at them. There are allusions in the later hymns to rites which lasted for very long periods and at which several priests were employed by the sacrificer. [A change] came over the spirit with which offerings were made to the gods in this period. What prompted the performance of sacrifices was no longer the thought of prevailing upon the gods to bestow some favor or ward off some danger; it was rather to compel or coerce them to do what the sacrificer wanted to be done. . . .*
>
> *There was a profound change in the conception of sacrifice, and*

consequently in that of the relation between gods and men. All that came to be insisted upon was a scrupulous carrying out of every detail connected with the various rites; and the good result accruing from them, whether here or elsewhere, was believed to follow automatically from it. . . . Ritualistic punctilio thus comes to be placed on the same level as natural law and moral rectitude.

You don't have to look far in the modern world to find similar conditions, Phædrus thought.

But what made the Hindu experience so profound was that this decay of Dynamic Quality into static quality was not the end of the story. Following the period of the *Brāhmaṇas* came the *Upaniṣadic* period and the flowering of Indian philosophy. Dynamic Quality re-emerged within the static patterns of Indian thought.

"*Ṛta*," Hiriyanna had written, "almost ceased to be used in Sanskrit; but . . . under the name of *dharma*, the same idea occupies a very important place in the later Indian views of life also."

The more usual meaning of *dharma* is, "religious merit which, operating in some unseen way as it is supposed, secures good to a person in the future, either here or elsewhere. Thus the performance of certain sacrifices is believed to lead the agent to heaven after the present life, and of certain others to secure for him wealth, children and the like in this very life."

But he also wrote, "It is sometimes used as a purely moral concept and stands for right or virtuous conduct which leads to some form of good as a result."

Dharma, like *ṛta*, means "what holds together." It is the basis of all order. It equals righteousness. It is the ethical code. It is the stable condition which gives man perfect satisfaction.

Dharma is duty. It is not external duty which is arbitrarily imposed by others. It is not any artificial set of conventions which can be amended or repealed by legislation. Neither is it internal duty which is arbitrarily decided by one's own conscience. *Dharma* is beyond all questions of what is internal and what is external. *Dharma* is Quality itself, the principle of "rightness" which gives structure and purpose to the evolution of all life and to the evolving understanding of the universe which life has created.

Within the Hindu tradition *dharma* is relative and dependent on the conditions of society. It always has a social implication. It is the bond which holds society together. This is fitting to the ancient origins of the term. But within modern Buddhist thought *dharma* becomes the phenomenal world—the object of perception, thought or understanding. A chair, for example, is not composed of atoms of substance, it is composed of *dharmas*.

This statement is absolute jabberwocky to a conventional subject-object metaphysics. How can a chair be composed of individual little moral orders? But if one applies the Metaphysics of Quality and sees that a chair is an inorganic static pattern and sees that all static patterns are composed of value and that value is synonymous with morality then it all begins to make sense.

It occurred to Phædrus that this was one answer, perhaps the basic answer, to why workmen in Japan and Taiwan and other areas in the Far East are able to maintain quality levels that compare so favorably to those in the West. In the past the mystics' traditional low regard for inorganic static patterns, "laws of nature" has kept the scientifically derived technology of these cultures poor, but since Orientals have learned to overcome that prejudice times have changed. If one comes from a cultural tradition where an electronic assembly is primarily a moral order rather than just a neutral pile of substance, it is easier to feel an ethical responsibility for doing good work on it.

Phædrus thought that Oriental social cohesiveness and ability to work long hard hours without complaint was not a genetic characteristic but a cultural one. It resulted from the working out, centuries ago, of the problem of *dharma* and the way in which it combines freedom and ritual. In the West progress seems to proceed by a series of spasms of alternating freedom and ritual. A revolution of freedom against old rituals produces a new order, which soon becomes another old ritual for the next generation to revolt against, on and on. In the Orient there are plenty of conflicts but historically this particular kind of conflict has not been as dominant. Phædrus thought it was because *dharma* includes both static and Dynamic Quality without contradiction.

For example, you would guess from the literature on Zen and its insistence on discovering the "unwritten *dharma*" that it would be intensely anti-ritualistic, since ritual is the "written *dharma*." But that isn't the case. The Zen monk's daily life is nothing *but* one ritual after another, hour after hour, day after day, all his life. They don't tell him to shatter those static patterns to discover the unwritten *dharma*. They want him to get those patterns perfect!

The explanation for this contradiction is the belief that you do not free yourself from static patterns by fighting them with other contrary static patterns. That is sometimes called "bad karma chasing its tail." You free yourself from static patterns by putting them to sleep. That is, you master them with such proficiency that they become an unconscious part of your nature. You get so used to them you completely forget them and they are gone. There in the center of the most monotonous boredom of static ritualistic patterns the Dynamic freedom is found.

Phædrus saw nothing wrong with this ritualistic religion as long as the rituals are seen as merely a static portrayal of Dynamic Quality, a sign-post which allows socially pattern-dominated people to see Dynamic Quality. The danger has always been that the rituals, the static patterns, are mistaken for what they merely represent and are allowed to destroy the Dynamic Quality they were originally intended to preserve.

Suddenly the foliage by the road opened up and there it was: the ocean.

He stopped for a second by the beach and just stared at the endless procession of waves moving slowly in from the horizon.

The south wind was stronger here and it cooled him. It was steady, like a trade wind. Nothing interfered with its flow toward him over the huge ocean. "Vast emptiness and nothing sacred." If ever there was a visible concrete metaphor for Dynamic Quality this was it.

The beach looked much cleaner here than on the other side of the hook and he would have liked to walk for a while, but he had to get back to the boat.

. . . And to Lila.

Where to start with her? That was the question. The *ṛta* interpretation of Quality would say that more ritual is what she needs—

not the kind of ritual that fights Dynamic Quality, but the kind that embodies it. But what ritual? She wasn't about to follow rituals of any kind. Ritual was what she was fighting.

But that could be an answer. Lila's problem wasn't that she was suffering from lack of Dynamic freedom. It's hard to see how she could possibly have any more freedom. What she needed now were stable patterns to *encase* that freedom. She needed some way of being reintegrated into the rituals of everyday living.

But where to start? . . .

. . . That doll, maybe. She had to give up that doll. She wasn't going to convert anyone to *that* religion. The longer she hung on to it the firmer the static pattern was likely to get. These defensive patterns were not only as bad as the patterns she was running from, they were worse! Now she's got *two* sets of patterns to break away from, the culture's and her own.

. . . He wondered if it was possible to put these defensive patterns to sleep by means of the doll. Just accept the idea that the doll is her real child and treat the doll in such a way as to quiet down all those longings. She says the doll, her baby, is dead. She thinks this is some sort of island. Why not bury the doll with full honors?

That would be a ritual, Phædrus thought. That's exactly what Lila needs. Don't fight her patterns. Amalgamate them. She already seemed to think of him as some sort of priestly figure. Why disappoint her? He could use this image to try to bury her insane patterns with the baby. It would be sort of theatrical and fake, he supposed, but that's what funerals were: theatre. They weren't for the corpse, certainly, but to help end the longings and old patterns of the living, who had to go on. The funeral would be real to Lila. That baby probably embodied just about every care she had.

Rta. That's what was missing from her life. Ritual.

Arriving at work Monday morning is *ṛta.* Getting paid Friday evening is *ṛta.* Walking into the grocery store and taking food off the shelf to feed one's children is *ṛta.* Paying for it with the money received on Friday is more *ṛta.* The entire mechanism of society is *ṛta* from beginning to end. That's what Lila really needed.

He could only guess how far back this ritual-cosmos relationship went, maybe fifty or one hundred thousand years. Cave men are usually depicted as hairy, stupid creatures who don't do much, but anthropological studies of contemporary primitive tribes suggest that stone age people were probably bound by ritual all day long. There's a ritual for washing, for putting up a house, for hunting, for eating and so on—so much so that the division between "ritual" and "knowledge" becomes indistinct. In cultures without books ritual seems to be a public library for teaching the young and preserving common values and information.

These rituals may be the connecting link between the social and intellectual levels of evolution. One can imagine primitive song-rituals and dance-rituals associated with certain cosmology stories, myths, which generated the first primitive religions. From these the first intellectual truths could have been derived. If ritual always comes first and intellectual principles always come later, then ritual cannot always be a decadent corruption of intellect. Their sequence in history suggests that principles emerge from ritual, not the other way around. That is, we don't perform religious rituals because we believe in God. We believe in God because we perform religious rituals. If so, that's an important principle in itself.

But after a while, as Phædrus walked along, his enthusiasm for the baby funeral started to go downhill. He didn't like this idea of going along with some ritual he didn't really believe in. He had a feeling that real ritual had to grow out of your own nature. It isn't something that can be intellectualized and patched on.

The funeral would be a pretense. How are you going to bring someone back to "reality" when the reality you bring them back to is a deliberate fake? That's no good. He had never gone along with that fakery in the mental hospital and he was sure it wouldn't work now. Santa Claus stuff. Sooner or later the lie breaks down . . . and then what's your next move?

Phædrus continued to think about it, leaning first one way and then another, until he got to a sign that indicated he was back at Horseshoe Cove.

When the cove came into view his boat was there all right, but another boat was alongside of it, rafted on.

A wave of very un-mystic anxiety came over him.

31.

As he got closer Phædrus saw that it was Rigel's boat. What a relief. But Rigel was supposed to be going to Connecticut. What was he doing here?

Then Phædrus remembered Lila had said Rigel was coming. How had she known *that*?

When Phædrus got to the dinghy he set down his tote bags of groceries and began to untie its painter from the steel spike in the log.

"Wait!" he heard.

He turned and saw Rigel standing on deck of his boat, his hands cupped over his mouth.

"I'm coming ashore," Rigel shouted.

Phædrus stopped untying the dinghy. He watched Rigel get down into his boat's dinghy. He wondered why Rigel didn't just wait for him to get there.

He watched Rigel row the short distance, looking over his shoulder slowly, his aristocratic features becoming closer and more distinct. He was smiling. When he got the boat beached, Phædrus helped him lift it up onto the sand.

"I just thought I'd come ashore and talk for a while with you," Rigel said. His smile was formal, calculated—a lawyer's smile.

"What's up?" Phædrus asked.

"Well, first of all I'm here to collect some money," Rigel said. "I paid your bill back at the marina."

"My God," Phædrus said, "I completely forgot about that."

"Well *they* didn't," Rigel said, and brought out a receipt from his pocket.

While Phædrus looked at the receipt and fished out his billfold, Rigel said, "I gave them a little extra to calm them down. They thought it was some sort of a drug transaction and didn't want to be involved in it. As soon as you were gone they calmed down and forgot about the whole thing."

"That's good," Phædrus said.

As Phædrus paid him, Rigel asked, "What have you been doing?"

"I've just been getting some groceries," Phædrus said, "enough to get us to Atlantic City, at least."

"Oh," Richard Rigel said. "That's good."

There was a pause and his face became a little tense.

"Where's Bill Capella?" Phædrus asked.

"He had to go back," Rigel said.

"That's too bad."

Rigel seemed to wait for him to go on talking but somehow he wasn't in the mood. As neither one of them said anything, Rigel seemed to get visibly nervous.

"Why don't we go for a walk for a while," Rigel said, "down this path here."

"Well you can if you want," Phædrus said. "I just want to get back to the boat. I've been going all day."

"There are some things I'd like to talk about," Rigel said.

"Like what?"

"Important things."

Rigel had always seemed bothered by something he wasn't talking about but now it seemed even worse. His verbal language and his body language seemed to go in different directions.

"You remember our conversation about Lila back in Kingston?"

"Yes," Phædrus replied, "I remember it well." He tried to say it flatly but it sounded sarcastic anyway.

"Since then," Rigel said, "what you said has been going round and round in my mind."

"Is that right?"

"I can't seem to stop thinking about it, and I'd like to talk about it some more and since we can't very well do that with Lila present, I thought perhaps we could go for a walk."

Phædrus shrugged. He retied the painter of the dinghy to the rusty spike and then with Rigel headed up the path away from the road.

The path in this direction was carpeted with wood shavings, and as they continued walking he saw it changed to a covering of fine black stone. A sign on one side that he hadn't noticed before said "U.S. Interior Dept." The marsh with the old day beacon in it looked the same as before but the white egret was gone.

"You remember that you said Lila has quality," Rigel said.

"That's right."

"Would you mind telling me just *how* you came to that conclusion?"

Oh for God's sake, Phædrus thought. "It wasn't a conclusion," he said. "It was a perception."

"How did you come to it?"

"I didn't 'come' to it."

They continued to walk quietly. Rigel's hands were clenched. He could almost hear wheels going around in his head.

Then he said exasperatedly, "What was there to *perceive!*"

"The Quality," Phædrus said.

"Oh, you're being ridiculous," Rigel said.

They continued to walk.

Rigel said, "Did she tell you something that night? Is that why you think she has Quality? You know she's mentally ill, don't you?"

"Yes."

"I just wanted to be sure. I'm never much sure of anything where she's involved. Did she tell you she's been chasing me all the way across New York ever since I left Rochester?"

"No, she didn't tell me that."

"Every damn bar. Every damned restaurant, wherever I turned there was Lila. I told her I didn't want anything to do with her. That case with Jim was over and I was done with it, but by now I'm sure you know how well she listens."

Phædrus nodded without adding anything.

"The reason she came to that bar in Kingston was because she knew I was there. That was no accident, you know, her taking up with you in the bar that night. She saw you were a friend of mine. I tried to warn you but you weren't listening."

Phædrus remembered now that Lila *had* asked a lot of questions about Rigel in the bar. That *was* true.

Then he remembered something else: "I was so drunk it's hard to remember anything that happened," he said, "but I vaguely remember one thing. Just as we were crossing the deck of your boat to get to ours I told her to be very quiet, not to make any noise because you were probably sleeping right under the deck. She said, 'Where?' and I pointed to the spot and then she picked up her suitcase way up over her head and slammed it down with all her might right on that spot."

"I *remember* that!" Rigel said. "It was like an explosion!"

"Why did she do it?"

"Because I wasn't having anything more to do with her!" Rigel said.

"Why was she chasing you?"

"Oh, that goes back forever."

"To the second grade, she said."

Rigel suddenly looked at him with an almost frightened look. Whatever he was so nervous about had something to do with this.

"She said she was the only one who was nice to you," Phædrus continued.

"That's not true," Rigel said.

Ahead, overgrown by bushes, was some unidentifiable concrete wreckage, like a modern sculpture growing in weeds. Rusted metal bolts emerged from concrete slabs broken up by goldenrod. It looked like the base of two steel cranes.

"She's different from what she used to be," Rigel said. "You wouldn't believe it now, but back in grade school Lila Blewitt was the most serene, pleasant-natured girl you could ever meet. That's why I was so shocked when you said she had 'quality.' I wondered if you saw something there."

"What happened to change her?"

"I don't know," Rigel said. "I suppose the same thing happens to all of us. She grew up and she discovered the world is not the place we think it is when we are children."

"Did you ever have sexual relations with her?" Phædrus asked. It was a shot in the dark.

Rigel looked at him with surprise. Then he laughed deprecatingly. "Everybody has!" he said. "You're no exception in *that* regard!"

"Did she become pregnant after that?" Phædrus asked.

Rigel shook his head and made a pushing-away motion. "No, don't jump to conclusions like that. That could have been anyone."

They walked on and Phædrus began to feel depressed. This path seemed to go on and on without getting anywhere. "We'd better turn around," he said.

He was beginning to feel like the detective at the end of the murder mystery, except that the detective gets a feeling of satisfaction from having finally run some quarry to the ground, and Phædrus wasn't getting any satisfaction from this at all.

He just really didn't want to have anything to do with this person any more.

They turned around, and as they walked back Rigel said, "There's still one other question to be taken up."

"What's that?"

"Lila wants to go back with me."

"*Now?*"

"Yes."

"Where?"

"To Rochester. I know her family and friends and can get her taken care of."

"Taken care of?"

"Certified."

Oh my God, Phædrus thought. Institutionalized.

A real wave of depression hit.

He just walked for a while, not saying anything because he didn't want to say anything wrong.

Finally he said, "I think that's an exceptionally poor idea. She's all right on my boat."

"She *wants* to go back."

"Because you talked her into it."

"Absolutely not!"

"The last time I talked to her she said she wants to go south, which is where we're heading."

"That isn't what she wants," Rigel said.

"I know what she wants," Phædrus said.

Now Rigel didn't say anything.

They continued to walk and before long the boats were back in sight again.

Rigel said, "I don't know quite how to tell you this. But you'd better hear it."

"Hear what?"

"Lila said she wants me to take her back to Rochester . . ." He paused. ". . . because you're trying to kill her."

Phædrus looked at him. This time Rigel looked straight back at him and his nervousness seemed gone. "So you see what the problem is," Rigel said.

"That's why I wanted to take this walk with you," Rigel continued. "I didn't expect this when I came down here. I just came to see if everything was all right. But under the circumstances . . . I rather got you into this . . . although I certainly tried not to. . . ."

"I'll talk to her," Phædrus said.

"She's already transferred her suitcase and other things onto my boat," Rigel said.

"Then I'll talk to her *there*!" Phædrus said.

This was a real disaster coming. But blowing up now would just make it more likely. He got into his dinghy and Rigel let him row ahead. He tied off on his own boat, went aboard, and on the other side crossed over the life-lines to Rigel's boat before he arrived.

When he looked down below he saw Lila's poor bruised face looking up at him with a smile. Then the smile disappeared. Maybe she'd thought he was Rigel.

He went down below and sat across from her. Now she looked as nervous as Rigel had been.

"Hello," he said.

"Hello," she said back.

"I hear you want to go back."

She looked down. Guilt. This was the first time he had ever seen her look guilty.

He said, "I think that's a very bad mistake."

She still looked down.

"Why are you going back?"

Lila looked up and then finally said, "I wanted to go with you. You don't know how bad. But now I've changed my mind. There are a lot of things I want to do first."

Phædrus said, "There's nothing but trouble waiting for you back there."

"I know that, but they need me."

"Who?"

"My mother and everybody."

He looked at her. "Well," he wanted to ask, "if they need you so badly then why the hell were you heading south in the first place?" But he didn't ask it. "What's changed," he wanted to ask. "Did Rigel put you up to this? Who put you up to this? Do you know what's going to happen to you back there? Is this some kind of suicide? My God, Lila, you haven't done one single solitary smart thing since the moment I met you, do you know that? When are you going to start?"

But he didn't say all this. He just sat there like a child at a funeral, watching her.

There was really nothing more he could say. She wanted to go back; there was nothing he could do about it.

"You're *absolutely sure?*" he said.

Lila looked at him for a long time. He waited for a flicker of doubt to appear and waited some more but she just sat there and then she said it so quietly he could hardly hear it. . . . "I'm all right. . . ."

Then he thought for a while longer, wondering, in what he knew would be the last chance, if there was something missing that he should say.

He couldn't think of anything.

Finally he got up and said, "Okay."

He climbed up to the deck where Rigel was standing. He said, "She wants to go. . . . When are you leaving?"

"Right now," Rigel said. "She wants to leave right away and I think that, under the circumstances, it's better."

As Phædrus watched him start up his boat's engine he felt somewhat dumbstruck. He crossed over to his own boat, helped Rigel cast off the lines and then watched with a strange sort of paralysis as Rigel's boat turned and then headed back north across the bay.

32.

It was going to take a while to get all this sorted out.

An hour ago he was planning to spend the rest of his life taking care of Lila. As of this minute he was never going to see her again. Wham. Wham. Just like that.

His mind felt like the beach out there, all full of old tires and derelict hulls and bleach bottles after the hurricane had passed through.

He guessed what he needed now was some time and silence to get back to where he was before.

All these events seemed to have completely cut off his past. Whatever was, was gone. It was really behind him. The ocean was right here now, just on the other side of this sand barrier. Here, now, this was a whole new life starting. Soon there'd be no trace of his ever having been here.

The boat swung a little in the breeze. It seemed empty now. Silent. He was all alone again. It was as though Lila had never been here. . . .

He supposed he should be overjoyed. He didn't know why he felt so let down. This was what he wanted. He should be celebrating. . . .

But it was really sad that she had to end it like that. Why did she tell Rigel he was trying to kill her? That was really bad. She knew he wasn't trying to kill her. Her whole attitude when she talked to him wasn't the attitude of someone who thought that.

. . . Of course he never *heard* her say he was going to kill her. He just heard Rigel *say* she said it.

. . . But Rigel wouldn't have lied about something like that. She must have said something of the sort.

. . . What made it so sad was it was the first really immoral thing she had done to him in all that time he was with her. Sure, she called a him a lot of bad names and stuff. But that had been more a defense of herself than any overt wickedness. She had just been trying to tell him the truth. But this time she was lying. That's why she wanted to get out of here so fast.

It was the first time he'd ever seen her look down like that. That's what was so sad to see. The thing that was most attractive about her was that straight-forward, eyes-ahead look of someone who's honest to themselves, whatever others might think. Now that was gone. It meant she was turning back to the static patterns she came from. She's sold out. The system beat her. It's made a crook out of her at last.

It was as though she had just one more step to take and she was out of hell forever, and then instead of taking that one step she turned back. Now she's really done for. That bastard will commit her for life.

Anyway, Phædrus supposed he would have to get busy and get ready to leave tomorrow. He'd get everything set to head out at daybreak. Possibly he could make it all the way to Barnegat Inlet if he could get in there. He'd have to look at the charts again.

Somehow he didn't feel like moving. He didn't feel like doing anything.

. . . He supposed he shouldn't be too hard on Lila. What had happened to her was very scary stuff. If she wants to go back to some place she thinks is safer who's to blame her?

. . . The funny thing was that when she said he was trying to kill her, that was insane—but it wasn't entirely incorrect. He *was* trying to kill her—not the biological Lila, but the static patterns that were *really* going to kill her if she didn't let go.

From the static point of view the whole escape into Dynamic Quality seems like a death experience. It's a movement from something to nothing. How can "nothing" be any different from death? Since a Dynamic understanding doesn't make the static distinctions necessary to answer that question, the question goes unanswered. All the Buddha could say was, "See for yourself."

When early Western investigators first read the Buddhist texts they too interpreted nirvana as some kind of suicide. There's a famous poem that goes:

> While living,
> Be a dead man.
> Be completely dead,
> And then do as you please.
> And all will be well.

It sounds like something from a Hollywood horror-film but it's about nirvana. The Metaphysics of Quality translates it:

> While sustaining biological and social patterns
> Kill all intellectual patterns.
> Kill them completely
> And then follow Dynamic Quality
> And morality will be served.

Lila was still moving toward Dynamic Quality. All life does. This breaking up of her life's patterns looked like it was part of that movement.

When Phædrus first went to India he'd wondered why, if this passage of enlightenment into pure Dynamic Quality was such a universal reality, did it only occur in certain parts of the world and not others? At the time he'd thought this was proof that the whole thing was just Oriental religious baloney, the equivalent of a magic land called "heaven" that Westerners go to if they are good and get a ticket from the priests. Now he saw that enlightenment is distributed in all parts of the world just as the color yellow is distributed in all parts of the world, but some cultures accept it and others screen out recognition of it.

Lila probably will never know what's happened to her and neither will Rigel or anyone else. She'll probably go through the rest of her life thinking this whole episode has been some kind of failure when in fact what had happened might not have been failure, but growth.

Maybe if Rigel hadn't shown up she would have killed all the bad patterns right here in Sandy Hook. But it's too late now to ever know.

. . . Strange that she'd come to Kingston on a boat called the "Karma." It was unlikely anyone aboard knew what that word really meant. It was like naming a boat "Causal Relationship." Of all the hundreds of Sanskrit words he had learned so long ago, *dharma* and *karma* had hung on longest and hardest. You could translate and pigeon-hole the others but these never seemed to stop needing translating.

The Metaphysics of Quality translated *karma* as "evolutionary garbage." That's why it sounded so funny as the name of a boat. It seemed to suggest she had arrived in Kingston on a garbage scow. *Karma* is the pain, the suffering that results from clinging to the static patterns of the world. The only exit from the suffering is to detach yourself from these static patterns, that is, to "kill" them.

A common way taken to kill them is suicide, but suicide only kills biological patterns. That's like destroying a computer because you can't stand the program it's running. The social and intellectual patterns that caused the suicide have to be carried on by others. From an evolutionary point of view it's a really a backward and therefore immoral step.

Another immoral way of killing the static patterns is to pass the patterns to someone else, in what Phædrus called a "karma dump." You invent a devil group, Jews or blacks or whites or capitalists or communists—it doesn't matter—then say that group is responsible for all your suffering, and then hate it and try to destroy it. On a daily personal level everyone has things or people they hate and blame for their suffering and this hatred and blame brings a kind of relief.

Back in Kingston Rigel's whole breakfast sermon was a karmadump. Lila's accusation just now was another one. That's what made it so sad. She'd received too much karmic garbage in her life and she couldn't handle it and that's what was making her crazy and now she's dumped some of it and that will probably make her less crazy, for a while at least, but that's not the moral solution.

If you take all this karmic garbage and make yourself feel better by passing it on to others that's normal. That's the way the world works. But if you manage to absorb it and not pass it on, that's the highest moral conduct of all. That really advances everything, not just you. The whole world. If you look at the lives of some of the great moral figures of history—Christ, Lincoln, Gandhi, and others—you'll see that that's what they were really involved in, the cleansing of the world through the absorption of karmic garbage. They didn't pass it on. Their followers sometimes did, but they didn't.

On the other hand, Phædrus supposed, when you're on the receiving end of some karma dump like that it sets you free. If he'd thrown Lila out when she was insane it would have bothered him afterward as something he shouldn't have done. But now, this way, with both Rigel and Lila rejecting him, there was no way he was going to feel guilty about her departure. The bond of obligation was broken. If Lila had been full of gratitude and attachment he would still be stuck with her. Now Rigel had that honor.

. . . Across the cabin, on the pilot berth, Phædrus saw that her suitcase was gone. There was a nice empty hole there. That was good. That meant he could get the trays of slips back out and have room to get to work on them again. That was good too. He remembered that PROGRAM slip he wrote to wait until Lila gets off the boat. He could cross that one off now.

He wondered if he really *did* want to go back to all those slips. In their own way they were a lot of karmic garbage too. Strictly speaking, the creation of any metaphysics is an immoral act since it's a lower form of evolution, intellect, trying to devour a higher mystic one. The same thing that's wrong with philosophology when it tries to control and devour philosophy is wrong with metaphysics when it tries to devour the world intellectually. It attempts to capture the Dynamic within a static pattern. But it never does. You never get it right. So why try?

It's like trying to construct a perfect unassailable chess game. No matter how smart you are you're never going to play a game that is "right" for all people at all times, everywhere. Answers to ten questions led to a hundred more and answers to those led to a thousand more. Not only would he never get it right; the longer he worked on it the wronger it would probably get.

. . . Then as he thought about this gloomily he saw something else in a shadow at the back of the berth:

It was the doll.

· · ·

She'd left it behind.

That was sort of sad too. After all the fuss she'd made over it, now she just walks off and leaves it. It left a feeling of immorality too. What do you think of a small girl who goes off and leaves her doll alone and abandoned? Will she do that when she grows up?

He got up and looked at it.

It was just an ordinary machine-molded rubber doll—not a very expensive one. It had no moving eyes. Its brown hair was part of the machine-molding. He saw that one spot on the head was abraded where it had evidently rubbed against something in the river for a long time. But probably if it had been glued-on hair it would have all come off by now.

There was something really sad about it, sitting there all bare-naked and sexless. Something innocent. Something wronged. He didn't like to look at it. He didn't want to be involved with it.

. . . What the hell was he going to do with it?

. . . He didn't want to keep it on the boat.

He supposed he could just throw it overboard. It'd look like all the other trash on the beach. No one would know the difference. Probably that's where it was headed anyway before Lila fished it out of the river.

Beside it was a shirt that didn't look like one of his. It looked new and clean. He picked it up. There was a sharp pin in it which he pulled out and set on the chart table. It must really be new, he thought, if it's still got pins in it.

When he tried to put it on he couldn't get the buttons buttoned without exhaling. It was too small. It couldn't be one of his. Lila must have left it. What was Lila doing with a man's new shirt? Now he was beginning to remember she had wrapped the doll in something that looked like this. That's probably where it came from. But why should she have bought a shirt for the doll? She really was into some kind of fantasy world.

Well, if that's what she bought it for, to cover up this doll, that seemed like a perfect use for it right now. Maybe it would help overcome this wronged feeling the doll gave off.

He slipped the shirt over the doll's head. It came down way over the doll's feet like a nightshirt. That looked better. He buttoned the collar around its neck. Something about this doll was giving it all kinds of Quality the manufacturer had never built into it. Lila had overlaid a whole set of value patterns on top of it and those values were still clinging to it. It was almost like some religious idol.

He set it on the edge of the pilot berth, and went back and sat down and stared at it for a while. It looked better with the shirt on.

An idol, that's what this doll was. It was a genuine religious idol of an abandoned religion of one. It had all those formidable characteristics that idols always have. That's what spooked him. Once they've been ritualized and adored, these idols change in value. You can no more throw them away casually than you can throw an old church statue on the dump.

He wondered what they actually did with old abandoned church statues. Did they have a desanctification ceremony of some sort? He remembered he'd been going to have a funeral for this idol for Lila's benefit. Maybe he ought to give it one for his own benefit. Just to put it somewhere without turning it into trash.

Funny feelings. Anthropologists could do a lot with idols. Maybe they already had. He seemed to remember a book he'd always wanted to read called *The Masks of God*. You could discover a lot about a culture by what it said about its idols. The idols would be an objectification of the culture's innermost values, which were its reality.

This doll represented Lila's innermost values, the real Lila, and it said something about her that completely contradicted everything else. It indicated there were two contradictory patterns conflicting with some enormous force and what had happened was some kind of shift in these tectonic plates that had produced a kind of high Richter-scale earthquake. The one pattern, the one Rigel denounced, was going one way. This doll represented a pattern that was going another way, and so this idol allowed Lila to objectify the other pattern and ease the pressures that were causing the earthquake. And now she's abandoned it—evidence that she's going back to something worse. Maybe not.

Maybe to keep from going to something worse himself he should bury it with dignity, he thought, just for his own benefit.

He heard a klunk and realized it was the dinghy. The groceries were still down there. Everything had happened so fast he'd forgotten all about them.

He went up on deck, lowered himself into the dinghy and then lifted the grocery bags up onto the deck of the boat. Now, with Lila gone, he had enough food to get to Norfolk, at least. It would probably go bad before then.

He got back on deck and lowered the canvas bags one by one down into the cabin where he set them on the berth and then brought out their contents and put them into the ice box. Then he looked at the doll-idol.

He picked it up and tucked it under one arm like a child of his own and brought it up on deck, where he set it down carefully. Then he stepped down into the dinghy again and brought the doll down and placed it on the stern thwart ahead of him and rowed ashore. Good thing he had this shirt to wrap over this idol if he needed to. If someone came along he'd have a hard time explaining.

The trail passed by low shrubs with small thick leaves and tiny blue-gray berries. It was paved with small orange-tan stones and sand, and there were pieces of dry grass on it—hollow round reeds broken into six-inch pieces, about a quarter of an inch thick, laid in whirligig patterns. He wondered if the hurricane had done that. Ahead, on one side by some fading goldenrod was a Department of Interior survey marker.

Later on was a nicely-made painted sign asking people to keep out of the marsh to protect the wildlife. It was good that the main road to town didn't have access to this area. It made it much more isolated.

He heard a honking of geese overhead. He looked up and saw about thirty or forty geese flying in a V-formation, northwest, the wrong way. . . . Crazy geese. This warm spell must have gotten to them.

Walking along with this idol Phædrus felt as if the two of them were sharing this experience, as though he were back in childhood again and this were some imaginary companion. Little children talk to dolls and grown-up adults talk to idols. He supposed that a doll allows a child to pretend he's a parent while an idol allows a parent to pretend he's a child.

He reflected on this for a while and then his mind framed a question: "What would you say," he asked the idol, "if we were in India now? What would you say to all this?"

He listened for a long time but there was no response. Then after a while into his thoughts came a voice that did not seem to be his own.

"All this is a happy ending."

Happy ending? Phædrus thought about it for a while.

"I wouldn't call it a happy ending," he said. "I'd call it an inconclusive ending."

"No, this is a happy ending for everyone," the other voice said.

"Why?"

"Because everybody gets what he wants," the voice said.

"Lila gets her precious Richard Rigel, Rigel gets his precious self-righteousness, you get your precious Dynamic freedom, and I get to go swimming again."

"Oh, you know what's going to happen?"

"Yes, of course," the idol said.

"Then how can you say it's a happy ending when you know what's going to happen to Lila?"

"It's not a problem," the idol's voice said.

"Not a problem? He's going to try to lock her up for life and that's not a problem?"

"Not for you."

"Then why do I feel so bad about it?" Phædrus asked.

"You're just waiting for your medal," the idol answered. "You think maybe they're going to turn around and come back and hand you a citation for merit."

"But he's going to *destroy* her."

"No," the idol said. "She isn't going to let him get *anything* on her."

"I don't believe that."

"She owns Rigel now," the idol continued. "He's *had* it. From here on he's putty in her hands."

"No," Phædrus said. "He's a lawyer. He isn't going to lose his head over her."

"He doesn't have to. His head's already lost," the idol said. "She's going to use all those morals of his against him."

"How?"

"She's going to become a *repentant sinner*. She may even join a church. She's just going to keep telling him what a wonderful moral person he is and how he saved her from your degenerate clutches, and what can he do? How can he deny it? There's no way he can fight that. That just keeps his moral ego blown tight as a balloon and as soon as it starts to sag he will have to come back to her for more."

Whew, this was some idol, Phædrus thought. Sarcastic, cynical. Almost vicious. Was that what he himself was really like underneath? Maybe it was. A theatrical ham idol. A matineé idol. No wonder somebody threw it into the river.

"You're the winner, you know," the idol said. ". . . by default."

"How so?"

"You did one moral thing on this whole trip, which saved you."

"What was that?"

"You told Rigel that Lila had Quality."

"You mean in Kingston?"

"Yes, and the only reason you did that was because he caught you by surprise and you couldn't think of your usual intellectual answer, but you turned him around. He wouldn't have come here if it hadn't been for that. Before then he had no respect for her and a lot for you. After that he had no respect for you, but some for her. So you gave something to her, and that's what saved you. If it hadn't been for that one moral act you'd be headed down the coast tomorrow with a lifetime of Lila ahead of you."

Phædrus didn't like it. Judgments of this sort from a branch of his own personality were very confusing—and somewhat ominous. He didn't want to hear any more of them.

"Well, idol," he said, "you may be right and you may be wrong but we are coming to the end of the road here."

They had arrived at what looked like the ruins of an old fortress. It looked somewhat the way old ruins in India looked, except those were many centuries old. It looked sort of like a castle but it was concrete and broken in places with thick rusted reinforcing rods emerging from the breaks in the concrete. Part of it looked like the wall of small amphitheater. Apparently it was the parapet of an old fort. In one area were remains of an overhead trolley system that might have been for hauling military shells. Huge rings were in a wall apparently to take the recoil of a large cannon that was now gone. There was a beautiful leafless tree growing out of the middle of the parapet like an enormous umbrella. It was only about ten feet tall but was much wider than that.

As he walked to the northwest he could see more clearly how the remains of the old concrete structure had broken into fragments, tilted to one side and fallen into the water.

There were square holes in the concrete you could fall through. It looked as though the cracks in the concrete under his feet were ready to break any time. Apparently the breaking up and erosion were being caused by settling and probably by the action of the sea. But he guessed that the real destroyer was not the sea but that great ravager of most military installations, lack of appropriations.

It was sort of wonderful to see this old fort, built to assert man's domination over the earth, slowly sinking into the Atlantic Ocean. It certainly looked like an auspicious place for the interment of this idol.

He found a gate that led below the concrete to a dark chamber where he could hear water down below gurgling loudly. He entered a door with vertical spiked iron posts and I-beams. It was dark inside like a grotto. The only illumination came from below.

He turned to the right by a pockmarked wall and descended five steps leading down to small drop-off. He descended the stairs, testing the concrete carefully with his foot, went left, went forward, and then right again, into a dark tunnel. There he saw that the light came through a smashed portion of the concrete under which swept the water of the Atlantic.

There was enough light to show a dark high-water mark of the tide against the wall. He set the idol against the wall in a sitting position facing the entrance to the sea and arranged the shirt around it carefully. Within a few hours the tide should come and lift it out of here.

His mind said to the idol, "Well, little friend, you've had quite a busy existence."

He stepped back, did a small bow with his hands clasped together in the manner he had once learned in India, and then, feeling that things were right at last, turned and left.

Back to daylight and good old sanity. A few crickets were chirping. He heard a roar in the sky and looked up and saw a Concorde airplane slowly circling to the south then rising and speeding.

Good old technology. All this twentieth century sanity wasn't as interesting as the old days of his incarceration but he was getting a lot more accomplished, at a social level at least. Other cultures may talk to idols and animal spirits and fissures in rocks and ghosts of the past but it wasn't for him. He had other things to do.

He had a feeling of freshness as he walked back to the boat. What a fantastic day this was. How many people are ever lucky enough to clean the slate like this? They're all stuck with their endless problems.

He stood on a mound of sand beside some juniper bushes and said "Ahhhh!" He threw out his arms. Free! No idols, no Lila, no Rigel, no New York, no more America even. Just free!

He looked up in the sky and whirled. Ahhh, that felt good! He hadn't whirled like that for years. Since he was four. He whirled again. The sky, the ocean, the hook, the bay, spun round and round him. He felt like a Whirling Dervish.

He walked back to the boat in a kind of relaxed, nothing-to-do way, thinking of nothing whatsoever. Then he remembered when he had been walking down a dirt road like this one near Lame Deer, Montana, on the Northern Cheyenne reservation. It was with Dusenberry and John Wooden Leg, the tribe's chief, and a woman named LaVerne Madigan from the Association of American Indians.

So long ago. So many things had happened. He would have to get back to the Indians someday. That was where he had started from and that was where he had to get back to.

He remembered it had been spring then, which is a wonderful time in Montana, and the breeze blowing down from the pine trees carried a fresh smell of melting snow and thawing earth, and they were all walking down the road, four abreast, when one of those raggedy non-descript dogs that call Indian reservations home came onto the road and walked pleasantly in front of them.

They followed the dog silently for a while.

Then LaVerne asked John, "What kind of dog is that?"

John thought about it and said, "That's a good dog."

LaVerne looked curiously at him for a moment and then looked down at the road. Then the corners of her eyes crinkled and as they walked on Phædrus noticed she was sort of smiling and chuckling to herself.

Later, when John had left, she asked Dusenberry, "What did he mean when he said 'That's a good dog.' Was that just 'Indian talk'?"

Dusenberry thought for a while and said he supposed it was. Phædrus didn't have any answer either, but for some reason he had been as amused and puzzled as LaVerne was.

A few months later she was killed in an airplane crash, and a few years after that Dusenberry was gone too and Phædrus' own hospitalization and recovery had clouded over all memory of that time and he'd forgotten all about it, but now suddenly, out of nowhere, here it was again.

For some time now he'd been thinking that if he were looking for proof that "substance" is a cultural heritage from Ancient Greece rather than an absolute reality, he should simply look at non-Greek-derived cultures. If the "reality" of substance was missing from those cultures that would prove he was right.

Now the image of the raggedy Indian dog was back, and he realized what it meant.

LaVerne had been asking the question within an Aristotelian framework. She wanted to know what genetic, substantive pigeonhole of canine classification this object walking before them could be placed in. But John Wooden Leg never understood the question. That's what made it so funny. He wasn't joking when he said, "That's a good dog." He probably thought she was worried the dog might bite her. The whole idea of a dog as a member of a hierarchical structure of intellectual categories known generically as "objects" was outside his traditional cultural viewpoint.

What was significant, Phædrus realized, was that John had distinguished the dog according to its Quality, rather than according to its substance. That indicated he considered Quality more important.

Now Phædrus remembered when he had gone to the reservation after Dusenberry's death and told them he was a friend of Dusenberry's they had answered, "Oh, yes, Dusenberry. He was a *good* man." They always put their emphasis on the *good*, just as John had with the dog. A white person would have said he was a good *man* or balanced the emphasis between the two words. The Indians didn't see man as an object to whom the adjective "good" may or may not be applied. When the Indians used it they meant that good is the whole center of experience and that Dusenberry, in his nature, was an embodiment or incarnation of this center of life.

Maybe when Phædrus got this metaphysics all put together people would see that the value-centered reality it described wasn't just a wild thesis off into some new direction but was a connecting link to a part of themselves which had always been suppressed by cultural norms and which needed opening up. He hoped so.

The experience of William James Sidis had shown that you can't just tell people about Indians and expect them to listen. They already *know* about Indians. Their cup of tea is full. The cultural immune system will keep them from hearing anything else. Phædrus hoped this Quality metaphysics was something that would get past the immune system and show that American Indian mysticism is not something alien from American culture. It's a deep submerged hidden root of it.

Americans don't have to go to the Orient to learn what this mysticism stuff is about. It's been right here in America all along. In the Orient they dress it up with rituals and incense and pagodas and chants and, of course, huge organizational enterprises that bring in the equivalent of millions of dollars every year. American Indians haven't done this. Their way is not to be organized at all. They don't charge anything, they don't make a big fuss, and that's what makes people underrate them.

Phædrus remembered saying to Dusenberry just after that peyote meeting was over, "The Hindu understanding is just a low-grade imitation of *this*! This is how it must have really been before all the clap-trap got started."

And he remembered that Franz Boas had said that in a primitive culture people speak only about actual experiences. They don't discuss what is virtue, good, evil, beauty; the demands of their daily life, like those of our uneducated classes, don't extend beyond the virtues shown on definite occasions by definite people, good or evil deeds of their fellow tribesman, and the beauty of a particular man, woman or object. They don't talk about abstract ideas. But Boas said, "The Dakota Indian considers goodness to be a noun rather than an adjective."

That was true, Phædrus thought, and that was very objective. But it was like an explorer noticing that there's a huge vein of pure yellow metal emerging from the side of a cliff, jotting the fact down in his diary, and then never expanding on the subject because he's only interested in facts and doesn't want to get into evaluations or interpretations.

Good is a noun. That was *it*. That was what Phædrus had been looking for. That was the homer, over the fence, that ended the ball game. Good as a noun rather than as an adjective is all the Metaphysics of Quality is about. Of course, the ultimate Quality isn't a noun or an adjective or anything else definable, but if you had to reduce the whole Metaphysics of Quality to a single sentence, that would be it.